The Cuckoo in the Nest by Margaret Oliphant

In Two Volumes

Margaret Oliphant Wilson was born on April 4th, 1828 to Francis W. Wilson, a clerk, and Margaret Oliphant, at Wallyford, near Musselburgh, East Lothian.

Her youth was spent in establishing a writing style and by 1849 she had her first novel published: Passages in the Life of Mrs. Margaret Maitland.

Two years later, in 1851 Caleb Field was published and also an invitation to contribute to Blackwood's Magazine; the beginning of a life time business relationship.

In May 1852, Margaret married her cousin, Frank Wilson Oliphant. Their marriage produced six children but, tragically, three died in infancy. When her husband developed signs of the dreaded consumption (tuberculosis) they moved to Florence, and then to Rome where, sadly, he died.

Margaret was naturally devastated but was also now left without support and only her income from writing to support the family. She returned to England and took up the burden of supporting her three remaining children by her literary activity.

Her incredible and prolific work rate increased both her commercial reputation and the size of her reading audience. Tragedy struck again in January 1864 when her only remaining daughter Maggie died.

In 1866 she settled at Windsor to be closer to her sons, who were being educated at near-by Eton School.

For more than thirty years she pursued a varied literary career but family life continued to bring problems. Cyril Francis, her eldest son, died in 1890. The younger son, Francis, who she nicknamed 'Cecco', died in 1894.

With the last of her children now lost to her, she had little further interest in life. Her health steadily and inexorably declined.

Margaret Oliphant Wilson Oliphant died at the age of 69 in Wimbledon on 20th June 1897. She is buried in Eton beside her sons.

Index of Contents

VOLUME I
CHAPTER I
CHAPTER II
CHAPTER III
CHAPTER IV
CHAPTER V
CHAPTER VI

The Seven Thorns was rather an imposing place for a little country inn. It was a long house, not very high, yet containing some good-sized bedrooms on the upper storey, and rooms below calculated for the entertainment of a much greater company than ever appeared now upon the deserted highroad. It had been an old coaching road, and there were stables at the Seven Thorns which could take in half the horses in the county; but that, of course, was all over now. The greater part of these stables were shut up and falling into decay. So was the large dining-room and half of the extensive accommodation downstairs. The great kitchen, and a little room on the other side of the doorway, which was called the parlour, were all that was ever wanted now in the Seven Thorns. Sometimes there would come some excursion parties from the neighbouring town in summer, and then a large table was placed outside, or, on the emergency of a wet day, in the kitchen. This was the only event which ever broke the quiet in these degenerate days.

The usual traffic was confined to the village; to now and then a pedestrian jogging along on foot, sometimes a tramp, sometimes a tourist; or to a farmer going by to market, who remembered the day when the Hewitts of the Seven Thorns were as substantial a family as his own. It was a house which had come down in the world, with a downfall as greatly felt, as much rebelled against, as the fall of the proudest family in the county could have been. The Hewitts had no pretension to be gentry, but they had been yeomen, farming their own land, and giving a large and well-paid hospitality to man and beast, which involved little that was menial to the family itself. The Richard Hewitt of the day had stood with his hands in his pockets, on his own threshold, talking to his guests about public matters, or the affairs of the county, while his ostlers looked after the horses, and his buxom maid, or rough waiter, brought the gentlemen their beer or more potent draught. He did not touch either horse or glass, but admired the one or shared the other, like any other rustic potentate; and if his pretty daughter glanced out of an upstairs window upon the group at the door, Sir Giles himself would take off his cap, and though perhaps there might be a touch of extravagance in the obeisance, which meant, in his intention, that Patty or Polly was not in the least upon his own level, yet the Patty or Polly of the moment remained completely unconscious of that exaggeration, and blushed, and retired from the window with a delighted sensation of being admired by the gentleman who was always so civil. Alas! these fine days were all past: and when Patience Hewitt now swept out the parlour briskly, as she did everything, and threw fresh wholesome sand upon the floor, and brought in the beer which the young squire, loitering upon the forbidden threshold of the great kitchen, had already several times asked for, the sense of that downfall was as strong in her mind as if she had been the old aunt Patty, old as the world itself, the girl thought, to whom old Sir Giles had taken off his cap.

"Patty! Patty! bring us some beer; and be done with that sweepin', and come, there's a ducky, and pour it out yourself."

"Go to the parlour, Mr. Gervase; that's your place and not here. If you will have beer in the morning, which is so bad for you, I'll bring it presently; but you know father won't have you here."

"If you'll have me, I don't mind old Hewitt, not that!" said Gervase, snapping his thumb and forefinger.

"But I do," said Patience, with a frown. "Old Hewitt is my father, and those that don't speak respectful of him had better get out of here, and out of there, too. I won't have a man in the house that don't know how to behave himself, if he was a dozen times the squire's son."

The young man in question was a lanky youth, long and feeble upon his legs, with light hair longer than is usual, and goggle eyes, in which there was no speculation. He was very much cowed by Patty's energetic disapproval, and looked as if about to cry.

"Don't go on at me like that, Patty, don't, now! I'll swallow old Hewitt, dirty boots and all, before I'll have you frown. And do, do have done with your sweepin' and bring us the beer. I never feel right in the morning till I have had my beer."

"If you didn't have too much at night, Mr. Gervase, you wouldn't want it in the morning."

"Well, and whose fault is that? I'll drink no more beer. I've promised you, if—"

"If!" said Patty: "it's a big 'if.' If I'll take you up on my shoulders, that ain't fit for such a job, and carry you through the world."

"Come, that's too bad," said the young man. "Do you think I can't take care of my own wife! I never had any intentions that weren't honourable, and that you well know."

"You well know," cried Patty, with a flush of anger, "that the mere saying you hadn't is enough for me to bundle you neck-and-crop out of this house, and never to speak to you again."

"Well!" said poor Gervase, "you're hard to please. If he can't say that he means well, I don't know what a fellow may say."

"If I were in your place, I'd say as little as possible," said the maid of the inn.

"What a one you are!" cried the young squire, admiringly. "When we're married I'll let you do all the talking. You'll bring round the father and mother a deal sooner than I should. Indeed, they never hearken to me; but, Patty, when you speak—"

"What happens when I speak?"

"The very rector turns round his head. I've seen him do it at the church door."

"Pooh! the rector!" said Patty. "Tell me something a little fresher than that."

For, in fact, this young woman scorned the rector as one whom she could turn round her little finger. Had not she, ever since the days when she was the quickest at her catechism, the readiest to understand everything, the sharpest to take any hint, the most energetic in action, been known as the rector's favourite and ally in all parish matters for miles around?

"Is that all you think of him? but he's of as good a family as we are; and I shouldn't wonder," said the young man, with a giggle, "if Mrs. Bethell were to die, as folk say, that he mightn't come a-wooing to Patty, of the Seven Thorns, same as me."

"I should like to know," said Patty, sharply, "what kind of company you've been keeping, where they dare to speak of me as Patty of the Seven Thorns? And I suppose you didn't knock the fellow down that said it, you poor creature! you're not man enough for that, though I know some—" said Patty, with an air of defiance. She had by this time carried out all her operations, and even drawn the beer, and waved off the thirsty customer before her, driving him, as if he had been a flock of geese, into the parlour, with its newly-sanded floor.

"There!" she said, setting down her tray with a little violence; "it's good stuff enough, but it puts no more heart and strength into you than if you was a mouse. Too much is as bad, or maybe worse, than none at all. And, I tell you, I know some that would no more hear me named disrespectful like that—or any way but Miss Hewitt, Mr. Hewitt of the Seven Thorns' daughter—than I would demean myself to carrying on like a barmaid with every one that comes for a glass of beer into this house."

"I beg your pardon, Patty," said the young man; "I meant no harm. When you're Mrs. Gervase Piercey there's never one of them will dare mention your name without taking off his hat."

"Oh, you block!" cried Patty, exasperated. She paused, however, with an evident sense that to make her meaning clear to him would be impossible; yet added, after a moment, "If I can't be respected as Miss Hewitt, I'll never seek respect under no man's name. There's your beer, Mr. Gervase; and as soon as you've drunk it I advise you to go back to your parents, for you'll get no more here."

"Oh! Patty, don't you be so cruel."

"I'll be as cruel as I think proper. And I'll draw father's beer for them as I think proper, and nobody else. You're the spoiled child at the Hall, Mr. Gervase, but no one cares that for you here!"

And she, too, snapped her thumb and forefinger, in scorn of any subjection to ordinary prejudices, and shone radiant, in her defiance, in the homely scene to which she gave so much life. Patty was not a beautiful girl, as perhaps you may suppose. She had bright eyes, very well able to flash with indignation when necessary, or even with rage. She had a fine country complexion, with the gift, which is not so usual among the lowly born, of changing colour as her sentiments changed: flashing forth in wrath, and calming down in peace; and when she was excited, with an angry sparkle in her eyes, and the colour rising and falling, there was a faux air of beauty about her, which impressed the minds of those who exposed themselves to any such blaze of resentment. Her features, however, were not very good, and there was a hardness in the lines, which, no doubt, would strengthen in later years. She had a trim figure, a brisk light step, an air of knowing her own mind, and fully intending to carry out all its purposes, which made a great impression upon the shiftless and languid generally, and upon Gervase Piercey in particular. Perhaps Patty had a little too much the air, in her sharp intelligence, of the conventional soubrette, to have charmed a squire's son of greater intellectual perceptions. But Gervase knew nothing about soubrettes, or any other types, theatrical or otherwise. He knew vaguely what he saw, but no more; and that sharp intelligence, that brisk energy, that air of knowing her own mind, was more captivating to him than anything he had ever seen. He, whom everybody snubbed, who was accustomed to be laughed at, who knew so much as to know that he never knew what to do until somebody told him, and often did not understand what was wanted of him then—threw himself upon Patty with all the heavy weight of his nature. He had never seen anything so admirable, so strong, or so fair. She never was afraid to do whatever she had a mind to. She never stood swaying from one foot to another unable to make up her mind. She was all swiftness, firmness, alertness—ready for anything. He almost liked her to be angry with him, though it sometimes reduced him to abject despair, for the sake of that sparkle, that flush, that exhibition of high spirit. Nobody, Gervase felt, would "put upon him" while Patty was near; nobody would push him aside, bid him to get out of the way. Even his father did this; and, what was still more, his mother too, when exasperated. But they would not, if Patty was there. Gervase was not only in love with her, which he was to the full extent of his abilities in that way, but he felt that his salvation lay in Patty, and that, with her to back him up, nobody would trample upon him any more.

He hoped to find her in a milder humour when he came back in the evening; for in the meantime it was beyond anything he could say or do to charm Patty back into good humour. She went back to her sweeping, making the corners of the kitchen floor ring with the energetic broom that pursued every grain of dust into its last refuge there. She would not stop, even to say good morning to him, when he lounged away. But after he was gone Patty relaxed in her fierce industry. She put away the broom, and stood at the window for a moment, with deep thought upon her brow. What was it she was thinking of, bending those brows, drawing in her upper lip in a way she had when her mind was busy? "To be, or not to be," that was the question. She was far, very far, from a Hamlet; but that momentous choice was before her, as much as if she had been the mightiest of spirits. When a woman pauses thus upon the threshold of her life, and questions which path she is to take, it is generally easy to guess that the question really is, which man will she marry? Patty was full of ambition as if she had been a princess. And she felt truly as much the child of a fallen house as if Richard Hewitt of the Seven Thorns had been a ruined duke. How far, how very far was she, Patience, the maid of the inn, drawing beer for the customers, compelled to serve every tramp who had twopence to spend—from the state of young Miss Patty at the upstairs window, sitting like a lady, doing vandykes of tape for her new petticoats (for she was informed of every incident of those times of family grandeur), to whom Sir Giles took off his hat. She had heard all her life of these once glorious circumstances, and her spirit burned within her to do something to restore herself that eminence; to achieve something that would make Aunt Patty hold her tongue, and own herself outdone. Ah! and here it was lying in her power. Sir Giles might have bowed to old Patty, but never did she have it in her power to become Lady Piercey, if she chose. Lady Piercey! with Greyshott Manor at her command, and all the grandeur which the very best of the previous Hewitts had only seen by grace of the housekeeper. And Patty might one day be the mistress of the housekeeper if she chose! The possibility was enough to thrill her from head to foot; but she had not yet made up her mind. No, splendid as the prospect was, there was yet a great deal to think of before she could make up her mind. She went to the door and gave a hurried glance out, to see the long, listless figure of Gervase Piercey strolling along across the wide stretch of broken land that lay between him and his home. He paused to look back several times as he went along, but Patty would not gratify him with the sight of her looking after him. He was not a lover to be encouraged by such signs of favour, but to be kept down at her feet until she should choose to hold out a gracious finger. Her thoughts were not flattering to him as she looked after him: the long, lazy, listless, useless being. If he did not care so much for me, beer would be the chief thing that Mr. Gervase would care for; coming here in the morning for his glass, the fool, instead of doing something! A man with horses to ride and carriages to drive, and an estate that he might see to, and save his father money! "Lord! lord!" said Patty to herself, "what fools these men are!" for the only thing he could do with himself, to get through the morning, was to walk across to the Seven Thorns for his morning beer, and then to walk back again. She who had a hundred things to do scorned him for this more than words could say. But yet, "first and foremost, before I settle anything," said Patty, "I'll see that he's cured of that. A man that's always swilling beer morning and evening, if he was a duke, he is not the man for me."

CHAPTER II

The parlour at the Seven Thorns was, in the evening, turned into a sort of village club, where a select number of the fathers of the hamlet assembled night after night to consume a certain amount of beer, to smoke a certain number of pipes, and then to retire at a not very late hour, not much the worse, perhaps, for their potations. It was not a vicious place, nor was it one of revelry. The talk was slow, like the minds of the talkers, and it was chiefly concerned with local events. If now and then there was a public measure which was wide enough, or descended sufficiently low to reach the level of those rustic folk, there might be occasionally a few heavy words on that subject. But this was of the rarest occurrence, and the humours of the heavy assembly were little perceptible to a superficial observer. What was going on at the Manor was of infinitely less interest to this rustic club than what was going on in the village, and unless Sir Giles had turned out his cottagers, or, what was worse, endeavoured to improve their tumble-down habitations, I cannot see why their minds should have been directed to him or his affairs. It is, perhaps, a delusion of the writer, most interested himself in the Squire's family, which lends to the rural public the same inclination. It is true that when young Gervase Piercey first began to appear among them, to be placed in the warmest corner, and served first with whatever he called for, the elders of the village took their pipes out of their mouths and stared. "What do he be a-wanting 'ere?" they said to each other with their eyes, and a head or two was shaken, not only over the inappropriateness of his appearance, but because the presence of the young Squire was more or less a check upon their native freedom as well as prolixity of talk. Gervase had been known to interrupt a lingering discussion with a "Speak up, old cock!" or with a silly laugh in the wrong place, which confused the speaker and made him forget whereabouts in his subject he was. It was some time, however, before it occurred to them what the young man's motive was, which was made plain by several signs: in the first place by the fact that Patty ceased to serve the customers in the parlour, old Hewitt getting up with many grumbles from the settle to supply their wants himself; then by the impatience of the young man, who had at first smoked his pipe contentedly in his corner, interrupting the conversation only by those silly laughs of his, or by an equally foolish question, which, though idiotic in itself, was the cause of discomfiture to a village orator accustomed to have everything his own way; and then it was observed that Gervase let his pipe go out and kept his eyes upon the door, and then that he became very uneasy when the brisk voice of Patty was heard outside, presumably talking with the younger frequenters of the place, who hung about the precincts of the Seven Thorns, or occupied the bench under the window of the parlour. When the young squire at last got up and went out, the sages said little, but they looked at each other or nudged each other, those who were close enough pointing with their long pipes over their shoulders, and finally burst forth into a slow roar, shaking their sides. "Softy if 'e be, 'e knows wat's wat as well as ere another," said the "Maestro de chi sanno," the sage of sages, the Aristotle of the village. This revelation slowly communicated itself over the parish, "The young squire, he be after Patty Hewitt o' the Seven Thorns; but Patty is one as will keep him in his place, and no mistake," was the popular verdict. The parish knew, even better than the gentry did, that Gervase—Sir Giles' only child—was a softy; it knew his habits, and that he was good for nothing, not even to take a hand at cards or field a ball at cricket, so that his dangling after Patty Hewitt caused nobody any anxiety. She knew how to keep him in his own place; no village story of lovely woman stooping to folly was likely to arise in her case. The Softy was a good creature enough, and harmed nobody, except by that exasperating laugh of his, which made the persons interrupted by it furious, but broke no bones, everybody allowed. So that it was more on Gervase's account than Patty's that the village concerned itself. "She do be making a fool of 'im," they said with gratification; for was not this a just revenge for other maidens wronged by other young squires of higher qualities than poor Gervase. Generally there was a slow satisfaction in the triumph of the people over the gentry, as thus exemplified; yet a general wish that Patty should not push that triumph too far.

On the evening of the day on which this story begins, he had kept in the parlour as long as his patience lasted, always looking for the moment when she should appear; for the mind of Gervase worked very slowly, and he had not yet begun to understand as a rule, what all the parish already knew, that Patty now entered the parlour no more in the evening. Gervase knew that he had not seen her for night after night, but he had no faculty for putting this and that together, and he did not draw the natural conclusion that she had so settled it with her father. Nor had he found much advantage in going out to the door, in following the sound of her voice, which seemed to flicker about like a will-o'-the-wisp, now sounding close at hand, now from a distance. When Patty was visible she was generally in close conversation with some one—Roger Pearson as often as not, was an antagonist whom Gervase had sense enough not to encounter. And, accordingly, it was the most rare thing in the world when he had any nearer view of the object of his admiration than the dim outline of her, in the dark, flitting about in front of the house with her tray, and not to be interrupted; or perhaps strolling off beyond the seven thorns which gave their name to the house, with another tall figure beside her. Roger Pearson was the athlete of the village. It was he who commanded the eleven got up between Greyshott and Windyhill, which had beaten almost every eleven that had met them, and certainly every other eleven in the county; and he was a leading volunteer, a great football player, everything that it is most glorious in English country life to be. Gervase did not venture to contest openly the favour of Patty with this stalwart fellow. He stood on the threshold with his mouth open, and his heart rung, and watched them stroll away together in the moonlight, losing sight of them in the shadow of the thorns: waiting till they emerged beyond upon the great flat of the moorland country among the furze bushes. Poor Softy! to see the lady of his love thus taken away from him by a stronger than he, was very hard upon him. Though he was a Softy, there was in Gervase so much of that feeling of the gentleman, which can be transmitted by blood and by the atmosphere of an ancient house—as made him aware that to make his possible wife the object of a brawl was not to be thought of, even had he felt any confidence in his own courage and muscles as against those of Roger. So that both these reasons held him back: the instinct of the weakling, and the instinct of the gentleman too. If he could have fought with and overthrown Roger on any other argument, how he would have rejoiced! He planned in his dreams a hundred ways of doing so, but never in his waking moments ventured to cross that hero's path: and he would not make a row over Patty. No! no! even if he could have seized Roger by the collar and pitched him to the other side of the moor, as Roger, he was convinced, would do to him if the opportunity ever arose, he would not have done it to bring in Patty's name and make her talked about. No! no! He said this to himself as he stood at the door and watched them with his mouth open and watering, and his heart sore. Poor Gervase; there was something in it, even if not so much as he thought.

But this evening, by a happy chance, Roger was not there. Gervase found Patty standing alone, wholly indifferent to the two or three vague figures which were dimly visible on the bench beneath the lighted window of the parlour. It was such a chance for Gervase as had never happened before. He whistled softly, but Patty took no notice; he called her by her name in a whisper, but she never turned her head. Was she regretting the other man, the fellow who had nothing to offer her but a cottage, and who was far too busy with his cricket matches and things ever to earn much money, or even to stay at home with his wife? Gervase ventured upon a great step. He came up behind her and seized Patty's hand, which was akimbo, firmly placed upon her side.

"Who's that?" she cried, throwing off the touch; "and what are you wanting here?"

"You know well enough who it is—it's Gervase come to have a word—"

"Oh!" said Patty, disdainfully, "it's the young gentleman from the Manor as has no right to be here."

"Yes, it is me," said Gervase, not quick enough to take up the scorn in her speech. "Come, Patty, let's take a little turn round the Thorns: do, now!—there's nobody else coming to-night."

"Much I care for any one coming! I can take my walk alone, thank you, Mr. Gervase, and you had better go home. I can't abide to see you spending your time here morning and night."

"Why shouldn't I come here, Patty? It is the nicest place in all the world to me."

"But it oughtn't to be," cried Patty; "your place is in Greyshott Manor, and this is only a little inn upon the edge of the downs. What pleasure can you find in this parlour, with all their pipes going, and the smoke curling about your head, and the silly talk about Blacksmith John at the smithy, and how he shod Farmer George's mare?"

"Well, if I don't object to the talk; and what reason have you against it? It's always good for trade."

"It's not even good for trade," said the girl. "Do you think they like you to be here, these men? No; not even father don't, though it's to his profit, as you say. It stops the talk: for there's things they wouldn't say before you: and it makes them think and ask questions. It ain't pleasant for me when they takes to ask each other, 'What's the young squire after for ever down here?'"

"Well, you can tell them," said Gervase, with his foolish laugh; "I make no secret of it. Patty's what I'm after, and she knows—"

They had gone down upon the open ground where the seven thorns, which gave the house it's name, stood in a cluster, ghostly in the white moonlight, some of them so old that they were propped up by staves and heavy pieces of wood. Patty had moved on in the fervour of her speech, notwithstanding that she angrily rejected his request to take a turn. With the blackness of that shade between them and the house, they might have been miles, though they were but a few yards, from the house, with its murmuring sound of voices and its lights.

"Look here!" said Patty, quickly. "No man shall ever come after me that goes boozing like you do at beer from morning to night."

Patty, though she generally spoke very nicely, thanks to the Catechism and the rector's favour, was after all not an educated person, and if she said "like you do," it was no more than might be expected from her ignorance. She flung away the arm which he had stolen round her, and withdrew to a distance, facing him with her head erect. "You're a dreadful one for beer, Mr. Gervase," she said; "it's that you come to our house for, it isn't for me. If there was no Patty, you'd want a place to sit and soak in all the same."

"That's a lie!" said the young man; "and I don't take more than I want when I'm thirsty. It's only you that are contrary. There's that Roger; you let him have as much as you like—"

"What Roger?" cried Patty, with a flash of her eyes, which was visible even in the moonlight. "If it's Mr. Pearson you mean, he never looks at beer except just to stand pots round for the good of the house—"

"If that's what pleases you, Patty, I'll—I'll stand anything—to anybody—as long as—as long as—" Poor Gervase thrust the hand which she would not permit to hold hers, into his pocket, searching for the coin that he had not. At which his tormentor laughed.

"As long as you've anything to pay it with," she said. "And you have not—and that makes all the difference. Roger Pearson—since you've made so bold as to put a name to him—has his pockets full. And you're running up a pretty high score, Mr. Gervase, I can tell you, for nobody but yourself."

"I don't know how he has his pockets full," Gervase said, with a growl; "it isn't from the work he does—roaming the country and playing in every match—"

"You see he can play," said Patty, maliciously; "which some folks couldn't do, not if they was to try from now to doomsday."

"But it don't get him on in his business, or make money to keep a wife," said the young man with a flash of shrewdness, at which Patty stared with astonishment, but with a touch of additional respect.

"Well, Mr. Gervase," she said, making a swift diversion; "I shall always say it's a shame keeping you as short as you are of money; and you the heir of all."

"Isn't it?" cried Sir Giles Piercey's heir. "Not a penny but what's doled out as if I were fifteen instead of twenty-five—or I'd have brought you diamonds, before now, Patty, to put round your neck."

"Would you, now, Mr. Gervase? And what good would they have been to me at the Seven Thorns? You can't wear diamonds when you're drawing beer," she added, with a laugh.

"I can't abide you to be drawing beer," cried the young man: "unless when it is for me."

"And that's the worst I can do," said Patty, quickly. "Here's just how it is: till you give up all that beer, Mr. Gervase, you're not the man for me. It's what I begun with, and you've brought me round to it again. Him as I've to do with shall never be like that. Father sells it—more's the pity; but I don't hold with it. And, if I had the power, not a woman in the country would look at a man that was fond of it: more than for his meals, and, perhaps, a drop when he's thirsty," she added, in a more subdued tone.

"That's just my case, Patty," said Gervase; "a drop when I'm thirsty—and most often I am thirsty—"

"That's not what I mean, neither. If you were up and down from morning to night getting in your hay, or seeing to your turnips, or riding to market—well, then I'd allow you a drink, like as I would to your horse, only the brute has the most sense, and drinks good water; but roaming up and down, doing nothing as you are—taking a walk for the sake of getting a drink, and then another walk to give you the excuse to come back again, and nothing else in your mind but how soon you can get another; and then sitting at it at night for hours together till you're all full of it—like a wet sponge, and smelling like the parlour does in the morning before the windows are opened—Faugh!" cried Patty, vigorously pushing him away, "it is enough to make a woman sick!"

Personal disgust is the one thing which nobody can bear; even the abject Gervase was moved to resentment. "If I make you sick, I'd better go," he said sullenly, "and find another place where they ain't so squeamish."

"Yes, do; there are plenty of folks that don't mind: neither for your good nor for their own feelings. You can go, and welcome. And I'm going back to the house."

"Oh, stop a moment, Patty! Don't take a fellow up so quick! It isn't nice to hear a girl say that, when you worship the ground she stands on—"

"The smell of beer," said Patty, sniffing audibly with her nostrils in the air, "is what I never could abide."

"You oughtn't to mind it. If it wasn't for beer—"

"Oh, taunt me with it, do!" cried Patty. "If it wasn't for beer, neither Richard Hewitt of the Seven Thorns, nor them that belongs to him, that once had their lands and their farms as good as any one, and more horses in their stables than you have ever had at the Manor, couldn't get on at all, nor pay their way—Oh, taunt me with it! It's come to that, and I can't gainsay it. I draw beer for my living, and I ought to encourage them that come. But I can't abide it, all the same," cried Patty, stamping her foot on the dry and sandy turf; "and I won't look at a man, if he was a prince, that is soaking and drinking night and day!"

She turned and walked off towards the house with her quick, springy step, followed by the unhappy Gervase, who called "Patty! Patty!" by intervals, as he went after humbly. At last, just before they came into sight of the loungers about the door, he ventured to catch at her sleeve.

"Patty! Patty! just for one moment! Listen—do listen to me!"

"What were you pleased to want, sir?" said Patty, turning upon him. "Another tankard of beer?"

"Oh, Patty," said the young man, "if I was to give it up, and never touch another blessed drop again—"

"It would be real good for you—the very best thing you could do."

"I wasn't thinking of that. Would you be a little nice to me, Patty? Would you listen to me when I speak?—would you—?"

"I always listen to them that speaks sense, Mr. Gervase."

"I know I ain't clever," said the poor fellow; "and whether this is sense I don't know: but you shall be my lady when father dies, if you'll only listen to me now."

Patty's eyes danced, and her pulses beat with a thrill which ran through her from head to foot. But she said:

"I'll never listen to any man, if he would make me a queen, so long as he went on like that with the beer!"

CHAPTER III

Greyshott Manor, to which Gervase directed his steps after the interview above recorded, was a large red brick mansion, no earlier than the reign of Anne; though there were traces in various parts of the house of a much older lineage. The front, however, which you could see through the wonderful avenue of beeches, which was the pride of the place, bore a pediment and twinkled with rows of windows, two long lines above the porticoed and pillared door, which also had a small pediment of its own. It looked old-fashioned, but not old, and was in perfect repair. When the sun shone down the beech avenue, which faced to the west, it turned the old bricks of the house into a sort of glorified ruddiness, blended of all the warmest tones—red and russet, and brown and orange, with a touch of black relieving it here and there. The effect in autumn, when all those warm tints which, by the alchemy of nature, bring beauty out of the chilly frost and unlovely decay—was as if all the colours in the rainbow had been poured forth; but all so toned and subdued by infinite gradation that the most violent notes of colour were chastened into harmony. It was not autumn, however, at this moment, but full summer,—the trees in clouds and billows of full foliage, dark on either side of that glory of the moon, which poured down like a silver river between, and made all the windows white with the whiteness of her light. The avenue was a wonderful feature at Greyshott, and even the mere passer-by had the good of it, since it was closed only by a great gate of wrought iron, which would also have been worth looking at had the spectator been a connoisseur. The fault of the avenue was that it was a short one—not above a quarter of a mile long—and it was now used only by foot-passengers, who had a right of way through the little postern that flanked the big gate. Important visitors drove up on the other side, through what was called the Avenue, which was just like other avenues; but the Beeches were the pride of Greyshott. To think that the one slim shadow that came into the moonlight in the midst of them, with a wavering gait and stooping shoulders, should be the future lord and master of all those princely older inhabitants, with the power of life and death in his hands! A few years hence, when old Sir Giles had come to the end of his existence, his son could cut them down if he pleased. He could obliterate the very name of the great trees, so much more dignified and splendid members of society than himself, which stood in close ranks on either side of the path: he so little and they so great, and yet this confused and bewildered mortal the master of all!

If Gervase walked with a wavering gait, it was not because of the beer against which Patty had made so strong a remonstrance. He had, indeed, had quite enough of that; but his uncertain step was natural to the Softy, as all the country called him. He went along with his head stooping, his hands in his pockets, his eyes traversing the path as well as his feet, keeping up an inane calculation of the white pebbles, or the brown ones, among the gravel. He had long been in the habit of playing a sort of game with himself in the vacancy of his mind, the brown against the white, counting them all along the level of the road, occasionally cheating himself in the interests of the right side or the left. This occupation had beguiled him over many a mile of road. But it had palled upon him since he had known Patty, or rather, since she had surprised him into that admiration and enthusiasm which had made him determine to marry her, whatever difficulties might be in the way. It was, perhaps, because of the rebuff she had given him that Gervase had again taken to his game with the brown and white pebbles in the road, which, indeed, it was not too easy to distinguish in the whiteness of the moon. He walked along with his head down, his hands in his pockets, his shoulders up to his ears, and the moon was very unhandsome in the matter of shadow, and threw a villainous blotch behind him upon that clear white line of way. There was a light in the front of the house to which Gervase was bound; a sort of querulous light, which shone keen in the expanse of windows, all black and white in the moon, like the eyes of an angry watcher looking out for the return of the prodigal, but not like the father in the parable. It was, indeed, exactly so: the light was in his mother's window, who would not go to bed till Gervase had come home. It was not late, but it was late for the rural household, which was all closed and shut up by ten o'clock. Sir Giles was an invalid, his wife old, and accustomed to take great care of herself. She sat up in her dressing-gown, angry, though anxious, with all the reproachful dignity of a woman kept up and deprived of her natural rest, ready to step into bed the moment her vigil was over; a large watch ticking noisily and also reproachfully on the table beside her, with a sort of stare in its large white face, seeming to say, late! late! instead of tick, tick—to the young man's guilty ear.

At least, it had once done so; but Gervase by this time was quite hardened to the watch that said late! and the mother whose tongue in the tschick, tschick! of angry remonstrance, hailed him for want of better welcome when he went in.

He directed himself to a little side door in the shadow, which was often left open for him by the old butler, who had less fear of his plate than of getting the boy, whom, Softy as he was, he loved, into trouble. But sometimes it was not left open; sometimes an emissary from above, his mother's maid, who loved him not, one of her satellites, turned the key, and Gervase had to ring, waking all the echoes of the house. He thought it was going to be so on this particular night, for when he pushed, it did not yield. Next moment, however, it opened softly, showing a tall shadow in the dimly-lighted passage. "O, Gervase, how late you are!" said a low voice.

"Why, it's you!" he said.

"Yes, it's me. My aunt is angry, I don't know why. And she says you are to go to her before you go to bed."

"I sha'n't!" said Gervase.

"Do, there's a dear boy. She has got something in her head. She will imagine worse than the truth if you don't go. Oh! why should you be so undutiful? They would be so good to you if you would but let them. Go to your mother, Gervase, and let her see—"

She paused, looking at him by the faint light as if she were not very sure that Gervase's mother would see anything satisfactory. There was not, indeed, anything exhilarating to see. His light eyes, which had shone with a certain brightness upon Patty, were opaque now, and had no speculation in them. His under lip hung a little, and was always moist. The sullen look was habitual to his face. "What does she want o' me?" he said in his throat, running his words into each other.

"She wants of you—what I'm afraid she'll never get," said the cousin with a tone of exasperation; "but at least go and say good-night to her, Gervase, and be as pleasant as you can. You may always do that."

"You're not one that thinks much o' my pleasantness, Meg."

"I've always been grateful for it when you've showed me any," she said with a smile. She was a tall woman, older than Gervase, a few years over thirty, at the age which should be the very glory and flush of prime, but which in a woman is usually scoffed at as if it were old age. Gervase frankly thought his cousin an elderly woman who did not count any longer in life. She was very plainly dressed in black, being a widow and poor, and had something of the air of one who is on sufferance in a house to which she does not naturally belong. She kept at a slight distance from her cousin, taking half a step back when he took one in advance: but her voice to him was soft and her meaning kind. She had no great affection, beyond the habitual bond of having known him all his life, for Gervase; but she was a bystander seeing both sides of the question, and she did not think that the treatment adopted in his home was judicious, which made her more or less, as a dependent may be, the partizan of the poor fellow, for whom nobody had any respect, and few people cared at all.

"Come," she said, in a persuasive tone; "I'll go with you, Gervase."

"What good'll that do?" he said, sullenly.

"Well, not much, perhaps: but you always liked when you were little to have somebody to stand by you: and if my aunt thinks I'm intruding, it will be all the better for you."

So saying, she led the way upstairs, and knocked lightly at a door on the gallery which went round the hall. "Here he is, aunt," she said, "quite safe and sound; and now you can get to bed."

"Who is quite safe and sound? and was there any doubt on that subject?" said a voice within. Lady Piercey sat very upright in an old-fashioned chair of the square high-backed kind, with walls like a house. The candle that looked so querulous in the window had inside a sharp, self-assertive light, as if it had known all about it all the time. She was in a dressing-gown of a large shawl pattern, warm and wadded, and had a muslin cap with goffered frills tied closely round her face. It is a kind of head-dress which makes a benign face still more benign, and a sweet complexion sweeter, and which also stiffens and starches a different kind of countenance. Lady Piercey was high featured, of that type of the human visage which resembles a horse, and her frills quivered with the indignation in her soul.

"I thought you were anxious about Gervase, aunt."

Mrs. Osborne interfered in this obviously injudicious way, with the object of drawing aside the lightnings upon herself, as it was generally easy to do.

"I don't know what you had to do with it," said Lady Piercey, roughly. "If I'm anxious about Gervase, it's not about life or limb. I'm not a fool, I hope. What did you give her, you block, to make her come and put herself before you like this?"

"I've got nothing to give," said the lout. There had been a trace of manhood, a gleam even of the gentleman in him when he was with Patty. Here, in his mother's room, he became a mere lump of clay. He pulled out his pockets as he spoke, which shed a number of small articles upon the floor, but not a coin. "I have a deal to give—to her or any one," he said.

"Where do you spend it all?" said the mother; "five shillings I gave you on Monday, and what expenses have you? Kept in luxury, and never needing to put your hand in your pocket. Goodness, Meg, what a smell! Is it a barrel of beer you've rolled into my room, or is it—is it my only boy?"

"By—Gosh!" said Gervase. He could not be gentlemanly even in his oaths. He would have said "By George!" or perhaps "By Jove!" even if he had been with Patty, but nothing but this vulgar expletive would come to his lips here.

"I've heard of you, sir," said Lady Piercey; "I've heard where you spend your time, and who you spend it with. A common beerhouse, and the woman that serves the beer. Oh, good gracious! good gracious! and to think that should be my son, and that he's the heir to an old estate and will be Sir Gervase if he lives!"

"Ay," said Gervase, with a laugh, "and you can't stop that, old lady, not if you should burst."

"Don't you be too sure I can't stop it," she cried. "Your father is not much good, but he is more good than you think; and if you suppose there's no way of putting an idiot out of the line, you're mistaken. There are plenty of asylums for fools, I can tell you; and if you are such a double-dyed fool as that—"

Gervase stared and grew pale; but then he took courage and laughed a weak laugh. "I may be a fool," he said, "you're always that nice to me, mamma: but there's them in the world that will stand up for me, and cleverer than you."

Lady Piercey stared also for a moment; and then turning to Mrs. Osborne, asked, "Meg! what does the ass mean?"

"Oh, have a little patience, aunt! He means—nothing, probably. He has been doing no harm, and he's vexed to be blamed. Why should he be blamed when he has been doing no harm?"

"Do you call it no harm to bring the smell of an alehouse into my room?" cried Lady Piercey; "you will have to open all the windows to get rid of it, and probably I shall get my death of cold—which is what he would like, no doubt."

Gervase laughed again, his lower lip more watery than ever. "Trust you for taking care of yourself," he said. "If that's all you have got to say, slanging a fellow for nothing, I'll go to bed."

"Stop here, when I tell you! and let me know this instant about that woman. Who is she that will have anything to say to you? Perhaps she thinks she will be my lady, and get my place after me—a girl that draws beer for all the ploughmen in the parish!"

"I don't know who you're speaking of," said Gervase. His face grew a dull red, and he clenched his fist. "By Gosh! and if she marries me, so she will, and nobody can stop it," he said.

"You had better banish this illusion from your mind," said Lady Piercey, with solemnity. "A woman like that shall never be my lady, and come after me. It's against—against the laws of this house; it's against the law of the land. Your father can leave every penny away from you! And as for the name, it's—it's forbidden to a common person. The Lord Chancellor will not allow it!—the Queen will not have it! You might as well try to—to bring down St. Paul's to Greyshott! Do you hear, you fool, what I say?"

Gervase stood with his mouth open: he was confounded with these big names. The Queen and the Lord Chancellor and St. Paul's! They mingled together in a something stupendous, an authority before which even Patty, with all her cleverness, must fail. He gazed at his mother with the stupid alarm which all his life her denunciations had inspired. St. Paul's and the Queen! The one an awful shadow, coming down on the moors; the other at the head of her army, as in a fairy story. And the Lord Chancellor! something more alarming still, because Gervase could form no idea of him unless by the incarnation of the police, which even in Greyshott was a name of fear.

"Look here," said Lady Piercey, "this is what it would mean; you wouldn't have a penny; you'd have to draw the beer yourself to get your living; you'd be cut off from your father's will like—like a turnip top. The Lord Chancellor would grant an injunction to change your name; for they won't have good old names degraded, the great officers won't. You might think yourself lucky if you kept the Gervase, for that's your christened name; but it would be Gervase Brown, or Green, or something;—or they might let you for a favour take her name—the beerhouse woman's; which would suit you very well, for you would be the beerhouse man."

Gervase's lip dropped more and more, his face grew paler and paler. Lady Piercey by long experience had grown versed in this kind of argument. She was aware that she could reduce him to absolute vacuity and silence every plea he might bring forth. He had no plea, poor fellow. He was so ignorant that, often as he had been thus threatened, he never had found out the absurdity of these threats. He fell upon himself like a ruined wall, as he stood before her limp and terrified. There was a grim sort of humour in the woman which enjoyed this too, as well as the sense of absolute power she had over him; and when she had dismissed him, which she did with the slight touch of a kiss upon his cheek, but again a grimace at the smell of beer, she burst into a wild but suppressed laugh. "Was there ever such a fool, to believe all I say?" she said to her niece who removed her dressing-gown, and helped her into bed; and then—for this fierce old lady was but an old woman after all—she fell a-whimpering and crying. "And that's my son! oh Lord! my only child; all that I've got in the world."

CHAPTER IV

Margaret found Gervase waiting for her in the darkness of the corridor, when she left his mother. Lady Piercey was a righteous woman, who would not keep her maid out of bed after ten o'clock; but her niece was a different matter. He caught his cousin by the arm, almost bringing from her a cry of alarm. "Meg," he said in her ear, "do you think it's all true?"

"Oh, Gervase, you gave me such a fright!"

"Is it all true?"

"How can I tell you? I don't know anything about the law," she said, with a sense of disloyalty to the poor fellow who was so ignorant; but she could not contradict her aunt, and if that was supposed to be for his good—

"If it should be," said Gervase, with a deep sigh: and then he added, "I couldn't let her marry me if it wasn't to be for her good."

"Oh, Gervase, why can't you show yourself like that to them?" his cousin said.

"I don't know what you mean. I make no difference," he answered dully, as he turned away.

Then there came another disturbance. The door of Sir Giles' room further on opened cautiously, and his servant, who was also his nurse, looked out with great precaution and beckoned to her. Sir Giles was in bed; an old man with a red face and white hair; his under lip dropped like that of Gervase, though there was still a great deal of animation in his little bright blue eyes. He called her to come to him close to his bedside, as if Dunning, his man, did not know exactly what his master was going to ask.

"Has Gervase come in?" he said.

"Yes, uncle."

"Is he drunk?"

"Oh, no," said Margaret eagerly, "nothing of the sort!"

"That's all right," said the old gentleman with a sigh of satisfaction. "Now I'll go to sleep."

Thus the whole household, though it was not to be called a sensitive or a loving household, held its watch over the poor lad who, in his patent stupidity, was its only hope.

Margaret Osborne went away to the end of the corridor to her own room where her little boy was sleeping. She was a few years over thirty, as I have said, and therefore was one of those whose day is supposed to be over. She would have said so herself from other reasons, with complete good faith. For was she not a widow, thrown back as wrecks are upon the shore, out of the storms and hurricanes of life? She might have added that she was cast upon a desert island, after a very brief yet sharp acquaintance with all those stirring adventures and hair-breadth escapes which sometimes make life a stormy voyage. She had married a soldier, and gone with him from place to place during a course of troubled years. They had been poor, and their marriage was what is called an imprudent one; but it was so much worse than that, that Captain Osborne had by no means intended it to be imprudent, but had remained convinced till the last moment that Sir Giles Piercey's niece must bring something substantial with her to the common stock. He had been warned over and over again, but he had not believed the warning; and when he found himself with a wife on his hands, whose utmost endowment was a very small allowance; enough, with economy, to dress her in the simplest manner, but no more—while he himself had little more than his pay to depend on, the disappointment was grievous. Captain Osborne was a gentleman, though not a very high-minded one, and he did his best to keep the knowledge of this shock from his wife, and to look as if he shared that joy in life and intoxicating delight of freedom with which Margaret, the unconsidered orphan of Greyshott, stepped forth into the fulness of existence with the man she loved. He was able to keep that up quite a long time, his despondencies and occasional irritabilities being attributed by Margaret to anything but the real cause of them; but at the last, in an unguarded moment, the secret slipped from him. Not anything to leave an indelible mark on her memory; not that he had married her with the intention of increasing his income, which would not have been true; but only an unintentional revelation of the disappointment which had been in his mind from the very day of their marriage—the failure of a prospect upon which his thoughts were bent. "I thought I should have been able to do you more justice, Meg; but if we've grubbed on in a poor way, you must remember it's that old curmudgeon of an uncle of yours that's to blame." She had asked what he meant, with a startled look, and gradually had elicited the story of his disappointment, which sunk into her heart like a stone. Not that she misjudged him or believed that he had married her for that only. Oh! no, no; but to think, when you have supposed your husband to be satisfied with your society as you with his; to find in you the fulfilment of all his hopes of happiness as you in him; and then to discover that from your very marriage day he has gone forth with a disappointment, with a grudge; with an unsaid reflection, "If I had but known!"—Margaret forgot it 'mid the many events that filled her existence, forgot even the bitter thought that, had he known, he need not have been subjected to those slights and scorns and forced self-denials that befall the poor; forgot everything but love and sorrow in those last sad scenes which have this one compensation—that they obliterate all that is not love from the mourner's heart. But, nevertheless, the mark that had been made on her life was always there. We may have forgotten when, and how, and even by whose hand we got the wound, but the scar remains, and the smoothness of the injured surface can never be restored.

But she had her little boy, who was her estate, her endowment, her dowry, whatever else might be lacking; and who had come to be the delight of the house in which she was received after her widowhood—oh! not unkindly—with a quite genuine compassion and friendliness, if not love. They were not a family of delicate mind; they did not think it necessary to spare a dependent any of those snubs or small humiliations which belong to her lot. They took her in frankly because she had nowhere else to go to, with an occasional complaint of their hard fate in having to receive and support other people's children, and an occasional gibe at the poor relations who were always a drag upon the head of the family. I do not say that she had not felt this, for she had a high spirit; and, perhaps, if she had been a woman educated as women are beginning to be now, she might have felt herself capable of achieving independence and throwing off the sore weight of charity which is so good for those who give, but generally so hard upon those who receive. But after many a weary thought she had given up the hope of this. She had not boldness enough to venture on any great and unusual undertaking, and there were no means for a woman of earning her living then, except in the way of teaching (which, at all times, must be the chief standby), for which she was not capable, having had no education herself. So that she had to accept the humiliations, to hear herself described as "my niece, you know, who has had to come back, poor thing, left without a penny. If she had not had her uncle's house to come back to, Heaven knows what would have become of her"; and to witness the visitor's pressure of Lady Piercey's hand, and admiring exclamation, "How good you are!" And it was true—they were very good. She had not a moment she could call her own, but was running their errands the whole day. She was sick-nurse, lady's maid, secretary, and reader, all in one. Sir Giles had moments when he remembered that to have such an invalid master was hard upon Dunning, and that so valuable a servant must have, now and then, an afternoon to himself; and Lady Piercey was very considerate of her maid, Parsons, and insisted, as we have seen, that she should always get to bed by ten o'clock. But to both of these good people it seemed quite natural that Meg should take the place thus vacated, and support the gouty old gentleman, and put the old lady to bed. Their own flesh and blood! like the daughter of the house! of course, it was she who came in naturally to fulfil all their needs. And Margaret never made an objection—scarcely felt one; was glad to be always busy, always at their service; but now and then, perhaps, in an idle moment, wondered, with a smile, how they could get on without her; felt a little indignation against Dunning and Parsons, who never showed any gratitude to her for the many fatigues she spared them—and thought within herself that the story of the niece, poor thing, who had come back without a penny, might be less frequently told.

But there had come into her life a great revenge—a thing which no one had thought of, unintentional, indeed undesired. The little boy, the baby, whom every one had called poor little thing!—as of the most unprotected and defenceless of God's creation—that little boy, Osy, such a burden on the poor niece who had not a penny! had become the king of the house! It was such a revolution as had never entered into any mind to conceive. Osy, who understood nothing about his proper place or his position, as entirely dependent on Sir Giles' charity, but did understand very well that everybody smiled upon him, delighted even in his very naughtiness, obeyed his lightest wish, fulfilled all his little caprices, took his little place as prince, as if it had been the most natural thing in the world. From old Sir Giles, by whom he sat on his little stool, patting the old gentleman's gouty foot, with the softest feather-touch of his little hand, and babbling with all manner of baby talk profound questions that could have no answer, and shrills of little laughter, while even Dunning, on the other side of the old man's chair, smiled indulgent, and declared that nothing do amuse master or take him out of himself like that child; and Lady Piercey, to whom he would run, hiding among her ample robes with full connivance on her part, when it was time to put him to bed—while Parsons stood delighted by, alleging that children was allays so when they was happy, and that the little 'un was fond of her ladyship, to be sure—there was but one thought little of Osy. He was a darling, he was, the housekeeper said, who was grim to Mrs. Osborne, and resented much being obliged occasionally to take my lady's orders from the poor niece without a penny. Gervase was the only one in the family who did not idolise Osy. He had liked him well enough at first, when he mounted the little thing on his shoulder to Margaret's terror, holding the child, who had twice his energy and spirit, with a limp arm in which there was no security. But after the time when Osy, with a fling, threw himself from his cousin's nervous hold, and broke his little head and plunged the house into a panic of alarm, all such pranks had been forbidden, and Gervase took no more notice of the child, who had already begun to share the contempt of the household for him.

"Why doesn't Cousin Gervase 'list for a soldier?" Osy had asked one day as he sat by Sir Giles. "Why should he 'list for a soldier?" asked the old gentleman; though Dunning grew pale, and Lady Piercey looked up with a sharp "Eh?" not knowing what treason was to follow. Dunning knew what had been said on that subject in the servants' hall, and divined that the child had heard and would state his authorities without hesitation. "Because—" said Osy—but then he made a pause—his mother's eye was upon him, and, perhaps, though he had not the least idea what she feared and probably in childish defiance would have done that precisely had he known, yet this glance did give him pause; and he remembered that he had been told not to repeat what the servants said. The processes in a child's mind are no less swift than those of a more calculating age. "Because," said the boy, lingering, beginning to enjoy the suspense on all these faces, "because—it would make his back straight. Mamma says my back's straight because the sergeant drilled me when I was a lickle, lickle boy."

"And the dear child is as straight as a rush, my lady," said Parsons, who was, as so often, arranging Lady Piercey's work. She, too, was grateful beyond measure to little Osy for not repeating the talk of the servants' hall.

"And what are you now, Osy," cried Sir Giles, with a great laugh, "if you're no longer a lickle, lickle boy?"

"I'm the king of the castle," said Osy, tilting at Dunning with the old gentleman's stick. "Bedone, you dirty rascal; let's play at you being the castle, Uncle Giles, and I'll drive off the enemy. Bedone, you dirty rascal;—det away from my castle. I'll be the sentry on the walls," said the child, marching round and round with the stick over his shoulder for a gun, "and I'll call out 'Who does there?' and 'What's the word'—and I'll drive off all the enemy. But there must be a flag flying." He called it a flap, but that did not matter. "Mamma, fix a flap upon my big tower. Here," he cried, producing from his little pocket a crumpled rag of uncertain colour, "this hankechif will do."

"But that's a flag of truce, Osy; are you going to give me up then?" said the old gentleman.

"We'll not have no flaps of truce," said Osy, seizing Sir Giles' red bandana, "for I means fightin'—and they sha'n't come near you, but over my body. Here! Tome on, you enemy!" Osy's thrusts at Dunning, who retreated outside a wider and a wider circle as the little soldier made his rounds, amused the old gentleman beyond measure. He laughed till, which was not very difficult, the water came to his eyes.

"I do believe that mite would stand up for his old uncle if there was any occasion," said Sir Giles, nodding his old head across at his wife, and trying in vain to recover the bandana to dry his old eyes.

These were the sort of games that went on in the afternoon, especially in winter, when the hours were long between lunch and tea. When the weather was fine, Osy marched by Sir Giles' garden chair, and made him the confidant of all his wonderings. "What do the leaves fall off for, and where do they tome from when they tome again? Does gardener go to the market to buy the new ones like mamma goes to buy clothes for me? How do the snowdrops know when it's time to come up out of the told, told ground?" Fortunately, he had so many things to ask that he seldom paused for an answer. Sir Giles laid up these questions in his heart, and reported them to my lady. "He asked me to-day if it hurt the field when the farmers ploughed it up? I declare I never thought how strange things were before, and the posers that little 'un asks me!" cried the old man. Lady Piercey smiled with a superior certainty, based upon Mangnall's Questions and other instructive works, that she was not so easily posed by Osy. She had instructed him as to where tea and coffee came from, and taught him to say, "Thank you, pretty cow," thus accounting for his breakfast to the inquisitive intelligence. But there was one thing that brought a spasm to Lady Piercey's face, especially when, as now and then happened, she hid the little truant from his mother, and saved Osy from a scolding, as he nestled down amid her voluminous skirts and lifted up a smiling, rosy little face, in great enjoyment of the joke and the hiding place. Sometimes as she laid her hand upon his curly head with that sensation of half-malicious delight in coming between the little sinner and his natural governor, which is common to the grand-parent, there would come a sudden contraction to her face, and a bitter salt tear would spring to her eye. If Gervase had a child like that to be his father's heir! Why was not that delightful child the child of Gervase, instead of being born to those who had nothing to give him? It was upon Margaret, who had not a penny, that this immeasurable gift was bestowed. And no woman that could be the mother of such a boy would ever marry Gervase! Oh! no, no—a barmaid, to give him a vulgar brat, who, perhaps—. But the thoughts of angry love and longing are not to be put into words.

Margaret went to the end of the gallery to her own room, where her child's soft breath was just audible as he slept. She went and looked at him in his little crib, a little head like an angel's, upon the little white pillow. But it was not only in a mother's tender adoration that she stood and looked at her child. To hurt any one was not in Margaret Osborne's heart, but there had come into it for some time back a dart of ambition, a gleam of hope: little Osy, too, was of the Piercey blood. She herself was a Piercey, much more a Piercey than Gervase, poor fellow. If an heir was wanted, who so fit as her boy? Far more fit than old General Piercey, whom nobody knew. Oh! not for worlds, not for anything that life could give, would she harm poor Gervase, or any man. But the barmaid and her possible progeny were as odious to Margaret as to Lady Piercey: and where, where could any one find an heir like Osy, the little prince, who had conquered and taken possession of the great house?

CHAPTER V

It has been stated by various persons afflicted with that kind of trouble, that to be enlightened above one's fellows is a great trial and misery. I don't know how that may be, but it is certainly a great trouble to be a Softy, to have a fluid brain in which everything gets disintegrated, and floats about in confusion, and never to be able to lay hold upon a subject distinctly either by head or tail, however much it may concern you. This was the case of poor Gervase the morning after he had received that evening address from his mother in her nightcap, which was so well adapted to confuse any little wits the poor fellow had. That his marriage might be forbidden, and his very name taken from him, and himself reduced to draw beer at the Seven Thorns for his living, instead of making a lady of Patty, and lifting her out of all such necessities, overwhelmed his mind altogether. If it was true, he had better, in fact, have nothing more to say to Patty at all. A forlorn sense that it might be well for her in such a case to turn to Roger, who at least would deliver her from drawing beer, lurked in the poor fellow's breast. Nothing would humiliate Gervase so much as the triumph of Roger, who had always been the one person in the world who pointed the moral of his own deficiencies to the unfortunate young squire; and there swelled in his breast a sort of dull anguish and sense of contrast, in which Roger's triumphant swing of the bat and kick of the football mingled with his carrying off of the woman whom poor Gervase admired and adored, adding a double piquancy to the act of renunciation which he was slowly spelling out in his own dumb soul. Nobody would try to take away that fellow's name. He had a cottage of his own that he could take her to, dang him! Gervase was beguiled for a moment into his old indignant thought that such a man playing cricket all over the county would probably come to the workhouse in the end, and that this was where Patty might find herself, if she preferred the athlete to himself; but he threw off the idea in his new evanescent impulse. She was too clever for that! She'd find a way to keep a man straight, whether it was a poor fellow who was not clever, or one that was too good at every kind of diversion. I am no great believer in heredity, and the house of Piercey was by no means distinguished for its chivalrous instincts or tendencies; yet I am glad to think that some vague influence from his ancient race had put this idea of giving up Patty, if he could bring only trouble and no bettering to her, into his dull and aching head. If he had been wiser, he would probably have kept away from her in this new impulse of generosity, but he was not wise at all, his first idea was to go to Patty, and tell her, and receive her orders—which no doubt she would give peremptorily—to go away from her. He never expected anything else. He was capable of giving her up, for her good, if he found himself unable to make a lady of her, in a dull sort of way, as a necessity; but he was not capable of the thought that she might stand by him to her own hurt. It seemed quite natural to him—not a thing to be either blamed or doubted—that as soon as it was proved that he could not make a lady of her, she would send him away.

It was a dull morning, warm but grey, the sky, or rather the clouds hanging low, and the great stretch of the moorland country lying flat underneath, its breadth of turf and thickets of gorse, and breaks of sandy road and broken ground all running into one sombre, greyish, greenish, yellowish colour in the flat tones of the sunless daylight. Such a day in weariness embodied, taking the spring out of everything. The very birds in the big trees behind the Seven Thorns were affected by it and chirruped dejectedly, fathers and mothers swiftly snubbing any young thing that attempted a bit of song. The seven thorns themselves, which were old trees and knocked about by time and weather and the passing of straw-laden carts, and other drawbacks, looked shabbier and older than ever: no place for any lovers' meeting. Gervase had not the heart to go into the house. He sat down on the bench outside, like any tramp, and neither called to Patty, nor attempted any way of attracting her attention. She had seen him, I need not say, coming over the downs. She had eyes everywhere—not only in the back of her head, as the ostler and the maid at the Seven Thorns said, but at the tips of her fingers, and in the handle of the broom with which she was as usual sweeping briskly out the dust and sand of yesterday, and striking into every corner. The weather did not affect Patty. It needed something more than a grey day to discourage her active spirits. But when she found that her suitor did not come in, did not call her, did not even beat with his knuckles on the rough wooden table outside, to let it be known that he was there, surprise entered her breast; surprise and a little alarm. She had never let it be known by any one that she was moved by Gervase's suit. In her heart she had always been convinced that the Softy would not be allowed to marry, and her pride would not allow her to run the risk of such a defeat. At the same time there was always the chance that her own spirit might carry him through, and the prospect was too glorious to be altogether thrown away; so that when Patty became aware that he was sitting there outside, with not heart enough to say Boh! to a goose—alarm stole over her, and to contemplate the possible failure of all these hopes, was more than she could calmly bear. She stood still for a minute or two listening, with her head a little on one side, and all her faculties concentrated upon the sounds from the door: but heard nothing except the aimless scrape of his foot against the sandy pebbles outside. Finally she went out, and stood on the threshold, her broom still in her hand.

"Oh! so it is you, Mr. Gervase! I couldn't think who it could be that stuck there without a word to nobody. You've got a headache, as I said you would."

"No—I've got no headache. If I've anything, it's here," said poor Gervase, laying his hand on what he believed to be his heart.

"Lord, your stomach, then!" said Patty with a laugh—"but folks don't say that to a lady; though I dare to say it's very true, for beer is a real heavy thing, whatever you men may say."

"I am not thinking of beer," said Gervase. "I wish there was nothing more than that, Patty, between you and me."

"Between you and me!" she cried with a twirl of her broom along the step, "there's nothing between you and me. There's a deal to be done first, Mr. Gervase, before any man shall say as there's something between him and Miss Hewitt of the Seven Thorns; and if you don't know that, you're the only man in the parish as doesn't. Is there anything as I can do for you? for I've got my work, and I can't stand idling here."

"Oh, Patty, don't turn like that at the first word! As if I wasn't down enough! You told me last night to give it up for your sake, and I meant to; and now you come and tempt me with it! If I must have neither my beer nor you, what is to become of me?" poor Gervase cried.

Patty felt that things were becoming serious. She was conscious of all the pathos of this cry. She leant the broom in a corner, and coming down the steps, approached the disconsolate young man outside. "Whatever's to do, Mr. Gervase?" she said.

"Patty, I'll have to give you up!" said the poor fellow, with his head upon his hand, and something very like a sob bursting from his breast.

"Give me up? You've never had me, so you can't give me up," cried proud Patty. She was, however, more interested by this than by other more flattering methods of wooing. She laughed fiercely. "Sir Giles and my lady won't hear of it? No, of course they won't! And this is my fine gentleman that thought nothing in the world as good as me! I told you you'd give in at the first word!" She was very angry, though she had never accepted poor Gervase's protestations. He raised his head piteously, and the sight of her, flaming, sparkling, enveloping him in a sort of fiery contempt and fury, roused the little spark of gentlemanhood that was in Gervase's breast.

"If I give in," he said, "it is because of you, Patty. I'll not marry you—not if you were ready this moment—to be the wife of a man without a penny that would have to draw beer for his living. I wouldn't; no, I wouldn't—unless I was to make you a lady. I wanted—to make a lady of you, Patty!"

And he wept; the Softy, the poor, silly fellow! Patty had something in her, though she was the veriest little egotist and as hard as the nether millstone, which vibrated in spite of her at this touch. She said, "Lord, bless the man! What nonsense is he talking? Draw beer for his living! Tell me now, Mr. Gervase, there's a dear, what is't you mean."

And then poor Gervase poured out his heart: how he had been threatened with the Lord Chancellor and even with the Queen; how they could take not only every penny but his very name from him, and so make him bring shame upon the girl he loved instead of honour and glory as he had hoped. And how, in these circumstances, he would have to give her up. Better, though it might kill him, that she should marry a man who could keep her up in every thing than one who would be thrown upon her to make his living drawing beer.

Patty listened patiently, and cross-examined acutely to get to the bottom of this mystery. She was a little overawed to hear of the Lord Chancellor, whose prerogatives she could not limit, and who might be able to do something terrible; but gradually her good sense surmounted even the terrors of that mysterious power. "They can't take your name from you," she said; "it's nonsense; not a bit. Your name? Why, you were born to it. It's not like the estate. Of course your name's yours, and nobody can't take it away."

"Not?" said Gervase, looking up beseechingly into her eyes.

"Not a bit. I, for one, don't believe it. Nor the property either! I, for one, don't believe it. They've neither chick nor child but you. What! give it away to a dreadful old man, a cousin, and you there, their own child! No, Mr. Gervase, I don't believe a word of it. They wanted to frighten you bad; and so they have done, and that's all."

"They sha'n't frighten me," said Gervase, lifting his pale cheek and setting his hat on with a defiant look, "not if you'll stand by me, Patty."

"How am I to stand by you," cried the coquette with a laugh, "if you're a-going to give me up?"

"It was only for your sake, Patty," he said. "I'd marry you to-day if I could, you know. That's what I should like—just to marry you straight off this very day." He got up and came close to her, almost animated in the fervour of his passion. His dull eyes lighted up, a little colour came to his face. If he could only be made always to look like that, it would be something like! was the swift thought that passed through her mind. She kept him off, retreating a step, and raising both her hands.

"Stand where you are, Mr. Gervase! You say so, I know; but I don't see as you do anything to prove it, for all your fine words."

A look of distress, the puzzled distress habitual to it, came over poor Gervase's face. His under lip dropped once more, "What can I do?" he cried; "if I knew, I'd do it fast enough. Patty, don't it all stand with you?"

"I never heard yet," cried Patty, "that it was the lady who took the steps; everybody knows there's steps that have to be took."

"What steps, what steps, Patty?" he cried, with a feeble glance at his own feet, and the trace of them on the sandy road. Then a gleam of shame and confusion came over the poor fellow's face. He knew the steps to be taken could not be like that, and paused eager, anxious, with his mouth open, waiting for his instructions—like a faithful dog ready to start after any stick or stone.

"Oh, you can't expect me to be the one to tell you," cried Patty, turning away as if to go back to the house; "the lady isn't the one to think of all that."

"Patty! I'm ready, ready to do anything! but how am I to know all of myself? I never had anything of the sort to do."

"I hope not," said Patty, with a laugh, "or else you wouldn't be for me, Mr. Gervase, not if you were a duke—if you had been married before."

"I—married before! Patty, only tell me what to do!" He looked exactly like Dash, waiting for somebody to throw a stone for him, but not so clever as Dash, alas! with that forlorn look of incapacity in his face, and the wish which was not father to any thought.

"Well, if you're so pressing, a clergyman has the most to do with it."

"I'll go off to the rector directly." He was like Dash now, when a feint had been made of throwing the stone: off on the moment—yet with a sense that all was not well.

"Oh! stop, you—!" Whatever the noun was, Patty managed to swallow it. "Come back," she cried, as she might have cried to Dash. "Don't you see? The rector; he's the last man in the world."

"Why?" cried Gervase. "He knows me, and you, and everything."

"He knows—a deal too much," said Patty; "he'd go and tell it all at the Hall, and make them send for the Lord Chancellor, or whatever it is."

Poor Gervase trembled a little. "Couldn't we run away, Patty, you and me together?" he said humbly; "I know them that have done that."

"And have all the parish say I'm not married at all, and be treated like a—wherever I showed my head. No, thank you, Mr. Gervase Piercey. I don't think enough of you for that."

"You would think enough of Roger for that," cried poor Gervase, stung to the heart.

"Roger!" she cried, spinning round upon him with a flush on her face. "Roger would have had the banns up long before this, if I had ever said as much to him."

"The banns!" cried Gervase. "Ah, now I know! that's the clerk!" The stone was thrown at last. "They'll be up," he said, waving his hand to her as he looked back, "before you know where you are!"

It was all that Patty could do to stop him, to bring him back before he was out of hearing. Dash never rushed more determinedly after his stone.

"Mr. Gervase," she shouted, "Mr. Piercey; sir! Hi! here! Come back, come back! Oh, come back, I tell you!" stamping her foot upon the ground.

He returned at last, very like the dog still, humbled, his head fallen, and discomfiture showing in the very attitude of his limp limbs.

"Is that not right either?" he said.

"The clerk would be up at the Hall sooner than the rector; the rector would understand a little bit, but the clerk not at all. Don't you see, Mr. Gervase, if it is to be—"

"It shall be, Patty."

"It must be in another parish, not here at all; and then you'd have to go to stay there for a fortnight."

"Go to stay there for a fortnight!" Dismay was in the young man's face. "How could I do that, Patty, with never having any money, and never allowed to sleep a night from home?"

"Well, for that matter," she said, "how are you to marry anybody if things are to go on so?"

He made no reply, but looked at her with a miserable countenance, with his under lip dropped, his mouth open, and lack-lustre eyes.

And here Patty made a pause, looking at her lover, or rather gazing in the face of fate, and hesitating for one dread, all-important moment: she was not without a tenderness for him, the poor creature who adored her like Dash; but that was neither here nor there. While she looked at him there rose between him and her a vision of a very different face, strong and sure, that would never pause to be told what to do, that would perhaps master her as she mastered him. Ah! but then there was a poor cottage on one side, with a wife whose husband would be little at home, in too much request for her happiness; and on the other there was the Hall and the chance of being my lady. She looked in the face of fate, and seized it boldly, as her manner was.

"Stop a bit," she said; "there's another way."

"What is it, what is it, Patty?"

"But it wants money; it costs a bit of money—a person has to go to London to get it."

"Oh, Patty, Patty, haven't I told you—"

"Stop!" she said; "I'm going to think it over; perhaps it can be done, after all, if you'll do what I tell you. Don't come near the Seven Thorns to-night; stay at home and be very good to the old folks; say you'd like to see London and a little life, and you're tired of here."

"But that would be a lie!"

"Oh, you softhead, if you're going to stick at that! Perhaps you don't want me at all, Mr. Gervase. Give me up; it would be far the best thing for you, far the best thing for you! and then there's nothing more to be said."

"Oh, Patty!" cried the poor fellow; "oh, Patty! when you know I'd give up my life for you."

"Then do as I say, and mind everything I say, and I'll see if it can't be done."

CHAPTER VI

Gervase went home as she had told him, not bounding after the stone like a dog who has got its heart's desire, but steadily, a little heavily, somewhat disappointed, yet full of expectation, and always faithful. Something was going to be done for him that would result in Patty's standing by him for ever, and helping him to all he wanted. He did not know what it was; he was by no means sure that he would understand what it was were he told; but she did, and that was enough. It was going to be done for him, while he had no trouble and would only reap the results. That was how it was going to be all the rest of the time. Patty would take the responsibility. She would face everything for him. She would stand between him and his mother's jibes and his father's occasional roar of passion. Gervase was dimly sensible that his people were ashamed of him, that they thought him of little account. But Patty did not feel like that. She, too, jibed at him, it is true; but then she jibed at everybody, even Roger. It was different, and she would let no one else jibe. She would take all the responsibility; with her beside him, standing by him, or perhaps in front of him, standing between him and all that was disagreeable, he should escape all the ills of life. He should not be afraid of any one any more. He went back to the hall determined to carry out his orders. For her sake he would make a martyr of himself all that evening; he would sit with the old folks and do his best to please them. He would talk about London and how he wished to see it. He would say he was tired of the country—even that, since Patty told him to do so. To be sure, if there was no Patty, he would be tired of it; if the Hall meant the country, yes, indeed, he was tired enough of that. He went home not in the least knowing what to do with himself; but faithful, faithful to his orders. Dash, when commanded to give up the wild delights of a run and watch a coat, or a stick, did it resignedly with noble patience, and so did Gervase now: he had, so to speak, to watch Patty's coat while she went and did the work; it is the natural division of labour when one of two is the faithful dog rather than the man.

He began, three or four times, as he went along, that game with the white pebbles against the brown, and then remembered that it was silly, and pulled himself up. He would not like Patty to know that he had a habit of doing that. He was aware, instinctively, that it would seem very silly to her. Three, four, and five; and a great big one that ought to count three at least for the right hand man. No; he wouldn't do it; it was silly; it was like a child, not a man. What, he wondered, was she going to do? Not go to the rector, because she had herself objected to that. Another way—he wondered what other way there could be—that dispensed with both parson and clerk? But that, thank Heaven, was Patty's affair, and she had promised that she would do it. Seven brown ones in a row; such luck for the left-hand man! But no, no; he would not pay any attention to that. Patty would think him a fool for his pains. What was she doing—she that knew exactly what it was best to do? What a woman she was, up to everything; seeing with one look of her eye what he never would have found out, that it was not the right thing to speak to the rector, nor to the clerk, who was still worse than the rector. How much better it was that it should be all in her hands! How was a man to know, who had never been married himself, who knew nothing about such things, how to put up banns? What were banns? He had heard people asked in church, but he was not sure about the other name. Was it something, perhaps, to hang up like a picture? These thoughts did not pass through Gervase's mind in so many words, but floated after each other vaguely, swimming in a dumb sort of consciousness. He had, perhaps, never had so many all turning round and crossing each other before. Generally it was only the pebbles he thought of as he walked unless when it was Patty. It gave him a strange sort of bewildering sense of life to feel how many things he was thinking of—such a crowd of different things.

In the beech avenue, going up and down in his chair, pushed by Dunning, and with Osy capering upon a stick before him, Gervase came upon his father taking his morning "turn." He remembered what Patty said about being agreeable to the old folks, and he also had a certain pleasure in wheeling his father's chair. So he stopped and pushed the servant away. "You go and take a rest, Dunning. I'll take Sir Giles along," he said. "You mustn't play any tricks, Mr. Gervase," said the man, resisting a little. "What tricks should I play? I can take care of my father as well as any one, I hope," cried Gervase, taking with energy the back of the chair. It went along a little more quickly perhaps, but Sir Giles did not mind that. "Young legs go faster than ours, Dunning," he said to his servant; "but stand you by, old man, in case Mr. Gervase gets tired." "Oh, I'll stand by. I'll not leave that Softy in charge of my master," Dunning said to himself. "Oh, I'll not get tired, father," said Gervase aloud. This was quite a delightful way of uniting obedience to Patty's commands with pleasure to himself. "I'll take you all round the grounds, father. Ain't you tired of this beastly little bit of an avenue? I'll take you faster, as fast as the carriage if you like." "No, my boy, this'll do," said Sir Giles; "fair and softly goes the furthest." Dunning came on behind shaking his head.

"You tan't ride so fast as me, Uncle Giles," cried little Osy, prancing upon his wooden steed.

"Can't he, though, you little beggar. He'd soon run you out of breath, if I was to put on steam!"

"Oh, tome on, tome on!" cried Osy, flourishing his whip; and off Gervase tore, sweeping the chair along, with Dunning after him panting and exclaiming, and Sir Giles laughing, but shaking with the wild progress of the vehicle which usually went so quietly. The old gentleman rather liked it than otherwise, though when Gervase stopped with a sudden jerk and jar, he was thrown back upon his pillows, and seized with a fit of coughing. "You see you cannot do everything, little 'un; there's some that can beat you," cried Gervase, waving his long arms, and drawing up his sleeves. Osy had been thrown quite behind, and came up panting, his little countenance flushed, and his little legs twisting as he ran, the child no longer making any pretence to be a prancing steed. "Are you game for another run?"

"Yes, I'm dame," cried little Osy, making a valorous struggle for his breath.

"No, no, that's enough," cried Sir Giles, coughing and laughing, "that's enough, Gervase. No harm done, Dunning—you need not come puffing like a steam engine; but halt, Gervase, no more, no more."

"Uncle Giles, I'm dame, tome on; Uncle Giles, I'm dame," shouted Osy flourishing his little cap.

This scene was seen from my lady's chamber with extremely mingled feelings. Lady Piercey sat in the recess of the window, where, in the evening, that querulous light had burned, waiting till Gervase came home. She had an old-fashioned embroidery frame fixed there, and worked at it for half an hour occasionally, with Margaret Osborne in attendance to thread her needles. Parsons had long since declared that her eyes were not equal to it, but with Mrs. Osborne there could be no such excuse. Lady Piercey had forgotten all about her work in watching. "There is my boy Gervase wheeling his father," she said; "look out, look out, Meg. Whatever you may say, that boy is full of feeling. Look! He has taken it out of Dunning's hands. See how pleased your uncle is; and little Osy acting outrider, bless him. Oh!" cried Lady Piercey with a shriek. Her terror made her speechless. She fell back in her chair with passionate gesticulations, grasped Margaret, and pulled her to the window, then thrust her away, pointing to the door. "Go! go!" she cried with a great effort, in a choked voice—which Parsons heard, and came flying from the next room.

"It's nothing, aunt; see, they've stopped. It's all right, Uncle Giles is laughing."

"Go! go!" cried the old lady, pointing passionately to the door.

"Go, for goodness gracious sake, Mrs. Osborne. My lady will have a fit."

"There is nothing—absolutely nothing, aunt. They've stopped. Dunning has taken his place again; there's no need for interfering. Ah!" Margaret gave just such a cry as Lady Piercey had done, and flinging down her little sheaf of silks upon the frame, turned and flew from the room, leaving the old lady and her maid exchanging glances of consternation. And yet the cause of Mrs. Osborne's sudden change of opinion was not far to seek; it was that Gervase had seized little Osy and swung him up to his shoulder, where the child sat very red and uneasy, but too proud to acknowledge that he was afraid.

"Put down my child this moment!" cried Margaret, descending like a thunderbolt in the midst of the group.

"He's as right as a trivet. I'm going to give him a ride. I haven't given him a ride for a long time. Hi! Osy, ain't you as right as a trivet, and got a good seat?"

"Yes, tousin Gervase," said the boy with a quaver in his voice, but holding his head high.

"Put him down this moment!" cried Margaret, stamping her foot and seizing Gervase by the arm.

"I'll put him down when he's had his ride. Now, old Dunning, here's for it. We'll race you for a sovereign to the gate. Sit tight, Osy, or your horse will throw you—he's as wild as all the wild horses that ever were made."

"Div me my whip first," cried the child. He was elated though he was afraid. "And I won't ride you if you haven't a bit in your mouff." Once more the little grimy pocket-handkerchief was brought into service. "Here's the bit, and I'm holding you in hand. Now, trot!"

Margaret stood like a ghost, while the wild pair darted along the avenue, Gervase prancing with the most violent motion, little Osy sitting very tight, holding on to his handkerchief with the tightness of desperation, his cheeks blazing and throbbing with the tumultuous colour of courage, excitement, and fright. They are things which consist with each other. The child was afraid of nothing, but very conscious that he had once before been thrown from Gervase's shoulder, and that the prospect was not a pleasant one. As for the spectators, Sir Giles in his chair and his wife at the window, they were in a ferment of mingled feeling, afraid for their pet, but excited by this new development on the part of their son. "Mr. Gervase is really taking great care," gasped Lady Piercey to her maid. "Don't you see? He's got the child quite tight—not like that other time; Master Osy is quite enjoying it."

"Oh yes, my lady," said Parsons, doubtfully; "he's got such a spirit."

"And his cousin is so kind, so kind. There's nobody," said the old lady, with a sob and a gasp, "so good to children as my Gervase. There! thank Heaven, he's put him down. Miss Meg—I mean Mrs. Osborne is making a ridiculous fuss about it," said Lady Piercey, now running all her words into one in the relief of her feelings, "as if there was any fear of the child!"

Little Osy had swung down through the air with a sinking whirl as if he had shot Niagara, but once on firm ground, being really none the worse, tingled to his fingers' ends with pride and triumph. He gave a smack of his little whip with his right hand, while with the other he clutched his mother's dress, trembling and glowing. "Dood-bye, dood horse; I'll—I'll wide you again another time," he shouted, with a slight quaver in his voice.

Sir Giles was half-weeping, half-laughing, in the excitement of his age and weakness. Now that the child was safe, he, too, was delighted and proud. "Good'un to go, ain't he, Osy?" he cried. "But I say, lad, you oughtn't to caper like that; he's a deal too fresh, Dunning, eh? wants to have it taken out of him."

"Yes, Sir Giles," said Dunning. ("And I'd just like to take it out of him with a cart whip," he murmured, between his closed teeth.)

Lady Piercey was weeping a little, too, at her window, calming down from her excitement. "How strong he is, bless him, and well-made when he holds himself straight; and wouldn't harm the child not for the world, or any one that trusts him. Oh, Parsons, what a joyful family we'd be if Master Osy had been my son's boy!"

"Bless you, my lady, he's too young to have a boy as big as that."

"So he is, the dear. If I could live to see him with an heir, Parsons!"

"And why not, my lady? You're not to call old, and with proper care and taking your medicines regular—one of these days he'll be bringing home some nice young lady." ("Some poor creature as will be forced to take 'im, or else Patty of the Seven Thorns," was Parsons' comment within herself.)

"And then that poor little darling!" said Lady Piercey, regretfully. "But," she added with a firmer tone, "Meg spoils the boy to such a degree that he'll be ruined before he's a man. Look at her petting him as if he'd been in any danger; but she never had an ounce of sense. Get me my things, Parsons; I'll go down and sit in the air a bit and talk to my boy."

Gervase had fallen out of his unusual liveliness before his mother succeeded in reaching the beech avenue, but he came forward at her call, and permitted her to take his arm. "I like to see you in spirits," the old lady said, "but you mustn't shake about your father like that. Dunning's safest for an old man."

"I'll drive you out in the phaeton, mother, if you like, this afternoon."

"No, my dear; I feel safest in the big carriage with the cobs, and old Andrews; but it's a pleasure to see you in such spirits, Gervase; you're like my own old boy."

"You see," said Gervase, with his imbecile, good-humoured smile, "I've promised to do all I can to please you at home."

"Ah!" cried the old lady, "and who might it be that made you promise that? and why?"

Gervase broke into a laugh. "Wouldn't you just like to know?" he said.

CHAPTER VII

"Osy," said Mrs. Osborne, "you mustn't let cousin Gervase get hold of you like that again."

"He's a dood horse," said the little boy, "when I sit tight. I have to sit vewey tight; but next time I'll get on him's both shoulders, and hold him like a real horse. He's dot a too narrow back, and too far up from the ground."

"But listen to me, Osy. It makes me too frightened. You mustn't ride him again."

"I'll not wide him if I can help it," said Osy, reddening with mingled daring and terror, "but he takes me up before I can det far enough off, and I tan't run away, mamma."

"But you must run away, Osy, when I tell you."

The child looked up at her doubtfully. "It was you that told me gemplemens don't run away."

"Not before an enemy, or that," said Margaret, taking refuge in the vague, "but when it's only for fun, Osy."

"Fun isn't never serous, is it, mamma?"

"It would be very serious if you fell from that fo—, from Cousin Gervase's shoulder, Osy. Go out for a walk this afternoon, dear, with nurse."

"I don't like nurse. I like Uncle Giles best. And I'm the outwider, telling all the people he's toming."

"You see Uncle Giles has got something else to do."

Gervase was still in the foreground of the picture, carrying out his consigne. The servant had brought out upon the terrace at the other side of the house a box containing a game of which, in former days, Sir Giles had been fond. It was Gervase who had proposed this diversion to-day. "I'll play father a game at that spinner thing," he had said, after the large heavy luncheon, which was Sir Giles' dinner. "I'd like that, lad," the old man cried with delight. It was a beautiful afternoon, and nothing could be more charming than the shady terrace on the east side of the house which in these hot July days was always cool. The sunshine played on the roof of the tall house, and fell full on the turf and the shrubs, and the flower garden at the south corner, but on the terrace all was grateful shade. The game was brought out, and many experiments were made to see at what angle Sir Giles could best throw the ball with which it was played—an experiment in which Dunning took more or less interest, seeing it saved him another weary promenade through the grounds, pushing his master's chair. The carriage was waiting round the corner, and Lady Piercey came sailing downstairs with Parsons behind her carrying a large cloak. "Meg! do you know I'm ready to go out?" cried Lady Piercey, in the tone of that king who had once almost been made to wait. "May I bring Osy, aunt?" cried Margaret. "No," was the peremptory answer. "I'll go without you if you don't be quick."

"And I don't want to go, mover," said Osy. "I'm doing to play with Uncle Giles."

"Come along, little duffer," cried Gervase; "I'll give you another ride when we've done playing."

"Meg, come this moment!" cried Lady Piercey; and Margaret, with agonised visions, was compelled to go. Bitter is the bread of those who have to run up and down another man's stairs, and be as the dogs under his table. "Oh!" Margaret Osborne said to herself, "if I had but the smallest cottage of my own! If I could but take in needlework or clear starching, and work for my boy!" Perhaps the time might come when that prayer should be fulfilled, and when it would not seem so sweet as she thought.

Lady Piercey took her usual drive in a long round through the familiar roads which she had traversed almost every day for the last thirty years. She knew not only every village, but every cottage in every village, and every tree, and every clump of wild honeysuckle or clematis flaunting high upon the tops of the hedges. By dint of long use, she had come to make that frequent, almost daily, progress without seeing anything, refreshed, it is to be supposed, by the sweep of the wide atmosphere and all the little breezes that woke and breathed about her as she went over long miles and miles of green country, all monotonously familiar and awakening no sensation in her accustomed breast. She thought of her own affairs as she made these daily rounds, which many a poorer woman envied the old lady, thinking how pleasant it would be to change with her, and see the world from the luxurious point of vantage of a landau with a pair of good horses, and a fat coachman and agile footman on the box. But Lady Piercey thought of none of these advantages, nor of the beautiful country, nor the good air, but only of her own cares, which filled up all the foreground of her life, as they do with most of us. After a while, being forced by the concatenation of circumstances, she began to discuss these cares with Margaret, which was her custom when Parsons, who knew them all as well as her ladyship, was out of the way. Mrs. Osborne was made fully aware that it was because there was no one else near, that she was made the confidant of her aunt's troubles; but she listened, nevertheless, very dutifully, though to-day with a somewhat distracted mind, thinking of her child, and seeing an awful vision before her of Osy tossed from Gervase's shoulder and lying stunned on the ground, with nobody but Dunning and Sir Giles to look after him. This made her perhaps less attentive than usual to all Lady Piercey's theories as to what would be the making of Gervase, and save him from all difficulties and dangers. The old lady was not deceived in respect to her son; she was very clear-sighted, although in a moment of excitement, as on that morning, she might be ready to credit him with ideal virtues; on ordinary occasions nothing could be more clear than her estimate, or more gloomy than her forecast, of what his future might be.

"I am resolved on one thing," said Lady Piercey, "that we must marry him by hook or crook. I hate the French: they're a set of fools, good for nothing but dancing and singing and making a row in the world; but I approve their way in marrying. They would just look out a suitable person, money enough, and all that, and he'd have to marry her whether he liked it or not. Are you listening, Meg? If your uncle had done that with you, now, what a much better thing for you than pleasing your fancy as you did and grieving your heart!"

"I'm not worth discussing, aunt, and all that's over and gone long ago."

"That's true enough; but you're an example, and if I think proper, I'll use it. I dare say Captain Osborne thought you had a nice bit of money when he first began to think of you, and was a disappointed man when he knew—"

"Aunt, I cannot have my affairs discussed."

"You shall have just what I please and nothing else," said the grim old lady. "I have had enough of trouble about you to have a right to say what I please. And so I shall do, whatever you may say. A deal better it would have been for you if we had just married you, as I always wished, to a sensible man with a decent income, who never would have left you to come back upon your family, as you have had to do. That's a heavy price to pay, my dear, for the cut of a man's moustache. And I'd just like to manage the same for my own boy, who is naturally much more to me than you. But then there's the girl to take into account; girls are so much indulged nowadays, they take all kinds of whimseys into their heads. Now I should say, from my point of view, that Gervase would make an excellent husband; if she was sensible, and knew how to manage, she might turn him round her little finger. What do you say? Oh, I know you are never likely to think of anything to the advantage of my boy."

"I think my cousin Gervase has a great many good qualities, aunt; whether you would be doing right in making him marry, is another matter."

"Oh, you think so! it would be better to leave him unmarried, and then when we die Osy would have the chance? For all so clever as you are, Meg, I can see through you there. But Osy has no chance, as you ought to know. There's the General, and his son, Gerald—a new name in the family, as if the Gileses and the Gervases were not good enough for a younger branch! If it was Osy, bless the child, I don't know that I should mind so much," the old lady said in a softened tone, with a tear suddenly starting in the corner of her eye.

"Thank you for thinking that," said Margaret, subdued. "I know very well it could never be Osy."

"But there might be another Osy," said Lady Piercey, putting away that tear with a surreptitious finger. "There never was a brighter man than your uncle, and I'm no fool; and yet you see Gervase—What's to hinder Gervase from having a boy like his father if the mother of it was good for anything? A girl, if she had any sense, might see that. What's one person in a family? The family goes on and swamps the individual. You may be surprised at me using such words; but I've thought a deal about it—a great deal about it, Meg. A good girl of a good race, that is what he wants; and, goodness gracious, if she only knew how to set about it, what an easy time she might have!"

To this, Margaret, being probably of another opinion, made no reply; and Lady Piercey, after an expectant and indignant pause, burst forth—"You don't think so, I suppose? You think the only thing he's likely to get, or that is fit for him, is this minx at the Seven Thorns?"

"I never thought so," cried Margaret, "nor believed in that at all—never for a moment."

"That shows how much you know," said the old lady, with a snort of anger. "I believe in it, if you don't. Who is he staying at home to-day and trying to please, the booby! that hadn't sense enough to keep that quiet? Don't you see he's under orders from her? Ah, she knows what's what, you may be sure. She sees all the ways of it, and just how to manage him. The like of you will not take the trouble to find out, but that sort of minx knows by nature. Oh, she has formed all her plans, you may be sure! She knows exactly how she is going to do it and baffle all of us; but I shall put a spoke in my lady's wheel. My lady!" cried Lady Piercey, with the irritation of one who feels her own dearest rights menaced; "she is calculating already how soon she'll get my name and make me the dowager! I know it as well as if I saw into her; but she is going a bit too fast, and you'll see that I'll put a spoke in her wheel! John! you can turn back now, and drive to the place I told you of. I want to ask about some poultry at that little inn. You know the name of it."

"The Seven Thorns, my lady?" said John, turning round on the box, with his hand at his hat, and his face red with suppressed laughter, made terrible by fear of his mistress—as if he and the coachman had not been perfectly well aware, when the order was given, what kind of wildfowl was that pretended poultry which took Lady Piercey to the Seven Thorns!

"So it is; that was the name," said the old lady. "You can take the first turning, and get there as quick as possible. You'll just see how I shall settle her," she added, nodding her head as soon as the man's back was turned.

"Do you mean to see the girl, aunt?" cried Margaret, in surprise and alarm.

"What's so wonderful in that? Of course I mean to see her. I shall let her know that I understand all her little plans, and mean to put a stop to them. She is not to have everything her own way."

"But, aunt, do you think a girl of that kind will pay any attention?—don't you think that perhaps it will do more harm than—"

"I know that you have always a fine opinion of your own people, Meg Piercey! and of me especially, that am only your aunt by marriage. You think there's nothing I can do that isn't absurd—but I think differently myself, and you shall just see. Attention? Of course she will pay attention. I know these sort of people; they believe what you tell them in a way you wouldn't do: they know no better. They're far cleverer than you in some things, but in others they'll believe just what you please to tell them," said Lady Piercey, with a fierce toss of her head, "if you speak strong enough; and I promise you I sha'n't fail in that!"

The carriage swept along with an added impulse of curiosity and expectation which seemed to thrill through from the men on the box, who formed an impatient and excited gallery, eager to see what was going to happen, to the calm, respectable horses, indifferent to such mere human commotions, who probably were not aware why they were themselves made to step out so much more briskly. The carriage reached the Seven Thorns at an hour in the afternoon which was unusually quiet, and which had been selected by Patty on that account for an expedition which she had to make. She was coming out of her own door, when the two cobs drew up with that little flourish which is essential to every arrival, even at a humble house like that of the Seven Thorns, and stood there for a moment transfixed, with a sudden leap of excitement in all her pulses at the sight of the heavy old landau, which she, of course, knew as well as she knew any cart in the village. Was it possible that it was going to stop? It was going to stop! She stood on her own threshold almost paralysed, stupefied—though at the same time tingling with excitement and energy and wonder. My lady in her carriage, the great lady of the district! the potentate whom Patty of the Seven Thorns, audacious, meant to succeed, if not to supersede! The effect upon her for the first moment was to make her knees tremble, and her strength fail; for the next, to brace her up to a boldness unknown to her, though she had never before been timid at any time.

"If you please, my lady," said John, obsequious, yet with his eyes dancing with excitement and curiosity, at the carriage door, "that is Miss Hewitt of the Seven Thorns on the doorstep, if it is her your ladyship wants. Shall I say your ladyship wishes to—"

"Look here! you've got to go off to the post-office at once to get me some stamps. I'll manage the rest for myself," said Lady Piercey, thrusting two half-crowns into the man's hand. Poor John! with the drama thus cut short at its most exciting moment! She waited till he had turned his back, and then she waved her hand to Patty, still standing thunderstricken on the threshold. "Hi!—here!" cried Lady Piercey, who did not err in her communications with the country people round her on the civil side.

If it had not been for overpowering excitement, curiosity, and the desire for warfare, which is native to the human breast, Patty would have stood upon her dignity, disregarded this peremptory call, and marched away. She almost tried to do so, feeling more or less what an immense advantage it would have given her, but her instinct was too strong—a double and complicated instinct which moved her as if she had not been at all a free agent: first, the impulse to obey my lady, which was a thing that might have been overcome, but second, the impulse to fight my lady, which was much less easy to master, and, last of all, an overpowering, dizzying, uncontrollable curiosity to know what she could have to say. She stepped down from her own door deliberately, however, and with all the elegance and eloquence she could put into her movements, and went slowly forward to the carriage door. She was in her best dress, which was not, perhaps, so becoming to Patty as the homelier attire, which was more perfect of its kind than the second-rate young ladyhood of her Sunday frock. Her hat was very smart with flowers and bows of velvet, which happened to be the fashion of the time, and she carried a parasol covered with lace, and wore a pair of light gloves, which were not in harmony with the colour of her dress—neither, indeed, were Lady Piercey's own gloves in harmony with her apparel, but that was a different matter. The old lady's keen glance took in every article of Patty's cheap wardrobe, with a comment on the way these creatures dress! as she came forward with foolish deliberation, as if to allow herself time to be examined from head to foot.

"You are Patty, that used to come out so well in the examinations," Lady Piercey said, with a breathlessness which showed what excitement existed on her side.

"I am Patience Hewitt, my lady, if that is what you're pleased to ask."

Margaret sat looking on trembling at these two belligerents: her aunt, who overbore her, Margaret, without any trouble silenced all her arguments and shut her mouth; and this girl of the village and public-house, the Sunday-school child whom she remembered, the pet of the rector, the clever little monitor and ringleader—Patty, of the Seven Thorns, something between a housemaid and a barmaid, and Lady Piercey of Greyshott! The looker-on, acknowledging herself inferior to both of them, felt that they were not badly matched.

"Ah!" said Lady Piercey, "yes, that's what I asked. You're Robert Hewitt's daughter, I suppose, who keeps the public-house on our property?"

"Begging your pardon, my lady, the old inn of the Seven Thorns is my father's property, and has been his and his family's for I don't know how many hundred years."

"Oh!" cried Lady Piercey with a stare, "you speak up very bold, young woman; yet you've been bred up decently, I suppose, and taught how you ought to conduct yourself in that condition in which God has placed you."

"If you wish to know about my character, my lady, the rector will give it you; though I don't know why you should trouble about it, seeing as I am not likely to wish a place under your ladyship, or under anybody, for that matter."

"No," cried Lady Piercey, exasperated into active hostilities; "you would like to climb up over our heads, that's what you would like to do."

Patty replied to the excited stare with a look of candid surprise. "How could I climb over anybody's head, I wonder? me that manages everything for father, and keeps house at the Seven Thorns?"

"You look very mild and very fine," said Lady Piercey, leaning over the side of the carriage, and emphasising her words with look and gesture, "but I've come here expressly to let you understand that I know everything, and that what you're aiming at sha'n't be! Don't look at me as if you couldn't divine what I was speaking of! I know every one of your plots and plans—every one! and if you think that you, a bit of a girl in a public-house, can get the better of Sir Giles and me, the chief people in the county, I can tell you you're very far mistaken." Lady Piercey leant over the side of the carriage and spoke in a low voice, which was much more impressive than if she had raised it. She had the fear of the coachman before her eyes, who was holding his very breath to listen, growing redder and redder in the effort, but in vain. Lady Piercey projected her head over the carriage door till it almost touched the young head which Patty held high, with all the flowers and feathers on her fine hat thrilling. "Look you here!" she said, with that low, rolling contralto which sounded like bass in the girl's very ears, "we've ways and means you know nothing about. We're the great people of this county, and you're no better than the dust under our feet: do you hear? do you hear?"

"Oh yes, I hear very well, my lady," said Patty, loud out, which was a delight to the coachman, "but perhaps I am not of that opinion." There was, however, a little quaver of panic in her voice. Lady Piercey was right so far that a person of the people, when uneducated, finds it difficult to free him-, and especially herself, from a superstition as to what the little great, the dominant class can do.

"Opinion or no opinion," said the old lady, "just you understand this, Miss Polly, or whatever your name is: You don't know what people like us can do—and will do if we're put to it. We can put a man away within stone walls that is going to disgrace himself: we can do that as easy as look at him; and we can ruin a designing family. That we can! ruin it root and branch, so that everything will have to be sold up, and those that offend us swept out of the country. Do you hear? Everything I say I can make good. We'll ruin you all if you don't mind. We'll sweep you away—your name and everything, and will shut him up that you are trying to work upon, so that you shall never hear of him again. Do you understand all that? Now, if you like to think you can fight me and Sir Giles, a little thing like you, a little nobody, you can just try it! And whatever happens will be on your own head. Oh, are you back already, John? What haste you have made! Good-bye, Patty; I hope you understand all I've said to you. Those chickens, I can tell you, will never be hatched. John—home!"

Patty stood looking after the carriage with her breast heaving and her nostrils dilating. The old lady had judged truly. She was frightened. Panic had seized her. She believed in these unknown miraculous powers. What could the Seven Thorns do against the Manor House? Patty Hewitt against Sir Giles and Lady Piercey? It was a question to freeze the very blood in the veins of a poor little country girl.

CHAPTER VIII

But it was not for nothing that Patty had put on her best things: quivering and excited as she was, she would not go in again, however discouraged, and take them off and return to the usual occupations, which were so very little like the occupations of the great folks of the Manor. She went on a little way towards the village very slowly, with all her fine feathers drooping, dragging the point of her lace-covered parasol along the sandy road. She was genuinely frightened by old Lady Piercey, whom all her life she had been brought up to regard as something more terrible than the Queen herself. For Her Majesty is known to be kind, and there are often stories in the newspapers about her goodness and charity; whereas Lady Piercey, with her deep voice and the tufts of hair on her chin, had an alarming aspect, and notwithstanding her Christmas doles and official charities, was feared and not loved in her parish and district. How was Patty to know how much or how little that terrible old lady could do? She was much discouraged by the interview, in which she felt that she had been cowed and overborne, and had not stood up with her usual spirit to her adversary. Had Patty known beforehand that Gervase's mother was to come to her thus, she would have proudly determined that Lady Piercey should "get as good as she gave." But she had been taken by surprise, and the old lady had certainly had the best of it. She was of so candid a spirit, that she could not deny this; certainly Lady Piercey had had the best of it. Patty herself had felt the ground cut from under her feet; she had not had a word to throw at a dog. She had allowed herself to be frightened and silenced and set down. It was a very unusual experience for Patty, and for the moment she could not overcome the feeling of having lost the battle.

However, presently her drooping crest began to rise. If Lady Piercey had but known the errand upon which Patty was going, the intention with which she had dressed herself in all her Sunday clothes, taken her gloves from their box, and her parasol out of its cover! The consciousness of what that object had been returned to Patty's mind in a moment, and brought back the colour to her cheeks. "Ah, my lady! you think it's something far off, as you've got time to fight against, and shut him up and take him away! If you but knew that it may happen to-morrow, or day after to-morrow, and Patty Hewitt become Mrs. Gervase Piercey in spite of you!" This thought filled Patty with new energy. It would be still sweeter to do it thus, under their very nose, as it were, after they had driven away triumphant, thinking they had crushed Patty. It was perhaps natural, that in the heat of opposition and rising pugnaciousness, the girl should have turned her bitterest thought upon the spectator sitting by, who had not said a word, and whose sympathies were, if not on her side, at least not at all on that of the other belligerent. "That white-faced maypole of a thing!" Patty said to herself with a virulence of opposition to the dependent which exists in both extremes of society. The old lady she recognised as having a right to make herself as disagreeable as she pleased, but the bystander, the silent spectator looking on, the cousin, or whatever she was—what had she to do with it? Patty clenched her hand, in which she had been limply holding her parasol, and vowed to herself that that Mrs. Osborne should know who was who before they had done with each other, or she, Patty, would know the reason why. Poor Margaret! who had neither wished to be there, nor aided and abetted in any way Patty's momentary discomfiture; but it frequently happens that the victim of the strife is a completely innocent person, only accidentally concerned.

Stimulated by this corrective of despondency, Patty resumed all her natural smartness, flung up her head, so that all her artificial flowers thrilled again, raised and expanded her parasol, and marched along like an army with banners, taking up with her own slim person and shadow the whole of the road. Humbler passersby, even the new curate, who was not yet acquainted with the parishioners, got out of her way, recognising her importance, and that sentiment as if of everything belonging to her that was in her walk, in her bearing, and, above all, in the parasol, which was carried, as is done still in Eastern countries, as a symbol of sovereignty. Mr. Tripley, the curate, stumbled aside upon the grassy margin of the road in his awe and respect, while Patty swept on; though there was something in her members—that love of ancient habit, scientifically known as a survival—which made the impulse to curtsey to him almost more than she could resist. She did get over it, however, as wise men say we get over the use of a claw or a tail which is no longer necessary to us. Patty went along the high-road as far as the entrance to the village street, and then turned down to where, at the very end of it, there stood a little house in a little garden which was one of the ornaments of the place. It was a house to a stranger somewhat difficult to characterise. It was not the doctor's or even the schoolmaster's, still less the curate's, unless he had happened (as was the case) to be an unmarried young man, who might have been so lucky as to attain to lodgings in that well-cared-for dwelling. But, no; it was to well cared for to take lodgers, or entertain any extraneous element; it was, in short, not to be diffuse, the house of Miss Hewitt, the sister of Richard Hewitt of the Seven Thorns, and aunt to Patty; the very Miss Hewitt in her own person, who had sat at the window upstairs making the vandyke in tape for her new petticoat, and to whom Sir Giles, in the days of his youth, and all the gentlemen had taken off their hats. Those had been the palmy days of the Seven Thorns, and the Hewitt of those times had been able to leave something to his daughter, which, along with a bit of money which she was supposed to have inherited from her mother, had enabled Miss Hewitt to establish herself in great comfort, not to say luxury, in Rose Cottage. It was a small slice of a house, which looked as if it had been cut off from a row and set down alone there. Its bricks were redder than any other bricks in the village, indeed they were reddened with paint as high up as the parlour window; the steps were whiter, being carefully whitened every day; the door was very shiny and polished, almost like the panel of a carriage, in green; the window of the parlour, at the side of the door, was shielded by hangings of spotless starched muslin, and had a small muslin blind secured across the lower half of it by a band of brass polished like gold. The door had a brass handle and a brass knocker. There was not a weed in the garden, which presented a brilliant border of flowers, concealing the more profitable wealth of a kitchen garden behind. Several great rose bushes were there, justifying the name of the cottage; but Miss Hewitt had taken down those which clustered once upon the walls, as untidy things which could not be kept in order. Rose Cottage was the pride, if also in some respects the laughing-stock, of the village; but it was the object of a certain adoration to the members of the clan of Hewitt, who considered it a credit to them and proof of their unblemished respectability far and near.

Patty knew too well to invade the virginal purity of the front door, the white step, or the brass knocker; but went round through the garden to the back, where her aunt was busy preparing fruit for the jam, for which Miss Hewitt was famous, with the frightened little girl, who was her maid-of-all-work, in attendance. All the little girls who succeeded each other in Miss Hewitt's service had a scared look; but all the same they were lucky little girls, and competed for by all the housekeepers round when they attained an age to be handed on to other service as certain to be admirably trained. She was a trim old lady, a little taller than Patty, and stouter, as became her years, but with all the vivacity and alertness which distinguished the women of that ancient house. She was a person of discernment also, and soon perceived that this was not a mere visit of ceremony, but that there was matter for advice in Patty's eye, and not that interest in the fruit, and its exact readiness for preserving, which would have been natural to a young woman in Patty's position had there been no other object in her mind. Miss Hewitt accordingly, though with regret, suspended her important operations, breathing a secret prayer that the delay might not injure the colour of her jam, and led the way into the parlour. To describe that parlour would occupy me gratefully for at least a couple of pages, but I forbear. The reader may perhaps be able to fill up the suggestion; if not, he (she?) will probably hear more about it later on.

"Well," said Miss Hewitt, placing herself in her high-backed chair, which no one else presumed to occupy, "what is to do? I could see as you'd something to tell me of before you were up to the kitchen door."

"I've more than something to tell you. I've something to ask you," said Patty.

"I dare say: the one mostly means the other; but you know as I'm not foolish, nor even to say free with my money, if that's it, knowing the valley of it more than the likes of you."

"I know that," said Patty; "and it ain't for anything connected with the house or the business that I'd ever ask you, auntie; but this is for myself, and I sha'n't go about the bush or make any explanations till I've just told you frank; it's a matter of thirty pounds."

"Thirty pounds! the gell is out of her senses!" Miss Hewitt cried.

"Or thereabouts. I don't know for certain; but you, as knows a deal more than me, may. It's for a marriage-licence," said Patty, looking her aunt full in the face.

"A marriage-licence!" Miss Hewitt repeated again, in tones of consternation; "and what does the fool want with a licence as costs money, when you can put up the banns, as is far more respectable, and be married the right way."

"I don't know as there's anything that ain't respectable in a licence, and anyway it's the only thing," said Patty, "for him and me. If I can't get it, I'll have to let it alone, that's all. A marriage as mightn't be anything much for the moment, but enough to make the hair stand upright on your head, Aunt Patience, all the same!"

"What kind of marriage would that be?" said the old lady, sceptical yet interested; "that fine Roger of yours, maybe, as is probable to be made a lord for his battin' and his bowlin'. Lord! Patty, how you can be such a fool, a niece of mine!"

"I ain't such a fool," said Patty, growing red, "though it might be better for me if I was. But anyhow I am your niece, as you say, and I can't—be that kind of fool; maybe I'm a bigger fool, if it's true as that old witch at the Manor says."

"What old witch?" cried the other old witch in the parlour, pricking up her ears.

"Aunt Patience," cried Patty, "you as knows: can they lock up in a madhouse a young man as isn't mad, no more than you or me; but is just silly, as any one of us might be? Can they put him out of his property, or send for the Lord Chancellor and take everything from him to his very name? Oh, what's the use of asking who he is? Who could he be? there ain't but one like that in all this county, and you know who he is as well as I do. Mr. Gervase Piercey. Sir Giles' son and heir! and they've got neither chick nor child but him!"

"Patty," said the elder woman, laying a grip like that of a bird with claws upon her niece's arm, "is it 'im as you want the thirty pounds for to buy the licence? Tell me straight out, and not a word more."

"It is him," said Patty, in full possession of her h's, and with a gravity that became the importance of the occasion. Miss Hewitt did not say a word. She rose from her chair, and, proceeding to the window, pulled down the thick linen blind. She then placed a chair against the door. Then she took from the recess near the fireplace an old workbox, full to all appearance, when she opened it with a key which she took out of her purse, with thread and needles of various kinds. Underneath this, when she had taken the shelf completely out, appeared something wrapt in a handkerchief half-hemmed, with a threaded needle stuck in it—as if it had been a piece of work put aside—which proved to be an old pocketbook. She held this in her hand for a moment only, gave Patty a look, full of suspicion, scrutiny, yet subdued enthusiasm; then she opened it and took out carefully three crisp and crackling notes, selecting them one by one from different bundles. Then with great deliberation she put notes, pocketbook, the covering shelf, of the workbox, and the box itself back into the place where it had stood before.

"Mind, now you've seen it, I'll put it all into another place," Miss Hewitt said; "so you may tell whoever you like, they won't find it there."

"Why should I tell?" said Patty; "it's more for my interest you should keep it safe."

"You think you'll get it all when I die," said the elder woman, sitting down opposite to her niece with the notes in her hand.

"I think, as I hope, you'll never die, Aunt Patience! but always be here to comfort and help a body when they're in trouble, like me."

"Do you call yourself in trouble? I call you as lucky as ever girl was. I'd have given my eyes for the chance when I was like you; but his father was too knowing a one, and never gave it to me. Here! you asked for thirty, and I've give you fifty. Don't you go and put off and shilly-shally, but strike while the iron's hot. And there's a little over to go honeymooning upon. Of course he's got no money—the Softy: but I know 'im; he's no more mad than you or me."

She ended with a long, low laugh of exultation and satisfaction which made even Patty, excited and carried away by the tremendous step in her life thus decided upon, feel the blood chilled in her veins.

"You think there's no truth, then, in what Lady Piercey said: that they could take everything from him, even to his name?" It was the hesitation of this chill and horror which brought such a question to Patty's lips.

Miss Hewitt laughed again. "The Manor estate is all entailed," she said, "and the rest they'll never get Sir Giles to will away—never! All the more if there's a chance of an heir, who ought to have all his wits about him, Patty, from one side of the house. Get along with you, girl! You're the luckiest girl as ever I knew!"

But, nevertheless, it was with a slower step and a chill upon all her thoughts that Patty went back, without even putting up her parasol, though the sun from the west shone level into her eyes, to the Seven Thorns.

CHAPTER IX

For a few days after Patty's visit to her aunt, that young lady looked out with some eagerness for the reappearance of Gervase at the Seven Thorns, but looked in vain. At first she scarcely remarked his absence, having many things to think of, for it was not without excitement that she planned out the steps by which she was to enter into a new life. The first evening was filled, indeed, with the events of the day; the mental commotion called forth by the visit of Lady Piercey, and the excitement, almost overwhelming, of her unexpected, enthusiastic reception by Miss Hewitt, and the sudden supply so much above her most daring hopes. Fifty pounds! it was more to Patty than as many thousands would have been to minds more accustomed—much more. For the possession of a great deal of money means only income, and an unknown treasure in somebody else's hands, whereas fifty pounds is absolute money, which you can change, and spend, and realise, and enjoy down to the last farthing. It gave her a great deal of anxiety how to dispose of it at first. The Seven Thorns was not a place where any thief was likely to come for money; it was not a house worth robbing, which was a point, as Patty with her excellent sense was aware, on which burglars are very particular, taking every care to obtain accurate information. But then, again, money is a thing that betrays itself—a secret that is carried by the birds of the air. Had there been any of these gentry about, he might have divined from the way in which she carried herself, that she had fifty pounds in her pocket. There was a little faint lightness about it, she thought, when she put it in her drawer—a sort of undeveloped halo, showing that something precious was in the old pocketbook which she had found to enshrine it in. Then she took it out of that formal receptacle, and placed it with scientific carelessness in an old envelope. But, immediately, that torn paper covering seemed to become important, too, among the pocket-handkerchiefs and cherished trumpery, beads and brooches in her "locked drawer." The "girl," who was the only servant, except the ostler, at the Seven Thorns, had always manifested a great curiosity (taken rather as a compliment to her treasures than as an offence by Patty) concerning the contents of that locked drawer. She had often asked to be shown the "jewellery," which Patty, indeed, had no objection to show. What if she would be tempted this night of all others to break open the drawer, to refresh her soul with gazing at them, and perhaps to throw the old dirty envelope away? It was highly improbable that poor Ellen, an honest creature, would break open the drawer. But still, everything is possible when you have fifty pounds to take care of. Patty took it out again and placed it first in her pocket—but she soon felt that to be quite too insecure—and then in her bosom under her trim little bodice. She felt it there, while she went about her usual occupations, carrying beer to her father's customers. Fancy carrying pots of beer to labourers that were not worth so much as the price of them, and thanking the clowns for twopence—a girl who had fifty pounds under the bodice of her cotton frock! She was glad to see that Gervase had obeyed her orders, and did not appear in the parlour among the dull drinkers there.

Next day Patty was much occupied in rummaging out the empty part of the house, the best rooms, once occupied by important guests, when the Seven Thorns was a great coaching establishment, but now vacant, tapestried with dust and cobwebs, rarely opened from one year's end to the other, except at the spring-cleaning, when it is the duty of every housekeeper to clear out all the corners. She got up very early in the summer mornings, before any one was stirring (and it may be imagined how early that was, for the Seven Thorns was all alert and in movement by six o'clock), and went in to make an inspection while she was secure from any disturbance. The best rooms were in the western end of the long house, quite removed from the bar and the parlour, the chief windows looking out upon the garden, and at a distance upon the retreating line of the high road, and the slope of the heathery downs. Patty's heart swelled with pleasure as she carefully opened the shutters and looked round at the old faded furniture. There was a good-sized sitting-room, and two or three other rooms communicating with each other, and separated by a long passage from the other part of the house. "A suite of apartments," she said to herself! for Patty had read novels, and was acquainted with many fine terms of expression. The early sunshine flooded all the silent country, showing a dewy glimmer in the neglected garden, and sweeping along the broad and vacant road, where as yet there was nothing stirring. A few cows in a field, one of which got slowly up to crop a morsel before breakfast, as fine ladies (and fine gentlemen, too) have a cup of tea in bed, startled Patty as by the movement of some one spying upon her unusual operations and wondering what they meant. But there was no other spectator, nothing else awake, except the early birds who were chattering about their own businesses in every tree, talking over their own suites of apartments, and the repairs wanted, before the professional occupations of the day began, and the pipes were tuned up. They were far too busy to pay any attention to Patty, nor did she mind them. Besides, they were all sober, married folks, with the care of their families upon their heads; while she was a young person all thrilling with the excitement of the unknown, and making a secret survey of the possible future nest.

Patty inspected these rooms with a careful and a practised eye. Any young couple in the land, she felt, might be proud to possess this suite of apartments. She examined the carpets to see whether they would do, whether they would bear a thorough beating, which they required, and whether by judicious application of gall, or other restoring fluid, the colour might be brought back to the part which had been most trodden; or whether it would be better to buy one of those new-fashioned rugs which were spread upon the matting in the Rectory—a poor sort of substitute for a carpet, Patty had always thought—but as it was the fashion, it might be adopted to cover deficiencies; or a nice round table with a cover might be placed upon that weak spot. Curtains would be necessary, but thin white muslin is cheap and could be easily supplied. Patty pulled the old furniture about, as the rector's wife had done on her first arrival, to give it a careless look, which does not suit the stern angles of early Victorian mahogany and haircloth; but Patty had great confidence in crochet and frilled muslin to cover a multitude of sins. She stood at the window and looked out upon the garden which was quite retired and genteel—as refined a view as could have been had in the Manor itself. The cow in the field had lain down again to finish her night's rest after that early cup of tea. It was so quiet: the morning's sunshine almost level in long rays on the grass, the sleek coat of the brown cow glistening, nobody stirring. It almost overawed Patty to look out upon that wonderful silence before the world was awake. There was no telling what might happen in that new day; there was no telling what might come to her in the new life upon the margin of which she stood. She did not, I need scarcely say, think of the ideal excellencies of her future husband, or of love, or any of the usual enchantments that brighten the beginning of life. She thought of the Manor; of the old people who would soon die and be out of the way; of Lady Piercey's carriage, which would be hers; of the coachman and John on the box, whom she had been at school with (John at least), and whom she would make to tremble before her when her turn came to be my lady. My lady! Patty's head turned round and round. She put her head upon the window-frame to support herself, turning giddy with the thought. Your ladyship! She could hear people say it reverentially who had called, as if she had been their servant, for Patty at the Seven Thorns.

This was the thought that filled her mind with something of that ineffable elation and delight in her own happiness which is supposed to be peculiar to people who are in love. Patty was in love; but it would be putting a scorn upon her intelligence to suppose that she was in love with Gervase. Poor Gervase, the Softy! Patty was resolved to be very good to him—she had even a kind of affection for him as being her own to do what she pleased with. He should never have any reason to regret her ownership. She would be good to him in every way, deny him nothing, consider all his silly tastes as well as his serious interests. But what Patty was in love with was the Manor, and the carriage, and the rents, and the ladyship. Lady Piercey! The thought of that tingled to her very feet; it turned her head like wine. The old people, of course, would make themselves very disagreeable. It would be their part to do so. Patty felt that she would think no worse of them for fighting against her, tooth and nail. But they would have to give in at the end; or still better, they would die and get out of her way, which was the most probable thing. Young people generally think of the death of old people without compunction; it is their business to die, just as it is the business of their successors to live. It is the course of nature. Patty no more doubted they would die than that Christmas would come in six months, whatever happened. What she would have chosen for pleasure and to enhance her triumph to the utmost, was that old Sir Giles should die, and the old lady survive to be called the Dowager, and to see Patty bearing the title of Lady Piercey.

This was what would be most sweet; and it was very likely to come to pass, for everybody knew that Sir Giles was a great invalid, whereas nobody knew that Lady Piercey had been attacked last year by a little, very little premonitory "stroke"—nobody, at least, except Parsons and Margaret Osborne and the doctor, with none of whom Patty had any communication. The greatest triumph she could think of was to see the Dowager bundled off to her dower-house, while she, Patty, the regnant Lady Piercey, took her place. She was not an ill-natured person on the whole, but she felt that there was here awaiting her a poignant joy.

In the meantime, however, this glory was still at a distance, and the first thing to do was to prepare a shelter for the young couple who would have to inhabit, for lack of other habitation, these rooms in the west end of the Seven Thorns. Patty interviewed her father on the subject as soon as he had eaten his breakfast. She told him that to leave these beautiful rooms unoccupied was a sin and shame, and that it was his plain duty to do them up and look out for a lodger for next summer. "Indeed, I'm not sure but we might hear of somebody this season still, if they were ready," she said. She showed him all the capabilities of the place, and how a disused garden door might be arranged so as to form a separate entrance, "for gentry won't come in by a public-house door. It ain't likely," she explained. "What do I care about gentry, and what do you know about 'em?" said her father. "I'll never spend my money on such nonsense." "But you like to see the colour of theirs," said Patty, "and it would be good for trade, too. For suppose you gave them their board for a fixed rate, there would always be a good profit. It would keep us going and them, too, so as we should pay nothing for our living, and that in addition to the rent: don't you see, father?" "I don't believe in them profits," said the old man; "gentry, as you call 'em, don't eat the same things as I likes." "But they'd have to, father," said Patty, softly, "if they couldn't get nothing else." This struck Mr. Hewitt's sense of humour, and he allowed that it might be possible so, with a chuckle of democratic enjoyment. "I'd like to see 'em sit down with their mincin' ways to beans and fat bacon," he confessed. Patty was very sure that it was not on beans and fat bacon that she would feed the future Sir Gervase and Lady Piercey; but she made no remark on this point, and ere the week was over, she had all her plans in operation—the new entrance by the garden, the rods put up for the new muslin curtains, the old rooms scrubbed and polished, and dusted till they shone again. "I think I'll take a run up to London, and buy two or three little things out of my own little bit of money," she said cautiously. And though her father demanded what little bit of money she had to spend, he made no objection to the expedition. Patty was very well to be trusted to look after herself, as well as the interests of the family. And thus she prepared, in every respect, the way.

But Gervase never appeared. Morning and night she looked out for him, pleased and half-amused, at first, with the faithfulness with which he obeyed her. But after a time Patty became a little anxious. She had, indeed, forbidden him to come to the Seven Thorns. But she had not intended this self-sacrifice to be of such long duration. What if his mother had got hold of him? What if he had been frightened into giving up his love? The old lady had looked very masterful, very full of power to do mischief. What if they had shut him up? Patty grew more and more anxious as day followed day. The fifty pounds which she had sewn up in a little bag, and wore suspended by a ribbon round her neck, began to lie like a blister upon her pretty white skin underneath her bodice. What would Aunt Patience say if all her plans came to nothing, if no licence was necessary, and no bridegroom forthcoming? Patty felt her heart sink, sink into unimaginable depths. The old woman would reclaim her money with a sneer enough to drive any girl mad. She would laugh out at the fool that had fancied the Softy was in love with her. His father, as had all his wits about him, might take a person in; but Lord bless us, the Softy! Patty knew exactly what her aunt would say. Miss Hewitt had given her the money, not for love of her, but that she might triumph over the great people, and avenge the wrongs of the other Patty who had gone before her. Patty grew hot and grew cold, as she stood at the door looking out along the road, and seeing nobody;

her heart sickened at every footstep, and leaped at every shadow on the way. One night, when she stood there with her face turned persistently in one direction, just as the soft summer twilight was stealing over the landscape, and everything was growing indistinct, a voice close to her made Patty jump. She had not even observed—so great was her preoccupation—another figure coming round the other corner. Roger Pearson had seated himself on the bench under the parlour window, and yet she had taken no notice. He broke the silence by a laugh of mockery, that seemed to Patty the beginning of the ridicule and scorn of the whole parish. "Looking out for some one, eh?" said the voice; "but he ain't coming, not to-night."

"Who is not coming, Mr. Pearson?" said Patty, commanding herself with a great effort; "some one you were expecting to meet?"

"You can't come over me like that, Patty," said Roger. "Lord, a nice lass like you that might have the best fellow in the village—a-straining and a-wearing your eyes looking after a Softy! and him not coming neither—not a step! They knows better than that."

"I don't know what you mean, Mr. Pearson," said Patty, feeling herself enveloped from head to foot in a flush of rage and shame. "I don't know as I ever was known as one that looked after Softies—meaning poor folks that have lost their wits, I suppose. You're one of them, anyhow, that speaks like that to me."

"I wouldn't if I were you," said the young man, in his deep voice—"a fellow that's not fit to tie your shoe, though he may be the squire's son. Don't you think that'll ever come to any good. They'll never let you be my lady; don't you think it. They'll turn him out o' doors, and they'll cut him off with a shilling; and then you'll find yourself without a penny and a fool on your hands instead of a man."

"Is this something out of a story book, or is it out of his own head?" said Patty looking round her as if consulting an impartial audience,—"anyway, it has nothing to say to me. I'll send Ellen to you for your orders, Mr. Pearson, for I've got a lot to do to-night, and I can't stand here to listen to your romancing. Ellen," she cried, "just see to that gentleman." She went off with all the honours of war, but Patty's heart was likely to burst. She marched upstairs with a candle to the rooms she had been arranging so carefully, and locked the door, and sat down upon the sofa and gave way to a torrent of tears. Was it all to come to nothing, after all her splendid dreams? She knew as well as any one that he was a fool and could be persuaded into anything. How did she know that his mother, if she tried, could not turn him round her little finger, as she, Patty, had been certain she could do? How could she tell, in the battle between Lady Piercey of Greyshott and Patty of the Seven Thorns, that it was she who would triumph and not the great lady? It was all Patty could do not to shriek out her exasperation, her misery and rage; not to pull down the curtains and dash the furniture to pieces. She caught her handkerchief with her teeth and tore it to keep herself quiet—and the fifty pounds in the bag burnt her breast like a blister. What if it was to come to nothing, after all?

CHAPTER X

The week had been a very long week to Gervase. To him, poor fellow, there was no limit of time; no thought that his obedience was intended, nay, desired to stop at a certain point. He went on dully, keeping at home, keeping indoors, trying in his fatuous way to please his parents. It was a very dull round to him who had known the livelier joys of the Seven Thorns, the beer and the tobacco in the parlour, and Patty flitting about, throwing him a word from time to time. It seemed but a poor sort of paradise to sit among the slow old topers in the smoky room and imbibe the heavy beer; but it is unfortunately a kind of enjoyment which many young men prefer to the fireside at home, even without any addition of a Patty; and the poor Softy was not in this respect so very much inferior to the best and cleverest. The fireside at home, it must be allowed, was not very exciting. To be sure, the room itself was a very different room from that of the Seven Thorns. It was not the drawing-room in which the Piercey family usually sat in the evening, for the drawing-room was upstairs, and Sir Giles could not be taken up without great difficulty in his wheeled chair. It was the library, a large long room, clothed with the mellow tones and subdued gilding of old books, making a background which would have been quite beautiful to an artist. There was a row of windows on one side veiled in long curtains, and between these windows a series of family portraits almost as long as the windows, full length, not very visible in the dim light, affording a little glimpse of colour, and a face here and there looking out from that height upon the little knot of living people below; but the Pierceys of the past were not remarkable any more than the present Pierceys. A shaded lamp was suspended by a very long chain from the high roof, which was scarcely discernible going up so far, with those glimmers of bookcases and tall old portraits leading towards the vague height above; beneath it was a small round table, at which Lady Piercey sat in a great chair with her bright-coloured work; on the other side was Sir Giles among his cushions, with his backgammon board on a stand beside him, where sometimes Margaret, sometimes Dunning played with him till bedtime. Parsons, on the other hand, was so frequently in attendance on her mistress that the two old servants might be taken as part of the family circle. When Margaret took her place at the backgammon board, Dunning had an hour's holiday, and retired to the much brighter atmosphere of the servants' hall or the housekeeper's room. And when Dunning played with Sir Giles, Margaret attended upon Lady Piercey to thread her needles, and select the shades of the silk, and Parsons was set free. The one who was never set free was Mrs. Osborne, whose evenings in this dim room between the two old people were passed in an endless monotony which sometimes made her giddy. The dull wheel of life went round and round for her, and never stopped or had any difference in it. From year to year the routine was the same.

Now, whether this scene, or the parlour at the Seven Thorns, where the sages of the village opened their mouths every five minutes or so to emit a remark or a mouthful of smoke, or to take in a draught of beer, was the most—or rather the least—enlivening, it would be hard to say. The sages of the village are sometimes dull and sometimes wise in a book. They were full of humour and character in George Eliot's representation of them, and they are very quaint in Mr. Hardy's. But I doubt much if they ever say such fine things in reality, and I am sure, if they did, that Gervase Piercey was not capable of understanding them. The beer and the tobacco and the sense of freedom and of pleasing himself—also of being entirely above his company, and vaguely respected by them—made up the charms of the humbler place to Gervase. And Patty—Patty had got by degrees to be the soul of all; but even before Patty's reign began he had escaped with delight from these home evenings to the Seven Thorns. Why? For Sir Giles, even in his enfeebled state, was better company than old Hewitt and his cronies; and Lady Piercey's sharp monologue on things in general was more piquant than anything the old labourers found to say; and Mrs. Osborne was a great deal handsomer than Patty, and would willingly have exerted herself for the amusement of her cousin. But this is a problem to which there is no answer. Far better and cleverer young men than Gervase make this same choice every day, or rather every evening; and no one can tell why.

But Gervase had turned over a new leaf. He went out to the door and took a few whiffs of his pipe, turning his back to the road which led to the Seven Thorns, that the temptation might not be too much for him, and repeating dully to himself what Patty had said to him. And then he went into the library, where they were all assembled, and pushed Dunning away, who was just arranging the board for Sir Giles' game. "Here! look out; I'm going to play with you, father," Gervase said. The old gentleman had been delighted the first night, pleased more or less the second, fretful the third. "You don't understand my play, Gervase," he said.

"Oh! yes, I understand your play, father: Dunning lets you win, and that's why you like Dunning to play with you; but I'm better, for I wake you up, and you've got to fight for it when it's me."

"Dunning does nothing of the sort," cried Sir Giles, angrily, "Dunning plays a great deal better than you, you booby. Do you let me win, Dunning? It's all he knows!"

"I ought to be good, Sir Giles, playin' with a fine player like you; but I never come up to you, and never will, for I haven't the eddication you have, Sir Giles, which stands to reason, as I'm only a servant," Dunning said.

"There! You hear him: go and play something with Meg; you're never still with those long legs of yours, and I like a quiet game."

"I'll keep as quiet as pussy," said Gervase. "Which'll you have, father, black or white? and let's toss for the first move."

Now, everybody knew that Sir Giles always played with the white men and always had the first move. Once again the old gentleman had to resign himself to the noisy moves and shouts of his son over every new combination, and to the unconscious kicks which the restlessness of Gervase's long limp legs inflicted right and left. Dunning stood behind his master's chair, with a stern face of disapproval, yet trying hard by winks and nods to indicate the course which ought to be pursued, until Gervase threw himself back in his chair, almost kicking over the table with the corresponding movement of his legs, and bursting into a loud laugh. "What d'ye mean, ye old fool, making faces at me over father's shoulder? Do you mean I'm to give him the game, like you do? Come on, father, let's fight it out."

"I never said a word, Sir Giles! I hope as I knows my place," cried Dunning, alarmed.

"Hold your tongue, you big gaby," cried Sir Giles; but presently the old gentleman thrust the board away, overturning it upon his son's long legs. "I'll not play any more," he said: "I've had enough of it. I think I was never so tired in my life. Backgammon's a fine game, but one can't go on for ever. Fetch me my drink, Dunning; I think I'll go to bed."

"It's all because he's losing his game," cried Gervase, with a loud ha! ha! He had something like the manners of a gentleman at the Seven Thorns, but at home his manners were those of the public-house. "The old man don't like to be beaten; he likes to have everything his own way. And Dunning's an old humbug, and lets you have it. But it ain't good for you to have too much of your own way. I've been told that since I was a little kid like Osy; and what's sauce for the goose is sauce for the gander, father, don't you know."

"Gervase, how dare you speak so to your papa? Come over here, sir, and leave him a little in peace. Where did you learn to laugh so loud, and make such a noise? Come here, you riotous boy. You always were a noisy fellow, making one's head ache to hear you. Sit down, for goodness' sake, and be quiet. Meg, can't you find something to amuse him? I dare say he'd like a game at cards. How can I tell you what game? If you can't, at your time of life, find something that will occupy him and keep him quiet—! Here, Gervase, hold this skein of silk while Parsons winds it, and Meg will go and get the cards, and perhaps you'd like a round game."

"I don't want a game, mother, not for Meg's sake, who doesn't count. I want to be pleasant to you—and to father, too," said Gervase, standing up against the fireplace, which, of course, was vacant this summer night.

Sir Giles was so far from appreciating the effort of his son, that he sat fuming in his chair, while Dunning collected the scattered "men," muttering indistinct thunders, and pettishly putting away with his stick the pieces of the game. "Make haste! can't you make haste, man?" he mumbled; "I want my drink, and I'm going to bed. And I won't have my evening spoiled like this again. I won't, by George, not for anything you can say. Four nights I've been a martyr to that cub, and I don't see that you've done much to keep him in order, my lady! It all falls upon me, as everything does, and, by George, I won't have it again. Can't you make haste, you old fool, and have done with your groping? You're losing your eyesight, I believe. Have one of the women in to find them, and get me my drink, for I'm going to bed."

"I'll find them, father," cried Gervase cheerfully, plunging down upon the carpet on his hands and knees, and pushing the old gentleman's stick back into his face.

"For goodness' sake, Meg, find something for him to do! and take that boy off his father, or Sir Giles will have a fit," cried Lady Piercey in Mrs. Osborne's ear.

"Get out o' my way, you young ass!" Sir Giles thundered, raising the stick and bestowing an angry blow upon his son's shoulders. Gervase sat up on his knees like a dog, and stared for a moment angrily, with his hand lifted as if he would have returned the blow. Then he opened his mouth wide and gave forth a great laugh. Poor old Sir Giles caught at Dunning's arm, clutching him in an ecstasy of exasperation. "Get me off, man, can't you? Get me out of sight of him; take me to bed," the old father cried, in that wretchedness of miserable perception which only parents know. His son—his only son! His heir, the last of the Piercey's!—this Softy sitting up like a dog upon the floor!

Lady Piercey fell back also in her chair, and whimpered a little piteously, like the poor old woman she was, as Sir Giles was wheeled out of the room. The backgammon board, overturned, lay on the floor, with the pieces scattered over the carpet, and Gervase scrambling after them, for Dunning had been too tremulous and frightened to pick more than half of them up. "Oh! my poor, silly boy! oh! you dreadful, dreadful fool!" the old lady cried. "Will you never learn any better? Can't you wake up and be a man?" She cried over this, for a little, very bitterly, with that terrible sense of the incurable which turns the poor soul back upon itself—and then she flung round in her big chair towards her niece, who stood silent and troubled, not knowing what part to take. "It's all your fault," she cried in a fierce whisper, "for not finding something for him to do. Why didn't you find something for him to do? You might have played something to him, or sung something with him, or got him to look at pictures, or—anything! And now you've let your poor uncle go off in a rage, which may bring on a fit as likely as not, and me worse, for I can't give in like him. Oh, Meg, what an ungrateful, selfish thing you are to stand there and never interfere when you might have found him something to do!"

When Lady Piercey's procession streamed off afterwards to bed, my lady leaning heavily on Parsons' arm and Margaret following with the work, Gervase was left still picking up the pieces, sprawling over the carpet and laughing as he followed the little round pieces of ivory and wood into the corners where they had rolled. Margaret went back to the library after being released by her aunt, and found him still there making a childish game of this for his own amusement, and chuckling to himself as he raced them over the carpet. He scrambled up, however, a little ashamed when he heard her voice asking, "What are you doing, Gervase?" "Oh, nothing," he said with his foolish laugh, stuffing the "men" into his pockets. She put her hand upon his shoulder kindly.

"Gervase, dear, you're quite grown up, don't you know; quite a man now. You mustn't be so mischievous, just like a boy. Poor Uncle Giles, you must not play tricks upon him; he likes a quiet game."

"Don't you be a fool, Meg. Why, that was what I was doing all the night, playing his quiet game. Poor old father, he got into a temper, but bless you 'twasn't my fault. It's that old ass, Dunning, that's always getting in everybody's way."

"Of course he would like you best, Gervase,—but Dunning knows all his ways. Your game might be better fun—"

"I should think so," said the poor Softy. "My game is the game, and Dunning spoils everything. It ain't my fault, though every one of you gets into a wax with me,"—Gervase's lip quivered a little as if he might have cried,—"and me giving up everything only to please them!" he said.

"I am sure they are pleased to see you always indoors and not spending your time in that dreadful place."

"What dreadful place? That is all you know—I'd never have come home any more but for them that's there. It was she that sent me to please the old folks. But I shan't go on much longer if you all treat me like this. I've tried my best to make the time pass for them, Meg, to give them a laugh and that. And they huff me and cuff me as if I was a fool. Why do they always call me a fool," cried the poor fellow with a passing cloud of trouble, "whatever I do?"

"Oh, Gervase!" cried Margaret, full of pity. "But why did she want you so particularly to please them just now?"

He stared at her for a moment, then laughed and nodded his head. "You'd just like to know!" he said, "but she didn't mean me to be nice to you, Meg; for she's always afraid I'll be driven to marry you—though a man must not marry his grandmother, you know."

Margaret repented in a moment of the flush of anger that flew over her. "You can make her mind easy on that point," she said gravely; "but oh, Gervase, I am afraid it will make them very unhappy if you go on with this fancy; they would never let you bring her here."

"Fancy!" he cried, "I'm going to marry her. You can't call that a fancy; and if you think you can put me off it, or the whole world!—Get along Meg, I don't want to talk to you any more."

"But I want very much to talk to you, Gervase."

Gervase looked at her with a smile of foolish complacency. "I dare say you think me silly," he cried, "but here's two of you after me. Get along, Meg; whatever I do I'm not going to take your way."

"You must do as you please, then," said Margaret in despair; "but remember, Gervase," she said, turning back before she reached the door, "your father is old, and you might drive him into a fit if you go on as you did to-night—and where would you be then?" she added, with an appeal to the better feeling in which she still believed.

"Why, I'd be in his place, and she'd be my lady," cried the young man, with a gleam of cruel cunning, "and nobody could stop me any more, whatever I liked to do."

But next evening there seemed to be in his mind some lingering regard for what she had said. Gervase left his father alone, and devoted himself to his mother, who was more able to take care of herself. He offered to wind her silks, and entangled them hopelessly with delighted peals of laughter. He took her scissors to snip off the ends for her, and put the sharp points through the canvas, until Lady Piercey, in her exasperation, gave him a sudden cuff on his cheek.

"You great fool!" she cried—"you malicious wretch! Do you want to spoil my work as well as everything else? I wish you were little enough to be whipped, I do; and I wish I had whipped you when you were little, when it might have done you some good. Margaret, what do you mean sitting quiet there, enjoying yourself with a book and me driven out of my senses? That's what he wants to do, I believe—to drive us mad and get his own way; to make us crazy, both his poor father and me."

"No, I don't," cried Gervase, "and you oughtn't to hit me—I'll hit back again if you do it again. It hurts—you've got a fist like a butcher, though you're such an old lady." He rubbed his cheek for a moment dolefully, and then again burst out laughing. "You look like old Judy in the show, mamma, when she hits her baby: only you're so fat you could never get into it, and your voice is gruff like the old showman's—not squeaky, like Mrs. Punch. I've cut all the silks into nice lengths for you to work with—ain't you obliged to me? Look here," he said, holding out his work. Poor Lady Piercey clapped her fat hands together loudly in sheer incapacity of expression. It made a loud report like a gun fired off to relieve her feelings, and Sir Giles looked up from his quiet game with Dunning, not without a subdued amusement that she should now be getting her share.

"What's the matter, what's the matter, my lady? Is that cub of yours playing some of his pranks? It's your turn to-night, it appears, and serves you right, for you always back him up."

"Oh, you fool, you fool, you fool!" cried the old lady in her passion. And then she turned her fiery eyes on her husband with a look of contempt and fury too great for words. "Meg!" she cried, putting out her hand across the table and grasping Mrs. Osborne's arm, "If you're ever driven wild like me, never you look for sympathy to a man! when they see you nearly mad with trouble they give you a look, and chuckle! that's what they always do. Put down the scissors, you, you, you—"

"Oh, and to think," she cried wildly, "that that's my only son! Oh, Giles, how can you play your silly games, and sit and see him—the only one we have between us, and he's a born fool! And me, that was so thankful to see him stay at home, and give up going out to his low company! And now I can't abide him. I can't abide to see him here!"

This happened on the night when Patty, frightened and dejected, shut herself up in the room which she had meant for her bridal bower, and cried her eyes out because of Gervase's absence. The poor Softy was thus of as much importance as any hero, turning houses and hearts upside down.

CHAPTER XI

A whole week, and nothing had been seen or heard of Gervase at the Seven Thorns. Even old Hewitt remarked it, with a taunt to his daughter. "Where's your Softy, that was never out of the house, Miss Patty, eh? Don't seem to be always about at your apron string, my lass, as you thought you was to keep him there. Them gentlemen," said old Hewitt, "as I've told you, Softy or not, they takes their own way, and there's no trust to be put in them. He's found some one else as he likes better, or maybe you've given him the sack, Patty, eh? And that's a pity, for he was a good customer," the landlord said.

"Whether I've given him the sack or he's found some one he likes better, don't matter much to any one as I can see. I'll go to my work, father, if you've got nothing more sensible than that to say."

"Sensible or not, he's gone, and a good riddance," said her father. "I ain't a fine Miss, thick with the rector and the gentry, like you; but I declare, to see that gaby laughing and gaping at the other side of the table, turned me sick, it did. And I hopes as we'll see no more of him, nor none of his kind. If you will have a sweetheart, there's plenty of good fellows about, 'stead of a fool like that."

Patty did not stamp her foot as she would have liked to do, or throw out her arms, or scream with rage and disappointment. She went on knocking her broom into all the corners, taking it out more or less in that way, and tingling from the bunch of hair fashionably dressed on the top of her head, to the toe of her high-heeled shoes, with suppressed passion. She would not make an exhibition of herself. She would not give Ellen, the maid-servant, closely observing her through the open door of the back kitchen, nor Bob, the ostler, who had also heard every word old Hewitt said as he bustled about with his pail outside the house, any occasion of remark or of triumph over her as a maiden forsaken, whose love had ridden away. They were all on the very tiptoe of expectation, having already made many comments to each other on the subject. "You're all alike—every one of you," Ellen had said to Bob. "You'd go and forsake me just the same, if you saw some one as you liked better." "It'll be a long day afore I do that," said the gallant ostler, preserving, however, the privilege of his sex. They were all ready to throw the responsibility of attraction upon the woman. It was more to her credit to keep her hold on the man by being always delightful to him than by any bond of faithfulness on his part. Patty felt this to the bottom of her heart. It was not so much that she blamed her Softy. She blamed herself bitterly, and felt humiliated and ashamed that she had not been able to hold him; that he had found anything he liked better than her society. She swept out every corner, banging her broom as if she were punishing the unknown rivals who had seduced him away from her, and felt, for all her pride, as if she never could hold up her head again before the parish, which would thus know that she had miscalculated her powers. Roger Pearson knew it already, and triumphed. And then Aunt Patience—but that was the most dreadful of all.

Even old Hewitt himself, the landlord of the Seven Thorns, was a little disappointed, if truth were told. He had liked to say to the fathers of the village, "I can't get that young Piercey out o' my house. Morning, noon, and night that young fellow is about. And I can't kick him out, ye see, old Sir Giles bein' the Lord o' the Manor." "I'd kick him out fast enough," the blacksmith had replied, who never had any chance that way, "if he come sneakin' after my gell." "Oh, as for that, my Patty is one that can take care of herself," it had been Mr. Hewitt's boast to say. And when he was congratulated ironically by the party in the parlour with a "Hallo, Hewitt! you've been and got shut of your Softy," the landlord did not like it.

Softy as Gervase was, to have got him thus fast in the web, old Sir Giles' only son, was a kind of triumph to the house.

In the afternoon, however, Patty resolved to take a walk. It was an indulgence which she permitted to herself periodically—that her best things and her hat with the roses, her light gloves and her parasol might not spoil for want of use. She put on all this finery, however, with a sinking at her heart. The last time she had worn them she had been all in a thrill with excitement, bent upon the boldest step she had ever taken in her life. And the high tension of her nerves and passion of her mind had been increased by the unexpected colloquy with Lady Piercey at the carriage-door. But that was a day of triumph all along the line. She had baffled the old lady, and she had roused her own aunt to a fierce enthusiasm of interest, which had reacted upon herself and increased her determination, and the fervour of her own. When she had walked back that evening with the fifty pounds, she had felt herself already my lady, uplifted to a pinnacle of grandeur from which no fathers or mothers could bring her down. But now! Gervase himself had not seemed a very important part of that triumph a little while ago. He had been a chattel of hers, a piece of property as much her own as her parasol. And if he had emancipated himself, if he had escaped out of her net, if his mother had obtained the mastery of him, or sent him away, Patty felt as if she must die of rage and humiliation. To take back that fifty pounds to Aunt Patience and allow that the use she had got it for was no longer possible; to submit to be asked on all sides, by Roger in triumph, by everybody else in scorn, what had become of him? was more than she could bear. She would rather run away and go to service in London. She would rather—there was nothing in the world that Patty did not feel herself capable of doing rather than bear the brunt of this disappointment and shame.

It must be added that the value of Gervase individually was enormously enhanced by this period of doubt and alarm. The prize that is on the point of being lost is very different from that which falls naturally, easily into your hands. Patty thought of the Softy no longer as if he were a piece of still life; no more—indeed, not so much—a part of the proceedings which were to end eventually in making her my lady as the marriage-licence which would cost such a deal of money. All that was changed now. Poor fellow! he who had never been of much importance to anybody had become of the very greatest consequence now. She would never, never be my lady at all, unless he took a principal part in it—the great fool, the goose, the gaby! But though her feelings broke out once or twice in a string of such reproaches under her breath, Gervase was too important a factor now to be thought of or addressed by contemptuous epithets. He could spoil it all; he could make all her preparations useless. He could shame her in the eyes of Aunt Patience, and even before the whole of her little world, although nobody knew how far things had gone. Therefore it was with an anxious heart that Patty made a turn round by the outskirts of the village as if she were going to pay a visit to her Aunt Patience—the last place in the world where she desired to go—and then directed her steps towards the Manor, meaning to make a wide round past the iron gate and the beech-tree avenue, which were visible to any passenger walking across the downs. She gave a long look, as she passed, at the great house, with all its windows twinkling in the afternoon sun, and the two long processions of trees on either side. Her heart rose to her mouth at the thought that all this might, yet might never, be her own. Might be! it had seemed certain a week ago; and yet might never be if that fool—oh, that imbecile, that ridiculous, vacant, gaping Softy—should take it into his foolish head to draw back now.

The road lay close under the wall of the park beyond the iron gate. Patty had got so anxious, so terrified, so horribly convinced that her chances of meeting him were small, and that, except in an accidental way, she could not hope to lay hands on him again, that her stout heart almost failed her as she went on. It was a very warm day, and she was flushed and heated with her walk, as well as with the suspense and alarm of which her mind was full, so that she was aware she was not looking her best, when suddenly, without warning, she came full upon him round the corner, almost striking him with her outstretched parasol in the suddenness of the encounter. Gervase did not see her at all. He was coming on with his head bent, his under-lip hanging, his hands in his pockets, busy with his old game—six white ones all in a heap. What a jump for the right-hand man! and hallo, hallo! a little brown fellow slipping along on the other side, driven by somebody's foot! He made a mental note of that before looking to see who the somebody was, which was of so much less importance. And then Patty's little cry of surprise and "Oh! Mr. Gervase!" went through him like a shot at his ear. He gave a shout like the inarticulate delight of a dog, and flew towards her as if he had been Dash or Rover, roused by the ecstatic sound of their master's voice.

"Patty! Lord, to think of you being here! and me, that hasn't had a peep of you for a whole week. Patty! Oh, come now, I can't help it. I'm so happy, I could eat you up. Patty, Patty!" cried the poor fellow, patting her on the shoulder, looking into her face with his dull eyes suddenly inspired, "you're sure it's you!"

"And a deal you care whether it's me or not, Mr. Gervase," cried Patty, tossing her head. But in that moment Patty had become herself again. Her anxiety was over, her bosom's lord sat lightly on his throne. The fifty pounds in the little bag no longer felt like a blister. She was the mistress of the situation, and all her troubled thoughts flew before the wind as if they had never been.

"A deal I care? Oh, I do care a deal, Patty, if you only knew! Never you do it again—to make me stay away like this. I've made a mull of it, as I knew I should, without you to back me up. Father turns his back on me. He won't say a word. And even mother, that was always my stand-by, she says she can't abide to see me there."

Again Gervase looked as if he would cry; but brightening up suddenly, "I don't mind a bit as long as I can see you, and you'll tell me what to do."

"Well," said Patty, "I could perhaps tell you if I knew what you wanted to do. But I can't stand still here, for I've come out for a walk, and if you wish to speak to me you must come along with me. I'm going as far as Carter's Wells, and the afternoon's wearing on."

"Oh!" said Gervase, discomfited, "you're going as far as Carter's Wells? I thought—I supposed—or I wanted to think, Patty—as you were coming to look for me!"

"What should I do that for, Mr. Gervase?" said Patty, demurely.

"I'm sure I don't know," said the poor Softy. "I just thought so. You might have had something you wanted to tell me, or—to say I might come back, or—"

"What should I have to tell you, Mr. Gervase?"

He looked piteously at her, all astray, and took off his cap, and pushed his fingers through his hair. "I'm sure I don't know; and yet there was something that I wanted badly to hear. Patty, don't you make a fool of me like all the rest! If I don't know what it is, having such a dreadful memory, you do."

"It's a wonder as you remembered me at all, Mr. Gervase," said Patty, giving him a little sting in passing.

"You! I'd never forget you if I lived to be a hundred. I'd forget myself sooner, far sooner, than I'd forget you."

"But it's a long time since you've seen me, and you've forgotten all you wanted of me," Patty said, with a sharp tone of curiosity in her voice.

"No, I don't forget; I do know what I want—I want to marry you, Patty. I've been obeying all your orders, and trying to please the old folks for nothing but that. But it don't seem to succeed, somehow," he said, shaking his head; "somehow it don't seem to succeed."

"They will never give their consent to that, Mr. Gervase!"

"No?" he said, doubtfully. "Well, of course you must be right, Patty. They don't seem to like it when I tell them it's because of you I'm trying to please them and staying like this at home."

"You should never have said that," she cried quickly; "you should have made them think it was all because you were so fond of them, and liked best being at home."

"But it would be a lie," said Gervase, simply, "and mother's awful sharp; she always finds out when you tell her a crammer. Say I may come to-night; do now, Patty,—I can't bear it any more."

"But you must bear it, Mr. Gervase," said Patty; "that is, if you really, really, want that to come true."

"What's that, Patty?" cried the young man.

"Oh, you—!"—it was only a breath, and ended in nothing. Patty saw that mincing matters was of no use. "I mean about us being married," she said, turning her head away.

"If I want it!" he cried, "when you know there is nothing in the world I want but that. Nobody would ever put upon me if I had only you to stand by me, Patty. Tell me what I am to do."

She unfolded her scheme to him after this with little hesitation. He was to continue his attendance at home for a little longer, and to propound to his parents his desire to go to London and see the fine sights there. It took Patty a considerable time to put all this into her lover's head—what he was to say, which she repeated over to him several times; and what he was to do afterwards, and the extreme importance of not forgetting, of never mentioning her nor the Seven Thorns, nor anything that could recall her to their minds. He was to say that the country was dull ("And so it is—especially at home, and when I can't see you," said Gervase), and that he had never seen London since he was a child, and it was a shame he never was trusted to go anywhere or see anything. ("And so it is a great shame.") When all this was well grafted into his mind, or, at least Patty hoped so, she announced that she had changed her intention and would go no more to Carter's Wells, but straight home to complete her preparations. And he was allowed to accompany her back almost as far as the high road, then dismissed to return home another way. Patty did not say that she was afraid of meeting Lady Piercey's carriage; but this was in her mind as she proceeded towards the Seven Thorns, with her head and her parasol high, like an army with banners, not at all afraid now, rather wishing for that encounter. It did take place according to her prevision when she was almost in sight of the group of stunted and aged trees which gave their name to her father's house. Why Lady Piercey should be passing that way, she herself, perhaps, could scarcely have told. She wanted, it might be, with that attraction of dislike which is as strong as love, to see again the girl who had so much power over Gervase, and of whom he said in his fatuous way, that it was she who was the occasion of his present home-keeping mood; or she wanted, as the angry and suspicious mind always hopes to do, to "catch" Patty and be able to report some flirtation or malicious anecdote of her in the hearing of Gervase. The old lady had strained her neck looking back at the Seven Thorns, which lay all vacant in the westering sunshine, the door open and void, nobody on the outside bench, nobody at the window—a perfectly harmless uninteresting house, piquing the curiosity more than if there had been people about. "I declare, Meg," Lady Piercey was saying, "that horrid house gets emptier and poorer every day. The man must be going all to ruin, with not so much as a tramp to call for a glass of beer; and serves him right, to bring up that daughter as he like has, all show and finery, and good for nothing about such a place." "The Rector has a great opinion of her," said Margaret; "they say she is so active and such a good manager." "Oh! stuff and nonsense," cried Lady Piercey, "you saw her with your own eyes in light gloves and a parasol, trailing her gown along the road; a girl out of a beershop, a girl—" But here Lady Piercey stopped short with a gasp, for close to the side of the carriage, and almost within hearing, was the same resplendent figure; the hat nodding with its roses; the gown a little too long, and trailing, as was the absurd fashion of that time; the light gloves firmly grasping the parasol, which was held high like an ensign, leaving the girl's determined and triumphant face fully visible. Patty marched past, giving but one glance to the inmates of the carriage, her colour high and her attitude martial; while the great lady almost fell back upon her cushions, overwhelmed with the suddenness of the encounter. Fortunately Lady Piercey did not see the tremendous nudge which John on the box gave to the coachman. She was too much moved by this startling incident to note any other demonstration of feeling.

"Did you see that?" she asked in a low tone, almost with awe, when that apparition had passed.

"Yes—I saw her. She is too fine for her station, but Aunt—"

"Don't put any of your buts to me, Meg! Do you think she could hear what we were saying? The bold, brazen creature! passing me by without a bend of her knee, as if she were as good as we are. What is this world coming to when a girl bred up in my own school, in my own parish, that has dropped curtseys to me since ever she was a baby, should dare to pass me by like that?" Lady Piercey, who had grown very red in sudden passion, now grew pale with horror at a state of affairs so terrible. "She looked as if she felt herself the lady, and us nobodies. Meg! do you think Gervase has it in him to marry that girl, and give her my name when your uncle dies! If I thought that, I think it would kill me! at least," she cried, sitting up with fire in her watery eyes—"it would put me on my mettle, and I'd mince matters no more, but get the doctor's advice and lock him up."

"My uncle would never consent to that."

"Your uncle—would just do what I wish. There's not many things he's ever crossed me in; and all he has have turned out badly. If I could make up my mind to it, it wouldn't be your uncle that would stop me. I have a great mind to send for the doctor to-night."

"But Aunt, is it not more likely they have quarrelled," said Margaret, "since he has been staying at home so faithfully, and never been absent day or night?"

"Do you think that's it, Meg? or do you think it's only policy to throw dust in our eyes? Oh, I wish I knew. I wish I knew. Oh, Meg, that I should say it! I feel as if I'd rather he should go out even to that horrible

Seven Thorns, than drive us all frantic with staying at home. If he goes on like that another night, I don't think I can bear it. Oh, it's all very well for you, sitting patient and smiling! If you were to see your only child sitting there like an idiot, and showing the very page-boy what a fool he is, and gabbling and grinning till you can hardly endure yourself, I wonder—I wonder what you'd say."

CHAPTER XII

Gervase went home still with his head bent, but no longer thinking of the white pebbles and the brown. It is true that his accustomed eye caught a big one here and there, which had rolled to the side of the path, and which he felt with regret would have come in so finely for the right or the left-hand man! but his mind was fixed on his consigne, and he was saying to himself over and over the words Patty had taught him—that he wanted to go to see London, and all the fine things there; that he was tired (mortal tired) of staying always at home; that it was a shame he never was trusted nor allowed to do anything (and so it was a shame). He could not even think of the pleasure of going to London, of meeting Patty at the station, and all that was to follow, so absorbed were his thoughts with what he had to say in the meantime. And it would not have been surprising had Gervase been overwhelmed by the thought of making such a wild suggestion to his parents, who had kept him hitherto like a child under their constant supervision. But his simple mind was not troubled by any such reflection as this. Patty had told him what to say, and no feeling of the impossibility of the thing, or of the strange departure in it from all the rules which had guided his life, affected him. If it did not succeed, all he had to do was to tell her, and she would think of something else. Better heads than that of poor Gervase have found this a great relief among the problems of life. As for him, he was not aware of any problems; he had a thing to say, and the trouble was lest he should forget it or say it wrong. To think of anything further was not his share of the business. He, too, met his mother just as she returned from her drive, so that he had taken a considerable time to that exercise, walking up and down the path that led under the wall of the park, conning his lesson. An impulse came upon him to say it off then and there, and so free his mind from the responsibility; but he remembered in time that Patty had said it was to be kept till after dinner, when his father and mother were both present. He was rather frightened, however, when the carriage suddenly drove up, and he was called to the door. "Hallo! mamma," he said, striding over a gorse bush that was in his way. Lady Piercey had jumped at the conclusion, as soon as she saw him, that there had been a meeting, as she said, "between those two." She called out quickly to take him by surprise, "Hi! Gervase! have you met anybody on the road?"

Now, Gervase was not clever, as the reader knows; but just because he was a Softy, and his brains different from other people's, he was better qualified to deal with such a question than a more intelligent youth might have been. "Met anybody on the road?" he said, gazing with his dull eyes and open mouth. "But I've not been on the road; I've only been up and down here."

"Oh, you—! but here is just the same as the road. Who have you been talking to?" the mother cried.

"There was the man with the donkey from Carter's Wells," said Gervase; "but I never said a word to him, nor he didn't to me."

"Was that the only person you saw? Tell me the truth," said Lady Piercey severely. Gervase put his head on one side, and seemed to reflect.

"If I'm to tell the dead truth," he said, "but I don't want to, mother, for you'll scold like old boots—"

"Tell me this instant!" cried Lady Piercey, red already with the rage that was ready to burst forth.

"Well, then, there just was—the ratcatcher with his pockets full of ferrets coming up from—"

"Home!" cried the lady, more angry than words could say. "Oh, you fool!" she said, shaking her fist at her son, who stood laughing, his moist lips glistening—no very pleasant sight for a mother's eye.

"I thought I was to tell you the truth," he cried after them, as the carriage whirled away.

"Do you think it was the truth, Meg?" Lady Piercey demanded, in a gasp, when they had swept into the avenue. A feeling of relief came as her anger quieted down.

"Dear Aunt—do you think he could invent so quickly, without any time to prepare?"

"You mean he couldn't because he's not clever? Heaven knows! They're as deep as the deep sea, and as cunning as—. But that ratcatcher is a man I will not have hanging, with those beasts in his pockets, about my house."

The ratcatcher gave occasion for a good deal of talk that afternoon, both in Gervase's presence and out of it; and by good luck he had been about, and Lady Piercey gave her orders as to his expulsion from the premises, whenever he should appear, with real satisfaction. "He's not company for Gervase, and that every one knows," she said at the dinner table, when old Sir Giles ventured to remonstrate on behalf of the ferrets and their owner.

"Mother always says that when it's any fellow I like to have a chat with," Gervase said.

"There's no harm in old Jerry," said Sir Giles. "A man shouldn't be too squeamish, my lady. A good-natured word here and there is what's wanted of a country squire."

"But not taking pleasure in low company," retorted Lady Piercey. "And I tell you again, I won't have that old wretch and his beasts about my house."

"But father knows it's rare fun sometimes, ain't it, father?" said the young man, kicking the old gentleman under the table. Fortunately, the kick touched only Sir Giles' stick, and he was not displeased to take Gervase's part for once against his wife.

"Hush, you young ass, can't you? We don't speak of these things before ladies," he said.

This little confidential aside put Sir Giles in good humour. But when the family retired into the library, which was done by no means in the usual order—for Sir Giles himself in his chair, wheeled by Dunning, led the way—it was evident that an uneasy alarm in respect to Gervase was the leading sentiment in everybody's mind. Sir Giles announced loudly that it was Dunning, and only Dunning, who should play with him to-night. "I've got to give the fellow his revenge," he said. "I beat him black and blue last night. Eh, Dunning, didn't I beat you black and blue? You're not a bad player, but not just up to my strength."

"No, Sir Giles," answered the man, setting the table in haste, and keeping carefully between it and the heir of the house. Lady Piercey, on her side, employed Parsons and Margaret, both of whom were in attendance, in covering up all her silks. "Put them in the basket," she said, "and take out one as I want it. That's always the best way." Thus defended, the parents kept a furtive watch upon the movements of their son, but with less alarm than before, while Lady Piercey kept on a running exhortation to Mrs. Osborne in an undertone. "Meg! get him to play something. Meg! why don't you take him in hand! Meg! the boy's sure to get into mischief for want of something to do."

"Should you like a game of cribbage, Gervase?" said poor Margaret, unable to resist the urgency of this appeal.

"Cribbage is the old-fashionedest game; they don't play it anywhere—even in the publics," said Gervase. He had put himself in the favourite attitude of Englishmen, with his back to the fireplace; his coat-tails gathered over his arms in faithful adherence to custom, though the cause for any such unseemly custom was not there.

"Or bézique?" said Margaret; "or perhaps you'll sing a song, Gervase, if I play it. Your mother would like to hear you sing: you haven't sung her a song for years."

"Do, Gervase, there's a dear," said Lady Piercey. "You used to sing 'The north winds do blow, and we shall have snow,' so pretty when you were quite a little thing."

"I ain't a little thing now, and I'm not going to sing," said Gervase loudly. "I'm going to say something to father and mother. You can go away, Meg, if you don't want to hear."

"What is it?" cried Lady Piercey, sitting up more bolt-upright than usual, and taking off her spectacles to see him the better, and to cow him with the blaze of her angry eyes.

"This is what it is," said Gervase. "It's mortal dull at home, now that I've turned over a new leaf and don't go out anywhere at night; and a fellow of my age wants a little diversion, and I can't go on sitting in your pocket, mother, nor playing father's game every night—and he don't like losing, neither, and no more don't I."

This preamble was quite new, struck off out of his own head from Patty's text. It was with a great elation and rising self-confidence that Gervase found it so. Perhaps they'd find out that he was not such a fool as he looked—once he had got free.

"Eh! what's the lad saying? That's true enough—that's true enough," Sir Giles said.

"Oh, hold your tongue, papa! You don't know what he's aiming at," Lady Piercey said.

"And I've never seen a thing, nor gone any-place," said Gervase. "Its d—d hard upon me—it's devilish hard. Oh," he cried, "I can speak up when I like! It's that dull nobody would stand it (and so it is)." He added his old parentheses, though he had dropped the original theme. "I mustn't talk a moment with any person, but mother's down upon me—even Jerry, the ratcatcher, that every one knows."

"That's true, my boy," cried Sir Giles, "your mother's too hard on you; that's quite true."

"Wait, you fool, till you know what he's aiming at," cried Lady Piercey, with her eyes on fire.

"And I can't play your game, father, nor take you for a walk, but there's a fright all round as if I was going to kill you; and old Dunning after me, looking like a stuck pig."

Here was a chance for Lady Piercey to approve, too, at her husband's expense; but she was magnanimous, and did not take it. "You're well meaning enough, Gervase," she said, "I don't deny it; but you're too strong, and you shake poor papa to bits."

"Well, then," said Gervase, raising his voice to talk her down, "it's clear as there is nothing here for me to do; and it's dreadful dull. Enough to kill a man of my age; and the short and the long of it is that I can't go on like this any more."

He had quite thrown Patty's carefully prepared speech away, and yet it came breathing over him by turns, checking his natural eloquence. She had never meant him to utter that outcry of impatience, and Gervase would have ruined his own cause, and gone on to say, "I am going to be married," but for the questions that were suddenly showered upon him, driving him back upon his lesson.

"You can't go on like this? And how are you going on?" cried his mother. "Everything a man can desire, and the best home in England, and considered in every way!" She went on speaking, but her voice was crossed by old Sir Giles' growl. "What do you want—what do you want?" cried the old man. "Dunning, be off to your supper, and take that woman with you. What do you want—what do you want, you young fool?"

"But I know what you want," Lady Piercey cried, becoming audible at the end of this interruption; "you want what you shall never have as long as I live, unless it's somebody of my choosing, and not of yours."

"I'll tell you what I want," said Gervase, the moisture flying from his mouth; "I want to have a—I want to get—I want P—." Then that long-conned speech of Patty's flew suddenly, like a cobweb, into his mind, and stopped him on the edge of the abyss. He stopped and stared at them for a moment, his eyes roaming round the room, and then he burst into a loud laugh. "I want to go to London," he said, "and see all the fine things there. I don't know what mother's got in her head—some of her whimseys—I've never been let go anywhere or do anything, and I want to go to London to look about and see all the grand things there."

"To London?" said Sir Giles with surprise. Lady Piercey had been wound up to too great a pitch to go easily down again. She opened her mouth with a gasp like a fish, but no sound came therefrom.

"I've never been let go anywhere," said Gervase, "and up and down from the Manor to the village ain't enough. I want to go to London and see the fine sights there; I want to see the Queen and all that; I want to see a bit of life. There never was a gentleman like me that was kept so close and never let go to see anything. I've not been in London since I was a little kid, and it is a shame that I am never trusted (so it is), and it's mortal dull here, especially at home, and not seeing anything; and I want to go to London and see a bit of life, and not be buried alive here."

"My lady," said Sir Giles, after the pause of awe which followed this long, consequent, and coherent speech, "there's reason in what the lad says."

"There's something underneath," cried Lady Piercey, "a deal more than what he says."

"Mother always thinks that," cried Gervase, with his big laugh; and there could not be any question that what he said was true.

"There's some plan underneath it all," repeated Lady Piercey, striking her hand on the table. "He hasn't the sense to make up a thing like that, that has reason in it; there's some deep-laid plan underneath it all."

"Pooh, my lady! Poor lad!" said Sir Giles, shaking his head; "he hasn't the sense to make up a plan at all. He just says what comes into his head, and what he says has reason in it, and more than that, I'm glad to hear him say it. And it gives me a bit of hope," said poor old Sir Giles, his voice shaking a little, "that when he comes fully to man's estate, the boy, poor lad, will be more like other boys, Mary Ann, God bless him! and, perhaps, for so little as we think it, a real comfort to you and me."

The old gentleman leaned back in his chair, and raised with a feeble hand his handkerchief to his eyes. It was not difficult nowadays to make Sir Giles cry. The fierce old lady had no such emotion to subdue. She sat very upright, staring at her son, suspicious, thinking she saw behind him the pert little defiant countenance under the parasol which she had met on the road. But she did not see how they could have met or communicated with each other, and she could not, on the spur of the moment, make out what connection there could be between his desire to go to London, and Patty of the Seven Thorns. Margaret stood behind her uncle's chair, patting him softly on the shoulder to soothe him and assure him of sympathy. She looked over Sir Giles' head at the boy who, he was able to flatter himself, might be like other boys when he came to man's estate. How strangely can love and weakness be deceived! Gervase stood there against the mantelpiece, his foot caught up awkwardly in his hand, his slouching shoulders supported against the shelf, his big, loose bulk filling the place. Man's estate! The poor Softy was eight-and-twenty and well grown, though he slouched and distorted himself. But still the father, and even the suspicious, less-persuadable mother, saw in him a boy, not beyond the season of growth—never beyond that of hope.

Fortunately for Gervase, he had not time to go on in his flush of triumph and success, for another moment of that elation might have broken down all precautions and betrayed the plan which his mother felt, but could not divine, underneath. In the meantime, however, it was bedtime, and neither Sir Giles nor my lady could bear any more. Lady Piercey sent off Parsons, and discussed the question with her niece in her bedroom for a full hour after. "There's something underneath, I know there is," Lady Piercey said, nodding her head in her big nightcap. "But I don't see what she can have to do with it, for she would never want to send him away. And then, on the other hand, Meg, it would be the best thing in the world to send him away. There's nothing like absence for blowing a thing like that out of a boy's head. If there was a man we could trust to go with him,—but all alone, by himself, in a big place like London, and among so many temptations! Oh, Meg, Meg, I wish I knew what was the right thing to do!"

"He is very innocent, Aunt; he would not understand the temptation," said Margaret.

"Oh, I'm not of that opinion at all," cried Lady Piercey. "A man always understands that, however silly he may be; and sometimes, the sillier he is, the more he understands. But one nail knocks out another," she added thoughtfully. Though Lady Piercey was not a woman of the world, but only a very rustic person, she was yet cynic enough for the remorseless calculation that a little backsliding, of which so many people were guilty, would be better than a dreadful marriage which would bring down the family, and corrupt the very race—which was her point of view.

Gervase roamed about the house in high excitement, immensely pleased with himself, while this colloquy was going on. Had he met even Dunning or Parsons, whom he did not love, the possibility was that he might have revealed his meaning to them in sheer elation of spirits. But neither of these persons came in his way, and in this early household most of the other servants were already in bed. Margaret, however, met him as usual when she came out of Lady Piercey's room with her candle in her hand.

"What's she been saying to you, Meg?" he asked, but burst out laughing before she could reply. "It's such a joke," he said, holding his sides, "such a joke, if you only knew! and I've half a mind to tell you, Meg, for you're a good sort."

"Don't tell me anything, Gervase, for Heaven's sake, that I can't tell them. For, of course, I shall do so directly," Margaret cried.

"Wouldn't you just like to know?" he said, and laughed again, and chucked her under the chin in convulsions of hilarity. She stood at the door of the room, escaping hastily from the possible confidence and the familiarity, and, trembling, saw him slide down the banisters to the half-lighted hall below, with a childish chuckle of triumph. A slip upon that swift descent, and all might have been over—the commotion and the exultation, the trouble and the fear. But Gervase came back again beaming, and kissed his hand to her as he disappeared into his own room. He felt that he had gained the day.

CHAPTER XIII

The household at Greyshott was much disturbed and excited by the new idea thus thrown into the midst of them. Lady Piercey discussed it all next morning, not only with Margaret but with Parsons, whose views on the subject were very decided. She thought, but this within herself, that to get quit of the Softy, even for a few days, would be a great blessing to the house—though what she said was chiefly to agree with her mistress that a change, and to see a little of life, would be the best thing possible for Mr. Gervase.

"'Tisn't good for any young man to be always at home," said Lady Piercey. "I remember a piece of poetry, or a hymn, or something, which I used to know, that had a line about home-keeping youths, and that they had but poor wits—that is, looked as if they had poor wits, because they had never seen anything, don't you know?"

"Yes, my lady," said Parsons; "that's just how it is."

"And the dear boy has come to feel it himself," continued the mother; "he sees all the rest of the young men rushing about from one end of the world to the other, and he's begun to ask himself, How's that? Don't you see, Parsons?"

"Yes, my lady, it's as plain as the eyes in one's head," said Parsons.

"Of course, it is all because of his being so delicate when he was a child," said the old lady.

"But what a blessing it is, my lady, to see how he's outgrown it now!"

"Yes, isn't it a blessing, Parsons! Just as strong as any of them—and well grown—a good height, and large round the chest, and all that."

"Yes, my lady," Parsons replied. She did not commit herself, but she chimed in most satisfactorily with all that her lady said.

Margaret was by no means so entirely to be trusted to. She was very doubtful of the proposed expedition, and even when she assented, as it was often necessary to do to what her aunt said, did so with so uncertain and troubled a look that Lady Piercey, by force of the opposition, was more and more rooted in her view.

"It would do him all the good in the world," she said. "I know you think he's silly, my poor boy—not that he's really silly, not a bit; but he does not know how to express himself; and how is he ever to learn, stuck up here at home between you and me and his poor father, Meg?"

Margaret was a little taken aback by this question, and in her confusion laughed inadvertently, which made Lady Piercey very angry.

"You think you are clever enough for anything, and could teach him—as well as the best!"

"No, indeed," cried Margaret; "not at all. I don't know how young men learn—to express themselves. I think, so far as I have seen, that there are a great many who know how to express themselves—much worse than Gervase," she added hastily; for after all, it was not poor Gervase's fault, whereas it was the fault of many other men.

The mother, in her jealousy for her son, was pacified by this, and shook her head. "Oh, yes," she said, "there are many of them that are a poor lot. Gervase is—one in ten thousand, Meg. He is a gentleman, my poor boy. He doesn't know how to bully or make himself disagreeable. You know I am saying no more than the truth. He would do far better in the world if he made more of himself."

This required from Margaret only a murmur of assent—which she gave without too much strain of conscience; but she was unprepared for the swift following up of this concession. "So it's your opinion, Meg—if your opinion were asked, which I don't think likely—that your uncle and I should let him go?"

"Let him go! But as you say, aunt, my opinion is not likely to be asked," Margaret said quickly, to cover her exclamation of dismay.

"I'm not too fond of asking anybody's opinion. I like to hear what they say, just to make sure of my own; but since you've given yours, as you generally do, without waiting to be asked,—and you're not so far wrong as usual this time,—he ought to have his freedom. He's never done anything to make us suppose that he wouldn't use it rightly. He is a boy in a thousand, Meg! He has no bad ways—he is only too innocent, suspecting nobody."

"That might be the danger," said Margaret.

"Yes, my dear, that is just the thing—you have hit it, though you are not so bright as you think. He suspects nobody. He would put his money or whatever he had into anybody's hands. He thinks every one is as innocent as himself."

It would have been hard upon the poor mother had Margaret said what she thought: that Gervase did not think at all, which was a danger greater still. Lady Piercey knew all there was to be said on that point, and she kept her eye upon her niece, waiting to surprise that judgment in her face. Oh, she knew very well not only all that could be said, but all the reason there was for saying it! Lady Piercey was not deceived on the subject of her son, nor unaware of any of his deficiencies. It is to be supposed, knowing all these, that she must have known the dangers to which he must be exposed if he were allowed to carry out this proposal; but many other things were working in her mind. She thought it was only just that he should see life; and she thought, cynically, with a woman's half-knowledge, half-suspicion of what that meant—that life as seen in London would cure him entirely of Patty and of the dangers that were concentrated in her. Finally, there was a dreadful relief in the thought of getting rid of him for a little while, of being exempt, if even for a few days, from his presence, when he was present, which was insupportable—and from the anxiety about his home-coming and where he was, when he was absent. The thought of having him comfortably out of sight for a time, so far off that she should be no longer responsible for him, even to herself; that she should no longer require to watch and wait for him, but could go to bed when she pleased, independent of the question whether Gervase had come home—that prospect attracted her more than words could say. Oh, the rest and refreshment it would be! the exemption from care, the repose of mind! Whatever he might do in London, she, at least, would not see it. Young men, when they were seeing life, did not generally conduct themselves to the satisfaction of their parents. They acted after their kind, and nobody was very hard upon them. Gervase would be just like the others—just like others! which was what he had never been hitherto, what she had always wished and longed for him to be. She sat for a long time at her embroidery, silent, working her mouth as she did when she was turning over any great question in her mind; and Margaret was too glad to respect her aunt's abstraction, to leave her at full liberty to think. At length Lady Piercey suddenly threw down her needle, and with a gesture more like a man than an old lady, smote her knee with her hand.

"I've got it!" she cried. "I've found just the right thing to do!"

Parsons stopped and listened at the other end of the room, and Margaret paused in her work too, and raised her eyes. Lady Piercey's countenance was in a flush of pleasure; she went on drumming on her knee in excitement, swaying a little back and forward in her chair.

"It is the very thing," she said. "He'll get his freedom, and yet he'll be well looked after. You remember Dr. Gregson, him that was at that poor little dingy chapel when we were in town? Oh! you never remember anything, Meg! Parsons, you recollect Dr. Gregson, the clergyman with the family—that was so poor?"

"Yes, my lady," said Parsons, coming a few steps nearer; her presence made legitimate, even during the discussion of these family matters, by this demand.

"Oh, you needn't stop work; I am talking to my niece. When I want you I'll call you," said Lady Piercey, ruthless, waving her away. "Meg," she said, after watching the woman's reluctant withdrawal, "servants are a pretty set, poking their heads into everything; but you always stand up for them. Perhaps you think I'd better have up the cook, and let the whole of 'em know?"

"No; if you ask my opinion, Aunt, I think they are better left out."

"Oh, you think they are better left out? Perhaps you think I'd better keep it all in my own mind, and not speak of my affairs at all? But it doesn't matter much, and that's a satisfaction, what you think," said Lady Piercey, grimly. Then she resumed the argument. "I see my way; I see how we can do it all! Mr. Gregson is as poor as a church mouse, and he'll do anything to get a little money. He shall meet Gervase at the station, and he shall look after him and show him life, as the poor boy says." She laughed a low, reverberating laugh, that seemed to roll round the room; and then she added, giving Mrs. Osborne a push with her elbow, "You don't seem to see the fun of it, Meg."

"I don't think Gervase will; nor, perhaps, the poor clergyman."

The old lady laughed with deep enjoyment, putting one hand on her side. "Gregson will like anything that puts a little money in his pocket. And as for Gervase—" It was some utterance of deep contempt that was on Lady Piercey's lips; but she remembered herself, and repressed it in time. During the rest of the morning she sat almost silent, with her mouth working, and, as if she were turning over an amusing thought, gave vent now and then to a chuckle of laughter. The idea of sending Gervase to see life under the auspices of the poor little Low Church incumbent of Drummond Chapel, Bloomsbury, was delightful. She felt her own cleverness in having thought of it almost as much as she felt the happy relief of being thus rid of her poor Softy without any harm—nay, with perfect safety to him. All the accessories were delightful—the astonishment of Dr. Gregson, the ludicrous disappointment of the weak young man, his probable seduction into tea-parties and Bible-classes, which would be much more wholesome for him than the other way of seeing life. It occurred to Lady Piercey, with a momentary check upon her triumph, that there had been little girls among the Gregsons who might have grown up into dangerous young persons by this time. But that gave her but a temporary alarm, for, to be sure, it would be easy enough to drop any entanglement of that kind, and a young Gregson might, in the most virtuous manner, supplant Patty, as well as the worst—and all would consequently work for good to the only person of any consequence, the only son and heir of Sir Giles Piercey, of Greyshott, for whom alone his mother was concerned.

When this brilliant idea was communicated to Sir Giles, he, too, smote his thigh and burst into such a roar of laughter, that notwithstanding her gratification in the success of this admirable practical joke of hers, Lady Piercey was afraid. He laughed till he was red, or rather crimson, with a tinge of blue in the face; his large, helpless frame heaving with the roar which resounded through the room. She was so frightened that she summoned Dunning hastily, though she had the moment before sent him away, and had entered her husband's room alone, without any attendant on her own side, to consult him on this all-important subject. When Dunning returned, triumphant in the sense that they could not do without him, and tingling with curiosity, which he never doubted he should now have abundant means of satisfying, he found Sir Giles in a spasmodic condition in his chair, laughing by intervals, while Lady Piercey stood by his side, patting him upon the back with unaccustomed hands, and saying, "Now, my dear; now, now, my dear," as she might have done to a restive horse. Sir Giles' exuberance faded away at the sight of Dunning, who knew exactly what to do to make him, as they said, comfortable. And thus it happened that this old pair, who were older than the parents of Gervase had any need to be, and looked, both, much older than they were, from illness and self-indulgence, and all its attendant infirmities—were left to consult upon the fate of their only child with the servant making a third, which was very galling to Lady Piercey's pride. Sir Giles did not pay any attention. Dunning was to him not a man, but a sort of accessory—a thing that did not count. He calmed down out of his paroxysms of laughter at Dunning's appearance, but still kept bursting out at intervals. "What if the fellow"—and then he stopped to cough and laugh again—"what if he falls in love with Miss Brown or Miss Jones?" he said. "And then, my lady, you would be out of the frying-pan into the fire."

"I am not afraid of Miss Smith or Miss Jones," she cried, making a sign to him over Dunning's head to be careful what he said. But Sir Giles was in the humour for speech, and cared nothing who was present.

"I think a deal of these ladies," he said, in his mumbling voice. "It's a great joke—a great joke. I should like to see old Gregson's face when he hears of it. By Jove! and the old plotter you are, my lady, to make it all up. But it can't be; it can't be."

"Why can't it be?" cried Lady Piercey sharply, and much provoked.

"Because it wouldn't be fair, neither to the one of them nor to the other. Not fair at all, by George. Fair play's a jewel. What are you after, Dunning? Let my legs alone. There's nothing the matter with my legs. And you can go and be dashed to you. Can't I talk to my lady without you here?"

"Don't send him away," cried Lady Piercey hurriedly. "I can't have you get ill, and perhaps do yourself harm, because of me."

"Do myself fiddlesticks," cried Sir Giles. "I'm as strong as a horse, ain't I, Dunning? Be off with you, be off with you; don't you hear? I'll throw my stick at you if you don't scuttle, you son of a—. Hey! you can tell my lady I'm as well as either you or she."

"Yes, Sir Giles," said Dunning, stolid and calm. But he did not go away.

"It wouldn't be fair," Sir Giles went on, forgetting what he had said. "I say fair play all the world over. Women don't understand it. It's a capital joke, and I didn't think you had so much fun in you. But it wouldn't be fair."

"Don't be a fool, Giles," said Lady Piercey angrily. "If you don't see it's necessary, why, then, you can't see an inch before your nose; and to argue with you isn't any good."

"No," he said, "perhaps it isn't. I'm an obstinate old fool, and so are you an obstinate old fool, Mary Ann. And between us both we've made a mess of it. It wasn't altogether our fault, perhaps, for it was Nature that began," said the old gentleman, with something like a whimper breaking into his voice. "Nature, the worst of all, for you cannot do anything with that. Not a thing! We've tried our best. Yes; I believe you tried your best, my lady, watching and worrying; and I've tried my best, leaving things alone. But none of us can do anything. We can't, you know, not if we were to go on till Doomsday; and we're two old folks, and we can't go on much longer. It's not altogether your fault, and neither is it mine; but we'll go to our graves, by-and-by, and we'll leave behind us—we'll leave behind us—"

Here the old gentleman, probably betrayed by the previous disturbance of his laughter, fell into a kind of nervous crying, half exclamations, half laughing, half tears.

"Don't you be upset, my lady," said Dunning; "Sir Giles, he do get like this sometimes when he's flurried and frightened. But, Lord! a little glassful of water, and a few of his drops, and he's all right again."

Lady Piercey sat bolt upright in her chair. She, too, wanted the ministrations to which she was accustomed: the arm of Parsons to help her up, or Margaret to turn to, to upbraid her for her uncle's state, or to consult her as to what to do. She had not the same tendency to tears, though a few iron drops came from time to time, wrung out by her great trouble. She sat and stared at her husband, and at Dunning's services to him, till Sir Giles was quite restored. And then she rose with some stiffness and difficulty, and hobbled away. Parsons met her at the door, and took her mistress to her room; but, though Lady Piercey clung to her, the maid was not at all well received. "What were you doing at Sir Giles' door? What do you want in this part of the house?" she cried, though she had seized and clung to the ready arm. "I'll not have you spying about, seeing what you can pick up in the way of news, or listening at a door."

"I never listened at a door in my life," cried Parsons, indignant. "And nobody ever named such a thing to me, my lady, but you!"

"Oh, hold your tongue, do!" cried Lady Piercey. And she, too, like Sir Giles, was obliged to have a restorative when she had been safely conveyed to her room. She was the ruler upstairs, and he below. She had the advantage of him in being able to move about, notwithstanding her rheumatism, and the large share she had of those ills which flesh is heir to—all those which were not appropriated first by her husband—in which she took a certain satisfaction, not tempered, rather enhanced, by the attendant pain.

The letters came in at the hour of luncheon, and were taken to Lady Piercey as they are usually taken to the master of the house. She opened all the family-letters, her husband's as well as her own, and even the occasional bill or note that came very rarely for Gervase. Among them that day came a letter stamped with the Piercey crest, at which she gazed for a moment before opening it, with an indignant, yet scared look, as if she had beheld a blasphemy, and which made her, when she opened it, almost jump from her seat. She read it over twice, with her eyes opening wider and wider, and the red flush of surprise and horror rising on her face, then flung it violently across the table to Margaret. "Then he must go, that's flat! and to-morrow morning, not one hour later," she cried. Gervase was in the room, paying no attention to this pantomime, and caring nothing for what letters might arrive; but he was roused by what she said. He cried, "That's me, mother; I'm going to-morrow," with his loud and vacant laugh.

CHAPTER XIV

The letter which Lady Piercey had received, and which quickened so instantaneously her determination that Gervase should be gratified in his desire to visit London, did not seem at the first glance to have anything to do with that question. It was a letter from Gerald Piercey, asking to be allowed to come on a visit of two or three days to see his relations at Greyshott. Now, Gerald Piercey was, after Gervase, the heir-at-law—or rather he was the son of the old and infirm gentleman who was the heir-at-law. He was a soldier who had distinguished himself in India, and got rapid promotion, so that he had several letters already tacked to his name, and was in every way a contrast to the unfortunate who stood between him and the honours of the house. It was natural, and I think it was excusable, that poor Lady Piercey should hate this successful and highly esteemed person. To be sure, he was much older than Gervase—a man of forty, so that there was, as she said indignantly, no comparison! and she herself was not old enough (or at least, so she said) to have had a son of the Colonel's age. But these circumstances, which should have lessened the sense of rivalry, only made it greater, for even if Gervase had not been a Softy, he would never have been a man of so much importance as this cousin of the younger branch who had made himself known and noted in the world by his own personal character and deserts. Colonel Piercey had not been at Greyshott since he was a youth setting out in life, when he had paid his relations a hasty and not very agreeable visit. Gervase was then a silly little boy; but there are many silly little boys who grow up into tolerable young men; and his parents, at least, had by no means made up their minds to the fact of his inferiority. But Gerald, a young man who had just joined his regiment and was full of the elation and pleasure in life which is never greater than in these circumstances, who resembled the family portraits and knew all about the family history, and who looked so entirely the part of heir of the house, awoke a causeless enmity even in the jovial breast of Sir Giles, then a robust fox-hunter, master of the hounds, chairman of quarter sessions, and everything that a country gentleman should be. Poor little Gervase was nothing beside him, naturally! for Gervase was but a child, however clever he had been. But this thought did not heal the painful impression, the shock of a sensation too keen almost to be borne. All the neighbours were delighted with Gerald. What a fine young fellow! what a promising young man! what a pity it was—and the visitors gave a glance aside at poor little Gervase, already, poor child, the Softy among all his childish companions. They did not utter that last half-formed regret, but Sir Giles and his wife perceived it on their lips, in their thoughts, and hated Gerald, which was wrong, no doubt, but very natural and almost pardonable, from a parent's point of view.

And here he was coming back! a guest whom they could not refuse, a credit to the family, a distinguished relation, while Gervase was what he was. But Gerald Piercey should not, Lady Piercey resolved, see Gervase as he was,—not for the world! He was coming, no doubt, to spy out the nakedness of the land—but what he should find would only be an account of her son enjoying himself in London, seeing life, doing as other young men did. If Gerald was a colonel and a C.B., Gervase should bear the aspect of a young man about town—a man of fashion, going everywhere; a man who had no occasion to go to India to distinguish himself, having a good estate and a baronetcy behind him at home. To keep up this fiction would be easy if Gervase were but absent. It would be impossible, alas! to do it in his presence. Lady Piercey exerted herself during that day, in a way she had not been known to do before for years. She wrote a long letter, bending over it, and working all the lines of her mouth like a schoolboy. It was labour dire and weary woe, for a woman who had long given up any exertion of the kind for herself. But in this case she would not trust even Margaret. And then she had Gervase's drawers emptied, and his clothes brought to her to make a survey. They were not fashionable clothes by any means; Lady Piercey, though she was not much used to men of fashion, and knew nothing of what "was worn" at the time, yet knew and remembered enough to feel that Gervase in these garments would by no means bear the aspect of a young man about town. But he would do very well in the Gregson world in Bloomsbury; everybody who saw him there would know that he was young Mr. Piercey of Greyshott, Sir Giles' only son. This is the sort of fact that covers a multitude of sins, even in clothes. And in Bloomsbury the first fashions were not likely to be worn. He would pass muster very well there, but not—not before the eyes of Gerald Piercey, the colonel, the C.B., the cousin and heir. "You don't see why I should be in such a hurry," said Lady Piercey, with one of those glances which only want the power, not the desire, to kill. "I know, then, and that's enough, Gervase, my boy. You'll remember to be very good and please your poor father and me, now we've consented to give you this great treat, and let you go."

"Oh, yes," said Gervase, with a laugh; "I'll remember, mother. I sha'n't be let go wrong, you take your oath of that."

"What does he mean by not being let? You've told him about Gregson, Meg! Well, my dear, you know that is the only comfort I have. You'll be met at the station, and you'll find your nice rooms ready; and very lucky you are, Gervase, to find so good a person to take care of you. Do everything he tells you; mind, he knows all about you; and he'll always lead you the right road, as you say."

Gervase, staring open-mouthed at his mother, burst into a great laugh. He was astonished at her apparent knowledge of the companion who would not let him go wrong, but the confusion of the pronoun daunted him a little. Did she think it was old Hewitt that was going with him? He had enough of cunning to ask no questions, but laughed with a great roar of satisfaction mingled with wonderment. Lady Piercey put up her hands to her ears.

"Don't make such a noise," she said. "You laugh like your father, Gervase, and you're too young to roar like that. You must try to behave very nicely, too, and don't roar the roof off a London house with your laughing. And don't make a noise in company, Gervase. We put up with everything here because we're so fond of you; but in town, though they'll be fond of you, it makes a difference, not being used to you from your cradle. You must remember all I taught you about manners when you were a little boy."

"Oh, mother, don't you be afraid; my manners will be well looked after, too. I sha'n't dare to open my mouth," said Gervase, with another laugh.

"Well, I believe they are very particular," said Lady Piercey, with a still more bewildering change of pronouns. "And, Gervase, there's young ladies there: mind that you are very nice and civil to them, but don't go any further than you can draw back."

"Oh, I'll be kept safe from the young ladies, you take your oath of that!" he cried, with another shout of a laugh.

"For goodness gracious sake," cried Lady Piercey, "take him away!—Meg, can't you take him away and give him a good talking to? You have no nerves, and I'm nothing but a bundle of 'em. That laugh of his goes up to the crown of my head and down to the soles of my feet. Take him off, and let me look over his things in peace. And mind, Gervase, you've to listen to what Meg says to you, just the same as if I were speaking myself; for she knows about men, having married one, and she can give you a deal of good advice. Go out to the beech avenue, and then I can see you from my window, and make sure that you are paying attention to what she says."

When Gervase was safely outside with his patient cousin, whose part in all these proceedings was so laborious and uninterrupted, though she was not permitted to do much more than look on—he plucked off his hat and flung it up into the air in triumph, executing at the same time a sort of dance upon the gravel.

"Does she mean what she says, Meg? and how has she heard of it? and what has made her give in? Lord! what will some folks say when they know that it's all with her will?"

"What is it you are going to do, Gervase? and what do you mean by 'some folks'?" Margaret cried.

The Softy looked at her for a moment irresolute, doubtful, it would seem, what he should reply; and then he laughed again, more loudly than ever, and said: "Shouldn't you like to know?"

"Yes, I should like to know. I do not believe that they know at all what you mean. You are too cunning for them. You are going to take some step—"

"More than one—many steps. I'm going to London to see all that's going on—to see life. I told 'em so; and instead of looking curious like you, mother, don't you see, she knows all about it, and wants me to do it. Mother's a trump! She is that fond of me, she will do whatever I say."

"The thing is, what are you going to do, Gervase? What do you mean by seeing life?"

He laughed longer than ever, and gave her a nudge with his arm. "Oh, get along, Meg!" he said,—"you know."

"No, Gervase; tell me. You have always been a good boy—you are not going to do any harm?"

"I never heard it was any harm; it's what everybody does, and rejoicings about it, and bells ringing, and all that. Don't you tell—I'm going—No; I said I wouldn't say a word, and I won't. You'll know when I come back."

"Gervase, you frighten me very much—you wouldn't deceive your father and mother that love you so." She drew a long breath of alarm; then added with relief: "But if he is met at the station and taken care of—"

"That's it," said Gervase. "I'm going to be met at the station, and everything done for me. I'll never be left to myself any more. I'm not very good at taking care of myself, Meg."

"No," she cried; "that is quite true. I am so glad you feel that, Gervase. Then you won't be rebellious, but do what your mother wishes, and what her friend tells you. It will make her so happy."

"Her friend! Who's her friend?" said Gervase; and then the peal of his laughter arose once more. "I like my own friend best; but my friend and my mother's friend being just the same, don't you see?"

"Are they the same?" said Mrs. Osborne, thoroughly perplexed.

"There ain't two of them that are going to meet me at the station? No? then there's only one. And mother's a trump, and I'll do everything I'm told, and never be without some one to guide me all my life. And to stand up for me—for I am put upon, Meg, though you don't seem to see it. I am; and made a jest of; and no money in my pocket; never given my proper place. Meg, how much is mamma going to give me for my pocket-money while I'm away?"

"I can't tell you, Gervase. There will be your travelling money, and probably she will send the rest to—to be given you when you are in town."

"I ought to have it now in my own pocket," said Gervase, with a cloud upon his brow. "Do you think a man can go like a man to London town, and no money? They are mad if they think that. Lend us something, Meg—you've got a little, and no need to spend it; with everything given you that heart can wish. Why, you never spend a penny! And I'll pay it all back when I come to my own."

"I have nothing," she said, faltering. To tell what was not strictly true, and to refuse what her cousin asked, were things equally dreadful to Margaret—and it was a relief to her when Lady Piercey's window was jerked open by a rapid hand, and the old lady's head appeared suddenly thrust out.

"You're not talking to him, Meg; you're letting him talk to you. Don't let us have more of that. You're there to give him good advice, and that's what we expect of you. Don't you hear?" And the window was snapt with another emphatic jerk.

"Gervase, I am to advise you," said Margaret, trembling, though the situation was ludicrous enough, and she might have laughed had the case been other than her own. The watchful eye upon her from the window, the totally unadvisable young man by her side, were not, however, ludicrous but dreadful to Margaret. Her sense of humour was obscured by the piteous facts of the case: the young man entirely insensible to any reason, and his mother, who had never lost her primitive faith that if some one only "talked to him," Gervase would be just as sensible as other men. "But how can I advise you? I am troubled about what you are going to do. I hope you will not do anything to grieve them, Gervase. They are old people—"

"Yes," said Gervase, with a nod and a look of wisdom; "they are pretty old."

"They are old people," said Margaret, "and they have a great many things to put up with: they have illnesses and weakness—and they have anxiety about you."

"They needn't trouble their heads about me. I've got some one to look after me. She said it wasn't I," cried Gervase with a chuckle.

"That is while you are in London; but they think of you all day long, and are always thinking of you. You will not do anything to grieve them, Gervase, while you are away?"

"How can I when I'm going to be looked after all the time, and somebody to meet me at the station?" cried Gervase, with his loud laugh.

Lady Piercey was very anxious afterwards to know what advice Margaret had given to her son. The "things" had all been looked over and packed; and it took Lady Piercey a long time to consider what money she could trust her son with when he went away. She had intended at first to send some one with him to pay his railway ticket, and to send what he would want in London to Dr. Gregson. But then, what if an accident happened? what if Gregson failed to meet him, or appropriated the money? which was a thing always on the cards with so poor a man, the old lady thought. It could not be that the heir of Greyshott, Sir Giles' son, should leave his home penniless. She took out her cash-box, for she was the manager of everything, and had all the money interests of Greyshott in her hands—and took from it a five-pound note, over which she mused and pondered long, weighing it in her hand as if that were the way of judging. Then she put it back, and took out a ten-pound note. Ten pounds is a great deal of money. Much good as well as much harm can be done with ten pounds. It is such a large sum of money that, if you trust a man with that, you may trust him with more. She took out another—wavering, hesitating—now disposed to put it back, now laying it with the other, poising them both in her hands. Finally, with a quick sigh, she shut up the cash-box sharply and suddenly, and gave it to Parsons to be put back in the cabinet, where it usually dwelt; and folding up the notes, directed her niece to put them in an envelope. "Twenty pounds!" she said, with a gasp. Her two supporters had been present during all this process, and Parsons was exactly aware how much money was to be trusted in the pockets of the Softy, and thought it excessive. Lady Piercey sat by grimly, and looked on while the money was enclosed in the envelope, and then she turned briskly to her companion. "You had a long talk, Meg," she said;

"and I suppose you gave him a great deal of advice. You ought to know, you that had as husband an officer, for they are always in the heat of everything. What advice did you give to my boy?"

CHAPTER XV

Colonel Piercey arrived next day in the afternoon, Gervase having gone away in a state of the most uproarious spirits in the morning. Margaret had been made to accompany him to the railway, to see that his ticket was taken properly, and that he got the right train, and was not too late so as to miss it, or too early so as to be lingering about the station; in which latter circumstance it seemed quite possible to his mother that "that girl" might become aware that her prey was slipping from her fingers, and appear upon the scene to recover him. She might save herself the trouble, Lady Piercey thought, for the boy's brain was full of London, and a country lass was not likely to get much hold of him; but still, it's best to be on the safe side. No suggestion of Patty's real intentions had occurred to any one; not even in the Seven Thorns, where they suspected much less than at Greyshott. In the little inn it was supposed that the Softy had been, after all, too clever for her, and had got clean away; and in the Manor it was also believed that he had escaped from her vulgar attractions. He had got London in his blood, he was thinking of how to enjoy himself as much as he was capable of thinking of anything, and the Rev. Gregson would take care of that, his mother reflected with a grim smile. And to have him safely away, transferred to some one else's responsibility, no longer for the moment a trouble to any one belonging to him, filled Greyshott in general, and his parents in particular, with a heavenly calm. The only one who was not perfectly at ease was Mrs. Osborne, who endeavoured in vain to make out what he meant by many of his broken expressions. Margaret was sure that Gervase meant something which was not suspected by his family: but she, too, believed that he had somehow cut himself adrift from Patty, and that whatever his meaning was, in that quarter he was safe; which showed that though she was very different from the rest of the household, her mind, even when awakened into some anxiety and alarm, had little more insight than theirs.

She was met upon the road by Osy and his nurse, and the little boy was delighted to be lifted into the carriage, an unusual privilege. His chatter was sweet to his mother's ears. It delivered her for the moment from those anxieties which were not hers, which she was compelled to share without any right to them; without being permitted any real interest. Osy was her refuge, the safeguard of her individuality as a living woman with concerns and sentiments of her own. To put her arms round him, to hear the sound of his little babbling voice, was enough at first; and then she awoke with a start to the consciousness that Osy was saying something in which there was not only meaning, but a significance of a most alarming kind—"Movver, Movver!" the little boy had been saying, calling her attention, which was so satisfied with him, that it was scarcely open to what he said. He beat upon her knee with his little fist, then climbed up on the seat and seized her by the chin—a favourite mode he had of demanding to be listened to: "Movver! has Cousin Gervase don to be marrwed? Where has he don to be marrwed—tell me; tell me, Movver!"

Mrs. Osborne started with a sudden perception of what he meant at last. "Osy, you must not be so silly; Gervase has gone to London to see all the fine things—the shops, don't you remember? and the theatres, and the beautiful horses, and the beautiful ladies in the park."

"Yes, I wemember; there was one beau'ful lady with an organ, that singed in the street. But you said I couldn't marrwey her, I was too little. Will Cousin Gervase marrwey a lady like that?"

"Hush, child! he is not going to marry at all."

"Oh yes, yes, Movver! for he told me. He made me dive him my big silver penny that Uncle Giles dave me, and he said, 'I'm doing to be marrwed, Osy.' I dave it to him for a wedding present, like you dave Miss Dohnson your silver bells."

"Osy, don't say such things! It is nurse that has put this nonsense into your head."

"'Tisn't nurse, and 'tisn't nonsense, Movver!" cried the child with indignation. "Will he bring home the beau'ful lady, or will he do away with her, and live in another place? I hope he will go and live in another place."

"Osy, this is all an invention, my little boy. You must be dreaming. Don't say such things before any one, or you will make Uncle Giles and Aunt Piercey very unhappy. It is one of your little stories that you make up."

"It isn't no story, Movver! I never make up stories about Cousin Gervase; and he tooked my big silver penny, and then I dave it him for a wedding present; for he said 'I'm doing to be marrwed.' He did; he did—Movver! I hope he'll do away and live in another house. I dave it to him," said Osy, with a little moisture on his eyelashes. "But he tooked it first. It was my big, big, silver penny, that is worth a great lot. I hope—"

"Hush, Osy: don't you know, my little boy, that Cousin Gervase is to his mother what you are to me? She would not like him to go away."

"I heard Uncle Giles say, 'T'ank God, we've dot a little time to breathe,' and Aunt Piercey dave a great, great, big puff, and sat down as if she was t'ankful, too. It is only you, Movver, that looks sad."

"Osy, did you ever hear of the little pitchers that have long ears?"

"I know what it means, too," said the child. "It means me; but I tan't help it when people say fings. Movver, are you fond of Cousin Gervase, that you looks like that? like you were doing to cry?"

Was she fond of Gervase, poor boy? Margaret could not even claim that excuse for being sad. Was she fond of any of the people by whom she was surrounded, who held her in subjection? At least, she was terribly perturbed by the cloud that hung over them—the possible trouble that was about to befall them. Poor Gervase was not very much to build hopes or wishes upon, but he was all they had; and if it were possible that he was meditating any such steps, what a terrible blow for his father and mother!—a stroke which they would feel to the bottom of their hearts. For himself, was it, indeed, so sad? Was it not, perhaps, the best thing he could do? Her mind went over the possibilities as by a lightning flash. Patty—if it was Patty—if there was anything in it—was probably the best wife he could get. She was energetic and determined; she would take care of him for her own sake. And who else would marry the Softy? Margaret's mind leapt on further to possible results, and to a sudden perception that little Osy, had he ever had any chance of succession, would be hopelessly set aside by this step, and the only possible reward of her own slavery be swept from her horizon. This forced itself upon her, through the crowd of other thoughts, with a chill to her heart. But what chance had Osy ever had? And who could put any confidence in the statement of Gervase to the child? Perhaps it was only "his fun." The little theft of the money was nothing remarkable; for Gervase, who never had any money, was always on the look-out for unconsidered trifles, which he borrowed eagerly. Perhaps this was all. Perhaps the half-witted young man meant nothing but a joke—one of his kind of jokes—for why should he have betrayed himself to little Osy? On the other hand, there were those allusions to some one who was to meet him, which he had laughed at so boisterously, and which she could not imagine referred to Dr. Gregson. Margaret's bewilderment grew greater the more she thought.

"Osy," she said, as they turned up the avenue, "you must forget all this, for it is nonsense."

"About my big, big, silver penny?" said the child, the water now standing in his eyes; for the more he thought of his loss, which he had carried off in childish pride with a high hand at first, the more Osy felt it. "It is not nonsense, Movver," he said, "for it is true."

"About what Cousin Gervase said? It was very wrong of him, but that is not true, Osy. He must have said it for a joke. Don't say anything. Promise me, dear! Not a word."

"Not to you, Movver?" said the little boy, two big tears dropping from his eyes; "for I tan't, tan't bear to lose my silver penny, and I would not mind if it was a wedding present. I want my silver penny back!"

"We'll find you another one, dear, that will be just as good."

"But it won't be my own one, and I want my own one," Osy said. He was still sobbing with long-drawn childish reverberation of woe when they got to the door; but there he took a great resolution. "I'll fink it was a wedding present," he cried, "and then I sha'n't mind. I'll fink he is going to be marrwed, and I'll never say a word, because nobody knows but me."

This valorous resolve exercised a great control, and yet was very hard to keep up during the long afternoon which followed. It rained in the later part of the day, and Sir Giles could not go out, so that Osy, restored to all the privileges which had been a little curtailed during Gervase's temporary reign, became once more a leading member of the party. And how often that important secret came bursting to the little fellow's lips! But he kept his word, like a gentleman. Margaret heard him singing it to himself as he capered about the room on Sir Giles' stick, "Doing to be marrwed, doing to be marrwed," which relieved his mind without betraying his knowledge. It even attracted Sir Giles' attention, who called to him to know what he was singing.

"It's a silly rhyme he has just picked up," said Margaret, interposing, which was a thing the old people did not like.

"He can tell me himself," said Sir Giles; "he's quite clever enough."

"No, it isn't a silly rhyme," said little Osy; "it's me myself, that am a gweat prince riding upon a noble steed, and I'm doing to be marrwed—I'm doing to be marrwed!"

"And who's the bride, Osy; who's the bride?" said Sir Giles, in high good humour.

"It is a beau'ful lady in London that singed in the streets, with a big napkin on her head. But Movver said I was too little to marrwey her. I'm a man now, and a soldier and a gweat, gweat knight; and I can marrwey any one I please."

"That's the thing!" said old Sir Giles; "don't you be tied to your mother's apron-strings, my boy. The ladies always want to rule over us men, don't they? and some of us must make a stand, you know." The old gentleman laughed at his joke till he cried, the old lady sitting grimly by. But she, too, smiled upon the little rebel: "You'll not find him such an easy one to guide when he grows up, Meg," she said, nodding her head. "He's got the Piercey temper, for all it's so amusing now. It ain't amusing when they grow up," said Lady Piercey, shaking her head. But she, too, encouraged Osy to defy his mother. He was a pretty sight careering round the dim library like a stray sunbeam, his little laughing face flushed with play and praise. Had the child been clever enough to invent that little fiction, innocent baby as he looked?—or had he really forgotten, as children will, and believed himself the hero of his little song? But this was one of the mysteries that seven years can hide from everybody as well as seventy, and Margaret could not tell. Now that Gervase was gone the boy seemed to fall into his place again, the darling of everybody, the centre of all their thoughts. And who could tell what might happen? Osy was not the next in succession, but he was not far out of the line. Margaret tried to put all such thoughts out of her mind, but it was difficult to do so, with the sight of Osy's triumph and sway over them—two old people who were so fond of him and could do so much for him—before their eyes.

There came a moment, however, no further off than that evening, when every furtive hope of this description died at a blow out of Margaret Osborne's heart. It was not that Osy was less admired and petted, or that he had offended or transgressed in any way. It was simply the arrival at Greyshott of Colonel Gerald Piercey that had this effect. It was she who met him first as he came into the hall, springing down from the dogcart that had brought him from the station, and at the first glance her heart had died within her. Not that there was anything alarming in his aspect. He had attained, with his forty years, to an air of distinction which Margaret did not remember in him; and a look of command, of easy superiority, of the habit of being obeyed. This habit is curiously impressive to those who do not possess it. The very sound of his step as he came in was enough. Not a man to lose anything on which his hand had once closed, not one to risk or relinquish his rights, whatever they might be. Osy, by the side of this man! Her hopes, which had never ventured to put themselves into words, died on the moment a natural death. She advanced to meet the stranger, as in duty bound, being the only valid member of the family, and said, holding out her hand with a smile which she felt to be apologetic: "You are welcome to Greyshott, Cousin Gerald. My uncle and aunt are neither of them very well, and Gervase is from home. You don't remember me. I am Margaret Osborne, your cousin, too."

"I remember you," he said, "very well; but pardon me if I did not remember your face. I fear that is a bad compliment for a lady."

"Not at all," she said; "a good compliment: for I am more, I hope, than my face."

He did not understand the look she gave him, a wondering look with an appeal in it. Would he be good to Osy? Margaret felt as if this man were coming in like a conqueror—sweeping all the old, and feeble, and foolish of the house away before him, that he might step in and reign. He, on his side, had no such thought. He had come to pay a duty visit, moved thereto by his father. He had not been at Greyshott for many years; he remembered little, and thought less, of Gervase, who had been a child on his previous visit. That he should ever be master of the place, or sweep anybody away, was far from his thoughts. He followed into the library the slim, serious figure of this middle-aged woman in a black gown, horrified to think that this was Meg Piercey, the lively girl of his recollection. This Meg Piercey! It was true that he remembered her very well, a madcap of a girl, ready for any mischief; but this was certainly not the face he remembered, the young, daring, buoyant figure. It might have wounded Margaret, accustomed as she was to be considered as nobody, if she had been aware of the consternation with which he regarded her. A middle-aged woman! though not so old by a good many years as himself, who was still conscious of being young.

The visit, however, began very successfully. As he had no arrière pensée, he was quite at his ease with the old people whom he neither meant to sweep away nor to succeed. He received, quite naturally, the long and elaborate apologies of Lady Piercey in respect to her son.

"Gervase will be very sorry to miss you, Gerald,—he's in town; there is not much to amuse a young man in the country at this season of the year. He's not fond of garden parties and so forth, the only things that are going on, and not many of them yet. He prefers town. Perhaps it isn't to be wondered at. We have all liked to see a little life in our day."

What "life" could it have been that Lady Piercey in her day had liked to see? the new-comer asked himself, with an involuntary smile. But he took the explanation with the easiest good humour, thinking no evil.

"Lucky fellow!" he said; "he has the best of it. I was out in India all my young time, and saw only a very different kind of life."

"Come," said Sir Giles, "you amuse yourselves pretty well out there. Don't give yourself airs, Gerald."

"Oh, yes; we amuse ourselves more or less," he said, with a pleasant laugh. "Enough to make us envy a young swell like Gervase, who, I suppose, has all the world at his feet and nothing to do."

There was a strange pause in the room; a sort of furtive look between the ladies; a sound—he could not tell what—from Sir Giles. Colonel Piercey had a faint comprehension that he had, as he said to himself, put his foot in it. What had he said that was not the right thing to say? He caught Margaret's eye, and there was a warning in it, a sort of appeal; but he had not an idea what its meaning was.

"I am sure," said Lady Piercey, with a voice out of which she vainly endeavoured to keep the little break and whimper which was habitual to her when she was moved, "my boy might have all the world at his feet—if he was that kind, Gerald. But he's not that kind; he's of a different sort. He takes things in a—in a kind of philosophical way."

"Humph!" said Sir Giles, pushing back his chair. "Meg, Gerald will not mind if I have my backgammon. I'm an old fogey, you see, my boy, with long days to get through, and not able to get out. I'm past amusement. I only kill the time as well as I can now."

"I'm very fond of a game of backgammon, too, Uncle Giles."

"Are you, boy? why, that's something like. Meg, I'll give you a holiday. Ladies are very nice, but they never know the rules of a game," the ungrateful old gentleman said.

CHAPTER XVI

That evening in the library at Greyshott was the most cheerful that had been known for a long time; Colonel Piercey made himself thoroughly at home. He behaved to the old people as if they had been the most genial friends of his youth. He told them stories of India and his experiences there. He played backgammon with Sir Giles, and let him win the game as cleverly as Dunning did, and with more grace. He admired Lady Piercey's work and suggested a change in the shading, at which both she and Parsons exclaimed with delight that it would make all the difference! He was delightful to everybody except Margaret, of whom he took very little notice, which was a strange thing in so apparently chivalrous and kind a man, seeing in what a subject condition she was kept, how much required of her, and so little accorded to her, in the strange family party of which the two servants formed an almost unfailing part. Margaret felt herself left out in the cold with a completeness which surprised her, much as she was accustomed to the feeling that she was of no account. She had no desire that Gerald Piercey should pity her; but it was curious to see how he ignored her, never turning even a look her way, addressing her only when necessity required. It has always been a theory of mine that there exists between persons of opposite sexes who are no longer to be classed within the lines of youth, middle-aged people, or inclining that way, a repulsion instead of an attraction. A young man tolerates a girl even when she does not please him, because she is a woman; but a man of forty or so dislikes his contemporary on this account; is impatient of her; feels her society a burden, almost an affront to him. He calls her old, and he calls himself young; perhaps that has something to do with it. Colonel Piercey was not shabby enough to entertain consciously any such feeling; but he shared it unconsciously with many other men. He thought the less of her for accepting that position, for submitting to be the souffre-douleur of the household. He suspected her, instinctively, of having designs of—he knew not what kind,—of being underhand, of plotting her own advantage somehow, to the harm of the two old tyrants who exacted so much from her. Would she continue to hold such a place, to expose herself to so much harsh treatment, if it were not for some end of her own? It was true that he could not make out what that end would be; that there should be any possibility of the child (who was delightful) supplanting or succeeding Gervase, was not an idea that ever entered his mind. Gervase was a young man of whom he knew nothing, whom he supposed to be like other young men. And, after Gervase came the old General, Gerald Piercey's father, and himself. There was no possibility of any intruder in that place. He supposed that it was their money she must be after—to get them to leave all they could to her. Meg Piercey! the girl whom he could not help remembering still, who was not in the least like this pale person: to think that years and poverty should have brought that bright creature to this!

"I almost wonder, Gerald," said Lady Piercey, as she sat among her silks with an air of ease diffused over all the surroundings, working a little by turns and pausing to watch benignantly the process of the backgammon,—"I almost wonder that you did not meet my boy at the station. His train would come in just before yours left, and I have been thinking since then that you might have met. He was to meet an old friend, an excellent old clergyman, with whom he was to spend a few days. Though he is full of spirit, my Gervase is very fond of all his old friends."

"Humph!" said Sir Giles; but that was only perhaps because at that moment he made an injudicious move.

"I should not have known him had I met him," said the Colonel, carefully making a move more injudicious still, to the delight of Sir Giles; "you forget he was only a child when I was here. I saw an old clergyman roaming about, looking into all the carriages: was that your friend, I wonder? He had found no one up to that time."

"You sent Gregson after him then, my lady?" said Sir Giles; "though I said it wasn't fair."

"Why Sir Giles says it wasn't fair is this, Gerald," said Lady Piercey; "and you can judge between us. He thought because the boy was going to enjoy himself he shouldn't be troubled with old friends; but I thought a good judicious old clergyman, that had known him from his cradle, couldn't be in any one's way."

"I see your point of view," said Colonel Gerald, "but I think for my part I agree with Uncle Giles. At Gervase's age I should have thought the old clergyman a bore."

"Ah! but my Gervase is one in a thousand," Lady Piercey said, nodding her head and pursing up her lips.

"I saw another group at the station that amused me," said Gerald: "a young country-fellow with something of the look of a gentleman, and a girl all clad in gorgeous apparel, who had not in the least the look of a lady. They got out of the train arm-in-arm, he holding her just as if he feared she might run away—which was the last thing I should say she had any intention of doing. Is there any hobereau about here with a taste for rustic beauties? They were newly married, I should think, or going to be married. He, in a loud state of delight, and she—I should think she had made a good stroke of business, that little girl."

"I don't know of any name like Hobero," said Lady Piercey; "but there are a great many stations between this and London. I dare say they didn't come from hereabouts at all. Girls of that class are dreadful. They dress so that you don't know what kind they are—neither flesh nor fish nor red herring, as the proverb is—and their manners—but they haven't got any. They think nothing is too good for them."

"The woman in this case, I should say, knew very well that the young fellow was too good for her, but had no thought of giving him up. And he was wild with delight, a silly sort of fellow—not all there." Colonel Piercey's looks were bent unconsciously as he spoke upon the writing-table which stood behind Sir Giles' chair, and on which some photographs were arranged; and from the partial darkness there suddenly shone out upon him, from the whiteness of a large vignette, a face which he recognised. He cried, "Hallo!" in spite of himself as it seemed, and then, with a sudden start, looked at Margaret. She had grown pale, and as he looked at her she grew red, and lifted a warning finger. The Colonel sank back upon his seat with a consternation he could scarcely disguise.

"What's the matter, Gerald?" said Sir Giles, who was arranging steadily upon the board the black and white men for another game.

"Only the sight of that old cabinet which I remember so well," cried the soldier, with a curious tone in his voice. "It used to be one of our favourite puzzles to find out the secret drawers. When Mrs. Osborne was Miss Piercey," he continued, to give him an excuse for looking towards her again. Margaret had bent her head over her work. Was that what it meant? he asked himself. Was this designing woman in the secret? Was this her plan to harm her cousin, and get him into trouble with his parents? His face grew stern as he looked at her. He thought there was guilt in every line of her attitude. She could not face him, or give any account of the meaning in her eyes.

"Ay, it's a queer old thing," said Sir Giles; "many a one has tried his wits at it, and had to give up. It's very different from your modern things."

"You should see my Gervase at it," said Lady Piercey. "He pulls out one drawer after another, as if he had made it all. I never could fathom it for my part, though I have sat opposite to it in this chair for five-and-thirty years. But Gervase has it all at his fingers' ends."

"Pooh! he's known it all his life," said Sir Giles. "Gerald, my fine fellow, we've just time for another before I go to bed."

"Surely, Uncle," said Gerald; but it seemed to him that he had become all at once conscious of another game that was being played; a tragic game, with hearts and lives instead of bits of ivory—a hapless young fellow in the hands of two women, one of whom he had been made to believe he loved, in order to carry out the schemes of the other who was planning and scheming behind backs to deprive him of his natural rights. Imagination made a great leap to attain to such a fully developed theory, but it did so with a spring. Colonel Piercey thought that the presence of this woman, pale, self-restrained, bearing every humiliation, was accounted for now.

"Why did Gerald Piercey look at you so, Meg?" asked Lady Piercey. She had said she felt tired, and risen and said good night earlier than usual, seizing her niece's arm, not waiting till Parsons should come at her ordinary hour. She was fatigued with all the strain about Gervase; getting him off at the right hour, and getting all his "things" in order; and making out that new wonderful character for him to dazzle the visitor. She had a right indeed to be tired, having gone through so much that was exciting, and succeeded in everything, especially the last of her efforts. "Why did he look at you and talk that nonsense about the old cabinet? Something had come into his head."

"I supposed he thought, Aunt, of the time when we used to make fun over it, and ask all the visitors to find it out."

"Perhaps he did," said the old lady; "but though he looked at you that once, you needn't expect that he's going to pay attention to you, Meg. He thinks you're dreadfully gone off. I saw that as soon as he came into the room. You can see it in a moment from the way a man turns his head."

"I don't doubt that he is quite right," said Margaret, with a little spirit.

"Oh, yes; he's right enough. You're a very different girl from what you used to be," said Lady Piercey. "But you don't like to hear it, Meg; for you don't give me half the support you generally do. I don't feel your arm at all. It is as if I had nothing to lean on. I wish Parsons was here."

"Will you sit down for a moment and rest, and I will call Parsons?"

"Why should I rest—between the library and the stairs? I want to get to my room; I want to get to bed. What—what are you standing there for, not giving me your arm? I'll—I'll be on my nose—if you don't mind. Give me—your arm, Meg. Meg!" The old lady gave a dull cry, and moved her left arm about as if groping for some support, though the other was clasped strongly in that of Margaret, who was holding up her aunt's large wavering person with all the might she had. As she cried out for help, Lady Piercey sank down like a tower falling, dragging her companion with her; yet turning a last look of reproach upon her, and moving her lips, from which no sound came, with what seemed like upbraiding. There was a rush from all quarters at Margaret's cry. Parsons and Dunning came flying, wiping their mouths, from the merry supper-table, where they had been discussing Mr. Gervase—and the other servants, in a crowd, and Gerald Piercey from the room they had just left. Margaret had disengaged herself as best she could from the fallen mass of flesh, and had got Lady Piercey's head upon her shoulder, from which that large pallid countenance looked forth with wide open eyes, with a strange stare in them, some living consciousness mingling with the stony look of the soul in prison. Except that stare, and a movement of the lips, which were unable to articulate, and a slight flicker of movement in the left hand, still groping, as it seemed, for something to clutch at, she was like a woman made of stone.

And all in a moment, without any warning; without a sign that any one understood! Parsons, wailing, said that she wasn't surprised. Her lady had done a deal too much getting Mr. Gervase off; she had been worried and troubled about him, poor dear innocent! She hadn't slept a wink for two nights, groaning and turning in her bed. "But, for goodness gracious sake!" cried Parsons, "some one go back to master, or we'll have him on our 'ands, too. Mrs. Osborne, Lord bless you! go to master. You can't be no use here; we knows what to do—Dunning and me knows what to do. Go back to Sir Giles—go back to Sir Giles! or we won't answer for none of their lives!"

"Cousin Gerald, go to my uncle. Tell him she's a little faint. I will come directly and back you up, as soon as they can lift her. Go!" cried Margaret, with a severity that was not, perhaps, untouched, even at this dreadful moment, by a consciousness of the opinion he was supposed to have formed of her. It was as if she had stamped her foot at him, as she half-sat, half-lay, partially crushed by the fall of the old lady's heavy body, with the great death-like face surmounted by the red ribbons of the cap laid upon her breast. Those red ribbons haunted several minds for a long time after; they seemed to have become, somehow, the most tragic feature of the scene.

Colonel Piercey was not a man to interfere with a business that was not his. He saw that the attendants knew what they were about, and left them without another word.

Sir Giles was fuming a little over the interruption to his game. "What's the matter?" he said, testily. "You shouldn't go and leave a game unfinished for some commotion among the women. You don't know 'em as well as I do. Come along, come along; you've almost made me forget my last move. What did Meg Osborne cry out for, eh? My old lady is sharp on her sometimes. She must have given her a stinger that time; but Meg isn't the girl to cry out."

"It was a—stumble, I think," said the Colonel.

"Ay, ay! something of that kind. I know 'em, Gerald. I'm not easily put out. Come along and finish the game."

Margaret came in, some time after, looking very pale. She went behind her uncle's chair, and put her hand on his shoulder, "May I wheel you to your room, Uncle, if your game's over, instead of Dunning? He asked me to tell you he was coming directly, and that it was time for you to go to bed."

"Confound Dunning," cried Sir Giles, in his big rumbling voice. "I'm game to go on as long as Frank here will play. I've not had such a night for ever so long. He's a good player, but not good enough to beat me," he said, with a muffled long odd laugh that reverberated in repeated rolls like thunder.

The Colonel looked up at her to get his instructions. He did not like her, and yet he recognised in her the authority of the moment. And Margaret no longer tried to conciliate him, as at first, but issued forth her orders with a kind of sternness. "Let me wheel your chair, sir," he said; "you'll give me my revenge to-morrow? Three games out of four!—is that what you call entertaining a stranger, to beat him all along the line the first night?"

Sir Giles laughed loud and long in those rumbling, long-drawn peals. His laugh was like the red ribbons, and pointed the sudden tragedy. "You shall have your revenge," he said; "and plenty of it—plenty of it! You shall cry off before I will. I love a good game. If it wasn't for a good game, now and then, I don't know what would become of me. As for Meg, she's not worth naming; and my boy, Gervase, did his best, poor chap; but between you and me, Gerald, whatever my lady says, my boy Gervase—poor chap, poor chap!" Here the old gentleman's laughter broke down as usual in the weakness of a sudden sob or two. "He's not what I should like to see him, my poor boy Gervase," he cried.

He was taken to his room after a while, and soothed into cheerfulness, and had his drink compounded for him by Margaret, till Dunning came, pale, too, and excited, whispering to Mrs. Osborne that the doctor was to come directly, and that there was no change, before he approached his master, with whom, a few minutes afterwards, he was heard talking, and even laughing, by the Colonel, who remained in the library, pacing up and down with the painful embarrassment of a stranger in a new house, in the midst of a family tragedy, but not knowing what part he had to play in it, or where he should go, or what he should do. Margaret had left him without even a good-night, to return to the room upstairs, where Lady Piercey lay motionless and staring, with the red ribbons still crowning her awful brow.

CHAPTER XVII

And where was Gervase? His mother lay in the same condition all the next day. There was little hope that she would ever come out of it. The doctor said calmly that it was what he had looked for, for a long time. There had been "a stroke" before, though it was slight and had not been talked about; but Parsons knew very well what he was afraid of, and should have kept her mistress from excitement. Parsons, too, allowed that she knew it might come at any time. But Lord! a thing that may come at any time, you don't ever think it's going to come now, Parsons said; and who was she to control her lady as was the head of everything? It was allowed on all sides that to control Lady Piercey would have been a difficult thing indeed, especially where anything about Gervase was concerned.

"Spoiled the boy from the beginning, that was what she always did," said Sir Giles, mumbling. "I'd have kept a stronger hand over him, Gerald; but what could I do, with his mother making it all up to him, as soon as my back was turned?"

Colonel Piercey heard a great deal about Gervase that he had never been intended to hear. Lady Piercey's fiction, which she had made up so elaborately about the young man of fashion, crumbled all to pieces, poor lady; while one after another made their confidences to him. The only one who said nothing was Margaret. She was overwhelmed with occupation; all the charge of the house, which Lady Piercey had kept in her own hands, falling suddenly upon her shoulders, and without any co-operation from the much-indulged old servants, who were all servile to their imperious mistress, but very insubordinate to any government but hers. It became a serious matter, however, as the days passed by, and the old lady remained like a soul in prison, unable to move or to speak, yet staring with ever watchful eyes at the door, looking, they all felt, for some one who did not come. Where was Gervase? There was more telegraphing at Greyshott than there ever had been since such a thing was possible. Mr.

Gregson replied to say that he had not found Gervase at the train, and had not seen him, news which brought everything to a standstill. Where, then, had he gone? They had no address to send to, no clue by which he might be traced out. He had disappeared altogether, nobody could tell where. Colonel Piercey's first impulse had been to leave the distracted family, thus thrown into the depths of domestic distress, but Sir Giles clung to him with piteous helplessness, imploring him not to go.

"After my boy Gervase, there's nobody but you," he cried, "and he's away, God knows where, and whom should I have to hold on by if you were to go too? There's Meg, to be sure: but she's got enough to do with my lady. Stay, Gerald, stay, for goodness' sake. I've nobody, nobody, on my side of the house but you; and if anything were to happen," cried the poor old gentleman, breaking down, "who have I to give orders, or to see to things? I don't know what is to become of me if you won't stay."

"I'll stay, of course, Uncle Giles, if I can be of any use," said Colonel Piercey.

"God bless you, my lad!" cried Sir Giles, now ready to sob for satisfaction, as he had before been for trouble. "Now I can face things, if I've you to stand by me."

The household in general took heart when it was known he was to stay.

"Oh! Colonel Piercey, if you'd but look up Mr. Gervase for my lady?—she can't neither die nor get better till she sees her boy," said the weeping Parsons; and "Colonel Piercey, Sir," said Dunning, "Sir Giles do look to you so, as he never looked to any gentleman before. I'll get him to do whatever's right and good for him if so be as he knows you're here." Thus, both master and servants seized upon him. And yet what could he do? He could not go out and search for Gervase whom he had never seen, knowing absolutely nothing of his cousin's haunts, nor of the people among whom he was likely to be. And he could not consult the servants on this point. There was but one person who could give him information, and she kept out of his way.

On the evening of the second day, however, Margaret came into the library after Sir Giles had been wheeled off to bed. It happened that Colonel Piercey was standing before the writing-table, examining that very photograph which he had discovered with such surprise, and which had made him break off so quickly in his story on the night when Lady Piercey was taken ill. She came suddenly up to him where he stood with the photograph, and laid her hand on his arm. He had not heard her step, and started, almost dropping it in his surprise. "Mrs. Osborne!" he exclaimed.

"You are looking at Gervase's picture? Cousin Gerald, help us if you can. I don't know how much or how little she feels, but it is Gervase my aunt is lying looking for—Gervase, who doesn't know she is ill even if he had the thought. Was it him you saw with—with the woman? I have not liked to ask you, but I can't put it off any longer. Was it Gervase? Oh! for pity's sake, speak!"

"How should I know," he said, "if you don't know?"

"Know? I! What way have I of knowing? You saw him, or you seemed to think you did."

"It was only for a moment. I had never seen him before; I might be mistaken. It seemed to me that it was the same kind of face. But how can I speak on the glimpse of a moment? I might be quite wrong."

"You are very cautious," she cried at last, "oh, very cautious!—though it is a matter of life and death. Won't you help us, then, or can't you help us? If this is so, it might give a clue. There is a girl—who has disappeared also, I have just found out. Oh! Cousin Gerald, you know what he is?—you must have heard enough to know: not a madman, nor even an imbecile, yet not like other people. He might be imposed upon—he might be carried away. There was something strange about him before he went. He said things which I could not understand. But they suspected nothing."

"Was it not your duty," said Gerald Piercey, almost sternly, "to tell them—if they suspected nothing, as you say?"

"You speak to me very strangely," she said with a forced smile; "as if I were in the wrong, anyhow. What could I tell them? That I was uneasy, and not satisfied? My aunt would have asked what did it matter if I were satisfied or not?—and Uncle Giles!" She stopped, and resumed in a different tone, "And the girl has gone up to London from the Seven Thorns—so far as I can make out, on the same day."

"What sort of a girl?"

Margaret described her as well as she was able.

"I cannot give you many details. I think she is pretty: brown hair and eyes, very neat and nice in her dress, though my aunt thinks it beyond her station. I think, on the whole, a nice-looking girl—not tall."

"The description would answer most young women that one sees."

"It is possible—there is nothing remarkable. She looks clever and watchful, and a little defiant. But I did not mean you to go into the streets to look for Patty. I thought you might see whether my description agreed."

"Mrs. Osborne, perhaps you will tell me what you suppose to have happened, and what there is that I can do."

"If we are to be on such formal terms," said Margaret, colouring deeply, "yes, Colonel Piercey, I will tell you. I suppose, or rather, I fear, that Gervase may have gone away with Patty Hewitt. She is quite a respectable girl. She would not compromise herself; therefore—"

"You think he has married her?"

"I think most likely she must have married him—or intends to do it. But that takes time. They could not have banns called, or other arrangements made—"

"They could have a special licence."

"Ah! but that costs money. They would not have money, either of them. I have been trying to make inquiries quietly. But time is passing, and his poor mother! It would be better to consent to anything," said Margaret, "than to have her die without seeing him; and perhaps if he were found, the pressure on the brain might relax. No, I don't know if that is possible; I am no doctor. I only want to satisfy her. She is his mother! Whatever he is, he is more to her than any one else in the world."

"She does not seem very kind to you, that you should think so much of that."

"Who said she was not kind to me? You take a great deal upon yourself, Colonel Piercey, to be a distant cousin!"

"I am the next-of-kin," he said. "I'd like to protect these poor old people—and it is my duty—from any plot there may be against them."

"Plot—against them?" She stared at him for a moment with eyes that dilated with astonishment. Then she shook her head.

"I don't know what you mean," she said. "If you will not help, I must do what I can by myself. And you are free on your side to inquire, and I hope will do it, and take such steps as may seem to you good. The thing now is to find Gervase for his mother. At another moment," said Margaret, raising her head, "you will perhaps explain to me what you mean by this tone—towards me."

She turned her back upon him without another word, and walked away, leaving Colonel Piercey not very comfortable. He asked himself uneasily what right he had to suspect her?—what he suspected her of?—as he stood and watched her crossing the hall. It was a sign of the agitation in the house, that all the doors seemed to stand open, the centre of the family existence having shifted somehow from the principal rooms downstairs to some unseen room above, where the mistress of the house lay. What did he suspect Meg Piercey of? What had he against her? When he asked himself this, it appeared that all he had against her was that she was a dependent, a widow, a middle-aged person—one of those wrecks which encumber the shores of life, which ought to have gone down, or to be broken up, not to strew the margins of existence with unnecessary and incapable things, making demands upon feeling and sympathy which might be much better expended elsewhere. Colonel Piercey was not a hard man by nature: he was, in fact, rather too open to the claims of charity, and had expended too much, not too little, upon widows and orphans in his day. But it had stirred up all the angry elements in his nature to see Meg Piercey in that condition which was not natural to her. She ought to have died long ago along with her husband, or she ought to have a position of her own: to see her here in that posture of dependence, in that black gown, with that child, living, as he said to himself harshly, upon charity, and accepting all the penalties, was more than he could bear. There is a great deal to be said for the Suttee, though a humanitarian government has put an end to it. It is so much more dignified for a woman. To a man of fine feelings, it is a painful thing to see how a person whose natural rôle is that of a princess, a dispenser of help to others, should come down herself into the rank of the beggar, because of the death of, probably, a very inferior being to whom she was married. It degraded her altogether in the scale of being. A princess has noble qualities, large aims, and stands above the crowd—a dependant does quite the reverse. Scheming and plotting are the natural breath of the latter; and that a woman should let herself come down to that wilfully, rather than die and be done with it, which would be so much more natural and dignified! Colonel Piercey was aware that his thoughts were very fantastic, and yet this is how they were—he could not help himself. He was angry with Margaret. It was not the place she was born to; a sort of Abigail about the backstairs, existing by the caprice of a disagreeable old woman. Oh, no! it was not a thing that a man could put up with. And, of course, she must have sunk to the level of her kind.

This was why he suspected her. The question remained, What did he suspect her of? And this was still more difficult to answer. Such a woman, of course, would live by sowing mischief in a family; by hurting in the most effectual way the superiors who kept her down, and were so little considerate of her. And their son was the way in which she could most effectively do this. Gerald Piercey had various thoughts rising in his mind about this young man, who probably was not at all fit to hold the family property and succeed Sir Giles in its honours. There was one point of view from which Colonel Piercey could not forget that he himself was the next-of-kin—that which made him, in his own eyes, the champion of Gervase—his determined defender against every assault. Perhaps the very strength of this feeling might push him beyond what was right and just; but it would be in the way of supporting and protecting his weak-minded cousin. That was a point upon which, naturally, he could have no doubt. If Meg Piercey was against him, it was Gerald Piercey's part to defend him. But the means were a little doubtful. He was not clear whether Meg was helping Gervase to marry unsuitably, to spite his parents, or whether her intention was to prevent this marriage, in order to deprive him of his happiness and the natural protection which the support of a clever wife might afford to the half-witted young man. Thus, he had a difficult part to play; having first to find out what Margaret's scope and meaning was, and then to set himself to defeat it. He had been but three days in the house, and what a tangled web he was involved in!—to be the Providence of all these people, old and young, whom he knew so little, yet was so closely connected with; and to defeat the evil genius, the enemy in the guise of a friend, whom he alone was clear-sighted enough to divine. But she puzzled him all the same. She had looks that were not those of a deceiver; and when she had raised her head and told him that at another moment she would demand an explanation of what his tone meant, something like a shade of alarm passed through the soldier's mind. He would not have been alarmed, you may be sure, if Margaret had threatened him with a champion, as in the older days. Bois-Guilbert was not afraid of Ivanhoe. But, when it is the woman herself who asks an explanation, and his objections have to be stated in full words, to her alone, facing him for herself, that is a different matter. It may well make a man look pale.

CHAPTER XVIII

The next morning after this, Gerald Piercey found himself in the front of the Seven Thorns. He had not known what it was: whether a hamlet, or a farm, or what he actually found it to be, a roadside inn. The aspect of the place was more attractive than usual. It was lying full in the morning sunshine; a great country waggon, with its white covering, and fine, heavily-built, but well-groomed horses, standing before the door, concentrating the light in its great hood. One of the horses was white, which made it a still more shining object in the midst of the red-brown road. The old thorns were full in the sunshine, which softened their shabby antiquity, and made the gnarled roots and twisted branches picturesque. The long, low fabric of the house was bathed in the same light, which pervaded the whole atmosphere with a purifying and embellishing touch. The west side, looking over the walled garden, which extended for some distance along the road, though in the shade, showed a row of open windows, at which white curtains fluttered, giving an air of inhabitation to that usually-closed-up portion of the place. The visitor felt, as he looked at it, that it was not a mere village public-house, that its decadence might have a story, and that it was possible that the daughter of such a house might not, after all, be a mere rustic coquette, or, perhaps, so bad a match for the half-witted Gervase. Colonel Piercey had never once thought of himself as the possible heir of Greyshott; he did not feel that he had any interest in keeping Gervase from marrying, and though it was intolerable that the heir of the Pierceys should marry a barmaid, his feelings softened as he looked at the old country inn, with its look of long-establishment. Probably there was a farm connected with it; perhaps there was a certain pride of family here, too, and the daughter of the house was kept apart from the drinking and the wayside guests. Meg Piercey might have divined that the young woman was really the best match that Gervase could hope for, and this might be the cause of her opposition. (He forgot that he had supposed it likely that Meg might be bringing the match about for her own private ends, one hypothesis being just as likely as another.) With this idea he approached slowly, and took his seat upon the bench that stood under the window of the parlour. The roads between Greyshott and the Seven Thorns were dry and dusty, and his boots were white enough to warrant the idea that he was a pedestrian reposing himself, naturally, at the place of refreshment on the roadside.

The landlord came to the door with the waggoner, when Colonel Piercey had established himself there, and his aspect could not be said to be quite equal to that of his house. Hewitt had a red nose and a watery eye. His appearance did not inspire respect. He was holding the waggoner by the breast of his smock, and holding forth, duly emphasising his discourse by the gesture of the other hand, in which he held a pipe.

"You just 'old by me," he was saying, "look'ee, Jack; and I'll 'old by you, I will. The 'ay's a good crop; nobody can't say nothing again that. But there's rain a-coming, and Providence, 'e knows what'll come of it all in the end. It ain't what's grow'd in the fields as is to be trusted to, but what's safe in the stacks; and there's a deal o' difference between one and the other. Look'ee here! you 'old by me, and I'll 'old by you. And I can't speak no fairer. I've calcilated all round, I 'ave—me and Patty, my girl, as is that good at figures; and if it's got in safe, all as I've got to say is, that this 'ere will be a dashed uncommon yeer."

"It's mostly the way," said the waggoner, "I'll allow, with them dry Junes. The weather can't 'old up not for ever."

"Nor won't," said old Hewitt, with assurance; "it stands to reason. Ain't this a variable climate or ain't it not? And a drop o' rain we 'aven't seen not for three weeks and more. Then we'll 'ave a wet July. You see yourself when I knocked the glass 'ow it went down. And that," he added, triumphantly, waving his pipe in the air, "is what settles the price of the 'ay."

"I shouldn't wonder if you was right, master," said the waggoner, getting under weigh.

Gerald Piercey sat and watched the big horses straining their great flanks to the work, setting the heavy waggon in motion, with pleasure in the sight which diverted him for a moment from his chief object of interest. Coming straight from India and the fine and slender-limbed creatures which are the patricians of their kind, the great, patient, phlegmatic English cart-horse filled him with admiration. The big feathered hoofs, the immense strain of those gigantic hind-quarters, the steady calm of the rustic, reflected with a greater and more dignified impassiveness in the face of his beast, was very attractive and interesting to him.

"Fine horses, these," he said, half to Hewitt at the door, half to the waggoner, who grinned with a slow shamefacedness, as if it were himself who was being praised.

"Ay, sir," said Hewitt, "and well took care of, as ever beasts was. Jack Mason there—though I say it as shouldn't—is awfull good to his team."

"And why shouldn't you say it?" said Colonel Piercey. "It's clear enough."

"He's a relation, that young man is, and it's a country saying, sir, as you shouldn't speak up for your own. But I ain't one as pays much 'eed to that, for, says I, you knows them that belong to you better nor any one else does. There's my girl Patty, now; there ain't one like her betwixt Guildford and Portsmouth, and who knows it as well as me?"

"That's a very satisfactory state of things," said the visitor, "and, of course, you must know best. But I fear you won't be able to keep Miss Patty long to yourself if she's like that."

At this Patty's father began to laugh a slow, inward laugh. "There's 'eaps o' fellows after 'er, like bees after a 'oney 'ive. But, Lord bless you! she don't think nothing o' them. She's not one as would take up with a country 'Odge. She's blood in her veins, has my girl. We've been at the Seven Thorns, off and on, for I don't know 'ow many 'undred years: more time," said Hewitt, waving his pipe vaguely towards Greyshott, "than them folks 'as been at the 'All."

"Ah, indeed! That's the Pierceys, I suppose?"

"And a proud set they be. But 'Ewitts was 'ere before 'em, only they won't acknowledge it. I've 'eard my sister Patience, 'as 'ad a terrible tongue of 'er own, tell Sir Giles so to his face. 'E was young then, and father couldn't keep 'im out o' this 'ouse. After Patience, to be sure; but he was a terrible cautious one, was Sir Giles, and it never come to nought." The landlord laughed with a sharp hee-hee-hee. "I reckon," he said, "it runs in the blood."

"What runs in the blood?"

"I don't know, sir," said the innkeeper, pausing suddenly, "if you've called for anything? I can't trust neither to maid nor man to attend to the customers now Patty's away."

"If you have cider, I should like a bottle, and perhaps you'll help me to drink it," said Colonel Piercey. "I'm sorry to hear that Miss Patty's away."

"In London," said Hewitt; "but only for a bit. She 'as a 'ead, that chit 'as! Them rooms along there, end o' the 'ouse, 'asn't been lived in not for years and years. She says to me, she does, 'Father, let's clear 'em out, and maybe we'll find a lodger.' I was agin it at first. 'What'll you do with a lodger? There ain't but very little to be made o' that,' I says. 'They don't come down to the parlour to drink, that sort doesn't, and they're more trouble nor they're worth.' 'You leave it to me, father,' she says. And, if you'll believe it, she's found folks for them rooms already! New-married folks, she says, as will spend their money free. And coming in a week, for the rest of the summer or more. That's Patty's way!" cried the landlord, smiting his thigh. "Strike while it's 'ot, that's 'er way! Your good 'ealth, sir, and many of 'em. It ain't my brewing, that cider. I gets it from Devonshire, and I think, begging your pardon, sir, as it's 'eady stuff."

"But how," said Colonel Piercey, "will you manage with your visitors, when your daughter is away?"

"Oh, bless you, sir, she's a-coming with 'em, she says in her letter, if not before. Patty knows well I ain't the one for lodgers. I sits in my own parlour, and I don't mind a drop to drink friendly-like with e'er a man as is thirsty, or to see a set of 'orses put up in my stables, or that; but Richard 'Ewitt of the Seven Thorns ain't one to beck and bow afore folks as thinks themselves gentry, and maybe ain't not 'alf as good as 'er and me. No, sir; I wasn't made, nor was my father afore me made, for the likes of that."

"It is very good of you, I'm sure, Mr. Hewitt, to sit for half an hour with me, who may be nobody, as you say."

"Don't mention it, sir," said Hewitt, with a wave of the pipe which he still carried like a banner in his hand: "I 'ope I knows a gentleman when I sees one; and as I said, I sits at my own door and I takes a friendly drop with any man as is thirsty. That ain't the same as bowing and scraping, and taking folks's orders, as is nothing to me."

"And Miss Patty, you say, is in London? London's a big word: is she east or west, or—"

"It's funny," said Hewitt, "the interest that's took in my Patty since she's been away. There's been Sally Ferrett, the nurse up at Greyshott, asking and asking, where is she, and when did she go, and when she's coming back? I caught her getting it all out of 'Lizabeth the girl. What day did she go, and what train, and so forth? 'Lizabeth's a gaby. She just says 'Yes, Miss,' and 'No, Miss,' to a wench like that, as is only a servant like herself. I give it 'em well, and I give Miss her answer. 'What's their concern up at Greyshott with where my Patty is?"

"That's true," said Colonel Piercey, "and what is my concern? You are quite right, Mr. Hewitt."

"Oh, yours, sir? that's different: you ask out o' pure idleness, you do, to make conversation; I understand that. But between you and me I couldn't answer 'em, not if I wanted to. For my Patty is one as can take very good care of 'erself, and she don't give me no address. She'll be back with them young folks, or maybe, afore 'em, next week, and that's all as I want to know. I wants her then, for I'll not have nothing to do with 'em, and 'Lizabeth, she's a gaby, and not to be trusted. Lodgers in my opinion is more trouble than they're any good. So Patty will manage them herself, or they don't come here."

"The family at Greyshott takes an interest in your daughter, I presume, from what you say," said Colonel Piercey.

Upon this Hewitt laughed low and long, and winked over and over again with his watery eye. "There's one of 'em as does," he said. "Oh, there's one of 'em as does! If so be as you know the family, sir, you'll know the young gentleman. Don't you know Mr. Gervase?—eh, not the young 'un, sir, as is Sir Giles's heir? Oh, Lord, if you don't know him you don't know Greyshott Manor, nor what's going on there."

"I have never seen the young gentleman," said Gerald; "I believe he is not very often at home."

"I don't know about 'ome, but 'e's 'ere as often as 'e can be. 'E'd be 'ere mornin', noon, and night if I'd 'a put up with it; but I see 'im, what 'e was after, and I'll not 'ave my girl talked about, not for the best Piercey as ever trod in shoe-leather. And 'e ain't the best, oh, not by a long chalk 'e ain't. Sir Giles is dreadful pulled down with the rheumatics and that, but 'e was a man as was something like a man. Lord bless you, sir, this poor creature, 'e's a Softy, and 'e'll never be no more."

"What do you mean by a Softy?" said Gerald, quickly; then he added with a sensation of shame, "Never mind, I don't want you to tell me. Don't you think you should be a little more careful what you say, when a young man like this comes to your house?"

"What should I be careful for?" said Hewitt; "I ain't noways beholdin' to the Pierceys. They ain't my landlords, ain't the Piercey's, though they give themselves airs with their Lords o' the Manor, and all that. Hewitts of the Seven Thorns is as good as the Pierceys, and not beholdin' to them, not for the worth of a brass fardin—oh, no! And I wouldn't have the Softy about my house, a fool as opens 'is mouth and laughs in your face if you say a sensible word to 'im; not for me! Richard Hewitt's not a-going to think twice what he says for a fool like 'im. Softy's 'is name and Softy's 'is nature: ask any man in the village who the Softy is, and they'll soon tell you. Lord, it don't matter a bit what I say."

"Still, I suppose," said Colonel Piercey, feeling a little nettled in spite of himself, "it is, after all, the first family in the neighbourhood."

"First family be dashed," cried Hewitt; "I'm as good a family as any of 'em. And I don't care that, no, not that," he cried, snapping his fingers, "for the Pierceys, if they was kings and queens, which they ain't, nor no such big folks after all. Old Sir Giles, he's most gone off his head with rheumatics and things; and my lady, they do say, she 'ave 'ad a stroke, and serve her right for her pride and her pryin'. And Mr. Gervase, he's a Softy, and that's all that's to be said. They ain't much for a first family when you knows all the rights and the wrongs of it," Hewitt said.

CHAPTER XIX

The poet's wish that we might see ourselves as others see us was, though he did not so intend it, a cruel wish. It might save us some ridicule to the outside world, but it would turn ourselves and our pretensions into such piteous ridicule to ourselves, that life would be furnished with new pangs. Colonel Piercey went back to Greyshott with a sense of this keen truth piercing through all appearances, which was half ludicrous and half painful, though it was not himself, but his relations, that had been exhibited to him in the light of an old rustic's observations. He had come upon this visit with a sense of the greatness of the head of his own family, which had, perhaps, a little self-esteem in it; for if the younger branches of the house were what he knew them in his own person, and his father's, what ought not the head of the house, Sir Giles, the lineal descendant of so many Sir Gileses, and young Gervase, the heir of those long-unbroken honours, to be? He had expected, perhaps a little solemn stupidity, such as the younger is apt to associate with the elder branch. But he had also expected something of greatness—evidence that the house was of that reigning race which is cosmopolitan, and recognises its kind everywhere from English meads to Styrian mountains, and even among the chiefs of the East. It was ludicrous to see, through the eyes of a clown, how poor, after all, these pretences were. Yet he could not help it. Poor old Sir Giles, helpless and querulous, broken down by sickness, and, perhaps, disappointment and trouble; the poor old lady, not much at any time of the rural princess she might have been, lying speechless in that lingering agony of imprisoned consciousness; and the son, the heir, the future head of the house! Was not that a revelation to stir the blood in the veins of Gerald Piercey, the next-of-kin? He was a man of many faults, but he was full both of pride and generosity. The humiliation for his race struck him more than any possible elevation for himself. Indeed, that possible elevation was far enough off, if he had ever thought of it. A half-witted rustic youth, taken hold of by a pert barmaid, with a numerous progeny to follow, worthy of both sides—was that what the Pierceys were to come to in the next generation? He had never thought, having so many other things to occupy him in his life, of that succession, though probably he began to think, his father had, who had so much insisted on this visit. But what a succession it would be now! He was walking along, turning these things over in his mind, going slowly, and not much observant (though this was not at all his habit) of what was about him, when he was sensible of a sudden touch, which was, indeed, only upon his hand, yet which felt as if it had been direct upon his heart, rousing all kinds of strange sensations there. It was a thing which is apt to touch every one susceptible of feeling, with quick and unexpected sensations when it comes unawares. It was a little hand—very small, very soft, very warm, yet with a grasp in it which held fast, suddenly put into his hand. Colonel Piercey stopped, touched, as I have said, on his very heart, which, underneath all kinds of actual and conventional coverings, was soft and open to emotion. He looked down and saw a little figure at his foot, a little glowing face looking up at him. "May I tum and walk with you, Cousin Colonel?" a small voice said. "Sally, do away."

"Certainly you shall come and walk with me, Osy," said the Colonel. "What are you doing, little man, so far from home?"

"It's not far from home. I walks far—far—further than that. Sally, do away! I'm doing to walk home with a gemplemans. I'm a gemplemans myself, but Movver will send a woman wif me wherever I do. Sally, do away!"

"I'll take care of him," said Colonel Piercey, with a nod to the maid. "And so you think you're too big for a nurse, Master Osy. How old are you?"

"Seven," said the boy; "at least I'm more than six-and-three-quarters, Cousin Colonel. Little Joey at the farm is only five, and he does miles, all by hisself. Joey is better than me many ways," he added, thoughtfully; "he dets up on the big hay-cart, and he wides on the big horse, and his faver sits him up high! on his so'lder. But I only have a pony and sometimes I does with Jacob in the dog-cart, and sometimes—"

"Would you like to ride on my shoulder, Osy?"

Osy looked up to the high altitude of that shoulder with a look full of deliberation, weighing various things. "I s'ould like it," he said, "but I felled off once when Cousin Gervase put me up, and I promised Movver: but I tan't help it when he takes me by my arms behind me. Sometimes I'm fwightened myself. A gemplemans oughtn't to be fwightened, s'ould he, Cousin Colonel?"

"That depends," said Gerald. "I am a great deal bigger than you, but sometimes I have been frightened, too."

Osy looked at the tall figure by his side with certain glimmerings in his eyes of contempt. That size! and afraid!—but he would not make any remark. One does not talk of the deficiencies of others when one is of truly gentle spirit. One passes them over. He apologised like a prince to Gerald for himself. "That would be," he said, "when it was a big, big giant. There's giants in India, I know, like Goliath. If I do to India when I'm a man, I'll be fwightened, too."

"But David wasn't, you know, Osy."

"That's what I was finking, Cousin Colonel, but he flinged the stone at him before he tummed up to him. Movver says it was quite fair, but—"

"I think it was quite fair. Don't you see, he had his armour on, and his shield, and all that; if he had had his wits about him, he might have put up his shield to ward off the stone. When you are little you must be very sharp."

Osy looked at his big cousin again, reflectively. "I don't fink I could kill you, Cousin Colonel, even if I was very sharp."

"I hope not, Osy, and I trust you will never want to, my little man."

"I would if we was fighting," said Osy, with spirit; "but I'll do on detting bigger and bigger till I'm a man: and you are a man now, and you tan't gwow no more."

"You bloodthirsty little beggar! You'll go on getting bigger and bigger while I shall grow an old man like Uncle Giles."

"I never," cried Osy, flushing very red, "would stwike an old gemplemans like Uncle Giles. Never! I wouldn't let nobody touch him. When Cousin Gervase runned away with his chair, I helped old Dunning to stop him. You might kill me, but I would fight for Uncle Giles!"

"It appears you are going to be a soldier, anyhow, Osy."

"My faver was a soldier," said Osy. "Movver's got his sword hanging up in our room; all the rest of the fings belongs to Uncle Giles, but the sword, it belongs to Movver and me."

The Colonel gave the little hand which was in his an involuntary pressure, and a little moisture came into the corner of his eye. "Do you remember your father," he said, "my little man?"

Osy shook his head. "I don't remember nobody but Movver," the child said.

What a curious thing it was! To hear of the dead father and his sword brought that wetness to Colonel Piercey's eye; but the name of the mother, which filled all the child's firmament, dried the half-tear like magic. The poor fellow who had died went to the Colonel's heart. The lonely woman with the little boy, so much more usual an occasion of sentiment, did not touch him at all. He did not want to hear anything of "Movver": and, indeed, Osy was by no means a sentimental child, and had no inclination to enlarge on the theme. His mother was a matter of course to him, as to most healthy little boys: to enlarge upon her love or her excellencies was not at all in his way.

"You walk very fast, Cousin Colonel," was the little fellow's next remark.

"Do I, my little shaver? What a beast I am, forgetting your small legs. Come, jump and get up on my shoulder, Osy."

Osy looked up with mingled pleasure and alarm. "I promised Movver: but if you holded me very fast—"

"Oh, I'll hold you. You mustn't be frightened, Osy."

"Me fwightened! But I felled down and hurted my side, and fwightened Movver. Huwah! huwah!" shouted the child. "I'm not fwightened a bit, Cousin Colonel! You holds me and I holds you, and you may canter, or gallop, or anyfing. I'll never be afwaid."

"Here goes, then," said the grave soldier. And with shouts and laughter the pair rushed on, Colonel Piercey enjoying the race as much as the child on his shoulder, who urged him with imaginary spurs, very dusty if not very dangerous, holding fast with one hand by the collar of his coat. He had not much experience of children, and the confidence and audacity of this little creature, his glee, his warm grip, in which there was a touch of terror, and his wild enjoyment at once of the movement and the danger, aroused a new sentiment in the heart of the mature man, who had known none of the emotions of paternity. Suddenly, however, a change came over his spirit: he reduced his pace, he ceased to laugh, he sank all at once—though with the child still shouting on his shoulder, endeavouring, with his little kicks upon his breast, to rouse him to further exertions—into the ordinary gravity of his aspect and demeanour. There had appeared suddenly out of the little gate of the beech avenue, a figure, which took all the fun out of Gerald Piercey, though he could not have told why.

"Movver, movver! look here: I'm up upon my horse. But you needn't be fwightened, for he's not like Cousin Gervase. He's holded me fast, fast all the way."

"Oh! Osy," cried Margaret, holding her breath—for, indeed, it was a remarkable sight to see the unutterable gravity of Colonel Piercey endeavouring solemnly to take off his hat to her, with the child, flushed and delighted, upon his shoulder. There was something comic in the extreme seriousness which had suddenly fallen upon Osy's bearer. "You are making yourself a bore to Colonel Piercey," she said.

"Not at all; we have been enjoying ourselves very much. He is a delightful companion," said Gerald, but in a tone which suggested a severe despair. "Will you get down, Osy, or would you rather I should carry you home?"

"I would wather—" said the child, and then he paused. "I tan't see your face," he said, pettishly, "but you feels twite different, as if you was tired. I fink I'll get down."

Colonel Piercey's comment to himself was that the child was frightened for his mother, but, naturally, he did not express this sentiment. He lifted Osy down and set him on the ground. "Where's the nurse now?" he said; "a long way behind. You see, Osy, it's good to have a basis to fall back upon when new operations are ordered by the ruling powers."

Could the man not refrain from a gibe at her, even to her child, Margaret thought, with wonder? But she was surprised to see that he stood still, as if with the intention of speaking to her.

"You are going out?" he said, in his solemn tones. "Is Lady Piercey better?"

"She is no better; but I must attempt, in some way, to get the news conveyed to Gervase. Her eyes turn constantly to the door. They are still quite living, though not so strong. She must see him, if it is possible. She must see him, if there is any way—her only child."

"But not, from all I hear, a child that does her much credit," he said.

"What does that matter? He is all she has," she added hastily. "Don't let me detain you, Colonel Piercey. I must not be gone long; and I must try if anything can be done."

"You mean that I am detaining you," he said, turning with her. "And I have something to tell you, if I may walk with you. I have been talking to old Hewitt, of the Seven Thorns. He says he has no address to communicate with his daughter; but there is a newly-married couple coming to occupy his rooms, and that she is returning with them next week."

"A newly-married couple!" cried Margaret, aghast. "Can it be they? Can it be Patty? Is it possible?"

"I thought it might be so, if it was he and she whom I saw."

"Oh, his mother! his mother! And this was what she was most afraid of. Why, why did she let him go."

"Yes, why did she let him go, if she were so much afraid to this, as you think? But, perhaps you are alarming yourself unnecessarily? Lady Piercey must have known tolerably well at his age what her son was likely to do?"

"Yes, I am perhaps alarming myself unnecessarily. The chances are she will not live to see it. It is only she who would feel it much. Poor Aunt Piercey! Why should one wish her to live to hear this?" Margaret paused a little, wringing her hands, uncertain whether to turn back or to proceed. At last she said to herself, "Anyhow, she wants him—she wants him. If it is possible, she must see her boy;" and went on again quickly, scarcely noticing the dark figure at her side. But he did not choose to be overlooked.

"I should like," he said, "to have a few things explained. You say nobody would mind this marriage—if it is a marriage—except Lady Piercey?"

"I said nobody would mind it much. My uncle would get used to it, and he could be talked over: and Patty Hewitt is a clever girl. But Aunt Piercey—!"

"Why should she stand out?"

"If you do not understand," cried Margaret, "how can I tell you? His mother! and a woman that has always hoped better things, and thought still, if he married well,—You forget," she cried vehemently, "that poor Gervase was not to her what he was to us. He was her only child! A mother may see everything even more keenly than others; but you hope, you always hope—"

"I presume, then, you did not think so? You did not object to this marriage."

"What does it matter whether I objected or not? Of what consequence is my opinion? None of us can like it. A girl like Patty to be at the head of Greyshott! Oh! who could like that? But," said Margaret more calmly, "my poor aunt deceives herself; for what nice girl, unless she were forced, as girls are sometimes, would marry Gervase? Poor Gervase! It is not his fault. She deceives herself. But I don't think she will live to see it. I don't think she will live to hear of it. If she could only have him by her before she dies. Patty could not oppose herself to that. She could not prevent that."

"Is it supposed, then, that she would wish to do so?"

"Colonel Piercey," cried Margaret, "you have come among us at a dreadful moment, when all the secrets of the family are laid bare. Oh, don't ask any more questions! I have said things I did not intend to say."

"I hope that I am to be trusted," he said, with his severe tone; "and if I can help, I will. To whom are you going? Is it to this old Hewitt? for nothing, I think, is to be learned from him."

"I am going to Miss Hewitt, her aunt. It is in despair. For she has a hatred of all of us at Greyshott; but surely, surely, when they hear that his mother is dying—"

"She cannot hate me. I will go," Gerald Piercey said.

CHAPTER XX

Old Miss Hewitt sat in her parlour, if not like a fat spider watching for the fly, at least like a large cat seated demurely, with an eye upon her natural prey, though her aspect was more decorous and composed than words could tell. She had been made aware by her little servant a few minutes before that "a gentleman" was coming up to the door, and had instantaneously prepared to meet the visitor. A visitor was a very rare thing at Rose Cottage.

"You're sure it ain't the curate, a-coming begging?"

"Oh, no," cried the little maid, "a tall, grand gentleman, like a lord. I think I knows a pa'son when I sees 'un!" she added, with rustic contempt. Miss Hewitt settled herself in her large chair; she gave her cap that twist that every woman who wears a cap supposes to put all aright. She drew to her a footstool for her feet, and then she said, "You may let him in, Jane." A smile of delight was upon her mouth; but she subdued even that in her sense of propriety, to heighten the effect. She had been waiting for this moment for thirty years. She had not known how it would come about, but she had always felt it must come about somehow. She had paid fifty pounds for it—and she had not grudged her money—and now it had come. She did not even know the shape it would take, or who it was who was coming to place the family of Piercey at her feet, that she might spurn them; but that this was what was about to happen, she felt absolutely sure. It could not be Sir Giles himself, which would have been the sweetest of all, for Sir Giles was too infirm to visit anybody; while she, whom he had scorned once, was hale and strong, and sure to see both of them out! Perhaps it was a solicitor, or something of the kind. What did she care? It was some one from the Pierceys coming to her, abject, with a petition—which she would not grant—no, not if they besought her on their knees.

The room seemed in semi-darkness to Gerald, coming in from the brightness of the summer afternoon. The blind was drawn down to save the carpet, and the curtains hung heavily over the window for gentility's sake. Miss Hewitt sat with her back to the light, by the side of the fireplace, which was filled up by cut paper. There was no air in the room; and though Colonel Piercey was not a man of humorous perceptions, there occurred even to him the idea of a large cat with her tail curled round her, sitting demure, yet fierce, on the watch for some prey, of which she had scent or sight.

"My name is Piercey," said the Colonel. "I am a relation of the family at Greyshott, who perhaps, you may have heard, are in great trouble at this moment. I have come to you, Miss Hewitt—and I hope you will pardon me for disturbing you—to know whether, by any chance, you could furnish us with Gervase Piercey's address."

"Ah, you're from the Pierceys," said Miss Hewitt. "I thought as much—though there ain't that friendship between me and the Pierceys that should make them send to me in their trouble. And what relation may you be, if a person might ask?"

"I am a cousin; but that is of little importance. The chief thing is that Mr. Gervase Piercey is absent, and his address is not known. His mother is ill—"

"I heard of that," said the old lady, drawing a long breath as of satisfaction. "She's a hard one, too, she is. It would be something sharp that made her ill. I suppose as she heard—"

"She heard nothing. There was no mental cause for her illness, if that is what you mean. She had been sitting, talking just as usual—"

"Oh—h!" cried Miss Hewitt, with an air of disappointment; "then it wasn't from the shock? And what's their meaning, then, Mister Piercey—if you call yourself Piercey—in sending to me?"

"That is precisely what I can't tell you," said Gerald, with much candour. "I confess that it seems absurd, but I supposed, perhaps, that you would know."

"And why should it seem absurd? I know a deal more about the Pierceys than you think for, or any fine gentleman that comes questioning of me, as if I were an old hag in the village. Oh! I know the way that you, as calls yourselves gentlemen, speak!"

"I hope," said Gerald, surprised, "that I don't speak in any unbecoming way, or fail in respect to any woman. It is very likely that you know much more than I do, and the question is one that is easily settled. Could you throw any light upon the question where Gervase Piercey is, and if so, will you tell me his address?"

She looked at him for a moment as if uncertain how to respond—whether to play with the victim any longer, or to make a pounce and end it. Then she said, quickly, "Did he send you himself?"

"Did who send me?"

"Giles—Sir Giles; don't you understand? Was it him as thought of Patience Hewitt? That's what I want to know."

"Miss Hewitt, Lady Piercey is very ill—"

"Ah! he never was in love with her," cried the old lady; "never! He married her—he was drawn in to do it; but I know as he hated it when he did it. It never was for her, if it was he has sent you. Not for her, but for—"

She stopped and looked at him again, with a glare in her eyes, yet resolved, apparently, not to pounce but to play a little longer. "Ah! so my lady's ill, is she? She's an old woman, more like an old hag, I can tell you, than me. She was thirty-five, if she was a day, when she married Sir Giles, and high living and nothing to do has made her dreadful. He never could abear fat women, and it serves him right. Some people never lose their figure, whatever their age may be."

She sat very upright in her chair, with a smile of self-complacence, nodding her head. "Well," she said, "and what's wanted of me? Not to go and nurse my lady, I suppose? They don't want me to do that?"

"They wish to know," said Colonel Piercey, restraining himself with an effort, "Mr. Gervase Piercey's address."

"Their son's address?" said Miss Hewitt. "He's the heir, you know. The village folks calls him the Softy, but there couldn't nothing be proved against him. He'll be Sir Gervase after his father, and nobody can't prevent that. And how is it as they don't know their own son's address? and for why should they send you to me? Me, a lady living quiet in her own house, meddling with none of them, how should I know their son's address?"

"I have told you I have not the slightest light to throw on this question. It appears that your niece is in London, and that she was seen, or it is supposed she was seen, with my cousin."

"And what then?" cried the old lady. "You think, perhaps, as that Softy led my Patty wrong. Ho, ho! ho, ho!" She laughed a low guttural laugh, prolonging it till Colonel Piercey's exasperation was almost beyond bearing. "You think as he was the gay Lotharium and she was the young Lavinyar, eh? Oh, I've read plenty of books in my time, and I know how gentlemen talk of them sort of things. No, she ain't, Mister Piercey. My Patty is one that knows very well what she is about."

"So I have heard, also. I believe it is supposed that as he is such a fool, your niece may have married him, Miss Hewitt."

"And so she have, just!" cried the old lady, springing from her chair. She waved her arms in the air and uttered a hoarse "Hooray!" "That is just what has happened, mister; exactly true, as if you'd been in all the plans from the first. You tell Sir Giles as there is a Patty Hewitt will be Lady Piercey, after all, and not the Queen herself couldn't prevent it. Just you tell him that from me; Patience, called for her aunt, and thought to be like me, though smaller—my brother being an ass and marrying a little woman. But that's just the gospel truth. She's Mrs. Gervase Piercey, now, and she'll be Lady Piercey when the time comes. Oh!" cried Miss Hewitt, sinking back in her chair, exhausted, "but I'd like to be there when he hears. And I'd like to tell her, I should," she added, with a fierce glare in her eyes.

Gerald had risen when she did, and stood holding the back of his chair. Fortunately, he had great command of his temper, though the provocation was strong. He was silent while she settled herself again in her seat, and rearranged her cap-strings and the folds of her gown, though the flowers in her head-dress quivered with excitement and triumph. He said, "I fear you will never have that satisfaction. Lady Piercey is dying, and, happily, knows nothing about this. Perhaps your revenge might be more complete if you would summon her son to see her before she dies."

Miss Hewitt was too much occupied by what she had herself said to pay much attention to him. It was only after some minutes of murmuring and smiling to herself, that she began to recall that he had made a reply. "What was you saying, Mr. Piercey—eh? If you was counting on succeeding you're struck all of a heap, and I don't wonder, for there's an end of you, my fine gentleman! There'll be a family and a large family, you take your oath of that. None of your marrying in-and-in cousins and things, but a fine, fresh, new stock. What was you saying? Dying is she, that woman? Well, we've all got to die. She's had her share above most, and taken other folks' bread out of their mouths, and she must take her share now. Nobody's a-going to die instead of her. That's a thing as you've got to do when your time comes for yourself."

"And, happily," said Gerald, "she knows nothing of all this. Perhaps if she were permitted to see her son—"

"Goodness gracious me!" cried Miss Hewitt, rousing up: "do you hate her like that? I think you must be the devil himself, to put that into a body's head. It's a disappointment to me, dreadful, that she should die and not know; but to send him to tell her, and the woman at her last breath—Oh! Lord, what wickedness there is in this world! Man! what makes you hate her like that?"

"Will you allow her to see her son?" Colonel Piercey asked.

The old woman rose up again in her agitation. One of the old Puritan divines describes Satan as putting so big a stone into the sinner's hand to throw at his enemy, that the bounds of human guilt were over-passed and the almost murderer pitched it at his tempter instead. This suggestion was to Patience Hewitt, in the sense in which she understood it, that too-heavy stone. The desire for revenge had been very strong in her. She had waited and plotted all her life for the opportunity of returning to Sir Giles the reward of his desertion of her, and she had attained her object, and a furious delight was in it. But to seethe the kid in his mother's milk is a thing about which the most cruel have their prejudices. To bring the Softy back to shout his news into the ear of the dying woman, that was a more fiendish detail than she had dreamed of. She rose up and sat down again, and clasped her hands and unclasped them, and turned over the terrible temptation in her mind. No doubt it would be the very crown of vengeance, to prove to Sir Giles' wife that she, whom she had supplanted, was the victor at the last. That was what she had hoped for all through. She had hoped that it was some rumour of what had happened that had been the cause of Lady Piercey's illness. A stroke! it was quite natural she should have a stroke when she heard; it was the vengeance of God long deferred for what she had done unpunished so many years ago. But between this, in which she felt a grim joy, and the other, there was a great gulf. To send for Gervase, in order that he, with his own hand, should give his mother her death-blow, the horrible thought made her head giddy and her heart beat. It was a temptation—the most dreadful of temptations. It seized upon her imagination even while it filled her with horror. It answered every wild desire of poetic justice in the untutored mind: never had been any vengeance like that. It was a thing to be told, and shuddered at, and told again. "Oh! for goodness gracious sake, go along with you, go along with you," she cried, putting out her hands to push the Colonel away, "for I think you must be the very devil himself."

It was almost with the same words that Gerald Piercey answered Margaret, who met him eagerly as he returned. Sir Giles was out in the garden with Dunning and Osy, and there was no one to disturb the consultation of these two enemies or friends. "Have you heard anything of him?" cried Margaret. Colonel Piercey answered almost solemnly, "I have seen the devil; if he ever takes a woman's form."

"I have heard that she was a dreadful old woman."

"And I have made a dreadful suggestion to her, which she is turning over in her dreadful mind. She hates poor old Lady Piercey with a virulence which—perhaps you may understand it, knowing the circumstances; I don't. She is terribly disappointed that it was not the news which was the cause of the illness. And I have suggested that if the bridegroom could be sent home, the old lady might still hear it before she dies."

"The news—the bridegroom! Then it is so? They are married!"

"That's better, I suppose," said the Colonel, "than if it had been worse."

Margaret coloured high at this enigmatical speech. "To everybody but Aunt Piercey," she said. "My uncle will get used to the idea; but his mother! It is better he should not come than come to tell her that."

"If he comes we can surely keep him silent," Colonel Piercey said. "I thought that was the one thing to be attained at all risks."

"And so it was. And I thank you, Cousin Gerald, and we can but do our best."

Lady Piercey turned her eyes towards the door as Margaret went into the room. A dreadful weariness was in those living eyes, which had not closed, in anything that could be called sleep, since her seizure. She had lain there dead, but for that look, for three days, unable to move a finger. But always her eyes turned to the door whenever it opened, however softly. Sometimes the film of a doze came over them; but no one came in without meeting that look—the look of a soul in prison, with no sense but that one remaining to make existence a fact. How much she knew of what was passing around her, they could not tell; or of her own condition, or of what was before her. All she seemed to know was that Gervase did not come. Sometimes her eyes fell upon Margaret with a look which seemed one of angry appeal. And then they returned to watch the door, which opened, indeed, from time to time, but never to admit her son. Oh, dreadful eyes! Mrs. Osborne shrank from encountering them. It was she, she only of whom they asked that question—she whom they seemed to blame. Where was Gervase? Why did he not come? Was he coming? Speech and hearing were alike gone. Her question was only in her eyes.

And thus the evening and the morning made the fourth day.

CHAPTER XXI

Patty's ambitious schemes were crowned with complete success, and the poor Softy was made the happiest and most triumphant man in the world, on the day on which his mother was taken ill. Was it some mysterious impalpable movement in the air that conveyed to Lady Piercey's brain a troubled impression of what was taking place to her only son? But this is what no one can tell. As for Gervase, his triumph, his rapture, his sense of emancipation, could not be described. He was wild with pleasure and victory. The sharp-witted, clear-headed girl, who had carried out the whole plot, was at last overborne and subjugated by the passion she had roused, and for a time was afraid of Gervase. She had a panic lest his feeble head might give way altogether under such excitement, and she be left in the hands of a madman. Luckily this wild fit did not last long, and Patty gradually brought the savage, which was latent in his undeveloped nature, into control. But she had got a fright, and was still a little afraid of him when the week was over, and her plans were laid for the triumphant return home. She had written to her aunt on the day of her marriage, proclaiming the proud fact, and signing her letter, not with her Christian name, but that of Mrs. Gervase Piercey, in her pride and triumph. Mrs. Gervase Piercey! That she was now, let them rave as they pleased! Nobody could undo what Aunt Patience's fifty pounds had done. Those whom God had joined together—or was it not rather Miss Hewitt, of Rose Cottage, and ambition and revenge? Patty, however, had no intentions appropriate to such motives in her mind. She was not revolted by the passion of Gervase, as another woman might have been. She felt it to be a compliment more or less; his noise and uproariousness, so that he could scarcely walk along a street without shoutings and loud laughter, did not in the least trouble her. She subdued him by degrees, bidding him look how people stared, and frightening him with the suggestion that the world in general might think him off his head, and carry him off from her, if he did not learn to suppress these vociferous evidences of his happiness: a suggestion which had a great effect upon Gervase, and made him follow her about meekly afterwards to all the sights which she thought it necessary in this wonderful holiday to see. She took him to the Zoological Gardens, which he enjoyed immensely, dragging her about from one cage to another, not letting her off a single particular. They saw the lions fed, they gave buns to the bears, they rode like a couple of children upon the camels and the elephant. Gervase drank deep of every pleasure which the resources of that Garden of Eden permitted. He had not been there since he was a child, and everything was delightful to him. The success was not so great when Patty took him to St Paul's and the Tower, which she considered to be fashionable resorts, where a bride and her finery ought to be seen, and where Gervase walked about gaping, asking like a child at church when he could get out? Nor at the theatre, where Patty, instructed by the novels she had read, secured a box, and appeared in full costume, with that intoxicating proof that she was now a fine lady and member of the aristocracy, a low dress—and with an opera-glass wherewith to scan the faces and dresses of the other distinguished occupants of boxes. She was herself surprised at various things which she had not learnt from books—the unimpressive character of the ladies' dresses, and the manner in which they gazed down into what she believed to be the pit, a part of the house which she regarded with scorn. It was not a fashionable house, for to Patty, naturally, a theatre was a theatre, wherever situated; but it was disappointing not to see the flashing of diamonds which she had expected, nor to have other opera-glasses fixed upon herself as a new appearance in the world of fashion, which was what she looked for. And Gervase was very troublesome in the theatre. He kept asking her what those people were doing on the stage, what all that talking was about, and when it would be time to go away. When the merchant of ices and other light refections came round, Gervase was delighted, and even Patty felt that an ice in her box at the theatre was great grandeur; but she was discouraged when she saw that it was not a common indulgence, and that Gervase, peeling and eating oranges, and flinging them about, attracted an attention which was not that sentiment of mingled admiration and envy which Patty hoped to excite. A few experiences of this kind opened her sharp eyes to many things, and reduced the rapture with which she had looked forward to her entry into town as Mrs. Gervase Piercey. But these disenchantments, and scraps of talk which her sharp ears picked up and her still sharper imagination assimilated, suggested to her another kind of operation next time, and left her full of anticipations and the conviction that it only wanted a little preparation, a little guidance, to ensure her perfect triumph.

This strange pair had what seemed to Patty boundless funds for their week in town. Twenty pounds over of Aunt Patience's gift after paying the expenses of the marriage, had seemed enough for the wildest desires; but when there was added to that twenty pounds more, his mother's last gift to Gervase, she felt that their wealth was fabulous; far, far too much to expend upon personal pleasure or sightseeing. She permitted herself to buy a dress or two, choosing those which were ready made, and of which she could see the effect at once, both on herself and the elegant young lady who sold them to her; and she put aside a ten-pound note carefully, in case of any emergency. On the whole, however, it was a relief to both parties when they went home, though it took some trouble to convince Gervase that he could not go back to the Manor, leaving his wife at the Seven Thorns. He was not pleased to be told that he too must go and live at the Seven Thorns: "Why, that's what mother said—and draw the beer!" he cried; "but nothing shall make me draw the beer," cried Gervase. "Nobody asked you," Patty said, "you goose. We're going to live in the west rooms, a beautiful set of rooms that I put all ready, where there's a nice sofa for you to lie on, and nice windows to look out of and see everything that comes along the road—not like Greyshott, where you never see nothing—the carts and the carriages and the vans going to the fairs, and Punch and Judy, and I can't tell you all what." "Well," said Gervase, "you can stay there, and I'll come to see you every day; but I must go home." "What, leave me! and us but a week married!" cried Patty. She made him falter in his resolution, confused with the idea of an arrangement of affairs unfamiliar to him, and at last induced him to consent to go to the Seven Thorns with her on conditions, strenuously insisted upon, that he was not to be made to draw beer. But Gervase did not feel easy on this subject, even when he was taken by the new side-door into the separate suite of apartments which Patty had prepared with so much trouble. When old Hewitt appeared he took care to entrench himself behind his wife.

"I'll have nothing to do with the beer or the customers, mind you," he cried nervously. Nobody, however, made any account of Gervase in that wonderful moment of Patty's return.

"What! it's you as is the new married couple? and you've gone and married 'im?" cried Hewitt, with a tone of indescribable contempt.

"Yes, father! and I'll thank you to keep a civil tongue in your head; I've married him, and I mean to take care of him," Patty cried, tossing her head.

Old Hewitt laughed a low, long laugh. His mental processes were slow, and the sight of the Softy with his daughter had startled him much; for notwithstanding all that had been said on this subject he had not believed in it seriously. Now, however, that it dawned upon him what had really happened, that his child, his daughter, was actually Mrs. Gervase Piercey, a slow sensation of pride and victory arose in his bosom too. His girl to be Lady Piercey in her time, and drive in a grand carriage, and live in a grand house! The Hewitts were a fine old family, but they had never kept their carriage and pair. A one-horse shay had been the utmost length to which they had gone. Now Patty—Patty, the child! who had always done his accounts and kept his customers in order—Patty, his own girl, was destined to the glory of riding behind two horses and being called "my lady." The thought made him burst into a long, rumbling subterraneous laugh. Our Patty! it did not seem possible that it could be true.

"That reminds me," he said a moment after, turning suddenly grave. He called his daughter apart, beckoning with his finger.

Gervase by this time was lolling half out of the open window, delightedly counting the vehicles in sight. "Farmer Golightly's tax cart, and Jim Mason's big waggon, and the parson's pony chaise, and a fly up from the station," he cried: "it's livelier than London. Patty, Patty, come and look here." Gervase turned round, and saw his wife and her father with grave faces consulting together, and relapsed into absolute quiet, effacing himself behind the fluttering curtains with the intention of stealing out of the room as soon as he could and getting away. His mother's threat about drawing the beer haunted him. Could not she, who could do most things, make that threat come true?

"Patty," said old Hewitt, "you've done it, and you can't undo it; but there'll be ever such a rumpus up there."

"Of course, I know that," she said calmly; "I'm ready for them. Let them try all they can, there's nothing they can do."

"Patty," said the old innkeeper again, "I've something to tell you as you ain't a-thinking of. About 'Er," he said, pointing with his thumb over his shoulder.

"What about her? I know she's my enemy; but you needn't be frightened, father. I've seen to everything, and there's nothing she can do."

"It ain't that as I want you to think of. It's more dreadful than that. It's 'in the midst of life as we are in death,'" said Hewitt. "That sort of thing; and they've been a-'unting for 'im far and wide."

"Lord, father, what do you mean?" Patty caught at a confused idea of Sir Giles' death, and her heart began to thump against her breast.

Hewitt pointed with his thumb, jerking it again and again over his shoulder. "She's—she's—dead," he said.

"Dead!" said Patty, with a shriek, "who's dead?"

Hewitt, less aware than she of Gervase's wandering and unimpressionable mind, shook his head at her, jerking his thumb this time in front of him at the young man lolling out of the window. "Usht, can't ye? Why, 'Er, 'is mother," he said, under his breath.

A quick reflection passed through Patty's mind. "Then, I'm her," she said to herself, but then remembered that this was not the case that Sir Giles' death alone could make her Lady Piercey. As this flashed upon her thoughts, a bitter regret came into Patty's mind—regret, keen as if she had loved her, that Lady Piercey was dead, that she should have been allowed to die. Oh, if she had but known! How quickly would she have brought Gervase back to see his mother! Her triumph, whenever it should come, would be shorn of one of its most poignant pleasures. Lady Piercey would not be there to see it! She could never now be made to come down from her place, made to give up all her privileges to the girl whom she despised. Patty felt so genuine a pang of disappointment that it brought the tears to her eyes. "I must tell him," she said quickly,—the tears were not without their use, too, and it is not always easy to call them up at will.

"I wouldn't to-night. Let 'im have 'is first night in peace," said the innkeeper, "and take 'is beer, and get the good of it like any other man."

"Go down, perhaps you think, to your men in the parlour, and smoke with them, and drink with them, and give you the chance to say as he's your son-in-law? and his mother lying dead all the time. No, father, not if I know it," cried Patty, and she gave her head a very decided nod. "I know what I'm about," she added; "I know exactly what he's going to do. So, father, you may go, and you can tell 'Liza that we'll now have tea."

"I tell 'Liza! I'll do none of your dirty errands," said old Hewitt; but his indignation answered Patty's purpose, who was glad to get rid of him, in order that her own duty might be performed. She went forward to the window where Gervase was sitting, and linked her arm in his, not without some resistance on the part of the Softy, who was wholly occupied with his new pleasure.

"Let alone, I tell you, Pat! One white horse on the off side, that counts five for me; and a whole team of black 'uns for the other fellow. Where's all those black horses come from, I should like to know?"

"Gervase dear, don't you do it; don't make a game with the black horses. It's dreadful unlucky. They're for a funeral, come from town on purpose. And oh! Gervase dear, do listen to me! for whose funeral do you suppose?"

"Is it a riddle?" said Gervase, showing his teeth from ear to ear.

"Oh hush, hush, there's a good boy! It's not like you to make a joke of such dreadful things."

"Why can't you say then what it is, and have done with it?" Gervase said.

"That's just one of the sensible things you say when you please. Gervase—you remember your mother?"

"I remember my mother? I should think I remembered my mother. You know it's only a week to-day—or was it yesterday?"

"It was yesterday. You might remember the day you were married, I think, without asking me," said Patty, with spirit. "Well, then, you parted from her that day. She wasn't ill then, was she, dear?"

Upon which Gervase laughed. "Mother's always ill," he said. "She has such health you never know when she's well, or, at least, so she says. It's in her head, or her liver, or her big toe. No!" he cried, with another great laugh, "it's father as has the devil in his big toe."

"Gervase, do be serious for a moment. Your mother has been very ill, dreadful bad, and we never knew—"

"I told you," he said calmly, "she's always bad; and you can never tell from one day to another, trust herself, when she mayn't die."

"Oh, Gervase," cried Patty, holding his arm with both her hands: "you are fond of her a little bit, ain't you, dear? She's your mother, though she hasn't been very nice to me."

"Lord," cried Gervase, "how she will jump when she knows that I'm here, and on my own hook, and have got a wife of my own! Mind, it is you that have got to tell her, and not me."

"A wife that will always try to be a comfort to you," said Patty. "Oh, my poor dear boy! Gervase, your poor mother (remember that I'm here to take care of you whatever happens),—Gervase, your mother will never need to be told. She's dead and gone, poor lady, she's dead and gone!"

Gervase stared at her, and again opened his mouth in a great laugh. "That's one of your dashed stories," he said.

"It isn't a story at all, it's quite true. She had a stroke that very day. Fancy, just the very day when we—And we never heard a word. If we had heard I should have been the very first to bring you home."

"What good would that have done?" Gervase said sullenly, "we were better where we were."

"Not and her dying, and wanting her son."

Gervase was cowed and troubled by the news, which gave him a shock which he could not understand. It made him sullen and difficult to manage. "You're playing off one of your jokes upon me," he said.

"I playing a joke! I'd have found something better than a funeral to joke about. Gervase, we have just come back in time. The funeral's to-morrow, and oh! I'm so thankful we came home. I'm going to send for Sally Fletcher to make me up some nice deep mourning with crape, like a lady wears for her own mother."

"She was no mother of yours," said Gervase, with a frown.

"No; nor she didn't behave like one: but being her son's wife and one that is to succeed her, I must get my mourning deep; and you and me, we'll go. We'll walk next to Sir Giles, as chief mourners," she said.

Gervase gave a lowering look at her, and then he turned away to the open window, to count as he had been doing before, but in changing tones, the white horses and the brown.

CHAPTER XXII

Patty sat up half the night with Sally Fletcher, arranging as rapidly and efficiently as possible her new mise en scène. To work all night at mourning was by no means a novel performance for Miss Fletcher, the lame girl who was the village dressmaker; and she felt herself amply repaid by the news, as yet almost unknown to the neighbours, of the Softy's marriage and Patty's new pretensions. It is true that it had a little leaked out in the evening symposium in Hewitt's parlour; but what the men said when they came home from their dull, long booze was not received with that faith which ladies put in the utterances of the clubs. The wives of the village had always a conviction that the men had "heard wrong"—that it would turn out something quite different from the story told in the watches of the night, or dully recalled next day, confused by the fumes of last night's beer. But Sally Fletcher knew that her tale would meet with full credence, and that her cottage next morning would be crowded with inquirers; so that her night's work was not the matter of hardship it might have been supposed. She was comforted with cups of tea during the course of the night, and Patty spent at least half of it with her, helping on the work in a resplendent blue dressing-gown, which she had bought in London, trimmed with lace and ribbons, and dazzling to Sally's eyes. The dressmaker had brought with her the entire stock of crape which was to be had in "the shop," a material kept for emergencies, and not, it may be supposed, of the very freshest or finest—which Patty laid on with a liberal hand, covering with it the old black dress, which she decided would do in the urgency of the moment. It was still more difficult to plaster that panoply of mourning over the smart new cape, also purchased in town: but this, too, was finished, and a large hatband, as deep as his hat, procured for Gervase, before the air began to thrill with the tolling, lugubrious and long drawn out, of the village bells, which announced that the procession was within sight.

It was a great funeral. All the important people of that side of the county—or their carriages—were there. An hour before the cortège arrived, Sir Giles' chair, an object of curiosity to all the village boys, was brought down to the gate of the churchyard, that he might follow his wife to the grave's side. And a great excitement had arisen in the village itself. Under any circumstances, Lady Piercey's funeral, the carriages and the flowers, and the mutes and the black horses, would have produced an impression; but that impression was increased now by the excitement of a very different kind which mingled with it. Patty Hewitt, of the Seven Thorns, now Mrs. Gervase Piercey, would be there; and there was not a house, from the Rectory downwards, in which the question was not discussed—what would happen? Would Patty receive the tacit recognition of being allowed to take her place along with her husband. Her husband! could he be anybody's husband, the Softy? Would the marriage stand? Would Sir Giles allow it? The fact that it was Sir Giles gave the eager spectators their only doubt—or hope. Had it been Lady Piercey, she would never have allowed it. She would have thrown back the pretender from the very church-door. She would have rejected Patty, thrust her out of the way, seized her son, and dragged him from the girl who had entrapped him. At the very church-door! Everybody, from the rector down to the sexton's wife, felt perfectly convinced of that.

But it would not be Lady Piercey she would have to deal with. Lady Piercey, though she filled so great a position in the ceremonial, would have nothing to say on the subject; and it was part of the irony of fate, felt by everybody, though none were sufficiently instructed to call it by that name, that she should be there, incapable of taking any share in what would have moved her so deeply—triumphed over in her coffin by the adversary with whom, living, she would have made such short work. There was something tragic about this situation which made the bystanders hold their breath. And no one knew what Patty was about to do. That she would claim her share in the celebration, and, somehow, manage to take a part in it, no one doubted; but how she was to accomplish this was the exciting uncertainty that filled all minds. It troubled the rector as he put on his surplice to meet the silent new-comer, approaching with even more pomp than was her wont the familiar doors of her parish church. There was not much more sentiment than is inseparable from that last solemnity in the minds of her neighbours towards Lady Piercey. She had not been without kindness of a practical kind. Doles had been made and presents given in the conventional way without any failure; but nobody had loved the grim old lady. There was nothing, therefore, to take off the interest in the other more exciting crisis.

"Rattle her bones
Over the stones,
She's only a pauper, whom nobody owns."

Far from a pauper was the Lady Piercey of Greyshott; but the effect was the same. There are many equalising circumstances in death.

It was imposing to witness the black procession coming slowly along the sunshiny road. Old Miss Hewitt from Rose Cottage came out to view it, taking up a conspicuous position on the churchyard wall. So far from wearing decorous black in reverence of the funeral, Miss Hewitt was dressed in all that was most remarkable in her wardrobe in the way of colour. She wore a green dress; she had a large Paisley shawl of many colours—an article with which the present generation is virtually unacquainted—on her shoulders, and her bonnet was trimmed with gold lace and flowers. She had a conviction that Sir Giles would see her, and that he would perceive the difference between her still handsome face, and unbroken height and carriage, and the old ugly wife whom he was burying—poor old Sir Giles, entirely broken down by weakness and the breach of all his habits and ways, as well as by the feeling, not very elevated perhaps, but grievous enough, of loss, in one who had managed everything for him, and taken all trouble from his shoulders! There might be some emotion deeper still in the poor old gentleman's mind; but these at least were there, enough to make his dull eyes, always moist with slow-coming tears, quite incapable of the vision or contrast in which that fierce old woman hoped.

The interest of the moment concentrated round the lych-gate, where a great deal was to take place. Already conspicuous among the crowd assembled there to meet the funeral were two figures, the chief of whom was veiled from head to foot in crape, and leant upon the arm of her husband heavily, as if overcome with grief. Patty had a deep crape veil, behind which was visible a white handkerchief often pressed to her eyes, and in the other hand, a large wreath. Gervase stood beside her, in black clothes to be sure, and with a deep hatband covering his hat, but with no such monumental aspect of woe. His light and wandering eyes strayed over the scene, arresting themselves upon nothing, not even on the approaching procession. Sometimes Patty almost bent him down on the side on which she leant, by a new access of grief. Her shoulders heaved, her sobs were audible, when the head of the doleful procession arrived. She moved her husband forward to lay the wreath upon the coffin and then lifting her great veil for a moment looked on with an air of agonising anxiety, while Sir Giles was lifted out of the carriage and placed in his chair, with little starts of anxious feeling as if he were being touched roughly by the attendants, and she could scarcely restrain herself from taking him out of their hands. It was a pity that poor old Sir Giles, entirely absorbed in his own sensations, did not observe this at all, any more than he observed the airs of Miss Hewitt equally intended for his notice. But when Sir Giles had been placed in his chair, Patty recovering her energy in a moment, dragged her husband forward and dexterously slid and pushed him immediately behind his father's chair, coming sharply in contact as she did so with Colonel Piercey, who was about to take that place. "I beg your pardon, we are the chief mourners," she said sharply, and with decision. And then Patty relapsed all at once into her grief. She walked slowly forward half-leading, half-pushing Gervase, her shoulders heaving with sobs, a murmur of half-audible affliction coming in as a sort of half-refrain to the words read by the clergyman. The village crowding round, watched with bated breath. It was difficult for these spectators to refuse a murmur of applause. How beautifully she did it? What a mourner she made, far better than any one else there! As for that Mrs. Osborne, her veil was only gauze, and through it you could see that she was not crying at all! She walked by Colonel Piercey's side, but she did not lean upon him as if she required support. There was no heaving in her shoulders. The mind of the village approved the demeanour of Patty with enthusiasm. It was something like! Even Miss Hewitt, flaunting her red and yellow bonnet on the churchyard wall, was impressed by the appearance of Patty, and acknowledged that it was deeply appropriate, and just exactly what she ought to have done.

But though Patty was thus overcome with grief, her vigilant eyes noted everything through the white handkerchief and the crape. When poor Sir Giles broke down and began to sob at the grave it was she who, with an energetic push and pressure, placed Gervase by his side.

"Speak to him," she whispered in his ear, with a voice which though so low was imperative as any order. She leaned herself over the other side of the chair, almost pushing Dunning out of the way, while still maintaining her pressure on Gervase's arm.

"Father," he said, putting his hand upon the old man's; he was not to say too much, she had instructed him! Only his name, or a kind word. Gervase, poor fellow, did not know how to say a kind word, but his dull imagination had been stirred and the contagion of his father's feeble distress moved him. He began to sob, too, leaning heavily upon Sir Giles' chair. Not that he knew very well what was the cause. The great shining oaken chest that was being lowered down into that hole had no association for him. He had not seen his mother placed there. But the gloomy ceremonial affected Gervase in spite of himself. Happily it did not move him to laugh, which was on the cards, as Patty felt. It made him cry, which was everything that could be desired.

And Sir Giles did not push away his son's hand, which was what might have happened also. The old gentleman was in precisely the state of mind to feel that touch and the sound of the wavering voice. It was a return of the prodigal when the poor old father's heart was very forlorn, and the sensation of having some one still who belonged to him most welcome. To be sure there was Colonel Piercey—but he would go away, and was not in any sense a son of the house. And Meg—but she was a dependant, perhaps pleased to think she would have nobody over her now. Gervase was his father's own, come back; equally feeble, not shaming his father by undue self-control. To hear his boy sob was sweet to the old man; it did him more good than Dunning's whispered adjurations not to fret, to "think of your own 'ealth," to "'old up, Sir Giles!" When he felt the hand of Gervase and heard his helpless son sob, a flash of force came to the old man.

"It's you and me now, Gervase, only you and me, my boy," he said loud out, interrupting the voice of the rector. It was a dreadful thing to do, and yet it had a great effect, the voice of nature breaking in, into the midst of all that ceremony and solemnity. Old Sir Giles' bare, bowed head, and the exclamation loud, broken with a sob, which everybody could hear, moved many people to tears. Even the rector paused a moment before he pronounced the final benediction, and the mourners began to disperse and turn away.

One other moment of intense anxiety followed for Patty. She had to keep her Softy up to the mark. All had gone well so far, but to keep him in the same humour for a long time together was well nigh an impossible achievement. When Sir Giles' chair was turned round, Patty almost pushed it herself in her anxiety to keep close, and it was no small exertion to keep Gervase steadily behind, yet not to hustle Dunning, who looked round at her fiercely. If there should happen to come into the Softy's mind the idea of rushing off with his father, which was his usual idea when he stood behind Sir Giles' chair! But some benevolent influence watched over Patty on that critical day. Gervase, occupied in watching the equipages, of which no man had ever seen so many at Greyshott, walked on quietly to the carriage door. He got in after Sir Giles as if that were quite natural, forgetting the "manners" she had tried to teach him; but Patty minded nothing at that moment of fate. She scrambled in after him, her heart beating wildly, and no one venturing to oppose. Dunning, indeed, who followed, looked unutterable things. He said: "Sir Giles, is it your meaning as this—this lady—?"

But Sir Giles said never a word. He kept patting his son's hand, saying, "Only you and me, my boy." He took no notice of the intruder into the carriage, and who else dared to speak? As for Patty's sentiments, they were altogether indescribable. They were complicated by personal sensations which were not agreeable. The carriage went slowly, the windows were closed on account of Sir Giles, though the day was warm. And she was placed on the front seat, beside Dunning, which was a position which gave her nausea, and made her head swim, as well as being highly inappropriate to her dignified position. But anything was to be borne in the circumstances, for the glory of being seen to drive "home" in the carriage with Sir Giles, and the chance of thus getting a surreptitious but undeniable entrance into the house. She said nothing, partly from policy, partly from discomfort, during that prolonged and tedious drive. And Gervase behaved himself with incredible discretion. Gervase, too, was glad to be going "home." He was pleased after all that had passed to be sitting by his father again. And he did Sir Giles good even by his foolishness, the poor Softy. After keeping quite quiet for half of the way, suffering his father to pat his hand, and repeat that little formula of words, saying "Don't cry, father, don't cry," softly, from time to time, he suddenly burst forth: "I say! look at those fellows riding over the copses. You don't let them ride over our copses, do you, father?"

"Never mind, never mind, my boy," said Sir Giles. But he was roused to look up, and his sobbing ceased.

"I wish you'd stop the carriage and let me get at them. They shouldn't ride that way again, I promise you," Gervase cried.

"You can't interfere to-day, Mr. Gervase," Dunning presumed to say. "Not the day of my lady's funeral, Sir Giles. You can't have the carriage stopped to-day."

"Mind your own business, Dunning," said Sir Giles, sharply. "No, my boy, never mind, never mind. We must just put up with it for a day. It don't matter, it don't matter, Gervase, what happens now—"

"But that isn't my opinion at all," said Gervase; "it matters a deal, and they shall see it does. Job Woodley, isn't it, and young George? They think it won't be noticed, but I'll notice it. I'll take care they sha'n't put upon you, father, now that you have nobody but me."

"God bless you, Gervase, you only want to be roused; that's what your poor dear mother used always to say."

"And now you'll find him thoroughly roused, Sir Giles, and you can depend upon him that he will always look after your interests," Patty said.

The old gentleman looked at her with bewildered eyes, gazing heavily across the carriage, only half aware of what she was saying, or who she was. And then they all drove on to Greyshott in solemn silence. They had come up by this time to the great gates, and entered the avenue. Patty's heart beat more and more with suspense and excitement. Everything now seemed to hang upon what took place in the next hour.

CHAPTER XXIII

Gervase went up the steps and into his father's house without waiting either for Sir Giles, whose disembarkation was a troublesome business, or his newly-made wife. For the moment he had forgotten all about Patty. She had to scramble out of the high old-fashioned chariot, which had been Sir Giles' state equipage for long, and which had been got out expressly for this high and solemn ceremony, nobody taking any notice or extending a finger to her—even the footman turning his back. Patty was too anxious and too determined on making her own entry to be much disturbed by this. To get her feet within the house was the great thing she had to consider; but—it need not be said that John Simpson, the footman, had his fate decided from that day, if indeed Mrs. Gervase established, as she intended to do, her footing in her husband's home.

Gervase stood on the threshold, carelessly overlooking the group, the men about Sir Giles' chair putting him back into it, and Patty not very gracefully getting down the steps of the carriage. His tall hat, wound with the heavy band, was placed on the back of his head, his hands were in his pockets, his eyes wandering, catching one detail after another, understanding no special significance in the scene. The other carriages coming up behind, waiting till the first should move on, aroused the Softy. He had forgotten why they were there, as he had forgotten that he had any duty towards his wife, who, in her hurry, had twisted herself in her long veil and draperies, and whom no one attempted to help. Patty was not the kind of figure to attract sentimental sympathy, as does the neglected dependant of fiction, the young wife of low degree in presence of a proud and haughty family. She was briskness and energy itself, notwithstanding that complication with the long veil, at which Gervase was just about to burst into a loud laugh when a sudden glance from her eyes paralysed him with his mouth open. As it took a long time to arrange Sir Giles, Patty had the situation before her and time to grasp it. She saw her opportunity at once. She passed the group of men about the chair, touching Dunning's arm sharply as she passed, bidding him to "take care, take care!" Then, stepping on, took the arm of Gervase, and stood with him on the threshold, like (she fondly hoped) the lady of the house receiving her guests. Dunning had nearly dropped his master's chair altogether at that insolent injunction and touch, and looked up at her with a countenance crimson with rage and enmity. But when Dunning saw the energetic figure in the doorway, holding Gervase's limp arm, and unconsciously pushing him to one side in so doing, placing herself in the centre, standing there like the mistress of the house, a cold shiver ran over him. "You could 'a knocked me down with a straw," he said afterwards confidentially to Parsons, in the mutual review they made later of all the exciting incidents of the day.

But this was not all: the opportunity comes to those who are capable of seizing upon it. Patty stood there with a heart beating so loudly that it sounded like a drum in her own ears, but with so full a sense of the importance of every act and look, that her excited nerves, instead of mastering her, gave support and stimulation to her whole being. She might have known, she said to herself, that Gervase would have been of no use to her, a thing which she resented, being now in possession of him, though she had fully calculated upon it before. "Stand by your wife, can't you!" she whispered fiercely, as she took hold of his arm and thrust him towards the wall. He grinned at her, though he dared not laugh aloud.

"Lord, you did look ridiculous, Patty, with that long thing twisting round you."

"If you laugh, you fool," said Patty, between her closed teeth, "you'll be turned out of the house."

When she had warned him she turned, bland but anxious, to the group below. "Oh, carry him gently, carry him gently!" she cried. When Sir Giles was set down on the level of the hall, she was the first to perceive his exhausted state. "I hope you have a cordial or something to give him, after all this fatigue?" she said. "You have nothing with you? Let the butler get it instantly—instantly!" She was quite right, and Dunning knew it, and made a sign that this unexpected order should be obeyed, with bitter anger in his heart. The old gentleman was very nearly fainting, after all the exertion and emotion. Patty had salts in her hand and eau de Cologne in her pocket ready for any emergency. She flew to him, while Dunning in his rage and pain called to the butler to make haste. And when the rest of the party followed, Patty was found in charge of Sir Giles, leaning over him, fanning him with her handkerchief impregnated with eau de Cologne, applying from time to time her salts to his nose. When the butler came hurrying back with the medicine, the first thing the surrounding spectators were conscious of was her voice sharply addressing Dunning, "You ought to have had the drops ready; you ought to have carried them with you; you ought never to be without something to give in case of faintness—and after such a dreadful day."

The woman, the creature, the alehouse girl (these were the names by which Dunning overwhelmed her in his private discourses), was quite right! He ought to have carried his master's drops with him. He ought to have been ready for the emergency. Margaret, who had come in in the midst of this scene, after one glimpse of Mrs. Gervase standing in the doorway, which had filled her with consternation, stood by helplessly for the moment, not doing anything. Mrs. Osborne would not have ventured to interfere with Dunning at any period of her residence at Greyshott. His authority with the family had been supreme. They had grown to think that Sir Giles' life depended upon him; that he knew better than the very doctor. To see Dunning thus assailed took away her breath, as it did that of all the servants, standing helplessly gaping at their master in his almost faint. And it was evident from Dunning's silence, and his hurried proceedings, that this audacious intruder was right—astounding discovery! Dunning did not say a word for himself. His hand trembled so, that Patty seized the bottle from him, and dropped the liquid herself with a steady hand. "Now, drink this," she said authoritatively, putting it to Sir Giles' lips, who obeyed her, though in his half-unconsciousness he had been feebly pushing Dunning away. This astonishing scene kept back all the other funeral guests who were alighting at the door, and among whom the most dreadful anticipations were beginning to breathe to the effect that it had been "too much" for Sir Giles. To see Margaret Osborne standing there helpless, doing nothing, gave force to their suppositions, for she must have been occupied with her uncle had there been anything to do for him, everybody thought. Patty's shorter figure, all black, was not distinguishable from below as she leant over Sir Giles' chair.

Gervase, who had been hanging in the doorway, reduced to complete silence by his wife's threats, pulled Margaret by her dress. "I say, Meg! she's one, ain't she? She's got 'em all down, even Dunning. Lord! just look at her going it!" the admiring husband said. He dared not laugh, but his wide-open mouth grinned from ear to ear. He did not know who the tall fellow was by Margaret's side, who stood looking on with such a solemn air, but he poked that dignitary with his elbow all the same. "Ain't she as good as a play?" Gervase said.

Colonel Piercey was in no very genial frame of mind. He was angry to see Mrs. Osborne superseded, and angry with her that she did not step forward and take the direction of everything. And when this fool, this Softy, as the country people called him, addressed himself with elbow and voice, his disgust was almost beyond bounds. It was not decorous of the next-of-kin: he turned away from the grinning idiot with a sharp exclamation, forgetting altogether that he was, more or less, the master of the house.

"Oh, hush, Gervase," said Mrs. Osborne. "Don't laugh: you will shock all the people. She is— very serviceable. She shows— great sense— Gervase, why is she here?"

He was on the point of laughter again, but was frightened this time by Margaret. "Why, here's just where she ought to be," he said, with a suppressed chuckle. "I told you, but you didn't understand. I almost told— mother."

Here the half-witted young man paused a little with a sudden air of trouble. "Mother; what's all this about mother?" he said.

"Oh, Gervase! she wanted you so!"

"Well," he cried, "but how could I come when I didn't know? Ask her. We never heard a word. I remember now. We only came back last night. I thought after all we might find her all right when we came back. Is it—is it true, Meg?"

He spoke with a sort of timidity behind Patty's back, still pulling his cousin's dress, the grin disappearing from his face, but his hat still on the back of his head, and his fatuous eyes wandering. His attention was only half arrested even by a question of such importance. It moved the surface of his consciousness, and no more; his eye, even while he was speaking, was caught by the unruly action of the horses in one of the carriages far down the avenue, which put a movement of interest into his dull face.

"I cannot speak to you about it all here. Come in, and I will tell you everything," Margaret said.

He made a step after her, and then looked back; but Patty was still busily engaged with Sir Giles, and her husband escaped, putting his cousin's tall figure between himself and her.

"I say, are all this lot of people coming here? What are they coming here for? Have I got to talk to all these people, Meg?"

He went after her into the library, where already some of the guests were, and where Margaret was immediately occupied, receiving the solemn leave-takings of the county gentry, who had driven so far for this ceremony, but who looked strangely at Gervase, still with his hat on, and who, in presence of such a chief mourner, and of the illness of poor Sir Giles, were eager to get away. A vague story about the marriage had already flashed through the neighbourhood, but the gentlemen were more desirous even of keeping clear of any embarrassment that might arise from it, than of getting "the rights of the story" to carry back to their wives—though that also was a strong motive. Gervase gave a large grip of welcome to several who spoke to him, and laughed, and said it was a fine day, with an apparent indifference to the object of their visit, which chilled the blood of the kindly neighbours. And still more potent than any foolishness he might utter was the sign of the hat on his head, which produced the profoundest impression upon the small solemn assembly, though even Margaret, in the excitement of the crisis altogether, did not notice it for some time.

"We feel that the only kindness we can do you, dear Mrs. Osborne, is to leave you alone as quickly as possible," said Lord Hartmore, who was a very dignified person, and generally took the lead—and he was followed by the other potentates, who withdrew almost hurriedly, avoiding Gervase as much as possible, as he stood swaying from one foot to another, with a half laugh of mingled vacuity and embarrassment. Gervase was rather disappointed that they should all go away. It was rarely that he had seen so many people gathered together under his father's roof. He tried to detain one or two of them who gave him a second grasp of the hand as they passed him.

"You're going very soon. Won't you stay and have something?" Gervase said.

Colonel Piercey was standing outside the door of the library as they began to come out, and Lord Hartmore gave him a very significant look, and a still more significant grasp of the hand.

"That," he said with emphasis, with a backward movement of his head to indicate the room he had just quitted, "is the saddest sight of all,"—and there was a little pause of the gentlemen about the door, a group closed up the entrance to the room, all full of something to say, which none of them ventured to put into words; all relieving themselves with shaking of heads and meaning looks.

"Poor Sir Giles! I have the sincerest sympathy with him," said Lord Hartmore, "the partner of his life gone, and so little comfort in the poor son."

They grasped Gerald Piercey's hand, one by one, in a sort of chorus, grouping round the open door.

It was at this moment that Patty found herself free, Sir Giles having been wheeled away to his own rooms to escape the agitating encounter of so many strangers. She walked towards them with the heroic confidence of a Joan of Arc. Probably nothing but the habits of her previous life, her custom of facing unruly men in various stages of difficulty, dissatisfied customers, and those of too convivial a turn, drunkards, whom she had to master by sheer coolness and strength of mind, could have armed her for such an extraordinary emergency. She knew most of the men by sight, but had hitherto looked at them from a distance as beings unapproachable, not likely ever to come within touch of herself or her life; and they all looked towards her, more or less severely,—some with surprise, some with concealed amusement, some with the sternest disapproval. So many men of might and dignity, personages in the county, not one among them sympathetic; and one small young woman, in a place the very external features of which were unknown to her, where every individual was an enemy, yet which she meant to take possession of and conquer by her bow and her spear, turning out every dissident! The gentlemen stood and stared, rather in astonishment than in curiosity, as she advanced alone, her long veil hanging behind her, her crape sweeping the carpet. They did not make way for her, which was scarcely so much from incivility as from surprise, but stood staring, blocking up the door of a room which Patty saw must be the first stronghold to be taken, from the mere fact of the group that stood before it. She came up quite close to them without saying a word, holding her head high. And then she raised her high, rather sharp voice:—

"Will you please to make room for me to pass? I want to join my husband," she said.

And then there was a start as simultaneous as the stare had been. Patty's voice gave the gentlemen of the county a shock as if a cannon had been fired into the midst of them. It was a challenge and an accusation in one. To accuse men of their class of a breach of civility is worse than firing a gun among them. They separated quickly with a sense of shame. "I beg your pardon" came from at least two voices. It would be difficult to explain what they thought they could have done to resist the intruder: but they were horrified by the suggestion of interference—as if they had anything to do with it! so that in fact Patty entered triumphantly through a lane formed by two lines of men dividing to make way for her. A princess could not have done more.

She walked in thus with flags flying, pale with the effort, which was advantageous to her appearance, and found herself in the great room, with its bookcases on the one hand and the tall portraits on the other. But Patty found here, against her expectations, a far more difficult scene before her. Two or three ladies had come to give Margaret Osborne the support of their presence, on what they called "this trying day," without in the least realising how trying it was to be. One of them, an old lady, sat in a great chair facing the door, with her eyes fixed upon it. Two others, younger, but scarcely less alarming, were talking to Mrs. Osborne, who in her own sole person had been supposed by Patty with natural enmity to be the chief of her adversaries. They stopped their conversation and stared at Patty, as with a sudden faltering, she came in. Gervase stood against the end window, fully outlined against the light, with his hands in his pockets, and his hat on his head, swaying from one foot to another, his lower lip hanging a little and very moist, his wandering eyes turned towards the door. Patty entering alone under the eyes of these ladies, with a consciousness that much had passed since she had last looked at herself in a glass, and that veil and mantle might easily have got awry—and with the additional excitement of surprise in finding them there when she had looked at the worst only for the presence of Mrs. Osborne—might well have called forth a sympathetic movement in any bosom. And when it is added to this that Gervase, standing there against the light, had probably never in all his life looked so idiotic before, and that he had his hat on his head, last and most dreadful climax of all, it may be dimly imagined what were the sensations of his bride. But there are circumstances in which an unusual exaggeration of trouble brings support. Patty looked for a moment and then rushed upon her husband in horror. "Oh, Gervase! do you know you have got your hat on, and ladies in the room?" she cried, with an almost shriek of dismay.

Gervase put up his hand to his head, took off the hat, and then carefully examined it, as if to find the reason of offence there. "Have I?" he said, with a laugh; "then I never knew it. You should stick by me if you mean me to behave. I don't think of such things."

"Then you ought," she cried, breathless, taking the hat from him with a wife's familiarity, "and you ought to beg pardon." She took him by the arm quickly and led him forward a step or two. "Ladies," she said, "I am sure me and my husband are very glad to see you. He meant no rudeness, I'm sure. He doesn't think about such little things. I am still," she added, "a sort of a stranger"—with an insinuating smile which, however, was very tremulous, for Patty's nerves were strained to the utmost. She paused a moment for breath. "A bride has the feeling that the friends of the family know her husband better than she does; and it's such a sad occasion to begin. But I'm sure I may say both for him and for me that we are pleased, and will always be pleased, to see old friends here."

The ladies sat and stared at her speechless. What reply could be made to a woman so manifestly within her rights?

CHAPTER XXIV

Patty felt, which was surely very natural, that the worst of her troubles were over after this scene; and when Mrs. Osborne went out with the ladies, going with them from sheer inability to know what to do—she threw herself into a great chair, which seemed to embrace and support her, with a sense at once of having earned and fully deserved the repose, and also of having been successful all along the line. She had encountered almost all who were likely to be her adversaries, and they had all given way before her. To be sure, there had not been much said to her: the gentlemen had stood aside to let her in, the ladies had stared and said nothing, only one of them had turned with a little compunction of civility to bow to her as she went away. The old lady, whom Patty knew to be Lady Hartmore, had waddled out, saying: "Well, Meg, we shall say all we have to say another time," and had not so much as looked again at Patty. Meg Osborne, as Patty had begun to call her, had kept her eyes on the ground, and had accompanied her friends to the door without a word. But still it was Patty who had driven them away, not they who had interfered with Patty. When one of the armies in an engagement encamps upon the field of battle, that belligerent is generally admitted to have won the day. And here was Mrs. Gervase resting in that large deep chair, which was such an one as Patty Hewitt had never seen before, enjoying a moment of well-earned repose in her own house. Was it her own house? Her pulses were all throbbing with the excitement of conflict and the pride of victory; but she was aware that her triumph was not yet assured. Nevertheless, everything was in her favour. This grand house into which she had made her way, and which was even grander than Patty had supposed, was certainly her husband's home, and she was his wife as legally, as irrevocably as if she had been married with the consent of all the parents in the world. Nothing could part her from her husband, neither force nor law, and though her heart still owned a thrill of alarm and insecurity, she became more at ease as she thought the matter over. Who dared turn her out of the house into which she had so bravely fought her way? Nobody but Sir Giles, who was not equal to the effort, who would not wish to do it, she felt sure. Patty had a conviction in her mind that she only required to be let alone and allowed access to him for a single day to get wholly the upper hand of Sir Giles. And who else had any right to interfere? Not Meg Osborne, who had herself no right to be at Greyshott, except as a humble companion and hanger-on. A niece! what was a niece in the house? Patty herself had a poor cousin who had been taken in at the Seven Thorns, as a sort of inferior servant, out of charity, as everybody said, and whose life Patty well knew had been a very undesirable one. What was Meg Osborne more than Mary Thorne? She had no right to say a word. Neither had the tall gentleman, of whom she was, however, more frightened, whom she had already discovered to be Colonel Piercey, the nearest relation. How persons like Patty do make such discoveries is wonderful, a science which cannot be elucidated or formulated in mere words. She knew by instinct, and she knew also that he could not interfere. The servants were more in Patty's way, and her hatred of them was sharp and keen—but she had already managed to discredit Dunning, and she was not afraid of the servants. What could they do? What would they venture to do against the son's wife? All these thoughts were passing through her mind as she rested in the great chair. And yet that repose was not without thorns. Gervase, though he stood still and stared while the ladies withdrew, did not rest as she was doing. He walked to the window, to look out, and stood there fidgetting, and eager to take part in all the commotion outside. "Lord!" he cried, "Hartmore's carriage is sent round to the stables, and my lord has got to wait, and Stubbins, the little parson, is offering his fly. Oh, I can't stay here, Patty, I must be in the fun. You can get on very well by yourself without me."

"What do you want with fun the day of your mother's funeral?" she said severely. "They'll all think a deal more of you if you stay quiet here."

Gervase's countenance fell at the suggestion of his mother's funeral. No doubt, had he been at home, had his dull mind acquainted itself with the preliminaries, he would have been more or less moved. But it was too great an effort of mind for him to connect the ceremony in the churchyard, the grave and the flowers, with Lady Piercey, whom he had left in her usual health, deciding everything in her usual peremptory way. He had a strong impression that she would presently appear on the scene as usual and settle everything; and a sort of alarm came over his face, and his spirit was overawed for a moment by the mention of her name. There succeeded accordingly, for about a minute, silence in the room, which left Patty time to go over the question again. Who could interfere with her? Nobody! Not Meg Osborne, not Colonel Piercey, not a mere housekeeper or butler. Oh dear no! Nobody but Sir Giles himself! Patty settled herself more and more comfortably in her chair. The funeral had been at an unusually late hour, and it was now almost evening. She thought that after a little interval she would ring the bell for tea. If any one had need of refreshment after the labour of the day, it was she. And after that there were many things to think of, both small things and great things. What should she do about dinner, for instance? Meg Osborne, no doubt, had got a full wardrobe of mourning, day dress and evening dress (at her, Patty's, expense!), while Mrs. Gervase Piercey had only the gown which she had on, an old dress plastered with crape. Should she wear this for dinner? The thought of going down to dinner, sitting down with a footman behind her chair, and all the etiquette involved, was almost too much for Patty, and took away her breath. Should she brush the skirt, and smarten up the neck and wear this? Or should she send down to the Seven Thorns for her black silk, and explain that she had not had time to get proper mourning? Gervase had begun to fidget again while she carried on this severe course of thought. She could hear him laughing to himself at the window, making occasional exclamations. "Oh, by Jove!" he called out at last. "There's lots more coming, one on the top of another. I'm going to see after them." She was so deep in her meditations, that he was gone before she could interfere. And thus she was left in the great silent library, a room such as she had never seen before, overawing her with the sight of the bookcases, the white marble faces looking down upon her of the busts that stood high up here and there, the full-length portraits that stared upon her from the other side. Many people, quite as little educated as Patty—or less so, for the sixth standard necessarily includes many things—had come and gone lightly enough, and thought nothing of the books or the ancestors. I doubt much whether Margaret Osborne had half so much general information as Patty had; but, then, their habits of mind were very different. Mrs. Gervase, when she was left alone, could not help being a little overawed by all she saw. Her husband was not much to hold on by, but yet he "belonged there," and she did not. Patty had felt increasingly, ever since the day on which she married him, how very little her husband was to be depended upon. She had fully recognised that before the marriage, and had decided that she should not mind. But now it seemed a grievance to Patty that he could not defend her and advise her; that she had nobody but herself to look to; that quite possibly he might even abandon her at the most critical moment. "There is never any calculating," she said to herself bitterly, "what a fool may do;" in which sentiment Patty echoed, without knowing it, all the philosophies of the subject. Who could have thought he would have slid away from her, on her first entrance into a house where she would have to fight her way step by step, for nothing at all—for the first novelty that caught his wandering eye?

Patty was tired, and she cried a little at this crisis, feeling that her fate was hard. To acquire a husband with so much trouble, and to find out at once how little help to her he was. He was very fond of her, she knew. Still, now he was used to her, and took her for granted as a part of the order of things, he could not keep his mind fixed even on his wife. He was only a Softy after all, nothing more! Patty roused herself briskly, however, from this line of thought, which was evidently not one to encourage, and rang the bell. It remained a long time unanswered; and then she rang again. This time the footman who had turned his back upon her at the carriage-door, came, looked in, said "Oh!" when he saw her sitting alone, and went away. Patty's fury was indescribable. Oh that dolt John Simpson, what a fate he was making for himself! While she waited, growing more and more angry, Mrs. Osborne came in again, with hesitation. She was still in her outdoor dress, and looked disturbed and embarrassed.

"The servants— have told me— that you had rung the bell," she said, faltering considerably. "Is there— anything— I can order for you?"

Margaret was very little prepared for her rôle, and was as profoundly aware of her own want of power as Patty could be.

"Order for me!" said Patty. "I rang for tea, as a proper servant would have known; and I wish you to know, Mrs. Osborne—if you are Mrs. Osborne, as I suppose, for no one has had the decency to introduce you—that it is my place to give the orders, and not yours."

Margaret was so much taken by surprise that she had no weapon with which to defend herself. She said mildly:—

"I do not often give orders; but the housekeeper, who was my aunt's favourite maid, is much overcome. I will tell them—what you want."

"Thank you, I can tell them myself," said Patty, ringing another, a louder, and more violent peal. It brought up the butler himself in great haste, and it startled the still lingering visitors, who again thought nothing less than that Sir Giles must be taken ill. "Bring up tea directly," cried Mrs. Gervase. "This is the third time I have rung. I pass over it now, owing to the confusion of the house, but it had better not occur again."

The butler stared open-mouthed at the new-comer. Patty Hewitt, of the Seven Thorns! He knew her as well as he knew his own sister. Then he looked at Mrs. Osborne, who made him a slight sign—and then disappeared, to carry astonishment and dismay into the servants' hall.

"Mrs. Osborne give me a nod," said the angry dignitary, "as I had better do it. Lord! saucing me as have known her since she was that high, setting up for my lady, as grand as grand, and the family giving in to her!"

"The family!" said the cook, tossing her head; "call Mrs. Osborne the family, that is no better nor you and me. Far worse! A companion as is nobody, eating dirt to make her bread."

"Oh, if my poor lady had been here!" said Parsons, "that creature would soon have been put to the door! She was too soft-hearted over Mr. Gervase, was my poor lady—but not to stand that. As for Miss Meg, she hasn't got the spirit of a mouse!"

"But what am I to do?" said Stevens, the butler. "Me, an old servant, ordered about and sauced like that! What am I to do, I ask you? Take up the tea—or what? Mrs. Osborne, she give me a nod—but Mrs. Osborne she's not like Sir Giles' daughter, and nobody has no authority. What am I to do?"

It was finally resolved in that anxious conclave that John should be sent up with the tea, much to John's mortification and alarm, who began to feel that, perhaps, it might have been better to be civil to Patty Hewitt. He went, but returned in a minute, flying along the passages, his face crimson, his eyes staring out of his head. "She says as I'm never to show in her sight again!" he cried. "She says as how Mr. Stevens is to come hisself and do his duty: nor she didn't say Mr. Stevens either," cried John, with momentary satisfaction, "but Stevens, short; and wouldn't let me so much as put down the tray!"

"Robert can take it," said the butler; but he was bewildered and hesitated. Presently he followed with a sheepish air. "I'll just go and see what comes of it," he said.

Patty was sitting up very erect in her chair, a flame of battle on her cheeks. She allowed herself, however, to show a dignified relief when Stevens came in following his inferior, who carried the tray. It was not to be supposed that so great a man could bear that burden for himself: Patty recognised this fact with instant sympathy. She nodded her head with dignity.

"Stevens," she said, with the air of a duchess, "you will see that that man never comes into my sight again."

Stevens did not, indeed, make any reply, but a sound of consternation burst from him, a suspiration of forced breath, which Patty accepted as assent. Margaret was standing at a little distance speechless, an image of confusion and embarrassment. She knew no more than the servants what to do. Gervase's wife—as there was no reason to doubt this woman was—how could Gervase's cousin oppose her? Margaret had no rights—no position in the household; but the wife of Gervase had certainly rights, however inopportune might be the moment at which she chose to assert them. Mrs. Osborne, however, started violently when she herself was addressed with engaging friendliness.

"Won't you come and have some tea? No? are you going? Then, will you please tell Gervase that tea is here, and I am waiting for him?" Patty said.

Margaret withdrew from the room as if a shot had been fired at her. Her confusion and helplessness were so great that they went beyond anything like resentment. She was almost overawed by the boldness of the intruder and the impossibility of the situation. Gervase stood in the doorway, excited and pleased, shouting for the carriages, talking about the horses to whoever would talk with him. She was glad of some excuse for calling him, taking him by the arm. Certainly he would be better anywhere than there.

"Gervase," she said, "tell me, is that your wife who is in the library?"

"Eh? What do you say, Meg? Patty? Why, of course! What did you think she could be? Patty! look here, you come and tell Meg—"

"Hush, Gervase, she wants you to go to her. Tea is ready, and she is waiting for you. Now go, Gervase, go—do go!"

"She's come over Meg, too!" said Gervase to himself with a chuckle; and, fortunately, his amusement in that, and the impulse of his cousin's touch on his arm, and the new suggestion which, whatever it happened to be, was always powerful with him, made him obey the call which now came out shrilly over the other noises from the library door.

"Gervase! Gervase! I'm waiting for you for tea."

Margaret crossed the hall into the morning-room, with a grave face. The consternation which was in her whole aspect moved Colonel Piercey, who followed her, to a short laugh. "What is to be done?" he said.

"Oh, nothing, nothing that I know of! Of course she is Gervase's wife—she has a right to be here. I don't know what my poor uncle will say—but I told you before he would be talked over."

"She showed herself very ready and with all her wits about her, at the door."

"Yes," said Margaret. "She has a great deal of sense, I have always heard. It may not be a bad thing after all."

"It frightens you, however," Colonel Piercey said.

"Not frightens but startles me—very much: and then, poor Aunt Piercey! Poor Aunt Piercey! her only child, and on her funeral day."

"She was not a wise mother, I should imagine."

"What does that matter?" cried Margaret. "And who is wise? We do what we think is the best, and it turns out the worst. How can we tell? I am glad she is gone, at least, and did not see it," she cried with a few hot tears.

Colonel Piercey looked at her coldly, as he always did. It was on his lips to say, "She was not very good to you, that you should shed tears for her," but he refrained. He could not refrain, however, from saying—which was perhaps worse—"I am afraid it is a thing which will much affect you."

"Oh, me!" she cried, with a sort of proud disdain, and turned and left him without a word. Whatever happened he was always her hardest and coldest judge, suggesting meanness in her conduct and thoughts even to herself.

CHAPTER XXV

No house could be more agitated and disturbed than was Greyshott on the night of Lady Piercey's funeral. That event, indeed, was enough to throw a heavy cloud over the dwelling, where the imperious old lady had filled so large a place, that the mere emptiness, where her distinct and imposing figure was withdrawn, touched the imagination, even if it did not touch the heart. The impression, however, on such an occasion is generally one of subdued quiet and gloom—an arrest of life; whereas the great house was quivering with fears and suppositions, with the excitement of a struggle which nobody could see the end of, or divine how it should turn. The servants were in a ferment, some of them expecting dismissal; others agreed that under new sway, such as seemed to threaten, Greyshott would not be a place for them. The scene in the housekeeper's room, where the heads of the female department sat together dismayed, and exchanged presentiments and resolutions, was tragic in its intensity of alarm and wrath. The cook had not given more than a passing thought to the dinner, which an eager kitchen-maid on her promotion had the charge of; and Parsons sat arranging her lists of linen with a proud but melancholy certainty that all would be found right, however hastily her reign might be brought to an end.

"I never thought as I should have to give them up to the likes of her," Parsons said, among her tears. "Oh, my lady, my poor lady! She's been took away from the evil to come."

"She'd never have let the likes of her step within our doors," said cook, indignant, "if it had only been poor Sir Giles, as is no better than a baby, that had been took, and my lady left to keep things straight."

"Oh, don't say that, cook, don't say that," cried Parsons, "for then he'd have been Sir Gervase, and she Lady Piercey, and my lady would have—bursted; that's what she would have done."

"Lord!" cried the cook, "Lady Piercey! But the Colonel or somebody would have stopped that."

"There's nobody as could have stopped it," said Parsons, better informed. "They might say as he hadn't his wits, and couldn't manage his property, or that—but to stop him from being Sir Gervase, and her Lady Piercey, is what nobody can do; no, not the Queen, nor the Parliament: for he was born to that: Softy or not it don't make no difference."

"Lord!" said the cook again: and she took an opportunity shortly after of going into the kitchen and giving a look at the dinner, of which that ambitious, pushing kitchen-maid was making a chef-d'œuvre. The same information filtering through the house made several persons nervous. Simpson, the footman, for one, gave himself up for lost; and any other member of the household who had ever entered familiarly at the Seven Thorns, or given a careless order for a pot of beer to Patty, now shook in his shoes. The general sentiments at first had been those of indignation and scorn; but a great change soon came over the household—a universal thrill of alarm, a sense of insecurity. No one ventured now to mention the name of Patty. She, they called her with awe—and in the case of some far-seeing persons, like that kitchen-maid, the intruder had already received her proper name of Mrs. Gervase, or even Lady Gervase, from those whose education was less complete.

The sensation of dismay which thus pervaded the house attained, perhaps, its climax in the rooms which Margaret Osborne shared with her boy, and where she had withdrawn after her brief intercourse with Patty. These rooms were little invaded by the rest of the household, the nurse who took care of Osy, doing everything that was needed for her mistress, and the little apartment making a sort of sanctuary for the mother and the child. She was sure of quiet there if nowhere else; and when she had closed the door she seemed for a moment to leave behind her all the agitations which convulsed and changed the course of life. The two rooms, opening into one another, in which Margaret's life had been spent for years, which were almost the only home that Osy had ever known, were still hers, though she could not tell for how short a time: the sword hanging over the mantelpiece, which Osy had described as the only thing which belonged to his mother and himself, hung there still, their symbol of individual possession. For years past, Margaret had felt herself safe when she closed that door. She held it, as it now appeared, on but a precarious footing; but she had not thought so up to this time. She had felt that she had a right to her shelter, that her place was one which nobody could take from her; not the right of inheritance, it is true, but of nature. It was the home of her fathers, though she was only Sir Giles' niece, and bore another name. She had been a dependant indeed, but not as a stranger would be. It was the home of her childhood, and it was hers as long as the old rule continued—the natural state of affairs which she had not thought of as coming to an end. Even Lady Piercey's death had not appeared to her to make an end. Sir Giles would need her more: there would be still more occasion for her presence in the house when the imperious, but not unkind, mistress went away. The old lady had been sharp in speech, and careless of her feelings, but she had never forgotten that Meg Piercey had a right to her shelter as well as duties to discharge there. There had been, indeed, a scare about Gervase, but it was a proof of the slightness of reality in that scare that Margaret had scarcely thought of it as affecting herself. She had been eager to bring back Gervase to his mother, if by no other means, by the help of Patty, thus recognising her position; but after Lady Piercey's death, when the necessity was no longer pressing, Margaret had thought of it no more. And, certainly, of all days in the world, it was not upon the day of the funeral that she had looked for any disturbance in her life.

But now in a moment—in the time that sufficed to open a door, to ring a bell, to give an order—Mrs. Osborne recognised that this life was over. It had seemed as if it must never come to an end, as all established and settled existence does; and now in a moment it had come to an end. At many moments, when her patience was strained to the utmost, Margaret had come up here and composed herself, and felt herself safe within these walls. As long as she had this refuge she could bear anything, and there had been no likelihood that it would be taken from her. But now, whatever she might have to bear, it seemed certain that it was not here she could retire to reconcile herself to it. It seemed scarcely possible to believe that the old order of affairs was over; and yet she felt convinced that it was over and could return no more. She did not as yet ask herself what she should do. She had never acted for herself, never inquired into the possibilities of life. Captain Osborne's widow had come back to her home as the only natural thing to do. She had been brought up to do Lady Piercey's commands, to be the natural, superfluous, yet necessary, person who had no duty save to do duty for everybody; and she had fallen back into that position as if it were the only one in life. Margaret did not enter into any questions with herself even now, much less come to any decision. It was enough for one day to have faced the startling, incomprehensible fact that her life was over, the only life—except that brief episode of her marriage—which she had ever known. Where was she to go with her little pension, her husband's sword, and her boy? But she could not tell, or even think, as yet, of any step to take. All that she was capable of was to feel that the present existence, the familiar life, was at an end.

Osy had been left in a secluded corner of the garden while the funeral took place, to be out of the way. It had not seemed necessary to his mother to envelop him in mourning, and take him with her through that strange ceremonial, so mysterious to childish thoughts; and while she sat alone, the sound of his little voice and step became audible to her coming up the stairs. Osy, who was willing on ordinary occasions to spend the whole of his time out-of-doors, had been impatient to-day, touched by the prevailing agitation, though he did not know what it meant. He came in, stamping with his little feet, making up for the quiet which had been exacted from him for a few days past, and threw himself against Margaret's knee.

"Movver," he said, breathless, "there's a lady down in the libery."

"Yes, Osy, I know."

"Oh, movver knows," he said, turning to his attendant, "I told you movver alvays knows. Very queer fings," said Osy, reflectively, "have tummed to pass to-day."

"What things, Osy?"

"Fings about Aunt Piercey," said the little boy, counting upon his fingers; "somefing I don't understand. You said, movver, she had don to heaven, but Parsons, she said you had all don to put her somewhere else, but I believe you best; and then there were all the carriages and the gemplemans, and the horse that runned away. But most strangest of all, the lady in the libery." He paused to think. "I fought she wasn't a lady at all, but a dressmaker or somefing."

"And then? you changed your mind?"

"No," said the little boy, doubtfully, "not me. But she looked out of the window, and then she called, 'Gervase! Gervase!'—she touldn't say, Gervase, Gervase, if she were one of the maids. I fink it's the lady Cousin Gervase went to London to marrwy. And I'm glad," Osy said, making another pause. He resumed, "I'm glad, because now I know that my big silver piece was a marrwage present, movver. He tooked it, but I dave it him all the same; and as it was a marrwage present, I don't mind scarcely at all. But that is not the funniest fing yet," said Osy, putting up his hand to his mother's face to secure her attention; "there's somefing more, movver. She tummed to the window, and she said, 'Gervase, Gervase, who is that ickle boy?'"

"Well, Osy, there was nothing very wonderful in that," said Margaret, trying to smile.

"Yes, mower, there was two fings wonderful." He held out the small dirty forefinger again, and tapped upon it with the forefinger of his other little fat hand. "First—there touldn't any lady tum to Greyshott and not know me. I'm not an ickle boy, I'm Osy; and another fing, she knows me already quite well; for she isn't a beau'ful lady from London, like that one that singed songs, you know. She is the woman at the Seven Thorns. Sally, tum here and tell movver. We knowed her quite well, bof Sally and me."

"It's quite true, ma'am, as Mr. Osy says, it's quite, quite—"

"That will do," said Margaret, "I want no information on the subject. Make haste, Sally, and get Master Osy's tea."

Osy stood looking up somewhat anxiously in his mother's face, leaning against her. He put one hand into hers, and put the other to her chin to make her look at him, with a way he had. "Movver, why don't you want in—in—formashun?" he said.

"Osy, my little boy, you know you mustn't talk before Sally of your Cousin Gervase or the family; you must tell me whatever happens, but not any of the servants. That lady is perhaps going to be the lady of the house, now. She is Mrs. Gervase, and she has a better right to be here than you or me. Perhaps we shall have to go away. You must be a very good, very thoughtful little boy; and polite, like a gentleman, to every one."

"I am never not a gemplemans, movver," said the child, with an air of offended dignity; then he suddenly grew red, and cried out, "Oh, I fordot! Cousin Colonel met me in the hall, and he said would I tell you to tum, please, and speak to him in the rose-garden, because he touldn't tum upstairs. Will you do and speak to Cousin Colonel in the garden, movver? He said, wouldn't I tum with him to his house?"

"Osy! but you wouldn't go with any one, would you, away from your mother?"

"Oh, not for always," cried the child, "but for a day, two days, to ride upon his s'oulder. He's not like Cousin Gervase. He holds fast—fast; and I likes him. Movver, run into the rose-garden; for I fordot, and he is there waiting, and he will fink I've broke my word. And I doesn't want you now," said Osy, waving his hand, "for I'm doin' to have my tea."

Thus dismissed, Margaret rose slowly and with reluctance. She did not run to the rose-garden as her son had bidden her. A cloud had come over her face. It was quite reasonable that Colonel Piercey should ask to speak with her in her changed position of affairs. It would be quite reasonable, indeed, that he should offer her advice, or even help. He was her nearest relation, and though he had not been either just or kind to herself, he had fallen under the charm of her little boy. It might be that, distasteful as it was, for Osy's sake she would have to accept, even to seek, Gerald Piercey's advice. Probably it was true kindness on his part to offer it in the first place, to put himself at her disposal. For herself there could be no such question; somehow, so far as she was concerned, she could struggle and live or die: what would it matter? But Osy must grow up, must be educated, must become a man. Margaret had been of opinion that she knew something already of the bitterness of dependence; it seemed to her now, however, that she had not tasted it until this day.

VOLUME II

CHAPTER XXVI

Colonel Piercey had been walking up and down somewhat impatiently for some time, at the corner of the rose-garden where Osy had left him. The child had not then seen the lady at the window who asked who was that little boy; and this incident and the account of it, which Osy had hastened to give to his mother, had naturally occupied some time. He was not much accustomed to wait, and did not like it. And when he saw Margaret come slowly along, some half-hour after he had sent, what he felt was a very respectful message to her, asking her to allow him a few minutes' conversation, the curious opposition and sense of inevitable hostility which he felt towards his cousin, was sharpened into a keen feeling of resentment. She had held him at bay all along, never treated him with confidence or friendliness; and if she chose to affect fine-lady airs of coyness and pride now! It was quite unconsciously to himself, and he was by nature a man full of generosity, who would have been more astonished than words could say, had he been charged with presuming upon adverse circumstances; and yet he was far more angry with Margaret in her dependent position than he would have been with any woman more happily situated. He felt that she, as women he believed generally did, was disposed to stand upon the superiority of being at so great a disadvantage, and to claim consideration from the very fact that she got it from no one. Why should she bear the spurns of all the unworthy, and mount upon that pedestal of patient merit to him? It was not that he felt it natural to treat her badly because other people did, but because the fact that other people did, gave her the opportunity of assuming that it would be the same with him. He would have liked to take her by the shoulders and shake out of her that aspect of injury, without knowing that he dared not have entertained that fierce intention towards any one who was not injured. Finally, he watched her coming towards him slowly, showing her reluctance in every step, with an impatience and disinclination to put up with it, which was almost stronger than any feeling of personal opposition he had ever felt in his life. She said, before she had quite come up to him: "I am sorry I have kept you waiting. Osy has only given me your message now."

It was on his lips to say: "You are not sorry to have kept me waiting!" but he subdued that impulse. A man like Colonel Piercey cannot give a woman the lie direct, unless in very serious circumstances indeed. He replied stiffly: "I fear I have taken a great liberty in asking you to meet me here at all."

Margaret answered only with a faint smile and wave of her hand, which seemed to Colonel Piercey to say as plainly as words: "Everybody offers me indignity; why not you, too?" which, perhaps, was not very far from the fact; though she was a great deal too proud to have ever said, or even implied, anything of the kind. He answered his own supposition hotly, by saying: "I know no other place where we should be safe from interruption, and I thought it my duty to—speak to you about the new condition of affairs."

"Yes?" said Margaret. "I am afraid I have very little light to throw on the position; but I shall be glad to hear what you have to say."

All that he said in the meantime was, with some resentment: "You don't seem so much startled by what has happened as I should have supposed."

"I was much startled to see Patty—I mean the person whom we must now call Mrs. Gervase—at the funeral. But of course, after that, one was prepared for all the rest. I don't know that I had much reason to be startled even at that. From the moment we found that she was absent while he was absent, I ought to have, and indeed I did, divine what must have occurred. However sure one is of such a thing, it is startling, all the same, when one comes to see it actually accomplished; but I ought not to say more than that."

"You take it with much philosophy," Colonel Piercey said.

"Do you think so? I should be glad to think I was so strong-minded; for there is probably no one to whom it will make so much difference as to me."

"That is why I felt that I must speak to you. Can nothing be done to prevent this?"

"To prevent what?" she said, with some surprise.

"The reign of this woman over Uncle Giles' house, in Aunt Piercey's place! It is too intolerable; it is enough to make the old lady rise from her grave."

"Poor old Aunt Piercey! She has been taken away from the evil to come. I am glad that she is dead, and has not had this to bear."

"I suppose women have tears at their will," cried Colonel Piercey, bursting forth in an impatience which he could restrain no longer. "She was not so kind to you that you should feel so tenderly for her."

"How do you know she was not kind to me? She was natural, at all events," cried Margaret. "It has all been quite natural up to this time; I went away and I came back, and whatever happened to me, I was at home. But you, Colonel Piercey, you are not natural. I have no right to accept contumely at your hands. You came here with a suspicion of Heaven knows what in your mind; you thought I had some design: what was the design which you suspected me of having against the happiness of this household? I warned you that you should have some time or other to explain what you meant—to me."

Colonel Piercey stood confronting her among the roses which formed so inappropriate a background, and did not know what reply to make. He had not expected that assault. Answer to a man for whatever you have said or seemed to say, and whatever may lie behind, that is simple enough; but to explain your injurious thoughts to a woman, who does not even soften the situation by saying that she has no one to protect her—that is a different matter. He grew red, and then grew grey. He had no more notion what to answer to her than he had what it was, actually and as a matter of fact, that he had suspected. He had not suspected anything. He had felt that a woman like this could never have accepted the position of dependence, unless—That such a person must be a dangerous and hostile force—that she had wrongs to redress, a position to make—how could he tell? It had been instinctive, he had never known what he thought.

"Cousin Meg—" he said, hesitating.

"From the moment," she said indignantly, "in which you set me up as a schemer and designing person in the home that sheltered me, these terms of relationship have been worse than out of place."

Poor Colonel Piercey! He was as far from being a coward as a man could be. If he did not write V.C. after his name, it was, perhaps, because the opportunity had not come to him of acquiring that distinction; he was the kind of man of which V.C.'s are made. But now, no expedient, save that of utter cowardice, occurred to him; for the first time in his life he ran away.

"I am very sorry you will not accord me these terms," he said, meekly; "I don't understand what you accuse me of. I think you a schemer and designing person! how could I? If you will excuse me, there is no sense in such a suggestion. Unless I had been a fool—and I hope, at least, that you don't consider me a fool—how could I have thought anything of the kind? You must think me either mad or an idiot," he went on, gaining a little courage. "I came here with no suspicions. I have been angry," he added, turning his head away, "to see my cousin, Meg Piercey, at everybody's beck and call, and to see how careless they were of you, and how exacting, and how—"

"All this," said Margaret, with surprise, "should have made you look upon me with compassion instead of something like insult."

"Oh, compassion," he cried, "to you! I should have thought that the worst insult of all. You are not a person to be pitied. However I may have offended, I have always felt that—"

The end of this statement was part of the process of running away. Indeed, he was very much frightened, and felt the falseness of his position extremely. He had not a word to say for himself. To upbraid her—at a moment when her home, her last shelter, was probably about to be taken from her, and herself thrown upon the world with her helpless child—he, perhaps, being the only person who had any right to help her—was the most impossible thing in the world. And though his opinion had no time or occasion to have changed, it had always been an opinion founded upon nothing. A more curious state of mind could scarcely be. He was dislodged from his position at the point of Margaret's sword, so to speak. And he had never had any ground for that position, or right to have assumed it; and yet he was still there in mind, though in word and profession he had run away. Margaret did not understand this complicated state of mind. She was half amused by the dismay in his face, by his too swift and complete change of front. The amende which he had made was as complete as any apology and confession could be, though it was an apology by implication, rather than a direct denial of blame. "How could I?" is different from "I did not." But she did not dwell upon this.

"Of course," she said, "I have no right not to accept what you say, though it is, perhaps, strangely expressed. And I scarcely know what there is I can explain to you. My aunt feared this that has taken place, before I did: she naturally thought less of her son's deficiencies. She was so imprudent, as I thought it, as to warn the girl of things she would do to prevent it. I believe there was really nothing that could have been done to prevent it. And then she was equally imprudent in letting him go to town, and thus giving him the opportunity. She thought she could secure him by putting him in the hands of the clergyman, who never saw him at all. I feared very much how it would be, and poor Gervase was several times on the point of betraying himself. Perhaps, if I had sought his confidence—But his mother would not have paid any attention to what I could say. And I don't know what could have been done to prevent it."

"Why, he is next to an idiot!"

"Oh no," cried Margaret, half offended. "Gervase is not an idiot. He has gleams of understanding, quite—almost, as clear as any one. He knows what he wants, and though you may think his mind has no steadiness, you will find he always comes back to his point. He has a kind of cleverness, even, at times. Oh no; Aunt Piercey examined into all that. They could not make him out incapable of managing his own affairs. To be sure, he has not had any to manage up to this time. And now that he has this sharp Patty behind him," said Margaret, with a half smile—

"Then you think nothing can be done?"

"What could be done? You could not do anything in Uncle Giles' lifetime to turn his only child out of his inheritance."

"It is you," said Colonel Piercey, "who are imputing intentions now. I had no such idea. I think my business as next-of-kin is to defend the poor fellow. But the woman; that is a different thing."

"The woman is his wife. I don't want to assume any unnatural impartiality. But, after all, is he likely ever to have had a better wife? I believe she will be an excellent wife to Gervase. One of his own class, I hope, would not have married him."

"Why do you say, 'I hope?' Is that not worse than anything that could be said?"

"Perhaps," said Margaret. "Poor Gervase is not an idiot, but neither is he just like other people. And a girl might have been driven into it, and then might have found—" She added, with a little shiver, "It is the best thing that could have happened for him to marry Patty. I hate it, of course. How could I do otherwise? But as far as he himself is concerned—"

"You are a great philosopher, Cousin Meg."

"Do you think so?" Half resentful as she was, and not more than half satisfied with Colonel Piercey's explanations, he was yet the only person in the world to whom she could speak with freedom; and it was a relief to her. "She will look after Uncle Giles' comfort, and he will get to like her," she continued. "She will rule the household with a rod of iron." Margaret laughed, though her face settled down the next moment into a settled gravity. "They will have no society, but they will not want it. She will keep them amused. Perhaps it is the best thing that could have happened," she said.

"And you? and the boy?" He stopped and looked at her standing among the roses, which were very luxuriant in the last climax of maturity, full blown, shedding their leaves, just about to topple over from that height of life into the beginning of decay. Margaret had no trace of decay about her, but she, too, was in the full height of life, the fulfilment of promise, standing at the mezzo di cammin, and full of all capabilities. She did not look up at him, but answered with a half-smile,—

"I—and the boy? We are not destitute. Perhaps it will be better for us both to set out together, and live our own life."

"You are not destitute? I hope you will pardon me. After what you think my conduct has been, you may say I have no right—"

Margaret smiled in spite of herself.

"But you say that your conduct has been—not what I thought."

"Yes, yes, that is so: I have not been such a fool. Cousin Meg, we were great friends in the old days."

"Not such very great friends—no more than girls and boys are when they are not specially attached to each other."

He thought that she intended to give him a little prick with one of those thorns which the matured rose still keeps upon its stalk; and he felt the prick, which, being still more mature than she, he ought not to have done.

"I think it was a little more than that," he said, in a slight tone of pique; "but anyhow—we are cousins."

"Very distant cousins."

"Distant cousins," he cried, impatiently, "are near when there are no nearer between. We are of the same blood, at least. You want to push me away, to make me feel I have nothing to do with it; but that can't be so long as you are Meg Piercey—"

"Margaret Osborne at your service," she said, gravely. "Forgive me, Cousin Gerald. It is true, we have had enough of this tilting. I don't doubt for a moment that you would give me a helping hand if you could; that you wish me well, and especially," she added, lifting her eyes with a half reproach, half gratitude in them, "the boy—as you call him."

"What could I call him but the boy?" said Colonel Piercey, with a sort of exasperation. "Yes, I don't deny it, it was of him I wanted to speak. He is a delightful boy—he is full of faculty and capacity, and one could make anything of him. Let me say quite sincerely what I think. You are not destitute; but you are not rich enough to give him the best of everything in the way of education, as—as—don't slay me with a flash of lightning—as I could. Now I have said it! If you would trust him to me!"

She had looked, indeed, for a moment as if her eyes could give forth lightning enough to have slain any man standing defenceless before her; but then these eyes softened with hot tears. She kept looking at the man, explaining himself with such difficulty, putting forth his offer of kindness as if it were some dreadful proposition, with a gradual melting of the lines in her face. When he threw a hasty glance at her at the end of his speech, she seemed to him a woman made of fire, shedding light about her in an astonishing transfiguration such as he had never seen before.

"This," she said, in a low voice, "is the most terrible demonstration of my poverty and helplessness that has ever been made to me—and the most awful suggestion, as of suicide and destruction."

"Meg!"

"Don't, don't interrupt me! It is: I have never known how little good I was before. I don't know now if it will kill me, or sting me to life; but all the same," she cried, her lip quivering, "you are kind, and I thank you with all my heart! and I will promise you this: If I find, as you think, that, whatever I may do, I cannot give my Osy the education he ought to have, I will send and remind you of your offer. I hope you will have children of your own by that time, and perhaps you will have forgotten it."

"I shall not forget it; and I am very unlikely to have children of my own."

"Anyhow, I will trust you," she said, "and I thank you with all my heart, though you are my enemy. And that is a bargain," she said, holding out her hand.

Her enemy! Was he her enemy? And yet it seemed something else beside.

CHAPTER XXVII

While these scenes were going on, Mr. and Mrs. Gervase Piercey were very differently employed upstairs. When Patty had finished her tea, and when she had made the survey of the library, concerning which her conclusion was that these horrid bookcases must be cleared away, and that a full-length portrait of herself in the white satin which had not, yet ought to have been, her wedding-dress, would do a great deal for the cheerfulness of the room, she took her husband's arm, and desired him to conduct her over the house. When Patty saw the drawing-room, which was very large, cold, and light in colour, with chairs and chandeliers in brown holland, she changed her mind about the library. She had not been aware of the existence of this drawing-room.

"This is where we shall sit, of course," she said.

"Father can't abide it," said Gervase.

"Oh, your father is a very nice old gentleman. He will have to put up with it," said the new lady of the house.

In imagination she saw herself seated there, receiving the county, and the spirit of Patty was uplifted. She felt, for the first time, without any admixture of disappointment, that here was her sphere. When she was taken upstairs, however, to Gervase's room, she regarded it by no means with the same satisfaction. It was a large room, but sparsely furnished, in no respect like the luxurious bower she had imagined for herself.

"Take off my bonnet here!" she said: "no, indeed I sha'n't. Why, there is not even a drapery to the toilet table. I have not come to Greyshott, I hope, to have less comfort than I had at home. There must be spare rooms. Take me to the best of the spare rooms."

"There's the prince's room," said Gervase, "but nobody sleeps there since some fellow of a prince—I can't tell you what prince—And I haven't got the keys; it's Parsons that has got the keys."

"You can call Parsons, I suppose. Ring the bell," said Patty, seizing the opportunity to look at herself in the glass, though she surveyed the room with contempt.

"Lord!" cried Gervase. "Parsons, mother's own woman—." Then he threw himself down in his favourite chair with his hands in his pockets. "You can do it yourself. I'm not going to catch a scolding for you."

"A scolding!" said Patty; "and who is going to scold you, you silly fellow, except me? I should like to see them try—Mrs. Parsons or Sir Giles, or any one. You can just say, 'Speak to my wife.'"

"There's mother, that you daren't set up your face to. I say," said Gervase; "Patty, what's all this about mother? Mother's—dead? She'll never have a word to say about anything any more?"

"Dear mother!" said Patty. "You must always say dear mother, Gervase, now: I'm sure I should have loved her—but, you see, Providence never gave me the opportunity. No, she'll never have a word to say: it's me that will have everything to say.—Oh, you have answered the bell at last! Send Mrs. Parsons here."

"Mrs. Parsons, ma'am—my lady?" the frightened little under-housemaid, who had been made to answer, said.

Patty gave her a gracious smile, feeling that at last she had found some one who understood what her claims were.

"What's your name?" she said.

"Ellen."

"Well, Ellen, I like your looks, and I've no doubt we shall get on; but you needn't call me my lady, not now,—for the present I am only Mrs. Gervase. Now, go and send Parsons here."

"Oh, my lady, Mrs. Parsons! she's in my old lady's room. I daren't disturb her, not for anything in the world; it would be as much as my place was worth."

"I see you are only a little fool after all," said Patty, with a frown. "Your place is just worth this much—whether you please me or not. Mrs. Parsons has as much power as—as that table. Goodness," cried Patty, "what a state this house has been in, to be sure, when one servant is afraid of another! but I shall soon put an end to that. Call Parsons! let her come at once."

The little housemaid came back while Patty still stood before the glass straightening the edge of her bonnet and arranging her veil.

"If you please, my lady, Mrs. Parsons is doing out my old lady's drawers—and she has her head bent down, and I can't make her hear."

"I'll make her hear," cried Patty, with an impulse which belonged rather to her previous condition than to her present dignity; and she rushed along the corridor like a whirlwind, with her draperies flying. It was, doubtless, instinct or inspiration that directed her to the right door, while Gervase followed on her steps to see the fun, with a grin upon his face. He remembered only now and then, when something recalled it to him, that his mother was gone. He was not thinking of her now; nevertheless, when Patty burst into that room, he stood in the doorway dumb, the grin dying out from his face, and gave a scared look round as if looking for the familiar presence he had so often encountered there.

"You perhaps have not heard, Mrs. Parsons," said Patty, with her sharp, decisive voice, "that I sent for you?"

Parsons had her head bent over the drawers. She said, without turning round, "That gaby, Ellen, said something about somebody wanting me"; and then began to count,—"Eight, nine, ten. Three dozen here and three dozen in the walnut wardrobe," said Parsons; "that makes it just right."

Patty's curiosity overcame her resentment. She came forward and looked over Parsons' shoulder. "Six dozen silk stockings," she cried; "is that what you are counting? What a number for an old lady! and fine, too, and in good condition," she said, putting her hand over the woman's shoulder and bringing forth a handful. They were mingled white and black, and Patty looked upon them with covetous eyes.

"Who are you as takes such a liberty?" cried Parsons, springing to her feet. She found herself confronted by Patty's very alert, firm figure and resolute countenance. Patty drew Lady Piercey's silk stockings through her hands, looking at the size of them. She held them up by the toes to mark her sense of their enormous dimensions.

"I could put both my feet into one of them," she said, reflectively, "so that they are no use to me. Oh, you are Parsons! Open the door, please, at once, of the best rooms. I want to settle down."

The woman looked at the intruder with a mixture of defiance and fear. She turned to Gervase, appealing against the stranger. Many a time had Parsons put the Softy out of his mother's room, bidding him be off and not aggravate my lady. But my lady was gone, and Gervase was the master, to do what he would; or, what was worse, it was Patty who was the mistress. Patty of the ale-house! Parsons looked at Gervase with an agonised appeal. "They're your mother's things," she said; "Mr. Gervase, will you see them knock about your mother's things?"

Patty's eyes were in the drawer remarking everything, and those eyes sparkled and shone. What treasures were there! Not only silk stockings too big for her, but linen, and lace, and embroidered handkerchiefs, and silks, such as Patty had never seen before. She went to the drawers and closed them one after another.

"I see there are some nice things here," she said. "We can't have them turned over like this by a servant. Some servants expect their mistress's things as their perquisites, but we can't allow that in this house. Lock them up, lock them up at once, and I'll take the keys."

"The keys—my keys!" cried Parsons almost beside herself.

"The late Lady Piercey's keys. I'll take them, please, all of them. There's a time for everything; and to go over my mother-in-law's things the very day of her funeral is indecent—that is what it is, indecent; I can find no other word."

"I'll never give up my keys!" cried Parsons, "that my dear lady trusted me with—never, never!" And then she burst into tears, and flung them down on the floor at Gervase's feet. "Take them all, then! all!" she cried; "I'll not keep one of them! Oh, my dear old lady, what a good thing she has not lived to see this day! But it never would have happened had she been here. You never, never would have dared to lift up your little impudent face.—Oh, Mr. Gervase! oh, Mr. Gervase, save me from her! She'll tear me to pieces!" Parsons cried. No doubt Patty's look was fierce. The woman seized hold upon Gervase and swung herself out by him, keeping his limp person between her and his wife. "Don't let her!" she cried, "don't let her! in your own mother's room."

"Mrs. Parsons," said Patty, over Gervase's body as it were, "do you think I would soil my fingers by touching you? You thought you would rob the poor lady that's dead, and that nobody would notice; but you did not know that I was here. Instead of rummaging Lady Piercey's drawers, you had better empty your own, and get ready for leaving. Have all your accounts ready and your keys ready; you shall leave this house by twelve to-morrow," Patty cried.

"Mr. Gervase, Mr. Gervase!" cried the unfortunate woman.

"I say, don't you go and touch me, Parsons. I don't mind your talking, but you sha'n't go and finger me as if I was clothes from the wash," said Gervase. He laughed at his own joke with enjoyment. "As if I was a basket of clothes from the wash," he said.

"Shut the door upon her, Gervase. I don't condescend to bandy words.—At twelve to-morrow," Patty said.

Parsons went downstairs mad with fury, and was told the tale of the tea, and how John Simpson had got his dismissal, and was never to appear before that upstart more. "We had better all give warning afore she comes to the rest of us," said cook. But it was a good place, with many perquisites, and as she spoke she exchanged with the butler a look of some anxiety. Perhaps they did not wish to present their accounts at a moment's notice. Perhaps they only thought regretfully of their good place. Parsons had carried things with a high hand over the younger servants for years. She had not always even respected the susceptibilities of cook. She had been her mistress's favourite and companion, doing, they all thought, very much what she liked with the internal economy of the house. No one had ventured to contradict, or even oppose, Lady Piercey's factotum. It was not in human nature not to be pleased, more or less, that she had found some one to repay to her in a certain degree the little tyrannies of the past. "What would Mr. Dunning say?" was what everybody asked.

The house was, however, in great agitation as the hour of dinner approached, and the drama of the family was about to be exposed to the searching observation of that keen audience which waits at table, and which had all its faculties sharpened for this, its chief moment of spectatorship. To have this mode and period of watching the crisis of life in other human creatures, must be a great dédommagement for any ills that may pertain to domestic service in these days. It is as good as a play, nay, better, seeing that there is no simulation in the history that is worked out under our servants' eyes. It was exciting to think, even, how many places should be laid at table; whether Patty, whose new dignity had not been formally announced to any one, and, who, for anything they knew, might shrink from appearing in the midst of the family, unsupported—might not withdraw from the ordeal of the common meal, or be too much overcome with grief to come downstairs. Patty's mind was greatly exercised on the same subject. She had chosen from among the unoccupied rooms those which pleased her best, which were not, however, the prince's rooms, but a suite adjoining which took her fancy, the size and the fittings of which, however, suggested innumerable new ideas to a mind open and eager to receive every indication of what was suitable to her new state. For one thing, they were lined with prodigious wardrobes: miles, Patty said to herself with awe, of old dark, gleaming, mahogany doors, behind which were pegs and shelves innumerable, to contain the dresses of the inhabitant. Patty could count hers—and only two, or at most, three of these were fit for the use of Mrs. Gervase Piercey—on one hand; and the long range of empty space at once depressed and excited her—a vacancy that must be filled. In like manner, the large dressing-table had drawers for jewellery, of which Patty had none. And in this great space, where her little figure was visible in glimpses in two or three tall mirrors, there was such evident need of a maid, that her alert spirit was overawed by the necessity. Then she had nothing that was needful for the toilet: no shoes, not even a fresh handkerchief to dry those tears, which were ready to come at the mention of her dear mother-in-law's name. The temptation to return to that dear mother-in-law's room, and equip herself with those articles which lay there in such abundance, and which certainly, it would harm no one to make use of, was very strong. But Patty was half-afraid, half-conscious, that on this evening, at least, it would be unwise so to compromise herself. It was not an evening, she reflected, for full dress, and her mourning would be an excuse for everything. What a wise inspiration that had been, to cover her old dress with crape! Patty undid a hook or two, and folded in the corners of her bodice at the neck. It showed the whiteness of that throat, and gave an indication that she knew what was required in polite society. And she drew on again with some difficulty, over hands which were not quite so presentable, the black gloves, which had not borne the strain of the morning, the heat, and the affliction, so well as might have been desired. Before doing this, however, she had written, by a sudden inspiration, a note to Sally Fletcher, requesting her to come to Greyshott at once with Mrs. Gervase Piercey's "things," and to remain as her maid till further orders. And then she took her husband's arm, and went solemnly downstairs.

Colonel Piercey was lingering in the hall, much at a loss what to do. Margaret had not yet appeared. The butler stood at the door of the dining-room, with Robert, not John Simpson, at his side. Patty knew that it was correct and proper for the party to assemble first in the drawing-room, but she waived that ceremony for to-night. She came downstairs very audibly, describing to Gervase what she intended to do.

"I can't bear the gloomy library," she said. "I don't mean to sit in it. We must have the real drawing-room made fit to live in. But all that will want a little time, and, of course, your dear papa must be consulted. I would not for the world interfere with his little ways."

"Where's father? ain't he coming to dinner?" said Gervase, breaking into this speech, which the audience for which it was intended had already heard, noted, and inwardly digested.

"No, Mr. Gervase. Mr. Dunning things as Sir Giles 'as 'ad enough excitement for to-day."

"Well," said Patty, "I don't think much of Dunning after his neglect, but he's right in that. I should have said so myself had it been referred to me. Early to bed and kept quite quiet—that is the only thing for your poor dear papa. Are we waiting for any one?" she said, looking round with majesty. J'ai failli attendre. Patty had never heard these words, but they were written on her face.

There was silence in the hall. Colonel Piercey had turned round from the engraving which he had been examining with quite unnecessary minuteness; but as he did not know either of the strange couple who by a sudden transformation had become his hosts, it was not possible that he could give any explanations; and the butler, who had not the training of a master of the ceremonies, and who had begun to shake in his shoes before that personage who, in her day, had drawn beer for him at the Seven Thorns—who had dismissed the great Parsons, and accused the greater Dunning of neglect—remained dumb, shifting from one foot to another, looking helplessly in front of him. He ventured at last to say, with trepidation, that "Mrs. Osborne, if you please, is just coming downstairs."

"Oh, Mrs. Osborne!" said Patty, and swept into the room. She stood looking for a moment at the expanse of the table laid with five places—one of them unnecessary. "I suppose I had better take my own proper place at once without ceremony," she said, with an airy gesture, half to Colonel Piercey, half to the butler. "And, Gervase, as your father isn't here, you had better sit in his place. We must make another arrangement when Sir Giles is able to come to table. Oh, Margaret Osborne! Is that where she sits? And here she is! I don't say anything, for we are a little unpunctual ourselves to-night. But I must warn you all that I am generally exact to the minute, and I never wait for anybody," Patty said.

CHAPTER XXVIII

It may easily be supposed that there was not much conversation at the table thus surrounded. Colonel Piercey and Margaret Osborne sat opposite to each other, but concealed from each other by the huge bouquet of flowers which occupied the central place; and neither of them, in the shock and strangeness of the occasion, found a word to say. They were both paralysed, so to speak, by the unimaginable circumstances in which they found themselves, overwhelmed with an amazement which grew as the meal went on. Gervase, in his father's seat, ate voraciously, and laughed a good deal, but said little. Patty was mistress of the occasion. One glance of keen observation had shown her that Mrs. Osborne's dress was not even open at the throat; it was not covered with crape. It was the simplest of black gowns, with no special sign of "deep" mourning, such as on the evening of a funeral ought to have been indispensable. If Patty had ever entertained any doubt of herself it now vanished. It was she who was fulfilling all the duties necessary. The others were but outsiders. She had secured triumphantly her proper seat and sphere.

"It is unfortunate for us, Gervase," she said, "to come home on such a sad day; and to think we knew nothing of all the dreadful things that were going on till we learned it all with a shock when we arrived! It is true, we were moving about on our wedding-tour; but still, if the house hadn't been filled with those as—that—didn't wish us well, we might have been called back; and you, dear, might have had the mournful satisfaction—"

"You always said, Patty," said Gervase, "that you would stay a week away."

"And to think of my poor dear mother-in-law looking for us, holding out her poor arms to us—and us knowing nothing," said Patty, drying her eyes—"as if there were no telegraphs nor railways! Which makes it very sad for us to come home now; but I hope your dear father, Gervase, if he's rightly watched and done for, won't be any the worse. Oh, I hope not! it would be too sad. That Dunning, who has been thought so much of, does not seem to me at all fit for his place. To think of him to-day, such an agitating day, with nothing to give his master! I shall take the liberty of superintending Mr. Dunning in future," Patty said.

Gerald Piercey and Margaret Osborne ate what was set before them humbly, without raising their eyes. They were ridiculously silenced and reduced to subjection; even if they could have encouraged each other with a glance it would have been something, but they had not even that alleviation. What to say! They were ignored as completely as if they had been two naughty children. Gervase, more naughty still, but in favour, took advantage by behaving himself as badly as possible. He made signs to the butler to pour him out wine with a liberal hand, and gobbled his food in great mouthfuls. "I say, Meg," he whispered, putting his hand before his mouth, "don't tell! she can't see me!" while his wife's monologue ran on; and then he interrupted it with one of those boisterous laughs by which the Softy was known.

"What is it?" Patty cried sharply from the head of the table.

"Meg knows—Meg and me knows," cried Gervase from the other end.

"I must request," said Patty, "Margaret Osborne, that you will not make my husband forget, with your jokes, what day it is. You mayn't think it, perhaps, for my poor dear mother-in-law was not very kind to me—but I feel it to be a very solemn day. And you may be very witty and very clever, though you don't show it to me—but I won't have laughing and nonsense at my table on poor dear Lady Piercey's funeral day."

What was Margaret to do? She could not defend herself from so grotesque an accusation. She looked up with some quick words on her lips, but did not say them. It was intolerable, but it was at the same time ludicrous; a ridiculous jest, and yet the most horribly, absurdly serious catastrophe in the world.

"The laughing seems all on your husband's side," said Colonel Piercey, unable to refrain.

"Oh!" said Patty, fixing upon him a broad stare: and then she, too, permitted herself a little laugh. "It's the strangest thing," she said, "and I can't help seeing it's ridiculous—though laughing is not in my mind, however it may be in other people's, on such a day—here's a gentleman sitting at my table, and everybody knows him but me."

"I don't know him," cried Gervase, "not from Adam; unless it's Gerald Piercey, the soldier fellow that mother was so full of before I went off to get married: though nobody knew I was going to get married," he said, with a chuckle, "except little Osy, that gave me—I say, where's little Osy, Meg?"

"I hope," said Patty severely, "that children are not in the habit of being brought down here after dinner as they are in some places. It's such bad style, and, I'm thankful to say, it's going out of fashion. It's a thing as I could not put up with here."

"Send some one upstairs," said Margaret, in a low voice to the footman who was standing by her, "to say that Master Osy is not to come down."

"What are you saying to the servant? I don't want to be disagreeable," said Patty, "but I object to a servant being sent away from his business. Oh, if the child comes usually, let him come, but it must be for the last time."

"If I may go myself," said Margaret, half rising, "that will be the most expeditious way."

"Not before you have finished your dinner," cried Patty; "oh, don't, pray. I should be quite distressed if you didn't have your dinner. And you had no tea. I know some ladies have trays sent upstairs. But I can't tolerate such a habit as having trays upstairs: so for goodness' sake, Margaret Osborne, sit still and finish your dinner here."

Colonel Piercey moved his chair a little; he managed to look beyond the bouquet at Margaret, sitting flushed and indignant, yet incapable of completing the absurdity of the situation by a scene at table before the servants. Colonel Piercey had run through all the gamut of astonishment, anger, and confusion; he had arrived at pure amusement now. The momentary interchange of glances made the situation possible, and it was immediately and unexpectedly ameliorated by the melodramatic appearance of Dunning behind in the half-darkness at the door.

"Mr. Gervase, if you please, Sir Giles is calling for you," the man said.

Patty sprang up from her seat. "Sir Giles? the dear old gentleman! Oh, I foresaw this! He is ill, he is ill! Come, Gervase!" she cried.

"Not a bit," said Gervase; "it's only Dunning's way. He likes to stop you in the middle of your dinner. There's nothing the matter with the governor, Dunning, eh?"

"There's just this, that he's a-calling for Mr. Gervase, and not no other person," Dunning said, with slow precision.

"Well, I'm Mrs. Gervase; I'm the same as Mr. Gervase. Come, come, don't let's lose a moment! Moments are precious!" cried Patty, rushing to her husband and snatching him out of his chair, "in his state of health and at his age."

Margaret and the Colonel were left alone, but the fear of the servants was upon them. They did not venture to say anything to each other. They were helped solemnly to the dish which had begun to go round, and for a moment sat in silence like two mutes, with the inexorable bouquet between them. Then Colonel Piercey said, in very bad French, "This is worse than I feared. What are we to do?"

"I shall go to my room to Osy before she comes back."

"I have no Osy to go to," he said with a short laugh. "What a strange scene! stranger than any in a book. I am glad to have seen it once in a way."

"Not glad, I hope," said Margaret. "Sorry for Uncle Giles and all the rest. But she is not so bad as that. No, no, she is not. You don't see—she wants to assert all her rights, to show you and me how strong she is, and how she scorns us. On ordinary occasions she is not like this."

"You are either absurdly charitable in your thoughts, or else you want to throw dust in my eyes, Cousin Meg."

"Nothing of the kind; I do neither. It is quite true. She is not bad in character at all. She will be kind to Uncle Giles, and probably improve his condition. We have all had a blind confidence in Dunning, and perhaps he doesn't deserve it. She wants to get Uncle Giles into her own hands, and she will do so. But he will not suffer; I am sure of it."

"Poor old gentleman! It is hard to be old, to be handed from one to another. And will he accept it?" Colonel Piercey said.

"She will be very nice and kind, and she is young and pretty."

"Oh, not—not that!"

"You are prejudiced, Cousin Gerald. She is pretty when you see her in her proper aspect, and there can be no doubt she is young. Her voice is nice and soft. It is almost like a lady's voice. Hush! I think I hear her coming back!" Margaret rose hurriedly. "Please say to Mrs. Piercey, Robert, that I am tired, and have gone to my room."

"Let me come too," said Gerald Piercey, following her into the hall. "I shall go away to-morrow, of course—and you, what are you going to do?"

"I cannot go to-morrow. I shall have to wait—until I am turned out, or till I can go."

"I wish you would come with me to my father's, where you would be most welcome: and he is a nearer relative than I am."

"Thank you; you go too far," said Margaret. "To think me a scheming woman only this morning, and at night to offer me a new home, where I might scheme and plot at my leisure? No, I will do that no more: I will go to nobody. We are not destitute."

"Meg! will you remember that you have nobody nearer to you than my father and me?"

"But I have," she said, "on my mother's side, and on my husband's side. We shall find relations wherever we go."

He answered by an impatient exclamation. "There is one thing, at least, on which we made a bargain a few hours since," he said.

The lamp in the hall did not give a good light. It was one of the things which Patty changed in the first week of her residence at Greyshott. It threw a very faint illumination on Margaret Osborne's face. And she did not say anything to make her meaning clear. She did nothing but hold out her hand.

Patty, meanwhile, had made her way, pushing her husband before her, to Sir Giles' door. She pushed him inside with an earnest whisper. "Go in, and talk to him nicely. Be very nice to him, as nice as ever you can be. Mind, I'm listening to you, and presently I'll come in, too."

The room was closely shut up, though it was a warm night, and scarcely dark as yet, and Sir Giles sat in his chair with a tray upon the table beside him. But he had pushed away his soup. His large old face was excited and feverish, his hands performing a kind of tattoo upon his chair. "Are you there, my boy? are you there, Gervase?" he said. "Come in, come in and talk to me a little. I'm left all alone. I have nobody with me but servants. Where's—where's all the family? Your poor mother's gone, I know, and we'll never see her any more. But where's everybody? Where's—where's everybody?" the old gentleman said with his unsteady voice.

"I'm here, father, all right," Gervase said.

"Sir Giles, sir, he's fretting for company, and his game, and all that; but he ain't fit for it, Mr. Gervase, he ain't fit for it. He have gone through a deal to-day."

"I'll play your game, father. I'm here all right," Gervase repeated. "Come, get out the table, you old humbug, and we'll throw the men and the dice about. I'm ready, father; I'm always ready," he said.

"No, no," said Sir Giles, pushing the table away; "I don't want any game. I'm a sad, lonely old man, and I want somebody to talk to. Gervase, sit down there and talk to me. Where have you been all this long time, and your mother, your poor mother, wanting you? What have you been doing? You can go, Dunning; I don't want you now. I want to talk to my boy. Gervase, what have you been doing, and why didn't you come home?"

"I've been—getting married, father," said Gervase, grinning from ear to ear. "I would have told you, but she wouldn't let me tell you. She thought you might have put a stop to it. A fellow wants to be married, father, when he's my age."

"And who has married you?" said the father, going on beating with his tremulous fingers as though keeping time to some music. "Who has married you, my poor boy? It can't be any great match, but we couldn't expect any great match. I saw—a young woman: I thought she was—that I had somehow seen her before."

"Well, she's—why, she's just married to me, father. She's awful proud of her new name. She signed her letter—for I saw it—Mrs. Gervase Piercey, as if she hadn't got any other name."

"She shouldn't do that, though," said the old man, "she's Mrs. Piercey, being the son's wife, the next heir. If Gerald had a wife, now, she'd be Mrs. Gerald, but not yours. I'm afraid she can't know much about it. Gervase, your poor mother was struck very suddenly. She always feared you were going to do something like that, and she had somebody in her mind, but she was never able to tell me who it was. Gervase, I hope it is somebody decent you have married, now your poor mother isn't here."

"Oh, yes, father; awfully decent," said Gervase, with his great laugh. "She would have given it to any one that wasn't civil. She was one that kept you on and kept you off, and as clever as Old Boots himself, and up to—"

Patty had listened to this discussion till her patience was quite worn out. She had waited for a favourable moment to introduce herself, but she could not stand and hear this description, so far beneath her merits as she felt it to be. She came in with a little rush of her skirts, not disagreeable to the old man, who looked up vaguely expectant, to see her sweep round the corner of the large screen that shielded him from the draught. "I must come and tell you myself who I am, Sir Giles," she said. "I'm Patience; and though, perhaps, I shouldn't say it, I'm one that will take care of that, and take care of the house, and see that you are not put upon by your servants, nor made to wait for anything, but have whatever you wish. And I'll be a very good daughter to you, if you'll let me, Sir Giles," she said.

The old gentleman had passed a miserable week. First his wife's illness, so dreadful and beyond all human commiseration, and then her death, and the gloom of the house, and the excitement of the funeral, and the neglect of everything that made life bearable to him. It is true, that his soup and his wine and whatever food was allowed to him were supplied regularly, and no actual breach of his comforts had occurred. But his room had been darkened, and his backgammon had been stopped, and there had been no cheerful faces round him. Even little Osy's company had been taken away. The child had been stated to be "too much" for him. Parsons and Dunning had held him in their hands and administered him, and they were both determined that he should do and say nothing that was not appropriate to his bereaved condition. The old man was not insensible to his wife's death. It brought into his mind that sense of utter desolation, that chill sensation of an approaching end, which is, alas! not more palatable in many cases to an old man than to a young one. And Parsons and Dunning both thought it the most appropriate thing for him to sit alone and think of his latter end. But Sir Giles was not of that opinion. His old life was strong in him, though it was hampered with so many troubles. He wanted, rather, to forget that death was waiting for him, too, round the next corner. Who could tell how far off that next corner might be? He wanted to forget, not to be shut up helplessly with that thought alone. And Mrs. Osborne, with all the prejudices and bonds of the household upon her, had not had courage to break through the lines which had been formed around her uncle. She had believed, as it was the law of the family to believe, that Sir Giles' faithful attendant knew best. And thus it was, that when the young woman who was Gervase's wife came boldly in—a young person who was not afraid of Dunning, a stranger bringing a little novelty, a little stir of something unaccustomed into his life—he looked up with a kind of light in his dull eye, and relief in his mind. "Oh! you are Patience, are you?" he said. "Patience! it is a queer sort of a name, and I think I remember to have heard it before."

Oh, poor Miss Hewitt, in her red and yellow bonnet! If she had but known that this faint deposit of recollection was all that remained in her old lover's mind!

"But I should like you to call me Patty, Sir Giles." She went down on her knees at his feet, while the old gentleman looked on in wonder, not knowing what was going to happen. "You have not got that bandage quite straight," she said, "and I'm sure you're not so comfortable as you ought to be. I can put it on better than that. Look you here, Gervase, hold the candle, and in a minute I'll settle it all right."

Sir Giles was so much taken by surprise that he made no opposition; and he was amused and pleased by her silent movements, her soft touch and manipulation. The novelty pleased him, and the young head bent over his suffering foot, the pretty hair, the pleasant shape, were all much more gratifying than Dunning. He thought he was relieved, whether he was really so or not. And he was contented, and the spell of the gloom was broken. "But I'm not to be settled so easy as my foot," he said. "How dared you to take and marry my boy here, Mrs. Patty, or whatever your name is, without saying a word to me?"

Mrs. Gervase Piercey, or Mrs. Piercey, as she henceforward called herself, walked that night into the great state-room in Greyshott—where Sally Fletcher awaited her, trembling, bringing Patty Hewitt's small wardrobe roughly packed in one small box—with the air of a conqueror, victorious along all the line.

CHAPTER XXIX

Colonel Piercey left Greyshott the next morning after these incidents. There was no reason why he should stay. Even old Sir Giles had changed his note when his kinsman took leave of him. Mental trouble does not keep its hold long on a mind which has grown weak with bodily disease and much nursing, that prevailing invalidism and necessity for taking care of one's self which absorbs every thought; and though the old gentleman was still ready enough to mourn for the loss of his life-long companion, yet he was easily soothed and diverted by the needs of that older companion still, himself. Besides, now that the funeral was over, there was no alarming prospect before him, no terror of being compelled to act for himself. He took leave of the Colonel not uncheerfully. "Going?" he said, when Gerald appeared in his room to say good-bye. "I'm glad you could stay so long; but it's been a sad visit. Another time, now there's young people in the house, they'll make it more cheerful for you, eh? Don't be long of coming again."

Colonel Piercey, somewhat stiffly—which was his nature, for he had not the understanding of human weakness which brings indulgence, and he could not forget that a few days before the old man had begged him with tears to stay—answered that he was glad to leave his uncle so much better and more satisfied about his son.

"Oh," said Sir Giles, "about satisfied I don't know, I don't know; I can't tell you at this moment, Gerald. She speaks fair, but then she's on her promotion, don't you see? Anyhow, she's young, and perhaps she'll learn; and she's nice-looking—and speaks not so badly for a girl without education; not so badly, does she, Gerald? We'll do; oh, I think we'll do. She'll look after Gervase, and keep him off me. And that's a great thing, don't you see? Though when I think what his mother would have said—Lord bless me, I tremble when I think what his mother would have said. She never would have borne it. She would have turned the house upside down and made everybody miserable; which makes me feel that being as it had to be, it's perhaps better—better, Gerald, though it's a hard thing to say, that his mother went first, went without knowing. You will say she suspected; and I believe she did suspect; she was a penetrating woman; but suspecting's not so bad as knowing; and I'm—I'm almost glad, poor soul, that she's gone. She would never have put up with it. And now this one may make something of Gervase—who knows? It is a kind of anxiety off my mind. Time for your train?" the old gentleman added cheerfully. "Well, thank you for your visit, my boy; I've enjoyed it—and come again, come soon again."

Sir Giles was as much delighted to be free of his visitor as he had been to welcome him to Greyshott. And it was evident that he was conforming his mind to the new state of affairs. Gerald had meant to appeal to his kindness for Margaret, but he had not patience or self-command enough to say anything. He had no thought of the anxieties that dwelt in the old man's mind—the dreariness of his conclusion that it was better his old wife was gone: the forlorn endurance of a state of affairs which he had no power to prevent. A little more sympathy might have made Sir Giles' endurance take a tragic aspect, the last refuge of a sanguine and simple spirit trying to be content with the hope that something might still be made of his only child. But Gerald Piercey only thought with mingled contempt and pity of the facile mind, and the drivel of old age, things entirely beyond his sympathy or thoughts.

He had an interview of a more interesting kind with Margaret before he went away. "I wish you could leave as easily as I do," he said.

"So do I—but that would be impossible in any case. I have Osy to think of. I must not allow myself to be carried away by any sudden impulse—even if it were for nothing else, for my poor old uncle's sake. He is fond of Osy. It might chill his poor old clouded life still more to miss the child."

"Oh, Uncle Giles! I think you may make your mind easy on that point. It's age, I suppose, and illness. One thing is just as good as another to him."

"I am not quite of your opinion," she said.

"I think you are never quite of any one's opinion except your own," he retorted, quickly.

"Well, that's best for me, don't you think?" she replied, with something of the same flash of spirit, "seeing that I have, as people say, nobody to think of but myself."

"And the boy? Meg, you have promised me that you will think of what I said about the boy. He should want for nothing. He should have all the advantages education could give, if you would trust him to me—or to my father, if that would give you more confidence."

"It is not confidence that is wanting," she said.

"Then, what is it? It cannot be that you think I speak without warrant. My father will write to you. I will pledge myself to you—as if he were my very own. His future should be my care; his education, his outset in the world—"

Margaret stood looking at him for some time in silence, a faint smile about her lips, which began to quiver, the colour forsaking her cheeks. What she said was so perfectly irrelevant, so idiotic, to the straight-forward mind of the man who was offering her the most unquestionable advantage, and asking nothing but a direct answer—yes, or no—that he could almost have struck her in his impatience. He did metaphorically, with the severity of that flash in his eyes.

"And how there looked him in the face
An angel, beautiful and bright;
And how he knew it was a fiend,
That miserable knight."

—This was what Margaret said.

"What do you mean?" he cried; "is it I that am the fiend, offering the best I can think of?"

"Oh, the angel," said Margaret; "and is it my own heart that is the fiend, that makes the other picture? Oh, God help me! I don't know. My child is my life. But there are things better than life, and that might be given up. Yet, he is my duty, too, and not yours, Gerald. Prosperity and comfort, and your great warm-hearted, honourable kindness; or poverty and nature, and a poor mother—and love? Which would be the best for him? We cannot see a step before us; and the issues are of life and death."

"It is better not to exaggerate," he said, with an almost angry impatience. "There need be no cutting off. You should, of course, see the child when you liked, for his holidays and that sort of thing. There's no question of life or death, but of a man's career for the boy, under men's influence, or—I know, I know! You would teach him everything that is good, and put the best principles into him, and sacrifice yourself, and all that. In short, you would make a perfect woman of him, had Osy been a girl; but, as he is a boy—!"

"Don't you think you're a little sharp, Gerald," she cried, "bidding me cut out my heart and give it you, and showing me all the advantages!" She laughed, with her lips quivering, holding her hands clasped, fiercely determined, whatever she did, not to cry, which is a woman's weakness.

"Meg, you are a sensible woman: not a girl, to know no better."

This was his honest thought: a girl, young and tender, is to be spared, though her youth has the elasticity of a flower, and springs up again to-morrow; but the woman who has passed that chapter, whose first susceptibilities are over, is a different matter. He was honestly bewildered when Margaret left him hurriedly with a choked "Thank you. Good-bye. I shall write"; and thus broke off the conversation, leaving him there astonished in the hall, with his coat over his arm, and his travelling bag in his hand: for this was how they had held their last consultation, the library and dining-room being both full of Patty, whose presence seemed to occupy the whole house, and who now came forth, with all the airs of the mistress of the house, to take leave of her guest.

"Well, Colonel Piercey, so you are going? I hope it is not because of the circumstances, though, of course, with a death and a marriage both in the house, it isn't very suitable for strangers, is it? But I'm not one that would ever wish to be rude to my husband's friends. I'm told you were going, anyhow, and I hope that's the case. And I'm sure you must feel I'm very thoughtful," said Patty, with a little laugh, "never to disturb you in your tender good-byes! Oh, I can sympathise with that sort of thing! I told Gervase, 'Don't disturb those poor things; there isn't a place where they can have a word quiet before they part.' But I hope you'll soon come and fetch her, Colonel Piercey. You and her, you are not like Gervase and me: you haven't any time to lose."

"I have not the honour of understanding you, Mrs. Piercey," said the Colonel, very stiffly. "I must leave with you my farewells to my cousin Gervase."

"Oh, you needn't; he's here, he's coming—he wouldn't be so wanting as not to see you off himself, though you're only a third or fourth cousin, I hear. But as for not understanding me, Colonel Piercey, I hope you understand Meg Osborne, which is more to the purpose, and that you've named the day. Marriage is catching, I've always heard, and you ain't going to treat a relation badly, I hope, in my house. I'm sure, after all the philandering and talking in corners, and—"

"I wish you good-day, Mrs. Piercey," the Colonel said. He jumped into the dog-cart with an energy which even the quiet fat horse of Greyshott training could scarcely withstand, and, seizing the reins from the groom's hands, drove that comfortable animal down the avenue at a pace to which it was entirely unaccustomed. To describe the ferment of mind into which he was thrown by Patty's last words would be impossible. He heard the loud, vacant laugh of Gervase, and a cry of "Hi! Hallo! Where are you off to?" sounding after him, but took no notice. He was a man of considerable temper, as has not been concealed, and there could be no doubt that it would have afforded him considerable satisfaction to take Patty by the arms and shake her, had that been a possible way of expressing his sentiments. He was furious, first, he said to himself, at the insult to Meg; but it is doubtful whether this really was so much the cause of his indignation as he believed. The causes were complicated, but chiefly had reference to himself, who was more interesting to him at present than Meg or any one else in the world. That he should be accused of philandering and talking in corners, or of treating a woman "badly," even by the most vulgar voice in the world, had something so exasperatingly inappropriate and unlikely in it that he said to himself it was laughable. Laughable, and nothing else! Yet he did not laugh; he felt himself possessed by the most furious gravity instead—ready to kill anybody who should so much as smile. Philandering—and with a middle-aged woman! This, no doubt, gave it a double sting. It had never occurred to Colonel Piercey, though he was forty, to think of himself as on an elderly level, or to imagine any connection of his name with that of any woman who was not young and fair, and in the first chapter of life. I have always been of opinion that men and women about the same age, when that age has passed the boundaries of youth, are each other's natural enemies rather than friends. They have fully learned that they are on opposite sides. There is a natural hostility between them. If some chance has not made them friends, and inclined to forget or pardon the difference of their sides, they are instinctively in opposition. To marry each other is the last thing that would occur to them. Of course, I am considering natural tendencies only, and not those of the fortune-hunter of either sex, or persons in quest of an establishment. The man of forty seeks a young bride; the woman of that age, or near it, finds devotion in a young man. (I don't say seeks it—for all women feel this question of age to be fantastically important.) Gerald Piercey had reached the Greyshott station, and flung himself and his bags and wraps into a carriage, before he had begun to get over the sting of the suggestion that he had been philandering (Heavens, what a word!), and that not with a girl—an imputation which he might have smiled at and pardoned—but with a widow, a mother, a middle-aged woman! Indignity could not go further. The little barmaid, the wretched little tavern flirt who had seized possession of the home of the Pierceys, had caught him full in the centre of his shield.

It was not till long after, when that heat had died away, that he recurred to what he had at first tried to persuade himself was the occasion of his wrath—the insult to Meg. Poor Meg! whose growing old he had himself so deeply and absurdly resented, as if it had been her own fault—how would she fare, left in the power of that little demon? She could not go off at a moment's notice, as he could. She would have to wait, he remembered with a horrified realisation, perhaps for her quarter-day, for the payment of her pension, before she would be able to budge at all. And, then, where would she go?—a woman who had been accustomed to Greyshott, which, though it was not very luxurious or refined, was still, in its way, a great house. Where would she go, with her hundred or two hundred, or some such nominal sum, a year? And, perhaps, not money enough in the meantime even to pay her journey, even to carry her away! She was a hot-headed, self-willed, argumentative woman; determined in her own opinions, caring not a straw for other people's; refusing, in the most unaccountable way, an advantageous suggestion—a proposal that would have left her free, without encumbrance, to get as much comfort as possible for herself out of her very small income; an entirely impracticable, unmanageable woman! but yet—to think of that little barmaid flouting her, insulting her, was too much for the Colonel. His wrath rose again, not so hot, but full of indignation—a creature not worthy to tie her shoe! He seemed to see her standing there, against the dark panelling of the wall, in her black dress. And, somehow, it occurred to him all at once that the slim, tall figure did not present the usual signs which distinguish middle age. How old was

Meg Piercey, after all? A dozen years ago, when he had been at Greyshott last, she was a girl in her teens. Twelve years do not make a girl of nineteen middle-aged. She had married at four or five-and-twenty—not earlier; and Osy was seven or thereabouts. Gerald found himself unconsciously calculating like an old woman. If she had married at twenty-four, and if Osy were seven, that did not make her more than two-and-thirty at the outside. At thirty-two one is not middle-aged; the Colonel did not feel himself so at forty. To be sure, a woman is different; but even for a woman, though it may not be so romantic as eighteen, it is not a great age—thirty-two. And to be turned out of her home; and to be left with next to nothing to live on; and to be insulted by that vulgar little village girl; and to be set down, even by a man, a relation, one bound to make the best of her, as almost an old woman—at thirty-two! Poor Meg Piercey! Poor Margaret Osborne! The home of her childhood gone, and the protection of her married life gone. And her child! What was the difficulty about her child? Something more, perhaps, when one came to think of it, than merely being left without encumbrance, freed from responsibility! When one came to think of it, and to think how other women were, with their children about them, perhaps, after all, it meant more than that. Poor Meg! poor Meg!

CHAPTER XXX

Mrs. Osborne realised very fully all the weight of the trouble which had fallen upon her, but it is to be doubted whether she would have liked that compassionate apostrophe to "poor Meg!" any more than other things which had fallen from Gerald Piercey's lips; or, indeed, whether she felt herself so much to be pitied as he did. Nobody knows like ourselves how hard and how heavy our troubles are; and yet, at the same time, our own case is generally less miserable to us than it is to the benevolent onlooker. The moment it becomes our own case it somehow becomes natural, and finds alleviations, or, if not alleviations, circumstances which prove it to be no such extraordinary thing. We change our position according to our lot, and even in the self-consciousness of crime become immediately aware of a whole world of people who are as badly off, or perhaps worse, than we are, without the same explanations of their conduct which exist in our case. Margaret, seeing what had befallen her, and what was about to befall her, instinctively changed her own point of view, and felt, along with the necessity, a new rising of life and courage. The long consideration of what she was to do, though perhaps a painful and discouraging deliberation, yet roused all her faculties and occupied her mind. At thirty-two (since we have arrived through Gerald Piercey's calculations at something like her exact age), the thought of a new beginning can never be wholly painful. None of the possibilities of life are exhausted; the world is still before us where to choose. Nevertheless it was a confusing and not encouraging subject of thought. Margaret's education, such as it was, had been completed before any new views about the education of women were prevalent; indeed, it would not have mattered much whether these ideas had been prevalent or not, for certainly it never would have entered into the minds of Sir Giles or Lady Piercey to send their niece to Girton, or even to any humbler place preparatory to Girton. They gave Margaret as little education as was indispensable, entertained reluctantly a governess for her for some years, and had her taught to play the piano a little, and to draw a little, and to have an awkward, not speaking acquaintance with the French verbs, which was all they knew or thought of as needful. What could she do with that amount of knowledge, even now, when she had supplemented it with a great deal of reading, and much thinking of her own? Nothing. No school would have her as a teacher, no sensible parent would trust her, all unaware of the technique of teaching as she was, with the education of their children. And what was there else that a woman, a lady, with all her wits about her, and the use of all her faculties, could do? That was the dreadful question. Margaret did not fall back with indignation on the thought that its chief difficulty arose from the fact that she was a woman; for she knew enough of life to be aware that a man of her own class in the same position, trained to nothing in particular, would be almost as badly off. There were "appointments" to be had, she knew, for men certainly, for woman too, occasionally, but she was perfectly vague about them, what they were. And the idea of going out to an office daily, which was her sole conception, and on the whole a just one, of what an "appointment" might mean, filled Margaret with a bewildering sense of inappropriateness and impossibility. It would not be she who could fill any such place. It would be something different from herself, a shadow or outward appearance of her, impossible for herself to realise. Impossible—impossible! She knew nothing but how to read, to think, to discharge the duties of a mother to her child, to live as English ladies live, concerned with small domestic offices, keeping life more or less in harmony, giving orders to the servants, and smoothing over the tempests and troubles which arose from the imperfect execution of these orders—and looking after the poor. To do all these things is to be a not unimportant servant to the commonwealth. Life would go far more roughly, with less advantage on both sides, were it not for functionaries of this kind: but then their services are generally to be had for nothing, and are not worth money; besides—which makes the matter more difficult still—these services lose a great part of their real value when they are done, not for love but for money, in which case the house lady of nature changes her place altogether and goes over to another and far less pleasing kind.

These thoughts had passed through Margaret's mind vaguely, and without any pressure of an immediate emergency, many times already in the course of her speculations as to the future for Osy and for herself. She had often said to herself that she could not remain at Greyshott for ever; that the time must come when she would have to decide upon something; that the old couple who were her protectors could not live for ever; and that the house of Gervase, poor Gervase, however it might turn out, would probably be no home for her. She had gone over all those suggestions of what she could do to increase her small income, and to educate her child, with a ceaseless interest, but yet without any sharpness or urgency, as of a thing that might happen at any moment. And there was always a vague ground of probability behind—that either one or other of the old people, who were so fond of Osy, might leave him something to make his first steps easier, that they would not go out of the world without making some provision even for herself, who had served them like their own child, and knew no home but under their wing. There would be that, whatever it was, to make everything more possible. She had not calculated on it, and yet she had felt assured that some such thing would be. But now all those prospects had come to an end in a moment. Lady Piercey had left no will at all, and Sir Giles was no longer a free agent, or would not be so any longer. The prospect was cut off before her eyes, all that shadowy margin gone, nothing left but the bare certainty. Two hundred a year! There are very different ways of looking at two hundred pounds a year. It is not very long since the papers were full of letters demonstrating the impossibility of supporting life with honesty and gentility on seven hundred a year. The calculations looked so very convincing, that one rubbed one's bewildered eyes if one had been accustomed to believe (as I confess I had) that there was a great deal of pleasant spending for two young people in seven hundred a year. On the other hand, I have just read a novel, and a very clever novel, in which it is considered quite justifiable for a young man to marry and take upon him the charge of his wife's mother and sister on a hundred and fifty pounds a year. Clearly there is a very great difference between these estimates, and I think it very likely that the author of the latter is more practically instructed as to what she is speaking of than the gentleman who made the other calculations. Who shall decide upon the fact that lies between these two statements? I can only say that Margaret Osborne's conclusion was not to waste her time in efforts to get work which she probably could not do well, and which would be quite inappropriate to her, but to try what could be done upon her two hundred pounds a year. Ah! how many, many millions of people would be thankful to have two hundred a year! How many honest, good, well-conditioned families, "buirdly chiels and clever hizzies," have been brought up on the half of it! But yet there are differences which cannot be ignored. The working man has many advantages over the gentleman, with his host of artificial wants—but, alas! we cannot go back easily to the rule of nature. Margaret was not so utterly unprovided for as her cousin Gerald had remorsefully imagined. She was not destitute, as she said. She had laid a little money aside for this always-threatening emergency; and she had spoken to Sarah, Osy's maid, who, though reluctantly and on a very distant and far-off possibility, had declared it possible that she might undertake to do the work of a small house. "But, oh! I wouldn't, ma'am," Sarah had said, "not if I was you; you would miss Greyshott and the nice big rooms, and nothing to do but ring the bell." Margaret had laughed at this conception of life, and laughed now as she recalled it. But no doubt it was true. She was not very apt at ringing of bells, nor did she require much personal service—still it would not be without a regret, a sense of the difference—but that was of too little real importance to be thought of now.

Indeed, all these thoughts were as nothing to the other which Gerald Piercey, in his desire to help her, had flung into her mind like an arrow of fire. To carry Osy away to that cottage, to deprive him of all those "advantages" which, even at his age, a child can understand—Osy would know very well what that sacrifice meant when he had no pony to ride on, no great rooms to run about in, no obsequious court of flatterers ready to carry him on their shoulders, to give him drives and rides on nobler animals, to bring him dainties, and all kinds of indulgences. Osy had been the favourite of the house, as well as of old Sir Giles and my lady. He had been as free of the housekeeper's room as of the library. There was nobody who had not bowed down before him and sought to please him. The child, though he was only a child, would understand what it was to relinquish all these, to have a small cottage, a little garden, nothing outside of them, and only a mother within. At seven years old to have this brought home to him, was early, very early. He would not understand how it was. If he heard, even at that early age, that he might have had another pony, another household to conquer by his pretty ways, and all the usual indulgences and pleasant things, but for his mother, would Osy's childish affection bear that test? Would he like her better than his pony? And, oh! still deeper, more penetrating question, was she better than the pony, better than the larger upbringing, the position of one who is born to command, the freedom of life, the influence of men, the "every advantage" of which Gerald Piercey had spoken? Would she, a woman not very cheerful, and who must in future be very full of cares and calculations how to make both ends meet, would she be better for him than all that? She? What question could be more penetrating? "It would be better for the child." Would it be better for him? Sometimes it comes about that in the very midst of the happiness of life, with every sail full, and the sun shining, and the horizon clear, there comes a sudden catastrophe, and some young woman whose life has been that of the group of children at her knee, has suddenly to stop and stand by with dumb anguish, and see one and another taken away from her by kind friends, kindest friends! benefactors only to be blessed and praised! while all around her other friends congratulate her, bid her feel that she must not stand in the way of the children, of their real advantage! Is it to their real advantage? Is it better to be the children of kindness or the children of love? to be brought up in your own home or in another's? Oh, poor little mother; often you have to smile out of your broken heart and bear it! Margaret Osborne had but one thing in the world; but she would have done like the others, and smiled and endured even to be severed from that only possession, had she been sure. Who can be sure? She said to herself that love, and his own home, and the ties of nature were best. And then Gerald Piercey's words came back and stung her like fiery serpents: "A man's career, under men's influence, or—" Or what? A poor woman's influence, a woman who was herself a failure, whom nobody cared much for under the sun. Which—which would be the best for Osy? This is the kind of argument that tears the heart in two. It is full of anguish while it is going on: and after the decision is made, it lays up poignant and dreadful recollections. If I had not done that, but the other—if I had not sent away my child into the careless hands of strangers; or, on the other hand, if I had not been so confident of myself; if I could but have seen how much better for him would have been the man's influence, the man's career!

This was the war that Margaret was waging with herself while she had to meet the immediate troubles of the day. It was inconceivable how soon the great house was filled with Patty's presence, how soon it became hers, from roof to basement, how she pervaded it in all the rooms at once, so to speak, so that nothing was out of her sharp sight for more than two minutes. Mrs. Osborne had retired upstairs with her heart full when she left Colonel Piercey in the hall; but in the restlessness of a disturbed mind she came down again about an hour afterwards, partly to put a stop, for a time, to that endless argument, partly to write a letter which she had promised, to inform Lady Hartmore of what had happened, and partly, perhaps, out of that curiosity and painful inclination to hasten a catastrophe which comes to the mind in the storms of existence. It is true that she had made up her mind to leave Greyshott, but she could not do so as Gerald, a visitor, did, nor was she sure how she could best arrange her retirement with dignity and composure. She felt that there must be no semblance of a quarrel, nor would she make matters worse for Gervase's wife by allowing it to appear to the county that her first act had been to drive Gervase's cousin out of the house. She had decided to wait a little, to endure the new régime until she could quietly detach herself without any shock to her old uncle or commotion in the house. Yet it cannot be denied that Margaret's nerves were very much disturbed, and that she was conscious of Patty's entrance while she sat writing her letter, and felt her heart jump when that active, bustling little step became again and again audible. Margaret was seated with her back to the door, but the sound of this step, returning and returning, betrayed to her very clearly the impatience with which her presence was regarded. And her letter did not make much progress. She foresaw the coming attack, and she did not forestall it as she might have done by going away. At last a voice as sharp as the step broke the listening silence of the room.

"Margaret Osborne! how long are you going to be writing that letter? The housemaids are waiting, and I must have this room thoroughly done out. It wants it, I am sure! Oh, take your time! but if you will let me know about when you are likely to be done—"

"I can finish my letter upstairs, if it is necessary," Margaret said, turning round.

"Well, I think generally that is the best way. The library's generally supposed to be the gentlemen's room in a house. I mean to have the drawing-room put in order, and to use that, as it ought to be used. But not just this week, and poor mother so lately buried. I don't know what your feelings may be, but I can't sit in a dingy place like this," Patty said. "Oh, take your time," she added, with fine irony; "but if you could tell me within half an hour or so when you are likely to have done—"

"I will finish my letter in my own room."

"If I was you," said Patty, "I'd write them all there in future. New folks make new ways. I am very particular about my house. I like everything kept in its proper place—and every person," she added significantly. "The servants can't serve two masters. That is in the Bible, you know, so it must be true."

"I do not think," said Margaret, with a faint smile, "that you will be troubled by their devotion to me."

"No; I suppose you have let yourself be put upon," said Patty; "because, though you think yourself one of the family, you ain't exactly one of the family, and, of course, they see that. It's not good for a houseful of servants to have a sort of a lady, neither one thing nor another, neither a mistress nor a servant, in the house. It teaches them to be disrespectful to their betters, because they know you can't do anything to them. I would rather pension poor relations off than have them about the house putting everything out."

"It will not be necessary in my case," cried Margaret, with a sudden flame of anger and shame enveloping her all over. "I had fully intended to leave Greyshott, but wished to avoid any appearance of—any shock to my uncle."

"Oh, take your time!" cried Patty, with a toss of her head; and she called to the housemaids, who appeared timorous and undecided at the door. "Come here, and I'll show how I wish you to settle all this in future," she said. "Oh, Mrs. Osborne's going! You needn't mind for her."

CHAPTER XXXI

It was not worth while to be angry. She had known, of course, all along, how it must be. There had been no thought in her mind of resistance, of remaining in Greyshott as Patty's companion, of appealing to her uncle against the new mistress of the house. It had not been a very happy home for Margaret at any time; though, while Lady Piercey lived, it was a sure one, as well as habitual,—the only place that seemed natural to her, and to which she belonged. Perhaps, she said to herself, as she went hurriedly upstairs, with that sense of the intolerable which a little insult brings almost more keenly than a great sorrow, it was better that the knot should thus be cut for her by an alert and decisive hand, and no uncertainty left on the subject. She went into her room quickly, with a "wind in her going," a sweep of her skirts, an action and movement about her which was unlike her usual composure. Sarah was alone in her room, not seated quietly at work as was her wont, but standing at the window looking out upon some scene below. There was a corner of the stable yard visible from one window of Margaret's rooms, which were far from being the best rooms in the house.

"Where is Master Osy?" Mrs. Osborne said.

"He is with Sir Giles, ma'am. I—I was just taking a glance from the window before I began my work—"

"Sarah," said Margaret, "we shall have to begin our packing immediately. We are going away." How difficult it was not to say a little more—not to relieve the burden of her indignation with a word or two! for, indeed, there was nobody whom she could speak to except this round-faced girl, who looked up half frightened, half sympathetic, into her face.

"Oh, ma'am, to leave Greyshott! Where are you a-going to?" Sarah said; and her open mouth and eyes repeated with dismay the same question, fixed upon Margaret's face.

"Shall you be so sorry to leave Greyshott?" said Mrs. Osborne.

Sarah hung her head. She took her handkerchief from her pocket, and twisted it into a knot; finally the quick-coming tears rolled over her round cheeks. "Oh, ma'am!" she cried, and could say no more. A nurserymaid's tears do not seem a very tragic addition to any trouble, and yet they came upon Margaret with all the force of a new misfortune.

"What is it, Sarah? Is it leaving Jim? is that why you cry?"

"Oh, we was to be married at Christmas," the girl cried, in a passion of tears.

"Then you meant to leave me, Sarah? Why didn't you tell me so? Well, of course, I should not hinder your marriage, my good girl; but Christmas is six months off, and you will stay with Master Osy, won't you, till that time comes?"

Sarah became inarticulate with crying, but shook her head, though she could not speak.

"No!—do you mean no? I thought you were fond of us," said poor Margaret, quite broken down by this unexpected desertion. It was of no importance, no importance! she said to herself; but, nevertheless, it gave her a sting.

"Oh, don't ask me, ma'am, don't ask me! So I am, fond: there never was a nicer lady. But how do I know as Jim—they changes so, they changes so, does men!" Sarah cried, among her tears.

"Well, well; you will pack for me, at least," said Margaret, with a faint laugh, "if that is how we are to part, Sarah,—but you must begin at once; no more looking out of the window, for a little while, at least. But Jim is a good fellow. He will be faithful—till Christmas." She laughed again; was it as the usual alternative to crying? or was it because there are junctures of utter forlornness and solitude to which a laugh responds better than any crying? not less sadly, one may be sure.

Sarah dried her streaming eyes, but continued to shake her head. "It's out o' sight out of mind with most of 'em," she said. "I'll have to go and get the boxes, ma'am, and I don't know who there is to fetch 'em up, unless I might call Jim—and the others, they don't like to see a groom a-coming into the house."

"Then let the others do it, Sarah."

"Oh, Mrs. Osborne! they won't go agin the—the new lady, as they calls her. Oh, they calls her just Patty and nasty names among themselves, but if you asks them to do a thing, they says, 'We wasn't hired to work for the likes of you and your Missus, Sal.' Not a better word from one o' them men," cried Sarah, "not one of 'em! They're as frightened of her already as if she was the devil, and she isn't far short. I'll call him, ma'am, when they're at their dinners; and, perhaps, you'd give him a word, just a word, to say as how you think he's a lucky fellow to have got me, and that kind of thing—as a true friend."

"Is that the office of a true friend?" said Margaret. It is a great thing in this life, which has so many hard passages, when you are able to be amused. Sarah's petition and the words which she kindly put into her mistress's mouth, did Margaret more good than a great deal of philosophy. She went away after a time to look for her boy and to tell her uncle of the decision she had come to. They were out, as usual, in the avenue, Sir Giles being wheeled along by a very glum Dunning, and Osy babbling and making his little excursions round and about the old gentleman's chair.

"When I am a man," Osy was saying, "I s'all be far, far away from here. I s'all be a soldier leading my tompany. I s'an't do what nobody tells me—not you, Uncle Giles, nor Movver, nobody but the Queen."

"And I sha'n't be here at all, Osy," said the old man. "When you come back a great Captain like your cousin Gerald, there will be no old Uncle Giles to tell you what you said when you were a little boy."

"Why?" said the child, coming up close to the chair. "Will they put you down in the black hole with Aunt Piercey, Uncle Giles?"

"Master Osy, don't you speak of no such dreful things," said Dunning.

"But Parsons said, 'She have don to heaven,'" said the child. "I like Parsons' way the best, for heaven's a beau'ful place. I'd like to go and see you there, Uncle Giles. You wouldn't want Dunning, you'd have an angel to dwive you about."

"Oh, my little man!" said Sir Giles, "I don't think I am worthy of an angel. I'm more frightened for the angel than for the black hole, Osy. I don't think I want any better angel than you are, my nice little boy. I hope God will let me go on a little just quietly with Dunning, and you to talk to your old uncle. Tell me a little more about what you will do when you are a man. That amuses me most."

"Uncle Giles, Cousin Gervase doesn't do very much though he's a man. He's only don and dot marrwed. I'm glad he's dot marrwed. I dave him my big silver penny for a marrwage present. If he hadn't been marrwed he would have tooked it, and a gemplemans s'ouldn't never do that. So I'm glad. Are you glad, Uncle Giles?"

"Never mind, never mind, my boy. Are you sure you'll go to India, Osy, and fight all the Queen's battles? She doesn't know what a great, grand champion she's going to have, like Goliath," said the old man with his rumbling laugh.

"Goliaf," said Osy, gravely, "wasn't a nice soldier. He was more big nor anybody and he bragged of it. It's grander to be the littlest and win. I am not very big, Uncle Giles, not at pwesent."

"No, Osy. That's true, my dear," said the old gentleman.

"But I'll twy!" cried the boy. "I'm not fwightened of big men. They're genewally," he added, half apologetically and with a struggle over the word, "nice to little boys. Cousin Colonel, he is wather like Goliaf. He dave me a wide upon his s'oulder; but when he sawed Movver tomin, he—Are big men ever fwightened of ladies, Uncle Giles?"

"Sometimes, Osy," said Sir Giles, with a delighted laugh.

"Then it was that!" cried Osy. "I touldn't understand. Oh, wait, Uncle Giles; just wait till I tatch that butterfly. I'll tatch him; I'll tatch him in a moment! I'm a great one," the child sang, running off—"for tatching butterflies, for tatching—Movver, movver, you sended it away."

"What did the little shaver mean by giving a wedding present?" said Sir Giles. "Where's my money, Dunning? have I got any money? If he gave my boy a wedding present, it was the—the only one. They'll come in now, perhaps, when it gets known; but I'll not forget Osy for that, I'll not forget Osy for that. Did you ever see a child like him, Dunning? I never saw a child like him, except our first one that we lost," said the old man with a sob. "Did I ever tell you of our first that we lost? Just such a child; just such a child! And my poor Gervase was the dearest little thing when he was a baby, before—. Children are very different from men—very different, very different, Dunning. You never know how the most promising is to grow up. Sometimes they're a—a great disappointment. They're always a disappointment, I should say from what I've seen, comparing the little thing with the big man, as Osy says. But, please God, we'll make a man of that boy, whatever happens. Ah, Meg! is it you? I was just saying we must make a man of Osy—we must make a man of him—whatever happens."

"I hope he will turn out a good man, Uncle Giles."

"Oh, we shall make a man of him, Meg! not but what, as I was saying, they're always disappointments more or less. Your poor aunt would never let me say that, when she was breaking her poor heart for our first boy that we lost. I used to say he might have grown up to rend our hearts—but she would never hear me, never let me speak. It broke her heart, that baby's going, Meg." This had happened a quarter of a century before, but the old gentleman spoke as if it had been yesterday. "You may think she did not show it, and looked as if she had forgotten; but she never forgot. I saw it in her eyes when she saw Gerald Piercey first. She gave me a look as if to say, this might be him coming home, a distinguished man. For he was a delightful child—he might have grown to be anything, that boy!"

"Dear Uncle Giles! You must try to look to the future—to think that there may be perhaps other children to love." Margaret laid her hand tenderly upon the old man's shoulder, which was heaving with those harmless sobs—which meant so little, and yet were so pitiful to the beholder. "I wanted to speak to you—about Osy, Uncle Giles."

"Yes, yes," said the old man, cheering up. "Did you hear that he gave my poor Gervase a wedding present? that little chap! and the only one—the only one! I'll never forget that, Meg, if I should live to be a hundred. And, please God, we'll pay it back to him, and make a man of him, Meg."

"It was precisely of that, Uncle, I wanted to speak." But how was she to speak? What was she to say to this old man so full of affection and of generous purpose? Margaret went on patting the old gentleman on the shoulder unconsciously, soothing him as if he had been a child. "Dear Uncle Giles, you know that now Gervase is married, they—he will want to live, perhaps, rather a different way."

"What different way?" said Sir Giles, aroused and holding up his head.

"I mean, they are young people, you know, and will want to, perhaps—see more company, have visitors, enjoy their life."

Sir Giles gave her an anxious, deprecating look.

"Do you think then, Meg, that—that she will do? that she will know how to manage? that she will be able to keep Gervase up to the mark?"

"I think," said Margaret, pausing to find the best words, "I think—that she is really clever, and very, very quick, and will adapt herself and learn, and—yes—I believe she will keep him up to the mark."

"God bless you for saying so, my dear! that is what I began to hope. We could not have expected him to make a great match, Meg."

"No, Uncle."

"His poor mother, you know, always had hopes. She thought some nice girl might have taken a fancy to him. But it was not to be expected, Meg."

"No, Uncle. I don't think it was to be expected."

"In that case," said Sir Giles—he was so much aroused and interested that there was a certain clearness in his thoughts—"in that case, it is perhaps the best thing that could have happened after all."

"Dear Uncle, yes, perhaps. But to give them every chance, to make them feel quite at ease and unhampered, I think they should be left to themselves."

"I will not interfere with them," he cried; "I will not meddle between them. Once I have accepted a thing, Meg, I accept it fully. You might know me enough for that."

"I never doubted you, Uncle; but there is more: I think, dear Uncle Giles, I must go away."

"You—go away!" he said, looking up at her, his loose lips beginning to quiver; "you—go away! Why, Meg, you can be of more use here than ever. You can show her how to—how to—why, bless us, we all know, after all, that though she's Mrs. Piercey, she was only, only—well, nobody, Meg! you know—don't bother me with names. She is nobody. She can't know how to—to behave herself even. I looked to you to—Dunning, be off with you: look after Master Osy. I know it's wrong to speak before servants, Meg, but Dunning's not exactly a servant, he knows everything; he has heard everything discussed."

"Too much, I fear," said Margaret half to herself. "Dear Uncle, perhaps you have not considered that mine has always been rather a doubtful position. I am your niece, and you have always been like my father, but Gervase's wife thinks me only a dependant. One can't wonder at it—neither mistress nor servant. She thinks a little as the servants do. I am only here as a dependant. She will not take a hint from me. She will be better without me here. For one thing, she would think I was watching her, and making unkind remarks, however innocent I might be. It is best, indeed it is best, dear Uncle, that I should go."

"Go! away from Greyshott, Meg!—why, why! Greyshott—you have always been at Greyshott."

"Yes, Uncle Giles, thanks to you; dear Uncle Giles, when I was an orphan, and had no one, you have done everything for me; but now the best thing I can do for you is to go away. Oh, I know it, and am sure of it; everything will go better without me. You may imagine I don't like to think that, but it is true."

There was an interval, during which the old man was quite broken down, and Dunning, rushing to his master's side, shot reproachful speeches, as well as glances, at Mrs. Osborne. "It appears," said Dunning, "that I'm never believed to know nothink, not even my own dooty to my master; but those as comes to him with disagreeable stories and complaints, and that just at this critical moment in the middle of his trouble, poor gentleman, knows less than me. Come, Sir Giles. Compose yourself, Sir Giles. I'll have to give you some of your drops, and you know as you don't like 'em, if you don't take things more easy, Sir Giles."

"I'm better," said the old gentleman, feebly; "better, better. But, Meg, you've got no money—how are you to live without money, Meg?"

"I have my pension, uncle."

"A pension! what is a pension? It isn't enough for anything. Even your poor aunt always allowed that."

"It is enough to live on, Uncle—for Osy and me."

"Osy, too," he cried—"Osy, that I was just saying we must make a man of! You are very, very hard upon me, Meg. I never thought you would be hard upon me." But already Sir Giles was wearied of his emotions, and was calming down.

"I hope there will be other children to make up to you, Uncle Giles."

"What!" cried the old man, "is there a prospect of that? Are there thoughts of that already, Meg? Now, that is news, that is news! Now you make up for everything. Whew!" Sir Giles uttered a feeble whistle, and then he gave a feeble cheer. "Hurrah—then there may be an heir to the old house still. Hurrah! Hurrah?"

"Shall I say it for you, Uncle Giles?" said Osy. "Stand out of the way, Movver, and let Uncle Giles and me do it. Hurrah!" cried the little fellow, waving his hat upon Sir Giles' stick. "Now, Uncle Giles, hip, hip, as the men do—hurrah! hurrah! hurrah!"

CHAPTER XXXII

This was about Osy's last performance in the house which was the only home he had ever known. He did not know what he was cheering for, but only that it was delightful to make a noise, and that his old uncle's tremulous bass, soon lost in an access of sobs and laughter, was very funny. Osy would willingly have gone on for half an hour with this novel amusement; but it must be allowed that when he found the great boxes standing about in the room that had been his nursery, and began to watch the mysteries of the packing, his healthy little soul was disturbed by no trouble of parting, but jumped forward to the intoxicating thought of a journey and a new place with eager satisfaction and wonder. Everything was good to Osy, whether it was doing exactly the same thing to-day as he had done every day since he was born, or playing with something that he had never done or known before. He was much more perplexed to be kept upstairs after dinner, and not allowed to go down to the library, than he was by the removal from everything he had ever known. And when next morning he was driven away in the big carriage to the railway station, he was as ready to cheer for the delight of the outset as he had been, without knowing why, for Uncle Giles' mysterious burst of self-gratulation. All things were joyful to the little new soul setting out upon the world.

Patty, however, was by no means delighted with Margaret's prompt withdrawal. She felt herself forestalled, which was painful, and the power of the initiative taken from her. She had intended to play for a little, as the cat plays with the mouse, with this fine lady, who had once been so far above Patty Hewitt, and to whom, in her schoolgirl days, she had been expected to curtsey as to the Queen. Patty's heart had swelled with the thought of bringing down pride (a moral process, as everybody knows), and teaching the woman who had no money, and therefore no right to set herself up above others, her proper place; and it vexed her that this fine rôle should be taken from her.

"Oh, you are going, are you?" she said. "I hope it isn't on my account. When I married Gervase I knew all that there was to put up with, and more than has turned out. I knew I shouldn't have my house to myself, like most new married ladies, and I had made up my mind to all that. I wouldn't have turned you out, not for the world—however you might have been in my way."

"I am afraid I have a strong objection," said Margaret, "to be in anybody's way."

"Ah, that's your pride," said Patty, "which I must say I wonder at in a person of your age, and that knows she has nothing to keep it up on. You've got a pension, haven't you, that's enough to live on? It's a fine thing having money out of all our pockets to spend as you please; but I never heard that a pension was much to trust to, and if you were to marry again you would lose it all. And your boy to bring up, too. My father-in-law has a tremendous idea of your boy. I think it's good for him, in one way, that you are taking him away; for it's ridiculous to bring up a poor child like that, who hasn't a penny, to think that he's as good as the heir, and treated by everybody as if he was really a gentleman's son, you know, with a good fortune at his back."

Margaret smothered with difficulty the indignation that rose to her lips, but she said quietly, "You must disabuse your mind of any such idea. Osy never could be my uncle's heir. The heir of Greyshott after Gervase—and, of course, Gervase's children—is not Osy, but Gerald Piercey, our cousin who has just gone away."

Though this was precious information to Patty, she received it with a toss of her head.

"I hope," she said, "I know a little about the family I've married into; but I can tell you something more, and that is, that it'll never be your fine Colonel's, for all so grand as he thinks himself; for it's all in father-in-law's power, and rather than let him have it he'll leave it all away. I wouldn't see a penny go to that man that gives himself such airs, not if I were to make the will myself to take it away."

"I hope," said Margaret, with an effort, "that there will be natural heirs, and that there need be no question on that point."

"Oh, you will stand up for him, of course!" cried Patty; "but I'd like you to know, if you're making up the match on that score, that it'll never come to pass. Me and Gervase is both against him, and father-in-law won't go against us both, not when he gets used to me. I'd rather see it all go to an 'ospital than to that man. I can't bear that man, looking down upon those that are better than himself, as if he was on stilts!" Patty grew red and hot in her indignation. Then she shook out her dress airily, as if shaking away the subject and the objectionable person. "Oh yes," she said, "natural heirs!" with a conscious giggle. "It's you that has gone and put that in father-in-law's old head. But I told him it was early days. Dear old man. It's a pity he is silly. I don't think he ever can have been much in his head, any more than—. Do you?"

"My uncle is in very bad health. He is ill, and his nerves are much affected. But he has always been a man quite—quite able to manage his own affairs. A man," cried Margaret, faltering a little with indignation and distress, "of very good sense and energy, not at all like—not at all—"

"Well, well," said Patty, "time shows everything, you know, and he's quite safe with me and Gervase; at all events, whatever comes after, his only son comes first, don't he? And me and Gervase will see that the dear old man isn't made a cat's-paw of, but kept quite square."

It was with a sensation half of disappointment, yet more than half of satisfaction, that Patty found herself next morning alone in what she called so confidently her own house. Alone, for Sir Giles, of course, was in his own room, and was much better there, she felt, and Gervase, so long as he was kept in good humour, was not very troublesome. To be sure, it cost a good deal of exertion on her part to keep him in good humour. He felt, as so many a wooer of his simple mind has done, the want of the employment of courtship, which had so long amused and occupied him. He could no longer go to the Seven Thorns in the evening, a resource which was entirely cut off from his vacant life, from the fact of having Patty always with him, without the exercise of any endeavour on his own part. The excitement of keeping free of his mother's scrutiny; the still greater excitement of fishing furtively for Patty's attention, making her see that he was there, persuading her by all the simple wiles of which he was master to grant him an interview; the alarm of getting home, with all the devices which had to be practised in order to get in safely, without being called to account and made to say where he had been—and inspected, to see what he had been doing: all this took a great deal of the salt out of poor Gervase's life. He did not know, now that he had settled down again at home, and all the annoying sensations of the crises were over, what to do with himself in the evenings. Patty and he alone were rather less lively than it had used to be when Sir Giles and Lady Piercey sat in their great chairs, and the game of backgammon was going on, and Meg about, and the child rampaging in all the corners. Even to have so many more people in the room gave it to him an air of additional animation. Patty told him it was the library that looked so dull. "Such a room for you all to sit in," she said, "so gloomy and dark, with these horrid old pictures, and miles of books. Wait till I have the drawing-room in order." But it didn't amuse Gervase to watch all the alterations Mrs. Patty was making, nor how she was having the white and gold of the great drawing-room furbished up. The first night they sat in that huge room, with all the lamps lit, and the two figures lost among all the gilding and the damask, and reflected over and over again, till they were tired of seeing themselves in the big mirrors, Gervase felt more lonely than ever. Never had Patty found so hard a task before her,—not when she had to attend to all the customers alone, and keep their accounts separate in her head, and to chalk up as much as was safe to the score of one toper, and cleverly avoid hearing the call of another who had exceeded the utmost range of possible solvability. Never, when she had all that to do, had she found it so heavy upon her as it was to amuse Gervase. She invented noisy games for him, she plied him with caresses when other methods failed, she endeavoured to revive the old teasings and elusions of the courtship; but as Gervase's imagination had never had much to do with his love-making, these attempts to return to an earlier stage were generally futile. He could not be played with—made miserable by a frown, brought back again by a smile, as had once been the case. And Patty had more than the labours of a Hercules in keeping her Softy in order. There was no one to defend him from now, no tyrannical mother to be defied, to make him feel the force of the wife's protection. When Sir Giles was well enough to come to the drawing-room after dinner, the task was quite beyond the powers of any woman; for it was needful to please the old gentleman, to give up everything for him, to represent to him that his company was always a delight to his children. Poor old Sir Giles had winked and blinked in the many lights of the great drawing-room. He had been dazzled, but he had not been ill-pleased.

"We never used this, you know, in your mother's time but for company," he said. It was Gervase whom he seemed to address, but it was Patty who replied.

"I thought it would be a little change for you," she said. "A change is always good, and there's more light and more air. You should always have plenty of air, and not the associations that are in the other room."

"Perhaps you are right, my dear," the old gentleman said with a sigh. It was she who was "my dear" now; and, indeed, she was very attentive to Sir Giles, never neglecting him, doing everything she could think of for his pleasure. It was on one of the evenings when she was devoting herself to him, playing the game he loved, and allowing him to win in the cleverest way, that Gervase, who was strolling about the room with his hands in his pockets, half jealous of his father, calling her, now in whispers, now loudly, to leave that and come to him, at last disappeared before the game was finished. Patty went on hurriedly with the backgammon, but she was on thorns all the while. She had established the habit of sending off Dunning, whom she was slowly undermining, less for any serious reason than because he was a relic of the past régime; and, therefore, she was now helpless; could not leave Sir Giles; could not interrupt the process of amusing and entertaining him. Where had the Softy gone? to prowl about the house looking for something that might amuse him; to fling himself dissatisfied upon his bed and fall asleep in the utter vacancy of his soul? An uneasy sense that something worse than this was possible oppressed Patty as she sat and played out the game of backgammon. Then there ensued another dreadful interval, during which Sir Giles talked and wondered what had become of his son. "He has gone to sleep somewhere, I shouldn't wonder," said Patty; "the nights are growing long, and poor dear Gervase wants a little amusement. I was thinking of suggesting, dear papa (this was the name she had fixed upon Sir Giles, who had resisted at first, then laughed, and finally accepted the title with the obedience of habit), that we should both play, he and I, against you. You are worth more than the two of us, you know."

"Nonsense, you little flatterer. You've a very pretty notion of the game. I had to fight for it that last round. I had, indeed. I had to fight for my life."

"Ah, dear papa!" said Patty, shaking her head at him. "You are worth far more than the two of us! but it would keep us all together, all the family together."

"I don't like Gervase to play with me," said Sir Giles fretfully. "He's too noisy, and he has no sense; he can't understand a refined game. I shouldn't wonder if he had gone out to some of his old haunts that his poor mother couldn't bear. The Seven—. I beg your pardon, my dear, I am sure," the old gentleman cried, colouring up to his eyes.

"Dear papa, why should you beg my pardon? But oh, no! Gervase has not gone to the Seven Thorns. He went there for me. That makes all the difference. Why should he go back now?"

"My dear," said Sir Giles again, "I must beg your pardon. I didn't intend to make any insinuation. Of course it was for you. But it's a dangerous thing to acquire a habit, especially for one that—for one that doesn't, don't you know, take in many ideas at a time."

"I know him better than that. I know where he is, the lazy boy. But, dear papa, fancy, it is ten o'clock; your bedtime. Oh, how soon ten comes when we have a pleasant game, and in such good company! I suppose I must ring for Dunning now."

"Yes, you had better ring for Dunning. If I am a little bit late, and should have a headache or anything, he throws it in my teeth. We have had a very pleasant game, and I must say that for you, my dear, that you know how to make the time pass. Well, Dunning, here I am, ready you see, ready to the minute, thanks to Mrs. Gervase, who is a great deal more careful of me than you are, you surly old beggar. Good night, my dear; but tell Gervase from me that it isn't good manners to break up the party; but he never was renowned for good manners, poor boy," the old gentleman said, shaking his head as he was wheeled away.

And then Patty had a bitter moment. She went to the library, where he sometimes took refuge, falling asleep upon the old sofa, where he had lain and kicked his heels as a child; and then to his room, where he sometimes went when he was dull, to throw himself upon his bed. But Gervase was not to be found in either place. He came stumbling to the old door which opened on the yew avenue, late at night, and she herself ran downstairs to admit him—angry, yet subduing herself. He had resumed his old habit, as his father had guessed: the habit which had been formed for Patty, and which she had so sharply shaken him out of with a power and mastery which she no longer possessed. Patty felt in that moment the first drawback of that unexampled elevation which she had attained with such unexpected ease. Had she married in her own class, the publican's daughter would not have been very deeply wounded by her husband's return on an occasion in such a plight. But when she stole down through the sleeping house and admitted the future master of Greyshott, and led him upstairs, hushing his broken speech and stumbling gait, that nobody might hear, Patty learned something which no other manner of instruction could have conveyed to her. She found that there were things that were harder upon a lady (such as she flattered herself she had become) than on a village woman. She coaxed and soothed him to bed, like a nurse with a child, that nobody should suspect what had happened; and she ground her teeth and vowed vengeance upon her father, who had dared to take the Softy in and treat him like this. And thus there arose before Patty a prospect which appalled even her brisk and courageous spirit. What if she should not be able to put this down summarily and with the strong hand? Then what would become of her hopes of winning a place in the county, and being acknowledged by all the great people as worthy to make her entrance among them? After the first unexpected triumph of becoming mistress of a great house and a number of servants, her ambition had risen to higher flights; and this was what that over-vaulting ambition aimed at. But what would become of that hope, or of many others, if the Softy, startled out of himself for a moment by his marriage, should fall back into the beerhouse society which suited him best? Patty fell from the height of her dreams when she saw that sight which is always a pitiful one for a young wife. She felt the burden of "the honour unto which she was not born" come down for the first time with a crushing weight upon her. Oh, it was not so simple after all—so easy, so pleasant to be a lady! She had begun already to forget that it was to Gervase she owed her advancement, and to feel the burden of keeping him amused and employed. Now she felt that the Softy had it in his power to mar that advancement still. She had cleared every hostile influence out of the house; she had got rid of every rival. She had conquered Sir Giles, and gained possession of the keys, and become the acknowledged mistress of Greyshott. What a great thing, what a wonderful thing, for Patty Hewitt! And yet she felt, in the bitterness of her heart, that it might be better to be still Patty Hewitt, with all the world before her, than to be Mrs. Piercey, of Greyshott, with that Softy to drag her down.

This was the first big thorn that pierced Patty's foot, and reminded her that she was mortal, as she was marching on in her victorious way.

CHAPTER XXXIII

Patty had been triumphantly successful in the first chapter of her career. She had an easy victory over her father-in-law. She had cleared the house of everybody whom she disliked or feared. First, Mrs. Osborne, and with her—not least in Patty's estimation—Sarah, Osy's maid, who had been at school with her, and whom she was still more anxious to get rid of than her mistress. Then Parsons, who knew a great deal too much of the family to be endurable for a moment; then the one servant in the house who had ventured to be rude to Gervase's wife, John the footman: a dreadful example, whose sudden fate had exercised the most salutary influence over the rest of the household. It is true that Dunning still remained Sir Giles' attendant, against whom there were the same objections as against Parsons; but for the moment, at least, Dunning was indispensable, and had to be borne with. She stood, however, after the first month of her sway on the very top-gallant of success, supreme in the house, her word a law, the oldest and most secure arrangements falling to pieces at her will, the entire order of affairs changed to please her. Everything had gone as she desired, and no head had been lifted up in rebellion. The great wardrobes were full of fine clothes. She had shuffled off Miss Fletcher, the village dressmaker, and procured the finest and most highly cultivated maid that ever advertised in the Times. Lady Piercey's stores of lace and linen, and even her old-fashioned jewellery, which was much more valuable than beautiful, were in Patty's hands. She had realised all her dreams, and more than all. But there is nothing perfect in human affairs, and now the reverse of her good fortune began to rise out of the mists before Patty's eyes.

The first trouble of all was, perhaps, the cutting off of her connection with her home and origin. Her father had come to see her very early in her story, had been received in the half-dismantled library for a short angry conference, and left with a crimson countenance and a volley of muttered oaths, and had never come again. But there was another member of the family who was less easy to get rid of. Miss Hewitt made a call in state, in her most splendid costume, with a bonnet still more exuberant in red and yellow than that in which she had witnessed the funeral of Lady Piercey. She descended upon Patty at an early hour, when Mrs. Gervase was still profoundly occupied with the restoration of the great drawing-room, and made her way there, regardless of the opposition of the polite butler. "Perhaps you are not aware that I am Mrs. Piercey's own aunt," that lady said fiercely; "I shall go to my niece wherever she is. I have no fear of not being welcome." The butler knew, also, too well who the visitor was, and he trembled for the consequences of his weakness as she pushed her way before him into the room where the carpenter and his apprentice and a couple of housemaids were executing Patty's orders, under her close superintendence. The men were on ladders cleaning the long mirrors, the maids were busy with the furniture, while Patty, seated in a gilt and brocaded chair sat in state looking on. "Place that table in the corner, there, and these two chairs beside it. Not that, you stupid; the deep gentleman's chair on one side, and this one without arms on the other—let me see. Yes, that will do, with a palm or a great fern behind." Patty held her head on one side to contemplate the effect, while the two housemaids stood looking on, not yet so much accustomed to the new sway that they did not exchange a glance, a "la! much she knows about it," when her attention was called away.

It was, indeed, with no small start and sensation that Patty's attention was called away. She was sitting thus, with her head on one side, contemplating the group of furniture, perhaps imagining herself in the chair without arms, with a silken train arranged about her feet (when her mourning should be over, for Patty was, in all things, a stickler for propriety), while some grand gentleman, a viscount at least, leant over the table entertaining her from the depths of the "gentleman's chair": when there suddenly burst upon her consciousness a bustle at the door, a quick throwing open, and a voice which was harsh and jarring, but alas, how well known and familiar!

"Patty, my pet, here I am! That man of yours wanted to put me in a waiting-room, but I said, Where she is there I'll go; and here I am, my little lovey, and a happy woman to see you in your own house."

"Oh!" cried Patty, rising quickly from her chair. Her wits were so much about her, even in this great and sudden shock, that she refrained from saying aunt in the hearing of that excited audience—which was foolish, indeed, since all the housemaids and all the carpenters in Greyshott parish knew very well that Miss Hewitt, of Rose Cottage, was Mrs. Piercey's aunt, and far the richest, consequently the most respectable of her kindred. Patty could not say much more, for she was enfolded in the heavy drapery of Miss Hewitt's Paisley shawl, and almost stifled in her close embrace. "And bless you, all's ended as I said it would; and ain't I glad I was the one to help you to it?" Miss Hewitt said in her enthusiasm, bestowing a large audible kiss on Patty's face.

"Oh, dear!" said Patty, as soon as she could speak. "This isn't the place to receive any one in. Jervis, why didn't you show the lady into the morning-room? I can't talk to you here, with all the servants about."

"Don't blame the man," said Miss Hewitt; "I wanted to see you free, without stopping whatever you were doing. It's not as if I were a mere visitor as couldn't make allowances. I just like to see everything, and what it was like before, and what you're doing. I know you, Patty. They won't know it for the same 'ouse afore you're done with it. Well, this is a nice room! but none too big for what you'll want when you get things your own way. Greyshott won't know itself with all the doings there'll be."

"Oh, but I can't receive any lady here," said Patty. "Let me take you into the morning-room; it's where I always sit in the morning. I couldn't possibly sit and talk with a caller before lunch in any other place. If you don't mind I'll show you the way."

The butler held the door open with an obsequious air in which there was, as that functionary was well aware, an over-acting of his part—but that did not occur to the ladies who swept out, Patty in advance, and to whom it would scarcely have seemed too much if Jervis had walked backwards before them. He stayed behind to make his comment with uplifted hands and eyes upon the spectacle. "Lord, ain't she a-going it!" said Jervis. It was, perhaps, not dignified for a person in his position to unbosom himself to the housemaids and the carpenter; but how could mortal man keep silent in circumstances so exciting? The ladies went to the morning-room in another frame of mind, both of them putting on silently their armour for the inevitable battle. When they had reached the room which was to be the scene of it, Miss Hewitt flung herself at once heavily into an easy chair. "Well! I call this a poky little place," she cried. "You might have sent the servants away, Patty. I liked that other place much better. Morning-room! why it's no better than my parlour," she cried.

"It would only hold the whole of your house, kitchen and all," cried Patty; "and it's where I choose people to come," she added decisively, "when they've that little sense as to come in the morning, when no lady receives."

"Oh, that's how I am to be met, is it?" said Miss Hewitt, "you little ungrateful wretch! It was nothing but dear aunt, and how good I was, when you came to me to help you. Ah! you had to come to me to help to secure him at the last—and him nothing but a Softy. If I had had somebody to stand for me like I did for you, Miss Patty, Greyshott would have been a very different place, and you'd never have got your nose in here!"

"Well, Aunt," said Patty, "if those are your ideas, you can't wonder that I shouldn't want you. For if you had married Sir Giles, which I suppose is what you mean, and would never have let me get my nose in, you'll understand that I don't want your nose in. I wouldn't have said it so plump if you hadn't begun. Though I don't believe Sir Giles ever thought of such a thing, now I know him well."

"He's not a Softy, you see," said the angry old lady, with a snort.

"No," said Patty, sedately; "he's not a Softy. I should think he'd had a good deal of common-sense in his day. But I don't want to quarrel," she added; "whatever you may do. No doubt you've come about your money, which is quite natural. You shall have your money, Aunt Patience. It wasn't so needful as I thought it would be, for Mr. Piercey had plenty for what was wanted; but, of course, I'm much obliged to you all the same."

"Oh, Mr. Piercey: that's what you call the Softy now!" cried Miss Hewitt, in high scorn.

"It's what I always called him, and it's his name and mine too. I'm Mrs. Piercey, as the heir's wife, and not Mrs. Gervase. My father-in-law says so, and he ought to know."

"Oh, your father-in-law," cried Miss Hewitt, with extreme bitterness; "you've changed all your relations, I see. When it comes to a person to disown their debts and their folks—"

"I do neither the one nor the other," cried Patty. "You shall have every penny of your fifty pounds—and interest, if you like, with that. And everybody knows my folks," she cried, with a toss of her head. "Oh, no fear that they'll ever be forgotten. Father's been here with the smell of beer about him like to knock you down, and when I told him I couldn't bear it, what does he do but fling out of the house cursing and swearing, and letting everybody see."

"Well, your father is a trial," Miss Hewitt allowed candidly. "I don't wonder, Patty, as you were hurt; but so was he, and he won't come back no more, won't Richard. You can't, anyhow, my pet, have the same objections to me."

Miss Hewitt held her head aloft, and her golden flowers nodded and rustled. The complacency of her smile, and the confidence that in her there was nothing to find fault with, was too much even for Patty. She could not say the words that came to her lips.

"Well, Aunt Patience," she said, in subdued tones, "I am treating you just the same as if you were Lady Hartmore."

"And no more than is my due, Patty. I might have been my lady many and many's the year if I'd had an Aunt Patience as would have done for me as I've done for you. Has she been to call already? She's one as always respects the rising sun."

"No," said Patty, still more subdued, "she has not been yet—but that's easy explained, where there's been so lately a death in the house."

"And a good thing for you, too! If ever there was a tyrant of a woman—But I see you're in deep crape, Patty, to show your grief."

"I hope I know better than to show any want of respect to my mother-in-law. And I think, Aunt Patience, you might have known better than to come to a house that's in such mourning with all these colours on your head."

"My bonnet!" cried Miss Hewitt. She caught sight of herself in a glass, and bridled and smiled at herself, instinctively arranging the bow of red ribbon that was tied under her chin. "I never had such a becoming bonnet in my life; and as for mourning, there's nobody could expect me to put on black for her."

"No," said Patty, "and that's why I hadn't expected even a call from you, Aunt Patience, during the mourning—not being in any way a real connection of the house."

Miss Hewitt fixed her eyes very wide open upon those of her niece, and the two maintained a silent combat by that method for at least a minute. It was the elder who gave in the first. "If that's how you're going to treat your own relations," she said, "Patty, you'll not see much of me. And I can tell you, as well as if it had happened already, you won't see much of other folks. There's none of the grand people as you're looking for that will come near the place. The rector'll call because he's bound to, and because you was once his show girl at the Sunday School; and the new curate will call to see if he can get a subscription for something, but, mark you my words: nobody else—no, not a soul! and when you've bundled everybody belonging to you out of your doors, then you'll see who you'll have to speak to. I'm sorry for you, Patty, I am indeed."

"Are you, Aunt Patience?" cried Patty, with defiance. "When it comes to that, I'll send for you back."

"It's a deal easier," said Miss Hewitt sentiously, "to whistle folks away than to bring them back."

But after this there was a cessation of hostilities, and in the end Miss Hewitt was taken over the house to see all its splendours, which, as much as possible, she depreciated. She was the only witness of her elevation whom Patty had as yet had, and though some sacrifice of pride and spirit was necessary, a natural longing to impress and dazzle her world, through the means of some spectator, was still stronger. Patty went so far as to offer her aunt some of those pairs of silk stockings which Parsons had been counting when her new mistress fell upon her. "They're such good stockings," Patty said, "but miles too big for me." "If you think I'll wear her old cast-off things!" cried Miss Hewitt, purple with rage, flinging them back into the drawers from which Patty had taken them. "And my foot, if anything, is a little smaller than yours," she added, with angry satisfaction. But when the visitor lingered and at last betrayed her desire to be asked to stay for "dinner"—a word which came out unadvisedly, and which she immediately corrected, with a blush—"Lunch, I suppose you call it,"—Patty assumed very high ground.

"My dear Aunt! if we were by ourselves of course it would not matter; but dear papa always takes his luncheon along with us."

"And who's dear papa?" asked Miss Hewitt, with natural derision.

"I mean Sir Giles, of course; he's in very delicate health, and we have to be very careful."

"Sir Giles," said Miss Hewitt grimly, "has seen me before."

"Yes—he said so when he heard my name—he said, Where have I heard that name before?"

"Patty, you're a little devil; he knows a deal more than that of me."

"Ah, well, perhaps once, Aunt; but his memory's gone now; and to bring in a stranger to the luncheon table! Perhaps you don't remember," said Patty severely, "that my poor dear mother-in-law has not yet been a fortnight in her grave."

Miss Hewitt was thus got rid of, though not without trouble; but Patty did not find it easy to forget what she had said, especially when it came true to the letter; for week after week went by and not a step, except that of the doctor, crossed the threshold of Greyshott. Patty took her place in the drawing-room every afternoon, with everything arranged very cleverly, and looking as like as an imitation could be to the little mise en scène of a young lady waiting for her guests; but no guests ever came. At length, after much waiting, there appeared—exactly as Aunt Patience had said—the rector! accompanied by his young daughter, for he was a widower. The rector called her Patty in the first moment of meeting, and though he amended that in a confused manner, and gave her finally her full honours as Mrs. Piercey, it was difficult to get over that beginning, which threw his young companion into utter discomfiture. And then, to make matters worse, he delivered a little lecture upon the responsibilities of her new position and the difficulty of the duties that would come upon her. "You must not let your mind dwell on your disadvantages," he said kindly; "everybody, after a while, will make allowances for you." "You are quite mistaken if you think I want to have allowances made for me," said Patty, provoked. And what could the rector reply? He said, "Oh!" thus showing the poverty of the English language, and how little a man in such a predicament can find to say for himself; and then he began hurriedly to talk parish talk, and ask Mrs. Piercey's patronage for various charities—charities by which Patty Hewitt might almost have been in a position to benefit so short a time ago. "That's well over," he said to his daughter, wiping his forehead, when they went out of the gates of Greyshott. And he did not come again, nor she—not even the girl. And nobody came; and of all the difficult things in the world Mrs. Gervase Piercey found nothing so difficult as to explain to her grand maid how it was that no visitor was ever seen at Greyshott. The thing itself was bad enough, but to explain it to Jerningham was still worse. "You see we are still in deep mourning," Mrs. Piercey said. "Yes, ma'am," said Jerningham, with a sniff of polite scepticism. For a lady who, however deep her mourning might be, had not a single friend to come to see her, was more than Jerningham could understand. And Patty sat alone in her fine drawing-room, and walked about her great house, and spoke to nobody but old Sir Giles and her own Softy; and thought many times, with a kind of alarm, of what Aunt Patience had said. Had it not already come true?

CHAPTER XXXIV

This, however, was after all but a small matter; it was not actual misfortune. Patty, indeed, felt it much, partly on account of Jerningham and the other servants, who she felt must triumph in this non-recognition of her claims; and also a little for herself, for it was an extraordinary change from the perpetual coming and going of the Seven Thorns, and all the admiration and respect which she had there, the jokes, and the laughter and the talk, which if not refined, were good enough for Patty Hewitt—to the condition of having no one to speak to, not a soul—except old Sir Giles and her own Softy, whose conversation clever Patty could not be said to have enjoyed at any time. It was very dull work going on from day to day with nothing better than poor old Sir Giles' broken talk, which was about himself and his affairs—not about her, naturally the most interesting subject to Patty. Many times she was tempted to go upstairs and sit with Jerningham to unbosom herself and relieve her mind of all the unspoken talk, and make a companion and confidante of her maid. Jerningham was a person much better trained and educated than Patty. She could have instructed her in many of the ways of the fine ladies which Mrs. Piercey could only guess at, or painfully copy out of novels; but perhaps, if her mistress had yielded to this impulse it would have been Jerningham who would have held back, knowing her place and desiring no confidences. Patty, however, also knew her place, and that to confide in a servant was a fatal thing, so that she never yielded to this temptation. But how dull it was! It is a fine thing to be the mistress of a great house, to have a large household under your orders, to be served hand and foot, as Patty herself would have said; but never to have a gossip, never a jest with any one, she for whom every passer-by had once had a cheerful word, to have nobody to admire either herself or her dresses, to envy her good fortune, to wonder at her grandeur! that takes the glory out of any victory. Would Cæsar have cared to come back with all the joy and splendour of a triumphal procession had there been nobody to look at him? Patty had succeeded to the extent of her highest dreams, but, alas! there was nobody to see.

That, however, was merely negative, and there was always the hope that it might not last. She took her seat in the drawing-room every day with perennial expectation, still believing that somebody must come; and, no doubt, in the long run, her expectation would have come true. But Patty soon had actual trouble far more important than any mere deprivation. She had been afraid of Sir Giles, over whom her victory had been easy, and she had been afraid of the servants, whom she had now completely under her foot; but she never had any fear about the Softy, her husband, who had been her dog—a slave delighted with his chains—who had desired nothing better than to do what she told him, and to follow her about wherever she went. That Gervase should become the only rebel against her, that he should escape her authority and influence, and take his own way in opposition to hers, was a thing which had not entered into any of her calculations—Gervase, whose devotion had been too much, who had wearied her out with his slavish dependence on her, how had he emancipated himself? It was inconceivable to Patty. She had felt sure that whatever happened she could always control him, always keep him in subjection, guide him with a look, be absolute mistress of his mind and all his wishes. The first revelation of something more in Softy which she had not calculated upon had come when she first found the difficulty of amusing him in the long evenings (lit with so many wax candles, surrounded with so many glories!). Then it was revealed to Patty that she was not enough even for that fool. Then it began to dawn upon her faintly that the Seven Thorns itself had something to do with the attraction, and the excitement of the suspense, and the restraint and expectation in which she had held him: all these adjuncts were over now; he had Patty all his own, and he did not find Patty enough. Was that possible? could it be true?

Perhaps there was something in the very ease of Patty's triumph that had to do with this. Had his mother lived, and had Gervase experienced that protection of having a wife to stand by him, which he had anticipated, it is very likely that this result would have been long delayed, if, indeed, it had ever appeared at all. But there was nobody now against whom Gervase required to be protected. His father had never opposed him, and now that Sir Giles was, like everybody else in the house, under Patty's sway, not even the faint excitement of a momentary struggle with him chequered the Softy's well-being. The consequence was that he, as well as Patty, found it dull. He had no one to play with him, he longed for the movement of the alehouse, the sound of the carts and carriages, the slow jokes in the parlour, the smoke and the fun—also the beer; and perhaps that most of all. It was hard work even when Patty was devoted to his constant amusement, for the Softy had no intervals; he wanted to be entertained all the time: and when she flagged for a moment, he became sullen and tugged at his chain. But when Sir Giles came on the scene, and Patty's attention was distracted and her cares given to the old man, offence and sullen disgust arose in the mind of Gervase. He would not join in the game, as Patty called him to do; neither father nor son indeed wanted a third in the game: and Gervase, duller than ever and angry too, went to sleep for a night or two, tried to amuse himself another evening or two with cat's cradle or the solitaire board—then flung these expedients aside in impatience, and finally strolled off, through the soft, warm darkness of the night, to the Seven Thorns. The Seven Thorns! it was poetic justice upon Patty, but that made it only the harder to bear.

Then there came upon Patty one of those curses of life which fall upon women with a bitterness and horror of which probably the inflictors of the pain are never fully aware. It would have been bad enough if this had befallen her in her natural position as the wife of a country tradesman or small farmer. Domestic misery is the same in one class as in another; yet it would be vain to deny the aggravations that a higher position adds to primitive anguish of this kind. The cottager is not so much ashamed of her husband's backslidings. In many cases they are the subject of the long monologue of complaint that runs through her life. They cannot be hid, and they become a sort of possession, the readiest excuse for every failing of her own. But that the young master should stumble night after night up to Greyshott; that he should be seen by all the neighbourhood drinking among the dull rustics at the Seven Thorns; that a crowd of servants should listen and peep to hear his unsteady step, and his boisterous laugh, and the stammerings of excuse or explanations, or worse still, of noisy mirth, bursting from him in the middle of the quiet night—was something more terrible still. Patty—on that first occasion, when, long after every one else was in bed, she stole downstairs to admit him by that little door near the beech avenue, to which his unsteady footsteps naturally turned—was horrified and angry beyond description; but she did not doubt she could put a stop to it. Not for a moment did she hesitate as to her power. It should never happen again, she said to herself. Once was nothing. Henceforward she would be on her guard. He should not escape from her another time. She did not even upbraid Gervase—it was her own fault, who had never thought of that, taken no precautions; but it should never, never, she said to herself, with, perhaps unnecessary asseverations, happen again.

Gervase, upbraided as in sport by his laughing wife for forsaking her, as if he had been a naughty child, did nothing but laugh and triumph in reply. "Weren't they just astonished to see me!" he said: "your father opened his mouth like this," opening his own large mouth with the moist hanging under-lip. "You should ha' seen him, you should ha' seen him, Patty—like I was a ghost! 'Hallo!' said he, and 'Hallo!' said I, 'here I am, you see.' There wasn't one of them could say a word; but afterwards I stood treat, and we had a jolly night."

"And, oh, how you did smell of beer, you naughty fellow, when you came in!"

"Did I? Well, not without reason, neither," said Gervase, with his loud laugh; "a set of jolly old cocks when you set them going. We only wanted you there in your old blue dress and your apron."

"That you will never see again, I can tell you; and it isn't very nice of you, Gervase, wishing your wife in such a place."

"It's a good enough place, and it's where you came from," said Gervase. "But I told 'em," he said, nodding his head, "what an awful swell you have grown—nothing good enough for you. Didn't the old fellows laugh and nod their old heads. Ho, ho! He, he!"

"Gervase, dear," said his wife, "you won't go there again? you won't go and leave me all by myself, longing and wondering when you'd come back? I thought you'd gone and fallen asleep somewhere. I thought every minute you'd come into the room. You won't go again, Gervase, dear, and leave your poor Patty alone?"

"Why, you had father," Gervase said.

"Oh, papa; yes, dear, and I kept on playing to amuse him, dear old gentleman, and to keep it from him that you had gone out. If he had known where you were, it would have vexed him sadly, you know it would."

"It vexed them both," said Gervase, "when I went there after you; but I didn't mind—nor you either, Patty."

"A young single man has to have his liberty," said Patty, "but when he's married—You wouldn't have gone off and left me—your Patty, whom you said you were so fond of—in those days?"

"Ah," said the Softy, with the wisdom of his kind, "but I've got you now fast, Patty, at home waiting for me; so I can take my pleasure a bit, and have you all the same." He looked at her with a cynical light in his dull eyes. He, and she also, felt the strength of the argument. No need to please her now, and conciliate her in her own ideas about beer and the parlour of the Seven Thorns. She could no longer cast him off, or leave him in the lurch. Consequently, Gervase felt himself free to indulge his tastes in his own way, whatever Patty might think. She was struck silent by that new light in his eyes. He was not capable of argument, or of anything but sticking to what he had once said, with all the force of his folly. She looked at him, and, for the first time, saw what was before her. It had never occurred to her before that he had the strength to resist her, or that she could not call him to her like a dog when her better sense saw it to be necessary. A docile fool is sometimes contemptible enough; but a fool resistant, a being whom reason cannot teach, who has no power of being convinced! Patty felt a cold dew come over her forehead. She saw what was before her with momentary giddiness, as if she had looked over the edge of a precipice. But she did not lose hope. She sent next day an imperative note to her father requiring his attendance: that he either should resist or refuse her call did not come into her mind. "Come up to Greyshott," she wrote, "at once, for I have something to say to you;" as she might have written to one of her servants. But Richard Hewitt was not a man who could be defied with impunity. He never appeared in obedience to her summons; he took no notice of it. He replied only by that silence which is the most terrible of all kinds of resistance. And it was not long before Gervase disappeared again. After the second catastrophe, Patty swept down upon the Seven Thorns in her carriage—an imposing figure in her silk and crape. But Hewitt was not impressed even by the sight of her grandeur. "I'll not refuse no customer for you—there! and you needn't think you can come over me," he cried. "By George! to order me about—what I'm to do and whom I'm to have in this house. It's like your impudence; but I tell you, Miss, I'll see you d—d first," the angry man roared, bringing his clenched fist down upon the table, and making all the glasses ring. Patty was cowed, and had not a word to say.

And then there began for the triumphant young woman an ordeal enough to daunt the stoutest heart. It was true that she had not, like many a wife in such circumstances, the anguish of love to give a sting to everything. Patty had used the Softy partly as the instrument of her own elevation; but his folly had not disgusted or pained her as it might have done under other circumstances. She had a sober affection for him even, as her own property, a thing that belonged to her, and felt strongly the impulse of protecting him from scandal and injury: more, he was so involved still in all her hopes of advancement, that she was as much alarmed for the betrayal of his bad behaviour, as if (like so many) she had feared the loss of a situation or work which brought in the living of the family. And it must be added for Patty that she did her very best to keep all knowledge of Gervase's conduct from his father. She sat and played his game of backgammon, inventing almost every evening a new excuse. "Isn't he a lazy boy? He's gone to sleep again," was at first the easiest explanation. But Patty felt that would not do always. "What do you think, dear papa? Gervase has taken to reading," she said; "I gave him a nice novel, all hunting and horses, and he got so interested in it." "He never was any good outside a horse himself," Sir Giles said, with a little grumble. But he was easily satisfied. He asked nothing more than to have his mind relieved from that care for Gervase which Lady Piercey had always insisted he should share. "He's got his wife to look after him, now," Sir Giles said, when Dunning hinted a doubt that Mr. Gervase was sometimes out of an evening. He was thankful to wash his hands of all responsibility. That apparent selfishness of old age, which consists very much of weariness and conscious inability to bear the burden, came over him more and more every day. Had such a thing been possible as that Gervase should have married a girl in his own position, and made her miserable, the good in Sir Giles would have been roused to support and uphold the victim. But Patty knew very well what she was doing. Patty had accepted all the responsibilities. She was able to take care of herself. He had his wife to take care of him, and to keep him off his father. Patty accepted her share of that tacit bargain honestly; and, as for Sir Giles, it must be said that he was easily satisfied—received her explanations, and gave her as little trouble as possible. He nodded his head, and went on with his game. Perhaps, if truth had been told, it was a relief to the old man when the Softy—strolling about restlessly from place to place, interfering with the play, calling off his wife's attention, always troublesome and always ungainly—was not there.

CHAPTER XXXV

Patty had been married only about four months, when an incident happened that brought this period of humiliation and trouble after her triumph to a climax. The summer had gone, the dark days and long nights of early winter had come back, and Gervase's almost nightly visits to the Seven Thorns were complicated by the storms and rains of the season, which, however, were rarely bad enough to keep him indoors. Had Patty been free to keep a constant watch upon him, it was her opinion that she could have prevented his continual escape into the night. She could have made him so comfortable at home. By moments she had visions of what she could do to reclaim her husband and satisfy him, if the dreadful restraint of the old man and his nightly game were withdrawn. Once or twice, when Sir Giles was indisposed, she had, indeed, managed to do this. She had brewed him hot and fragrant drinks to take the place of the beer, and exhausted herself in talk to amuse him. Poor Patty! she thought to herself that surely she must, at least, be as amusing as the old fellows in the parlour at the Seven Thorns. Many a woman has thought the same: a brilliant young creature, full of knowledge and spirit, and wit and pleasantness, might not she think herself as attractive as the dull gossip of the club? But it is a dangerous conflict to enter into, and the race is certainly not to the swift nor the battle to the strong in this respect. And Patty was not an amusing conversationalist. She knew the methods of rustic flirtation, and how to hold off and call on a provoked and tantalised lover; and she could be very lively in talk about herself and what she meant to do; but the first was no longer a method to be employed with Gervase, who was now brutally conscious of being Patty's proprietor; and he was not even so much interested in what she meant to do as he once had been. He much preferred the heavy jokes, the great guffaw, the half-mocking attention that was paid to himself in the parlour at the Seven Thorns. He was not in the least aware that the big laugh that went round, and in which he himself joined with a sensation of truly enjoying himself, was chiefly at him and his folly. And his freedom to do what he liked, to drink as much as he liked, and babble and maunder at his pleasure, was very sweet to Gervase: he liked it better than anything else in the world; perhaps not better than Patty if there had been a conflict between the two—but then, as he said, he had Patty all the same whatever he might do, and why shouldn't he enjoy himself when it was so entirely in his power?

But when Patty sat the whole evening through playing backgammon with Sir Giles, her ears on the alert for every sound, her hopes sometimes raised by a footstep on the stairs to imagine that he had not gone out after all, or her fears excited by some noise to the terror of believing that he had come back earlier than usual, and was coming in—like the fool he was, to betray himself to his father! it was not wonderful if she looked sometimes with a suppressed bitterness at her old father-in-law fumbling at his game. What good was his life to that old man? He could not walk a step without assistance. He was bound to that chair whatever happened. He had nobody of his own age to speak to, no one except people of another generation, whom he was keeping out of what Patty called "their own." "Oh, if the old man were out of the way, how soon I could put everything right!" Patty said to herself. Though she had indeed failed, and received a grievous defeat, her confidence in herself was not shaken. It was only circumstances, she thought, that were to blame. If she had things in her own hands, if her evenings were unencumbered, if she could devote herself to her husband as she had intended to do, let us see how long the Seven Thorns would have stood against her! And, oh, what good was his life to that old man! If he were to die, what a blessed relief it would be! Full of aches and pains, his nerves shattered, unable to keep from crying when he talked, unable to think of anything except his walk (walk! in his chair driven by Dunning), and his dinner, which was chiefly slops, and his cups of beef tea, and his drops, and his game at night, which he was allowed to win to please him! Poor Sir Giles! It was not, indeed, a very pleasing programme: but it is to be supposed that it did not seem so miserable to him as to Patty, for Sir Giles showed no inclination whatever to die. He might have thought, if he had been an unselfish old man, that he was a burden, that he kept the young people from enjoying their lives, while getting so little good out of his own—that if he were but out of the way Patty would be my lady, and free to look after her own husband and keep him straight; but he did not do so. She sat all the evening through, and said: "Yes, dear papa," and "How capitally you play!" and "What luck you have!" and "I am nowhere beside you, dear papa," smiling and beaming upon him, and, to do her justice, exerting all her powers to amuse him; but all the time saying to herself, "Oh, what good is his life to him! Oh, how can he go on like this, keeping Gervase out of his right place, and keeping me that I can't do anything for my own husband! Oh, that we had the house to ourselves and I were free to keep Gervase straight!"

One evening, Patty had been feeling more keenly than usual this keen contrariety and hindrance of everything. Sir Giles had sat longer than he generally did, sending off Dunning when he appeared, demanding an hour's grace and another game. He was in higher spirits than usual. "Come, Patty," he said, "you're not tired. Have your revenge and give me a good beating. I'm in high feather to-night. I don't care that! for Dunning. Come back in an hour, and perhaps I'll go to bed."

"'Alf an hour, Sir Giles: and that's too long," Dunning said.

"Half an hour, dear papa—you must not really tempt Providence by staying any longer," said Mrs. Gervase. "Have my revenge? Oh, no! but I'll give you another chance of beating me all to atoms. Isn't Sir Giles well to-night, Dunning? He looks ten years younger."

"He's excited with all that play," said Dunning. "I don't 'old with so much backgammon. If he's ill in the morning I wash my hands of it. He knows well enough hisself he didn't ought to be so late."

"The white for me as usual," said Sir Giles. "I'm a sad, selfish, old fellow, always appropriating the winning colour, eh, Patty? Never mind, you are coming on beautifully—you play a very pretty little game. I'm training you to beat myself, my dear, if not to-night, well, some other night. Come along, don't let's waste any time if that old curmudgeon gives us only half an hour."

Patty drew her chair to the table again with her most smiling aspect. "Here I am, dear papa," she said. The renovated drawing-room, if it was, perhaps, in the taste of a past time and a little heavy and ungraceful, was a handsome room, abundantly lighted, with an atmosphere of warmth and luxurious comfort; and Patty in her black silk, with her hair carefully dressed à la Jerningham, and her dress from a fashionable mantua-maker, recommended by that accomplished attendant—was as good an imitation of what a lady at home ought to be, as it would be easy to find; and as she sat there ministering to her old father-in-law, keeping him in comfort and good humour, giving up her time and her attention to play over again the same monotonous unending game—the picture, both moral and physical, was one that would have gained the admiration of any spectator. But as she drew her chair again towards the table, there flashed across Patty's mind a remembrance of another scene: the parlour at the Seven Thorns full of a cloud of smoke and a smell of beer; the rustic customers, with their slow talk, holding forth each to his neighbour, calling with knocks upon the floor and table for further supplies; while she, Patty, the same girl, hastened to see what was wanted, and to bring them what they called for—she, Mrs. Piercey, the wife of the heir of Greyshott, the mistress of all this great house! And it was only four months ago. How clearly she saw that scene! The same thing would be going on to-night while she played backgammon with Sir Giles, and smiled, and talked to her dear papa—and with a thrill of mingled rage, vexation, and anxiety, Patty felt herself deserted and her husband there! It gave her a pang which was all the more keen from her confidence in what she could do, and her sense of the bondage which prevented her from doing it. Oh, why should this old man go on with his cackle and his dice, and his life which was no good to any one? Why, why couldn't he die and set her free? "Here I am, dear papa," she said.

"Perhaps that sleepy fellow, Gervase, will wake up and appear before we've done," said Sir Giles. "I wouldn't humour him too much, my dear. It's one thing to be devoted to your husband, and another thing to let him muddle his brains away. He sleeps a great deal too much, that's my opinion. He's not too bright at the best of times, and if you let him drowse about like this it'll do him harm—it'll do him harm. I don't see that he gets up any earlier in the morning for sleeping like this at night. His poor mother would never have permitted it. Sixes, my dear. No, no, you mustn't humour him too much."

"What luck you have, dear papa! Oh, yes, I know, I know, he's humoured too much. But some need more sleep than others: and don't you think, on the whole, it does him good? His mind comes out so much; he's so sensible when you talk to him. I couldn't wish for better advice than Gervase gives."

"I'm very glad to hear you say so, my dear; there's a great deal in him, poor boy; I always said so; more than anybody knows. But I wouldn't let him sleep like that. What, Dunning, you old rascal, here again already? It can't be half an hour yet."

"Oh, yes, dear papa," said Patty, "it is the half-hour; and that last throw has quite made an end of me. Good-night, and I hope you'll sleep well. And I'll go, as you say, and wake up that lazy boy. He is a lazy boy. But I'll try and break him of it now you've told me. I thought it was best to humour him. But I'll break him of it, now I know what you think."

"Do, my dear, do!" said Sir Giles, nodding his head at her as he was wheeled away. Dunning gave Mrs. Gervase a look behind his master's chair. Ah, you may keep such a secret from those whom it affects most, but to keep it from the servants is more than any one can do! Dunning knew well enough where Gervase was. He knew how Gervase returned home, at what hour, and in what condition. Dunning, in addition, thought he knew that it was Patty's doing, part of some deep-laid scheme of hers, and could not divine that the poor young woman's heart was beating under that fine gown with terror and anxiety. She gave a little gasp of relief when the sound of Sir Giles' chair died away, and his door was closed audibly. And then she rang to have the lights put out, telling the butler that Sir Giles and Mr. Piercey had both gone to bed; and then Patty, heroic as any martyr, placed herself under Jerningham's hands to have her hair brushed, going through all the routine that nobody might think from her demeanour that anything was wrong. She was quivering with anxiety in every limb when she sent the maid away; and then, in her dressing-gown, stole downstairs to open the side door, and strain her ears for the heavy footstep stumbling through the blackness of the night.

Poor Patty! what thoughts went through her mind as she kept that vigil! Fury and determination to do something desperate, to stop it at all hazards—and that this should be the last time, the very last! She would take him by the shoulder and shake the very life out of him rather than that this should go on. She would fling herself at his feet and implore him—alas, Patty knew very well that to implore and to threaten were alike useless, and that the fool would only open his moist mouth and laugh in her face. What could she do? what could she do? She would make an appeal to her father, she would threaten him with the loss of his licence, she would bribe him with all the money she could scrape together, she did not know what she would not do—but to bear this longer was impossible! And then she fell into a dreary calm, and thought over all that had happened, her wonderful triumph, the change in everything, the contrast. And yet what advance had she made if she never, never could separate herself from the Seven Thorns? Whether it was she who was there or her husband, what did it matter? Who would ever acknowledge them or give them their own place if this were to go on? Oh, if these county people had but done as they ought, if they had but shown themselves friendly and taken some notice of the young pair, people who had known Gervase all his life, and ought to have felt for him! Patty shed a few hot tears over the unkindness of the world, and then, as is so natural, her mind went back upon her own hopes, and the ideal she had formed of her life which, as yet, was so little realised. She had thought of herself as driving about the country, paying visits at those grand houses which had been to her as the abodes of the blest; her husband at her side, well-dressed and well set up, with everybody saying how much he had improved! And invitations raining upon them, and fortune smiling everywhere. Sir Gervase and Lady Piercey! how delightfully it had seemed to sound in her fortunate ears! To be sure all this could not be realised until poor old Sir Giles had been fully convinced that it was not for his advantage to live any longer; but that might have happened any day. Oh, if he could but be convinced of it now, and leave her free to care for her husband! Was not Gervase her first duty? Why should this old man go on living, keeping his son out of his own?

And then Patty's mind went back to the Seven Thorns, that place from which it appeared she could not get free. She saw herself there before anything was yet settled, while all her life was before her. As she sat alone and shivered and listened, the image of Patty, light-hearted and free, came up before her like a picture. How busy she had been, how everybody had admired her, even the old fellows in the parlour! And the young ones, how they had watched for a word with her, and some had almost come to blows! Roger, for instance, who had made so much fun of the Softy, who had looked such a gallant fellow in his brown velveteen coat and his red tie! She remembered how he had appealed to her not to do it, not to bind herself to a fool. The impudent fellow! to talk so of Gervase—Sir Gervase Piercey that was soon to be! Oh, poor Gervase, poor Gervase! he was not, perhaps, very wise, but he could still be set right again and kept straight if she were but free to give herself up altogether to the care of him. Roger Pearson could never have been anything but a country fellow living in a cottage. It was true that he was handsome, and all that. Patty seemed to see him, too, though she did not wish it, with the light in his eyes, looking at her with his air of mastery, the Adonis of the village. Every girl in the place had wanted Roger, but he had eyes for only her. Why did he come before her now? She did not want to see him or to think of him—far from that. There was not a fibre of the wanton in Patty's nature. She had no understanding of the women who, with husbands of their own, could think of any other man. And if she had the choice to make over again, she knew that she would do the same; but still she could not help thinking of Roger Pearson, though she had no idea why.

This effect, however, was shortly after explained to her in the most trying way. The night grew darker and darker, and colder and colder. The Seven Thorns must have been closed long ago, and all its revellers dispersed to their homes. What could have happened to Gervase? where could he have gone? Could he have taken so much that he was made to stay there, as unable to take care of himself, a thing which Patty could remember to have happened in her time? She became afraid to look at her watch or to listen to a clock, in the sickness of her heart. It was impossible but that he must have reached home long ago had he left the Seven Thorns in the natural way. Oh, where was he? where was he? Where had he gone? what had happened to him? Patty dared not go upstairs to bed, even when she was convinced that he could not be coming now; for her father, she was sure, would turn him out in the early morning if this was what had happened. Yet how could she remain up, and on the watch, when the servants would be stirring, revealing what had happened to the whole household? Patty is, perhaps, not a person for whom to appeal to the reader's sympathies, but she was very unhappy, very anxious, not knowing what to think.

At last, in the blackest hour of the night, about three o'clock or so in the morning, her anxious ear heard, or seemed to hear, a faint sound. Steps, and then a pause, and then steps again, and the sound of the little side gate in the beech avenue pushed open. Patty was immediately on the alert, with unspeakable relief in her mind. But the sounds were not those of one man stumbling home. Sometimes there was a noise as of something being tugged along the grass, then another stop, and the steps again making the gravel fly, and then the sound as of a fall. In her terror she stole out into the darkness, fearing she knew not what, and at last, by faint perception through the gloom, by sound, and by almost contact in the stifling dark, perceived how it was—her husband, scarcely conscious, being dragged and hustled along through the dark by another man.

"Is it you, Gervase? oh, is it you, Gervase?" she cried.

Oh, poor Patty! is there any one so hard-hearted as to refuse to pity her in her misery? The voice that answered her out of the blackness of the night was not that of Gervase. He uttered no sound but that of heavy breath. Yet it was a well-known voice, a voice that made her heart jump to her throat with intolerable horror, anger, and shame—to hear how sober, manful, energetic, and capable it was.

"There's nothing wrong with him," it said, clearly and quickly, "except that he's drunk. Show a light and I'll get him in. I've had such a job, but I'll manage now; only for goodness' sake look sharp and show a light."

It was the voice of Roger Pearson, whom she had been thinking of, whose presence had sent some subtle intimation through the air to bring him to her thoughts.

Patty hurried back to the open door and brought out the candle, which burned steadily in the motionless blackness of the air. She said not a word. Of the pang it gave her to see the man whom she had rejected bringing back the man whom she had married she gave no sign. If she could have covered her face that he might not see her, she would have done so; but that being impossible, Patty never flinched. She held the light to direct him, while now and then roused to take a step of his own accord, but generally dragged by the other, Gervase was got in. She led the way to the library, which was on the same level, stepping with precaution not to be heard, shading the light with her hand, with all her wits about her. There was not a tinge of colour on Patty's face. She was cold, shivering with excitement and distress. It was not till Gervase had been laid upon the sofa that she spoke.

"I am sorry you have had this trouble," she said. "I hope you have not over-strained yourself with such a weight. Can I get you anything?" She looked at him courageously in the face. It was right to offer a man something who had brought, even were it only a strayed dog, home.

And he, too, looked at her, and for a moment said nothing. He stretched his arms to relax them.

"I'm not a man that cares for the stuff," he said, "but perhaps I'd be none the worse for a drop of brandy to take off the strain. He's safe enough there," he added. "You needn't be anxious. He'll wake up before the daylight, and then you can get him upstairs."

Patty did not say a word, but led the way to the dining-room, where there was brandy to be got. It was a thing any lady might have done, she said to herself, even through the wild beating of her heart, and the passion in her breast—the passion of rage, and exasperation, and shame. He was cool enough, thinking more of stretching and twisting himself to ease his muscles than of the silent anguish in which she was. When he had swallowed the brandy he advised her, with rough friendliness, "Take a little yourself. It's hard on you; you want something to give you a little strength!"

"Will you take any more?" said Patty, sharply.

"No, I don't want no more. It's awful good stuff; it runs through a man like fire. I'd been at a bit of an 'op over there by Coulter's Mill, and I nigh fell over him lying out on the moor. He might have got his death; so when I saw who it was, I thought I'd best bring him home. But he'll take no harm; the drink that's in him will keep the cold out."

"I am much obliged to you," said Patty. "If there's any reward you'd take—"

"Meaning money?" he said, with a suppressed roar of a laugh. "No, I won't take no money. I might say something nasty to you after that, but I won't neither. It ain't very nice for you, poor girl, to have your man brought home in that state by your old sweetheart. I feel for you; but you always had a sharp tongue, and you never would give in. I advise you to take more care of the Softy now you've got him back," he said as he went away.

Patty shut and locked the door with an energy of rage and humiliation which almost overcame the horror of being heard. And then she went into the library and sat beside her husband till he had sufficiently recovered from his stupor to be taken upstairs. What hours of vigil! All the sins of her triumph might have been expiated while she sat there and shivered through the miserable night.

CHAPTER XXXVI

Patty had thoughts enough, surely, to occupy her that night, but it is doubtful whether there were any that came into her mind with the same reality—repeated again and again, as if by accident the recollection had been blown back upon her by a sudden wind—as those careless words uttered by Pearson when he had described how he had found Gervase: "I had been at a little hop at Coulter's Mill;" he said 'op, but though Patty had never used that manner of speech herself it did not hurt her. A little hop at Coulter's Mill. Such things were going on while she was shut up in the dismal grandeur of Greyshott. Girls were whirling round with their partners, receiving their attentions, which, though they might be rough and not very refined, were all that Patty knew of those delights of youth; while she, Patty, whom they all envied, who was now so far above them, sat and played backgammon with an old dotard, or watched half the night for her Softy's return. There were still such things, and Roger Pearson went to them! Patty had a soft place in her heart for Roger; she wished him no harm, and it might very well have been, had not Gervase and ambition come across her path, that she should have been his wife; and though she wished him nothing but good, Patty did hope that she had more or less broken his heart. She thought he would never have wished to go to those sort of places again, where every tune that was played and every dance would remind him of her. His careless speech took her, therefore, full in the breast, with a stupefying surprise. And he did not say it as if it was anything wonderful, but only as the calm ordinary of life, "I'd been at a little 'op at Coulter's Mill." And he was returning about two o'clock in the morning, which showed that he had amused himself well. Could such things be, and she out of them all? Every time this thought crossed her mind it gave her a new shock. It seemed almost impossible that such things could be.

But at all events, it was a comfort that Gervase at last was roused and got safely to his room before the servants were stirring, which it had been Patty's fear would not be possible. She had made up her story what to say in case she had been surprised by the early housemaid. She meant to keep the door closed, and to say that Mr. Piercey had been ill in the night and could not sleep, and now had fallen asleep on the sofa, and must not be disturbed. Happily, however, it was not necessary to burden her conscience with this additional fib. She got him upstairs safely, and to bed, and lay down herself upon the sofa with great relief. What a night! while all the girls who had been at the dance at Coulter's Mill would still be sleeping soundly, and if they ever thought of Patty, would think of her with such envy! Poor Patty, she was very brave. She snatched a little sleep, and was refreshed before Jerningham came to the door with that early cup of tea, which Patty understood all the fine ladies took in the morning. For once she was glad of that unnecessary refreshment. She told Jerningham that Mr. Piercey had been ill, and that she feared he had taken a bad cold; and then Patty closed the door upon the maid, who guessed, if she did not already know exactly, the character of the illness, and began to think steadily what she should do. She would tell Gervase that another night, if it happened again, he would be brought in dead, not alive. He would die, she would tell him, on the roadside like a dog. His was not a mind that could take in milder imaginations, but he would understand that. And Patty made up her mind to have another conversation with her father equally trenchant. She would tell him that if anything happened to Gervase she would have him tried for manslaughter. There would be abundant evidence, which she would not hesitate to bring forth, that the victim was half-witted, that he had been taken advantage of, and that the man who plied him with drink and then turned him out, his poor brain more clouded than ever, to find his way home, was his murderer and nothing else. Patty said to herself that she did not mind what scandals she would raise in such circumstances. If Richard Hewitt were brought to the scaffold she would not mind, though he was her father. She would tell him that she would drag him there with her own hands. She set here fierce little teeth, and vowed to herself that she would ruin him were he ten times her father, rather than let this go on. She would frighten Gervase to death; but before she was done she would set her foot on the ruins of the Seven Thorns.

Gervase, however, was too ill to be threatened the day after that dreadful vigil. He had caught cold lying out upon the moor, and he was very ill and in a high fever, quite unable to get up, or to have anything but nursing and kindness. Patty had the confidence of a woman well acquainted with the consequences of a debauch, that this would wear off in a short time and leave no particular results. She gave him beef-tea and gruel and kept him quiet, and told him, like a child, that he would be better to-morrow. "Gervase has caught a bad cold," she told Sir Giles, "but you must not be anxious, dear papa. I am keeping him in his warm bed, and he'll be all right to-morrow." "Right, right, my dear," said Sir Giles. "Bed is the best place. There is nothing like taking a cold in time, nothing like it. And we must remember he was always delicate. There's no stamina in him, no stamina." "He'll be all right to-morrow," Patty said, and she kept running up and down between the games to see if he was asleep, if he was comfortable, if he wanted anything. "Good creature!" said Sir Giles, half to himself, half to Dunning, who silently but consistently refused to appreciate Mrs. Piercey. "Now, what would you and I have done with the poor boy if he had been ill, and no wife on the spot to look after him?" "Maybe he wouldn't have had the same thing the matter with him," said Dunning, significantly. "Eh, what do you mean? What's the matter with him? He's got a bad cold," cried Sir Giles. "There are colds and colds," said the enigmatical Dunning. But Patty came back at the moment, saying that Gervase was quite quiet and asleep, and resumed her place for the second game. It was a longer game than usual, and Patty played badly, wishing her dear papa we will not venture to say how far off. But it came to an end at last, as everything does. "I hope you'll have a good night, my dear, and not be disturbed with him," the old gentleman said kindly. "Oh, I feel sure," cried Patty, "he'll be better to-morrow." But, as a matter of fact, she was not at all sure. The fumes of the drink ought to have died off by that time, but the fever had not died off. He was ill, and she was frightened and did not know what to do. And instead of being better in the morning, poor Gervase was worse, and the doctor had to be sent for, to whom, after various prevarications, poor Patty was obliged to confess the truth. Impossible to look more grave than the doctor did when he heard of this. "It was enough to kill him," he said. Patty understood (with a private reserve of vengeance against her father, who had been the cause of it) that Gervase was really ill and had escaped something still worse. But she was confident in her own powers of nursing, and did not take fright. She was really an excellent nurse, having a great deal of sense, and the habit of activity, and no fear of giving herself trouble. She devoted herself to her husband quite cheerfully, and even during the two first nights went down in a very pretty dressing-gown to play his game with Sir Giles. "We must not look for any change just yet, the doctor says, but he'll soon be well, he'll soon be well," she said; and believed it so thoroughly that Sir Giles, too, was quite cheerful, notwithstanding that Dunning, in the background, shook his head. Dunning would have shaken his head whatever had been the circumstances. It was part of his position to take always the worst view. And the household in general also took the worst view. Nobody had said anything about that fatal lying out on the moor. Mrs. Gervase certainly had not said a word (except to the doctor), and Roger Pearson had resisted every temptation to betray his share in the matter; yet everybody knew. How did they know? It is impossible to tell. The butler shook his head like Dunning, and so did the cook. "He have no constitution," they said.

But it was not till some days after that Patty began to take fright. She said "He'll be better to-morrow," even after she saw that the doctor looked grave—and resisted the aid of a nurse as long as she could, declaring that for a day or two longer she could hold out. "For he's not going to be long ill," she said, cheerfully. "Perhaps not," the doctor replied, with a tone that was exasperating in its solemnity. What did he mean? "You must remember, Mrs. Piercey," he continued, "that your husband has no constitution. Fortunately he has had no serious illness before, but he has always been delicate. It's common in—in such cases. He never had any stamina. You cannot expect him to throw off an attack such as this like any other man."

"Why not like any other man?" cried Patty. She was so familiar with Gervase that she had forgotten his peculiarities. Except when she thought of it as likely to serve her own purpose with her father, she had even forgotten that he was the Softy. He was her husband—part of herself, about whom, assuredly, there was no fibre of weakness. "Why shouldn't he shake it off like any other man?" she cried angrily.

The doctor gave her a strange look. "He has no constitution," he said.

The words and the look worked in Patty's mind like some strange leaven, mingling with all her thoughts. She could not at first imagine what they meant. After a while, when she was relieved by the nurse and went into another room to rest, instead of going to sleep, as she had, indeed, much reason to do, she sat down and thought it all over in the quiet. No constitution—no stamina. Patty knew very well, of course, what these words meant; it was the application of them that was difficult. Gervase! He was a little loose in his limbs, not very firmly knit perhaps, with not so much colour as the rustics around—but he was young, and healthy, and strong enough. Nobody had ever imagined that he was not strong. As for being a little soft, perhaps, in the mind, that was because people did not know him; and even if they did, the mind had nothing to do with the body, and it was all in his favour, for he did not worry and vex himself about things as others did. Like other men—why wasn't he like other men? He was as tall as most, he was not crooked or out of proportion, he was—

Did it mean that he might die?

Patty rose from her chair and flung her arms above her head with a cry. She was not without natural affection; she liked her husband, and was not dissatisfied with him, except in that matter of going to the Seven Thorns. She did not object to him because he was a fool; she was fond of him in a way. But when it suddenly flashed upon her that this might be the meaning of what the doctor said, it was not of Gervase's fate that she thought. Die! and deprive her of what she had made so many efforts to secure! Die! so that she never, never should be Lady Piercey, should she live a hundred years! Patty stood for a moment all quivering with emotion as she first realised this thought. It was intolerable, and not to be borne. She had married him, coaxed him, kept him in good humour, given up everything for him—only for this, that he should die before his father, and leave her nothing but Mrs. Piercey—Mrs. Piercey only, and for ever! Patty raised her hands unconsciously as if to seize him and shake him, with a long-drawn breath and a sobbing, hissing "Oh!" from the very bottom of her heart. She had it in her mind to rush to him, to seize him, to tell him he must not do it. He must make an effort; he must live, whatever happened. It was inconceivable, insupportable that he should die. He must not, should not die before his father, cheating his wife! She stood for a moment with her hands clenched, as if she had in reality grasped Gervase by his coat, and then she flung herself upon her face on the sofa in a passion of wild weeping. It could not, could not be; it must not be. She would not allow the possibility. Before his father, who was an old man—leaving all the honours to—anybody, whoever happened to be in the way, Margaret Osborne, for anything she knew—but not Patty, not she who had worked for them, struggled for them! It could not, and it must not be.

Patty did not sleep that day, though she had been up all night and wanted sleep. She bathed her face and her eyes, and changed her dress, and went back to her husband's bedside with a kind of fierce determination to hold by him, not to let him die. There was no change in him from what there had been when she left him, and the nurse was half offended by her intrusion. "I assure you, ma'am, I know my duties," she said, "and you'll break down next if you don't mind. Go, there's a dear, and get some sleep; you can't nurse him both by night and day. And there's no change, nothing to make you anxious."

"You are sure of that, nurse?"

"Quite sure. He's quite quiet and comfortable, so far as I can see."

"But they say he has no constitution," said Patty, gazing into the woman's face for comfort.

"Well, Mrs. Piercey; but most times it's the strongest man with whom it goes hardest," the nurse said.

And this gave Patty great consolation; it was the only comfort she had. It was one of those dicta which she had heard often both about children and men, and therefore she received it the more willingly. "It goes harder with the strong ones." That was the very commonest thing to say, and perhaps it was true.

The old women often knew better than the doctors, she said to herself. Indeed, there was in her mind a far greater confidence in such a deliverance than in anything the doctors could say.

And nothing could exceed the devotion with which poor Gervase was nursed. His wife was by his side night and day. She never tired—never wanted repose; was always ready; the most careful and anxious of nurses.

"He's much better to-day, don't you think?" was her greeting to the doctor when he came. And Dr. Bryant said afterwards that Mrs. Piercey looked as if she would have flown at his throat when he looked grave. She could not bear to be contradicted or checked in her hopes. And every day she went downstairs and assured Sir Giles that his son would soon be better.

"We can't expect it to pass in a day," she said, "for it is a very serious attack."

"And he has no stamina, no stamina; we always knew it—we were always told that," said the old gentleman.

Mrs. Piercey looked fiercely at her father-in-law, too. She could not bear to hear this repeated.

"Dear papa," she said, "it comes hardest always on the strongest men."

"God bless you, my dear!" cried old Sir Giles, falling a-sobbing, as was his wont when his mind was disturbed, "I believe that's true."

Oh, how could he go on living—that old man for whom nobody cared; who did nothing but keep the younger ones out of their own! What had he to live for? Patty wondered, with a wild, yet suppressed rage which no words could express; old, helpless, not able to enjoy anything except that wretched, tedious backgammon, and keeping others out of their own; yet he would live and see Gervase die! He would go on, and on, and see his only child buried, as he had seen his wife, and forget all about it after a week, and play his backgammon, and be guarded by Dunning from every wind that blew. Dunning! Was it Dunning, perhaps, that kept him alive; that knew things which the doctors don't know? It was natural to Patty's education and training to think this, and that some private nostrum would do more than all the drugs in the world.

"Shall I send down a nurse to you for a moment," she said to Sir Giles suddenly, "and will you let Dunning come up and look at him?" Dunning could not refuse to go, but he looked at Patty suspiciously, as if she meant to betray him into some trap.

"I don't know nothing about that kind of illness," he said.

"Oh, but you don't know what kind of illness it is till you see him," cried Patty. She hastily led the man to her husband's bedside, and watched his looks while he stood awkwardly, holding as far aloof as he could, looking down upon the half-sleep, half-stupor, in which the patient lay.

"Oh, Dunning, what do you think?"

"I think as he looks very bad," Dunning said, in a subdued and troubled voice.

"That's not what I want you to tell me. I want you to think if there is anything we could give him to rouse him up. What he wants is to be roused up, don't you see? When you are roused to see the need of it, you can do a deal for yourself, however ill you may be. What could we give him, Dunning, to rouse him up?"

Dunning could see nothing but some unintelligible trap that was being laid for him in those words.

"I'm not a doctor," he said, sullenly. "I know what's good for Sir Giles, as is chronic; but I don't know anything about the like of this. I should say there's nothing to give him, but just wait and—trust in God," said Dunning.

"Oh, God!" said Patty, in the unintentional profanity of her hot terror and distress. He was so far off; so difficult to get at; so impossible to tell what His meaning was! whereas she had felt that this man might have known something—some charm, some medicine which could be given at once.

"You had better go back to Sir Giles," she said, shortly, and sat down herself by that hopeless bed. But it was not hopeless to Patty. As soon as Dunning was gone she began to take a little comfort even from what he had said: "Wait, and trust in God." Patty knew all that could be said in words about trusting in God, and she knew many collects and prayers; but, somehow, even she felt that to ask God by any means, whatever happened, to exert His power that she might be Lady Piercey in the end—that the old man might die and the young man live for this purpose—was a thing not thought of in any collect: her mouth was stopped, and she could not find a word to say.

CHAPTER XXXVII

It was with nothing less than consternation that the county received the intelligence of Gervase Piercey's death, which flew from house to house nobody could tell how; told by the early postman on his rounds, conveyed with the morning's rolls from the villages, brought up at a pace much accelerated by the importance of the news by grooms with letter-bags, and every kind of messenger. Gervase Piercey was dead: the Softy of the village—poor Sir Giles' only son. Though he was a fool, he was Sir Giles' only child! There were ladies in the county who had wondered wistfully whether, if he were "taken up" by some capable woman, he might not have been so licked into shape as to have justified that capable woman in marrying him to her daughter. Nobody had been so brave as to do it, but several had speculated on the subject, thinking that, after all, to preserve a good old family from the dust, and hand on Greyshott to better heirs, might be worthy the sacrifice of a few years of a girl's life. These ladies, though none of them had been brave enough to take the necessary steps, felt doubly outraged by his marriage when it took place; and the consternation in their minds at the receipt of this last piece of news was tinged with something like remorse. Oh, if they had but had the courage! Maud or Mabel, if she had been forced to marry that unfortunate simpleton, would, as they now saw, have been so swiftly released! but it is needless to go back upon what might have been, after the contrary events. And now what a conjunction was this—what a terrible position for the poor old father! his only son taken from him; left alone with that woman in the house! Nobody knew anything about Patty; it was enough that she was Patty, and that she had married that poor half-witted young man. And then the question arose in a great many houses—What were they to do? They had not called upon Mrs. Gervase—nobody had called upon Mrs. Gervase—but how were they to approach Sir Giles now, with that woman there? Poor old Sir Giles! he had allowed her to take possession of his house for his son's sake, no doubt, and for peace, not being strong enough for any struggle, and what would he do now? Would he send her away, and thus be accessible again to his old friends, or what would he do? This question occupied the mind of the neighbourhood very much for the day or two after the news was received, and it became apparent that something must be done. The old man could not be left alone in his trouble, unsolaced by any friendly word; the details must be inquired into—the time of the funeral, so that proper respect might be paid. Many people sent cards, and servants to make the necessary inquiries, but one or two gentlemen went themselves, Lord Hartmore in particular, who as virtually the head of the county, and actually a very old friend, felt it incumbent upon him to carry his sympathy and condolence in person. Lord Hartmore was received by a young lady in very deep mourning, already covered in crape from top to toe, and crowned with the most orthodox of widows' caps. She was very quiet, but very firm.

"I cannot allow any one to disturb Sir Giles," she said; "he is very much broken down. Absolute quiet, and as little reference as possible to the details of our great trouble, are indispensable, the doctor says."

Lord Hartmore was much surprised at the self-possession of the young woman, and at her language.

"The tone of the voice was of course a little uneducated," he said, "but she talked, my dear, she talked as well as you or I, and made use of the same expressions!"

"Why, what other expressions could any one make use of?" cried Lady Hartmore.

"I said an old friend like myself should surely be made an exception; but she didn't give in. 'My father-in-law has seen none of his old friends for a long time,' she said quite pointedly; 'he is not accustomed to seeing them. It would be a great agitation to him, and I am charged to see that he is not disturbed.' I assure you," said Lord Hartmore, "I didn't know what to say. We have all deserted him in the most horrid way. The young woman was right: to put in an appearance just at this moment, not having shown since poor Lady Piercey's funeral, might quite probably be very discomposing to the old man!"

"And what about the funeral?" was the next question that was asked.

"There, again," said Lord Hartmore, "I can't blame her. She's met with no attention from us, and why should she take any trouble about us? The funeral is to be on Thursday; but she said, 'My father-in-law will not go. I can't put him to such a trial. I will follow my husband to his grave myself, and I don't know that I wish anybody else to take the trouble.' She carries things with a very high hand, but I can't blame her, I can't blame her," Lord Hartmore said. It must be added that the consternation of the county neighbours was increased by this report. Their consternation was increased, and so were their doubts as to what they should do; but at the same time their curiosity was piqued, and a certain sense of compunction rose in their bosoms. If it was merely the recklessness of disappointment and despair which moved Patty, or if it was severe and subtle calculation, at least her policy was wonderfully successful. There was a large attendance at poor Gervase's funeral, at which she appeared alone, occupying by herself the blackest of mourning coaches, and in such a depth of crape as never widow had worn before. But Mrs. Gervase was exceedingly digne in her woe. She made no hysterical demonstration. She had none of her own people in attendance upon her, as had been expected, though Richard Hewitt occupied a conspicuous position in the crowd, thrusting himself in among the county gentlemen in the procession. Patty stood by the grave all alone, and saw her hopes buried with real anguish. She fulfilled the part so well that Lord Hartmore (a candid man, as has been seen) could not contain himself for pity, and stepped quietly forward to her side and offered his arm. She took it silently, but with a trembling and evident need of support which went to the good gentleman's heart. Poor thing, poor thing! then she had been really fond of him after all. Lord Hartmore reflected silently that to a girl in her position the defects of the poor half-witted fellow might not be so apparent, and if she loved him, strange as that seemed! He led her back to her carriage with an almost fatherly friendliness, the whole village looking on, all the other gentlemen a little ashamed of themselves, and Richard Hewitt's red face blazing through the crowd. "My wife will call to inquire for you," he said, as he put her in, "and I hope that I may be admitted soon to see my dear old friend, Sir Giles." Patty answered only by a bow. It was all that could be expected of the poor young new-made widow, who had fulfilled this sad duty alone with no one to stand by her. The spectators were all impressed, and even overawed, by Patty's loneliness and her crape and her youth.

And she did in reality feel her downfall too much to get the good of Lord Hartmore's civility, or indulge the elation which sprang up in her mind, instinctively accompanying the consciousness that everybody saw her leaning upon Lord Hartmore's arm. Ah! what a thing that would have been a month ago! but now was it only a tantalising flutter before her eyes of what might have been, at present when all the reality was over? It would be unkind to Patty to say that no regret for poor Gervase in his own person was in her heart. She had not been without affection for Gervase, and the thought of his early death had been very sad to her at the moment. Poor Gervase, so young, and just when better things might have been in store for him! But the mind very soon familiarises itself with such an event when there is no very strong sentiment in question. It was not Gervase, but herself, whom Patty chiefly mourned. After all she had done and all she had gone through, to think that this was what was left to her—a position as insecure as that of any governess or companion, at the mercy of an old and ailing man, with one of her enemies at his ear. Oh, that it should be that old man, that useless, ailing old man, that should live and Gervase die! There seemed no justice in it, no equity, no sense of right. Sir Giles had lived his life and had all its good things, and there was no advantage to him or to any one in his continuance; whereas Gervase, Gervase! He, poor fellow, had it in his power to make his wife Lady Piercey, to secure her position so that nobody could touch it. And it was he that had gone, and not his father! Patty wept very real tears as she drove slowly home alone—real! they were tears of fire, and made her eyelids burn. Oh, how different from the last time when she drove along that same road, thrust in anyhow, clambering up without a hand to help her, sitting by Dunning's side—but with all the world before her, and the sense of a coming triumph in her veins! Patty did not deceive herself about her position now. A son's widow is a very different thing from a son's wife. The latter must be received, and has her certain place; the other is a mere dependant, to be neglected at pleasure. And it all rested with Sir Giles what was to become of her. He might keep her there as the mistress of his house, or he might make her a little allowance and send her away, desiring to see no more of her. Patty was altogether dependent, she felt, on the caprice of the old man. She had as good as nobody but he in the world, for she said to herself that nothing would induce her ever to speak to her father again, who had murdered Gervase and all her hopes. She would never look at him with her free will, never speak to him. That he should have dared to come to the funeral was a sin the more. Never, never! Patty said to herself she would rather go out to service, rather starve! These five months had placed a gulf between her and the Seven Thorns which nothing could ever bridge over. If it was suggested to her that she should return home, as young widows often do, she would say that she had no home, and it would be true. She would rather be a servant, rather starve!

And then her mind went back to Sir Giles. What would he do with her? The old man liked her, she felt sure. And she had been good to him. Whatever her motives had been, whether they would bear scrutiny or not, she had been good to him. She had kept pain away from him as far as she could. She had taken care of all his comforts. She had not permitted him to be disturbed. Dunning and all the rest would have thought it essential that he should go to the funeral and undergo all the misery and excitement of that ceremony. But Patty had prevented that. He had reason to be grateful to her; but would he be grateful? This was the tremendous question. Would he keep her there as the mistress of his house, or would he send her away? Patty had in her jewel-case, carefully locked up, a letter from Margaret Osborne to her uncle, which she thought it wisest to keep back. If Sir Giles received it, it might make him think that Mrs. Osborne was the best mistress for his house, which she was not, Patty felt sure. She put it aside, saying to herself that some time, when the excitement was over and everything had settled down, she would give it—but not now: to what purpose now? Poor Sir Giles wanted to forget his trouble, not to have it forced upon him by condolences. Margaret had written to Patty also a short note full of sorrow for poor Gervase, and asking whether it would be desirable that she should come to Greyshott for his funeral; to which Patty had replied explaining that everything was to be very quiet in consequence of the condition of "dear papa." "It is he that must be considered in everything," Patty wrote; "I have the doctor's orders to keep him as much as possible from all emotion. I will bury my dear husband myself. Nobody else, as you know, has ever been very fond of him, and I shall not ask anybody to come for the form's sake. If possible, dear papa is not to be told even the day. He is very broken and miserable, but when he is let alone and not reminded, he forgets." Margaret had accepted this as a refusal of her visit, and she had asked no more. It would have been a painful visit in any case. Colonel Piercey was abroad. There were, therefore, no relations to come to make the occasion more difficult for Patty, and yet there had been no want of "respect." The county magnates had all attended the melancholy funeral—where the young wife alone was chief mourner. "Why did not Margaret come?" they all asked, and blamed her. But a feeling of sympathy arose for Patty all over the neighbourhood. The doctor spoke with enthusiasm of her devotion as a nurse, and her intelligence and understanding. Poor thing! Poor thing! Whatever her antecedents had been, and however she had acquired that place, she had certainly behaved very well; and now what was to become of her? people asked with pity. It was assumed that she would return to her friends, as other young widows did—though not in this case to her father's house.

If they had but known how anxiously she was herself debating that question as she drove along in her crape and her woe, with the blinds down, and every symptom of desolation! Dunning had not allowed his master to dine out of his own rooms, or to indulge in any diversion in the evening, since the death of his son. If other people did not know or care what was right, Dunning did, and at all events poor Mr. Gervase should be respected in his own house as long as he lay there. Above all, on the evening of the funeral day, Dunning was determined there should be no relaxation of that rule. He was disposed to think, as were the rest of the servants, that Patty's reign was over; but the others were more wary than Dunning, and did not show any signs of emancipation as yet. He did so with premature exultation, rejecting almost roughly her suggestion that Sir Giles should dine as usual on that gloomy evening. "Master's not equal to it," said Dunning, "and if he was he didn't ought to be. I don't hold with folks that dance and sing the day they've put their belongings in the grave—or eat and drink, it's just the same."

"You forget what the doctor says, that nothing must be allowed to upset him. I hope you don't talk to Sir Giles on—melancholy subjects," Patty said, with all the dignity of her widow's cap.

"I don't know what subjects there can be but melancholic subjects in this 'ouse of mournin'," Dunning said.

"Then I will come and see him myself," said Patty. She went to Sir Giles' room accordingly, after his too simple dinner had been swallowed, and devoted herself to him.

"I think we'll send Dunning away for a little, dear papa," she said. "We have things to talk of, haven't we?—and Dunning has been on duty a long time, and a little society will make him more cheerful."

"I beg your pardon, Sir Giles," said Dunning, "but whatever some folks may think I don't 'old with being cheerful, not on the day of a funeral."

"What does he say, my dear? what does he say?" said Sir Giles. "But look you here, Dunning, whatever it is I won't have Mrs. Piercey contradicted. Do you hear, sir? Do as Mrs. Piercey tells you," and he struck his stick upon the floor.

Dunning in consternation withdrew, for when Sir Giles was roused he was not to be trifled with.

"She's found out some d—d trick to come over the old man," he said in the housekeeper's room to which he retired. But this was a mistake; for it was Sir Giles himself who had invented the trick. He turned to Patty with great tenderness when the man disappeared, and took her by both hands and drew her to a chair beside him.

"My dear," he said, "I've forgotten, like an old sinner, what Meg Osborne told me. I've been allowing you to do all sorts of things and wear yourself out. But it sha'n't happen again, it sha'n't happen again. Now that my poor dear boy is gone we must be more careful than ever—for it's our last hope both for you and for me to have an heir for the old house."

CHAPTER XXXVIII

It was Sir Giles himself who had found this charm which had so great an effect on the after-history of Greyshott. Patty, among other qualities which were not so praiseworthy, had the almost fierce modesty of the young Englishwoman, and would not have spoken on such a subject to a man, even so harmless a person as an old man like Sir Giles, for any inducement. She did not even understand what he meant at first, and the same impulse of farouche modesty made her ashamed to explain, or do more than blush deeply and remonstrate, "Oh, dear papa!" as she would have done probably in any case, whether his supposition had been false or true. The old gentleman in his melancholy and confused musings over Gervase, had suddenly remembered, the thought being recalled by some merest trifle of association, the hurrahs of little Osy which had mingled with his own feeble cheer on some forgotten occasion. He remembered it suddenly as the strangest contrast to his feelings now. What had the old father, desolate and childless, to cheer about? What had he heard that could have produced that cheer? It was when Meg was going away—when she had told him she was going to take Osy away from him. That was nothing to cheer about. What was it that had made him forget Osy, but which the dear little fellow had caught up and shouted over, though it was an unkindness to himself? and then he recollected all at once. What Mrs. Osborne had said had been the most common and ordinary wish that children might arise in the old house, which was the most natural thing, the most certainly to be expected. She had meant no more: but Sir Giles had at once attributed to Meg a knowledge which was at the moment impossible, without reflecting either that she was the last person to receive the confidence of Patty. He forgot now that it was months since this had been said, and only remembered that it had been said, and that the prospect was like life from death. Life from death! That was what it would be—from his dead son an heir, in whom the old house might blossom and grow glad again. He took up the idea where he had dropped it with a sudden exhilaration which drove away all sorrow. An heir to the old house, a thing all made of hope, with none of poor Gervase's deficiencies, a being whom the old man fondly hoped to "make a man of" even yet before he died.

And it would not be too much to say that the first feeling of Patty, when she understood what the old gentleman meant, was one of consternation. She did not know how to answer him, how to tell him that she had no such hope. Her lips were closed partly by the tradition of silence on such subjects which an unsophisticated Englishwoman seldom surmounts, and partly because she was so utterly astonished and taken aback by the suggestion. She did not even see the advantage in it, nor how it placed this feeble old man whose life hung on a thread in her hands. It was not till after she had left him and was alone, and could think, that these advantages occurred to Patty; and there was probably no suggestion of a treacherous kind which it would have seemed to her so impossible to make use of. The scruples of life are very much things of circumstance, that seeming quite legitimate and right to one which is the height of immodesty and indelicacy to another. Patty had one distinct object in her mind, now that all her hopes were over, which was to induce her father-in-law, by whatever means were possible, to make a provision for her. He was really, she felt, the only one to whom she could now cling, her sole support and protection, and she meant to be also his protector, to take care of him as he had never been taken care of before. All this she steadfastly intended, meaning nothing but good to the ailing and desolate old man; but she also intended that he should provide for her, as was her right as his son's wife. Should Sir Giles die at the present moment, Patty was strongly and painfully aware that she would be in no way the better for having taken that step which had seemed so prodigious a one, which had raised her so high above all her antecedents and belongings, by becoming Gervase Piercey's wife. She was Mrs. Piercey, but she was without a penny, poorer by the burden of that name than Patty Hewitt could ever have been. Her first duty, her first determination was to be provided for, in whatever manner it might be most possible to do that. But it is only just to her to say that this way of influencing her father-in-law, and of moving him to do what she wished, had never occurred to her, and even when thus suggested it was very repugnant to her—the last thing she desired to do. But Patty, shut up in her room of widowhood and mourning, with her cap with its long, white streamers visible upon the table, and everything black about her, even the dressing-gown which she had put on to sit by the fire, and her mind so alert and unfatigued going over everything, speculating how best to pluck from the nettle danger the flower of safety, could not shut out the suggestion from her thoughts. It might even yet prove to be so, she said to herself, blushing hotly, even though she was alone. And if not, why shouldn't she permit Sir Giles to think so? It would give him a great deal of pleasure, poor old gentleman. It would tide him over the worst time, the immediate crisis of his son's death, and it would double her every claim upon him, and make it more than ever necessary that he should put her at once beyond the reach of want or suffering of any kind. Still, it was with reluctance that she accepted this weapon which had been thrust into her hand.

Sir Giles could not get his new discovery out of his head. He told Dunning of it before he went to bed. It was whispered all through the house in the morning; and though some of the women scoffed and declared it to be an invention, yet it was, of course, the most natural idea in the world. From Patty not a word came, either in assertion or denial. She said nothing; she understood no hints; she never allowed herself to be betrayed into reference to her supposed hopes. Sir Giles alone talked to her on the subject with joyous laughter and chuckles, and a loudly expressed determination that she should be obeyed and not contradicted, which was of priceless value to Patty, at the moment when her sway was a little uncertain, and when expectation was strong in the household that she should be displaced and Mrs. Osborne sent for in her place. The household by no means desired Mrs. Osborne in Patty's place. Margaret had been too much and too long a dependant to be popular among the servants; and Patty, who was so peremptory, who had acted upon her convictions, and managed to turn out everybody whom she feared or disliked, had powerful recommendations in her imperious authority. She meant what she said, and could not be driven or persuaded out of it; and she knew when work was well done, and gave the capable housemaid or cleaner of plate the praise which was his or her due. And she was not unjust, save in the case of personal disrespect to herself, which she never pardoned—a quality which the servants' hall entirely approved. Mrs. Osborne could be got to "look over" anything by judicious entreaty or representation, especially if it was a mere offence against herself, and was less respected and considered in consequence. It was not, therefore, in any way desired that she should take up the reins; yet, all the same, it made a great difference to Patty that Sir Giles had taken it into his head that she must not be contradicted. It established her once more firmly in her seat.

And the little group in the great drawing-room in the evening was all the more cheerful in consequence. It was, to look at, a forlorn group enough: the old gentleman, more feeble than ever, with Dunning behind his chair, ready to move it according to his caprice, and the young widow in her deep crape, a black spot upon the white and gold of the room. Patty had been requested by Sir Giles to "take that thing off her head," and did so obediently in her father-in-law's presence, though she was far too determined to do her duty by her dead husband to dispense with that symbol of grief on any other occasion. They sat with the backgammon-board between them, playing game after game. There was in Patty's mind unutterable relief from the misery and suspense which she had suffered in Gervase's lifetime; but other thoughts, scarcely less anxious, occupied her fully. Yet she talked to the old gentleman with an endeavour to please and amuse him which was heroic. It was a great strain upon Patty. She could talk of herself without difficulty; she could have talked, had she thought it expedient, of her father and aunt, and their sins against her; she could have talked of Gervase; but these subjects being all tabooed, it was very hard upon Patty to find anything to say. She knew nobody whom Sir Giles knew. She could not tell him the news, for she knew none, except the affairs of the village, which interested herself, and which she seized on greedily from every possible channel. But Patty could not talk on any other subject. She had to talk about the backgammon, to remind him of the wonderful stroke he had played last night, and the wonderful luck he had always; and how it was such an amazing chance for her to play, a poor ignorant thing as she was, with such an accomplished player as dear papa. This was but a scanty thread to spin through night after night, and had it not been made up so much of applause it is very doubtful how long it would have sufficed. But there is nothing of which the ordinary mind can swallow so much as praise; and when the interest of life is reduced to a game, the player thinks as much of his lucky chances and his skilful movements as if it were something of the highest importance; so that, on the whole, this talk did very well and kept them going. But still Patty had not ventured to introduce her great subject—that provision for herself which she felt became more and more important every day; for who could tell whether any morning Sir Giles might not be found to have passed away from this life altogether, or to be enclosed in the living tomb of paralysis, unable to act or devise anything more.

Lady Hartmore did not call next day as her lord had promised, but she did call, and was received by Patty in full panoply of mourning and with a heart that beat loudly with suppressed excitement. Lady Hartmore was neither so much touched by the sight of the young widow, nor so sympathetic as her husband had been. She examined Patty curiously, with searching eyes, full not only of the superciliousness of rank, but of the experience of a much older woman, which Mrs. Gervase would have opposed with defiance, but for the false pretence which, though she had never put it forth, and though it had arisen most innocently, gave her something of a sensation of guilt. This, however, though Patty was not aware of it, did her service with the great lady. It subdued her natural determination, and gave an apparent softness to her aspect which did not belong to it by nature. Lady Hartmore put a great many questions to the young widow: did she think of remaining at Greyshott, which must be so melancholy a place nowadays? did she think this last shock had very much shaken Sir Giles? did she not feel it a great responsibility to be left in charge of him? and many other such questions. To these Patty replied very properly that she could not possibly leave Sir Giles alone; that he had been very kind to her, like a father, and that nothing would induce her to desert him; that he was very well on the whole, "quite himself," and that she tried to be as cheerful as she could on his account. She took no notice of the question about leaving Greyshott. It was not indeed necessary to reply to it, when she had already made that answer about the impossibility of leaving Sir Giles.

"But you must want somebody to speak to,—somebody to take care of you, too," said the great lady, meaning more than she said.

"Oh, no," said Patty; "I have always had very good health, I have never been delicate. I am very fond of my dear father-in-law. He does not want very much—he is very easily amused, and so kind, always so kind. We do very well all by ourselves—as well," Patty added, with a sigh, "as in the circumstances we could possibly do."

What could any one say to such perfect sentiments? Lady Hartmore was baffled in her inquisitions. "Still," she said, "I should have thought that some one who was a relation—some one of your own family—a woman to speak to—"

"I am sure," said Patty, "that Lady Hartmore knows my family are not likely to be welcome at Greyshott; and I have but an old aunt who was never married, and therefore has no experience." She blushed as she said this, and Lady Hartmore was very quick to take up the inference for which she was prepared. But Patty was too wise to be led into any further disclosures or to answer any of the searching questions which her ladyship proceeded to put.

"How did you find the poor thing?" her husband asked when he joined her in the carriage—for Lord Hartmore had visited Sir Giles while Lady Hartmore thus did her duty by Patty.

"I found the poor thing very well and extremely well able to take care of herself," said the lady. "I don't think you need waste so much sympathy upon her." But Lord Hartmore was full of feeling, and could not be persuaded to take this view.

"The poor old fellow is quite exultant," he said. "It is a wonderful blessing for him, whatever you may think of it in any other connection. It has given him a new lease."

"I don't believe a word of it," said Lady Hartmore.

"Oh, come!" cried her husband. "It is one thing to trust your own judgment, which is an excellent one, I don't gainsay it—but quite another to set it up against those who must know the facts best. By the way, he bewildered me by saying Meg told him. Has Meg been here?"

"Not that I know of; but she may have made a hurried run to see her uncle. If Meg told him—" said Lady Hartmore, in subdued tones. She added after a pause, "I shall think more of her if Meg is her confidante."

Thus on the whole the impression was favourable to Patty, even though the grounds upon which it was formed were false.

After this visit Patty took her first active step towards the accomplishment of her desires. Sir Giles, who had been pleased with the Hartmore visit and augured great things from it, opened the way by asking if she had not liked Lady Hartmore and found her kind? "A nice woman, a good-hearted woman," he said.

"Yes, dear papa; but one thing she said gave me a great deal of pain; for she seemed to think I should go back to my family, and leave you," she said, putting her handkerchief to her eyes.

"Leave me? nonsense!" said Sir Giles, "I sha'n't let you leave me, my dear. I shouldn't have sent you away, anyhow, you may be sure; no, no, I shouldn't have sent you away; but in present circumstances, my dear—Why, you're all our hope at Greyshott, you're all our stand-by, you're—you're our sheet-anchor."

"How kind, how kind you are, dear papa! I try to do my best to keep everything straight, though I never could pretend to be of so much consequence as that. But people feel free to speak," said Patty, with a sigh, "because they know I have no ground to stand on. I wasn't dear Gervase's equal when he married me, and there were no settlements or anything, you know; and I am quite dependent, quite dependent, as much as a servant—but without any wages," Patty added, with a faint laugh.

It was at one of the rare moments when Dunning was absent, intervals of which Patty eagerly took advantage. Dunning was, indeed, a thorn in her flesh, though after mature deliberation she had decided that it was wiser to retain him, that he might take the responsibility of Sir Giles' health.

"Dependent!" cried Sir Giles, "nonsense, nonsense! A servant, my dear? Don't let me hear such a word again. No, no; no, no; never could have been so, for you've been quite a daughter, quite a daughter. But, in the present circumstances—"

"Ah, dear papa, don't let us think of that. I love to be with you—it's the only comfort I have; but still I can't forget that I have no provision. I might have to go away and work for my living, if somebody were to over-persuade you, or if you were—ill or anything. A Mrs. Piercey having to work for her living—or perhaps take a situation! I shouldn't mind it for myself, but when I think, dear papa, of your name."

"Good Lord!" cried Sir Giles, "you must be out of your mind, my dear, to think of such a thing. My poor boy's wife, and a good wife to him, too, if he had but lived to profit by it. That's all nonsense, all nonsense, my dear."

"Ah, dear papa! but it would not be nonsense if I had not you to trust to," cried Patty, laying her hand upon his arm. "It is you who are my sheet-anchor. I have not a penny of my own, not even to pay for my mourning; and I can't earn any for myself, don't you know, because of dear Gervase and your name—the first in the county. I couldn't take in needlework, could I, in Greyshott? and a woman, you know, has always little expenses—"

"My dear," said Sir Giles, "have all the fal-lals you can set your face to, and send in the bills to me; you've nothing to do but send in the bills to me."

"Dear papa! as if I ever doubted your kindness. It is not fal-lals I am thinking of; this," cried Patty, holding up her crape, "is not much of a fal-lal, is it? But what I am thinking of is the time to come, when I shall require to have a little provision or income or salary of my own."

"Do you mean," cried the old man, in the half-sobbing tone into which he was betrayed by any emotion, "when—when—I'm no more; when I'm dead? Is that what you mean?"

Patty stooped down and laid her face against the large old limp hand, which reposed on the arm of Sir Giles' chair. "I hope I'll be dead, too, before that," she said; "for what should I have to live for then?"

This, it need not be pointed out, was no answer to his question; but it seemed so, and Sir Giles was much affected and sobbed, which Patty echoed with a deep sigh or two which seemed to give a more refined expression to his feeling. He put his other hand upon her head.

"Please God, we'll see better days before that," he said.

And then Dunning came back, and a new game was begun.

CHAPTER XXXIX

It was not till some days after this, that Sir Giles referred to the subject again. Patty thought it had entirely failed to make any impression on his mind, and that she must herself renew the conversation, when he surprised her by saying suddenly, as if there had been no interval, "It won't be necessary, my dear, it won't be necessary. As his mother, everything will be in your hands."

"Dear papa!" she cried, with a quite natural start; "how you frightened me!"

"I don't want to frighten you, my dear; anything but that—anything but that! But you must see that any little arrangements we might make would be all needless, quite needless. Of course, everything will go to the natural heir. There will probably be a long minority, for you know, my dear, with the best intentions in the world, an old fellow like me—though I would give half my kingdom to see him come of age—half my kingdom! But no, no, that's a selfish thought; for I should wish him to have the property unimpaired, if not added to—if not added to. You'll take great care of it, I am sure. You're quite a woman of brains." Sir Giles spoke very fast, to get through this long effort of thought and consideration before Dunning came back. Then he added, with his usual mingled outburst of laughing and sobbing, patting her arm with his large old nerveless hand, "So you see it's needless, needless, my dear, for everything will be in your hands."

"Dear papa!" cried Patty. She was silent for some time in confusion and embarrassment. Then, "There's nothing certain in this world," she said.

"What, what?" cried Sir Giles. "Nothing's happened—nothing's happened, my dear? I hope you don't mean to tell me that?"

"Nothing has happened, dear papa," cried Patty, with a painful flush upon her face. She had not meant to deceive him, and certainly not in this way. It was indeed hard upon her that she had, without any fault of hers, this fiction to keep up. "But there's nothing certain in this world," she said. "Who would have thought five months ago that I should need to be thinking of a little provision for myself—I, that was Gervase's wife, and had no need to think of anything? I married him without a thought of having anything settled on me, or even wanting a penny but what he gave me." Patty put her handkerchief to her eyes to absorb some real tears, for though her grief for poor Gervase could scarcely be expected to be very profound, her pity for herself was sincere and lasting. "Dearest papa! I can't bear to ask for myself. I've always been used to work, and I could get my own living at any time. It is just that I can't bear, being Mrs. Piercey, that I should have to do it in that way—Gervase's widow, with your name."

"Don't, my dear, don't! For goodness' sake don't agitate yourself! Don't cry, my dear, don't cry!" said Sir Giles, anxiously.

"Oh, I wouldn't cry if—if I could help it. I would do nothing to vex you, dear papa. But when I think of all that has happened—oh, who should know so well as I that there's nothing certain in this world!"

"My dear, my dear, I'll send for Pownceby to-morrow. You must not upset yourself—you mustn't, indeed. What should I do, and everybody, if—if anything was to happen?" Sir Giles cried. And he became so excited in his anxiety to calm her, that Patty was compelled to conquer herself and regain her self-command. She looked up with a mournful smile from her pocket-handkerchief. "Dear papa," she said, "we are two of us that mustn't do that. If you get upset it will upset me, and that will upset you still more; so we must each hold up for the sake of the other. Suppose we have another game?"

"You always know exactly what I want," said the old gentleman, his sob turning into a laugh, as his laugh so often turned into a sob. There was not, in fact, much difference between the two; and the rest of the evening was passed as usual in admiring exclamations on Patty's part as to his wonderful play and wonderful luck, so that even Dunning did not suspect that there had been anything more.

Patty reminded her father-in-law next morning when she went to him, as she had begun to make a practice of doing, to see if he wanted any letters written, that he had spoken of some Mr. Pownceby who was to be written to. "I don't know who Mr. Pownceby is, but you said something about him, dear papa!" And the result was that in a day or two Mr. Pownceby came, the family solicitor, whom Patty indeed did not know, but of whose faculties and position in the matter she had a shrewd guess. She had to entertain the little gentleman to luncheon after he had been closeted with Sir Giles all the morning; and Mr. Pownceby was much impressed by Mrs. Piercey's dignified air, and her crape and her widow's cap. "I suppose it's within the range of possibilities that a girl in that position might be fond even of a poor fellow like Gervase Piercey," he said to himself doubtfully; and he made himself very agreeable to the young widow. He informed her that he had received instructions to charge the estate with an annuity of a thousand pounds a year for her, of which the payments were to begin at once. "A very proper arrangement," he said, and he was impressed by the composure with which Patty received the information. She was not indeed at all elated by it. A thousand pounds a year was a great thing for Patty Hewitt of the Seven Thorns. She would have thought it a princely revenue when she became Gervase Piercey's wife; but a few months' familiarity with the expenditure of Greyshott had made a great change in Patty's views. To descend into a small house like the Rectory, for instance (she had once thought the Rectory a palace), and to do without a carriage, was far from an agreeable prospect. "How shall I ever do without a carriage?" Patty said to herself, and she thought with scorn of the little basket-work pony-chaise which was all the rector could afford. Was it possible that she should ever come down to that? Mr. Pownceby, when he went away, held her hand for a moment, and asked whether a very old friend of the family, who had known poor dear Gervase from his birth, might be permitted to say how pleased and thankful he was that there were hopes—? which made Sir Giles so very happy, poor old gentleman? "And I fear, I fear, my dear old friend has not many days before him," the lawyer said; "he's quite clear in his mind, but it was not to be expected that a worn-out constitution could bear all those shocks one after another. We'll not have him long, Mrs. Piercey, we'll not have him long!"

"Does the doctor say so?" asked Patty.

"My dear lady, the doctor says he has the best of nursing; and everything so much the better for a lady in the house." It was with this douceur that the solicitor took his leave, being a man that liked to please everybody. And there can be no doubt that a softened feeling arose in the whole neighbourhood about Patty, who was said to be such a good daughter to Sir Giles. "Thrown over her own people altogether—no crowd of barbarians about the house, as one used to fear; and quite gives herself up to her father-in-law; plays backgammon with him half the day, which can't be lively for a young woman; and expects—" These last were the most potent words of all.

Patty was, indeed, very good to her father-in-law, and that not altogether for policy, but partly from feeling; for he had been kind to her, and she was grateful. The winter was dreary and long, and there were sometimes weeks together when Sir Giles could not get out, even into the garden, for that forlorn little drive of his in the wheeled chair. Patty gave herself up to his service with a devotion which was above all praise. She bore his fretfulness when weakness and suffering made the old man querulous. She was always at hand, whatever he wanted. She looked after his food and his comfort, often in despite of Dunning and to the great offence of the cook, but both these functionaries had to submit to Patty's will. Had she not carried everything with a very high hand, it is possible that her footing might not have been so sure; for the women soon penetrated the fiction, which was not indeed of Patty's creation, and Dunning even ventured upon hints to Sir Giles that all was not as he thought. The old gentleman, however, got weaker day by day; one little indulgence after another dropped from him. March was unusually blustery, and April very wet. These were good reasons why he should not go out; that he was more comfortable in his chair by the fire. Then he got indifferent to the paper, which Dunning always read to him in the morning, and only took an interest in the scraps of news which Patty repeated to him later on.

"Why did not Dunning read me that, if it is in the paper? The fellow gets lazier and lazier; he never reads the paper to me now! He thinks I forget!" When Dunning would have remonstrated Patty checked him with a look.

"You must never contradict Sir Giles!" she said to him aside.

"And he says I'm never to contradict her!" Dunning said indignantly in the housekeeper's room, where he went for consolation; "between them a man ain't allowed to say a word!"

The women all cried out with scorn that Sir Giles would find out different from that one o' these days.

"Then he'll just die," said Dunning. Things had come to a very mournful pass in the old melancholy house.

By degrees the backgammon, too, fell out of use. Patty sat with him still in the evening, but it was in his own room, often by his bedside, and many, many conversations took place between them, unheard by any one. Dunning would catch a word now and then, as he went and came, and gathered that Sir Giles was sometimes telling her of things he would like to have done, and that sometimes she was telling him of things she would wish to be done.

"As if she had aught to do with it!" Dunning said with indignation. Dunning, observing everything, imagined, too, that Sir Giles began to grow anxious about those expectations which were so long delayed. His attendant sometimes heard mutterings of calculation and broken questioning with himself from the old gentleman.

"It's a long time to wait—a long time—a long time!" he said.

"What is a long time, Sir Giles?" Dunning ventured to ask—but was told to hold his tongue for a fool.

One day, towards the end of April, he suddenly roused from a long muse or doze by the fire, and called to Dunning to send a telegram for Pownceby.

"Tell him to come directly. I mayn't be here to-morrow," Sir Giles said.

"Are you thinking of changing the air, Sir Giles?" said the astonished servant.

The rain was pouring in a white blast across the park, bending all the young trees one way, and pattering among the foliage.

"Air!" said the old man; "it's nothing but water; but I'm soon going to move, Dunning, as you say."

"Well, it might do you good, Sir Giles, a little later—when the weather's better."

Sir Giles made no reply, but Dunning heard him muttering: "She always says there's nothing certain in this world."

Mr. Pownceby came as quick as the railway could bring him.

"Is there anything wrong?" he asked of Mrs. Piercey, who met him at the door.

"Oh, I am afraid he's very bad," said Patty; "I am afraid he's not long for this world."

"Why does he want me? Does he want to change his will?"

"I don't know—I don't know. Oh, Mr. Pownceby, I don't know how to say it. I am afraid he is disappointed: that—that you said to me last time—"

"Was not true, I suppose?" said the father of a family, who was not without his experiences, and he looked somewhat sternly at Patty, who was trembling.

"I never said it was," she said. "It was not I. He took it into his head, and I did not know how to contradict him. Oh, don't say to him it's not true! rather, rather let him believe it now. Let him die happy, Mr. Pownceby! Oh, he has been so good to me! Say anything to make him die happy!" Patty cried.

The lawyer was angry and disappointed, too; but Patty's feeling was evidently genuine, and he could not help feeling a certain sympathy with her. Sir Giles was sitting up in bed, ashy white with that pallor of old age which is scarcely increased by death.

"I'm glad you're come in time, Pownceby—very glad you're come in time. I'm—I'm going to make a move; for change of air, don't you know, as Dunning says. Poor Dunning! he won't get such an easy berth again. My will—that's it. I want to change—my will. Clear it all away, Pownceby—all away, except the little legacies—the servants and that—"

"But not Mrs. Piercey, Sir Giles? If—if she's been the cause of any—disappointment; it isn't her fault."

"Disappointment!" said the old man. "Quite the contrary. She's been just the reverse. It was a good day for me when she came to the house. No, I don't mean that it was a good day, for it was my poor wife's funeral; but if anybody could have made a man of Gervase she would have done it. She would have done it, Pownceby. Yes, yes; sweep her away! sweep everybody away! I give and bequeath Greyshott and all I have—all I have, don't you know? Gerald Piercey can have the pictures if he likes; she won't care for them to—"

The old man was seized with a fit of coughing, which interrupted him at this interesting moment. Mr. Pownceby sat with his pen in his hand and many speculations in his mind. To cut off his daughter-in-law's little income even while he praised her so! And who was the person to whom it was all to be left without regard for the rest? Meg Piercey, perhaps, who was one of the nearest, though she had never been supposed to have any chance. The lawyer sat with his eyes under his spectacles intently fixed upon Sir Giles, and with many remonstrances in his mind. Mrs. Gervase might be wrong to have filled the poor man with false hopes; but to leave her to the tender mercies of Meg Piercey, whom she had virtually turned out of the house, would be cruel. Sir Giles began to speak before his coughing fit was over.

"She says, poor thing," and here he coughed, "she s—says that there's nothing—nothing certain in this world. She's right, Pownceby—she's right. She—generally is."

"There's not much risk in saying that, Sir Giles."

"No, it's true enough—it's true enough. It might grow up like its father. God grant it otherwise. You remember our first boy, Pownceby? Wasn't that a fellow! as bold as a lion and yet so sweet. His poor mother never got over it—never; nor I neither, nor I neither—though I never made any fuss."

Was the old man wandering in his mind?

"I hoped it would have been like him," said Sir Giles, with a sob. "I had set my heart on that. But none of us can tell. There's nothing certain, as she says. It might grow up like its father. I'll make all safe, anyhow, Pownceby. Put it down, put it down—everything to—"

"Sir Giles! to whom? Everything to—?"

"Why, Pownceby, old fellow! Ah, to be sure he doesn't know the first name. Sounds droll a little, those two names together. Quick! I want it signed and done with, in case I should, as Dunning says—don't you know, change the air."

"But, Sir Giles!" cried the lawyer, in consternation: "Sir Giles!" he added, "you don't mean, I hope, to leave the property away from the family and the natural heir?"

"What a muddlehead you are, Pownceby!" said Sir Giles, radiant. "Why, It will be the natural heir. It will be the head of the family. And it will grow up like our first boy, please God. But nothing is certain; and supposing it was to turn out like its father? My poor boy, my poor Gervase! It wasn't as if we weren't fond of him, you know, Pownceby. His poor mother worshipped the very ground he trod on. But one can't help hoping everything that's good for It, and none of the drawbacks—none of the drawbacks. Make haste, Pownceby; draw it out quick! You're quicker than any clerk you have, when you'll take trouble. Nothing's certain in this world; let's make it all safe, Pownceby, however things may turn out."

"I'll take your instructions, Sir Giles—though I don't like the job. But it's a serious matter, you know, a very serious matter. Hadn't you better think it over again? I'll have the will drawn out in proper form, and come back to-morrow to have it signed."

"And how can you tell that you'll find me to-morrow? I may have moved on and got a change of air, as Dunning says. No, Pownceby, draw up something as simple as you like, and I'll sign it to-day."

The solicitor met Mrs. Piercey again in the hall as he went out. He had not been so kind on his arrival as she had found him before; but now he had a gloomy countenance, almost a scowl on his face, and would have pushed past her without speaking, with a murmur about the train which would wait for no man. Patty, however, was not the woman to be pushed aside. She insisted upon hearing his opinion how Sir Giles was.

"I think with you that he is very ill," he replied, gloomily, "and in mind as well as in body—"

"Oh no," cried Patty, "not that, not that! as clear in his head, Mr. Pownceby, as you or me."

He gave her a dark look, which Patty did not understand. "Anyhow," he said, "he's an old man, Mrs. Piercey, and I don't think life has many charms for him. We have no right to repine."

Mr. Pownceby had known Sir Giles Piercey all his life, and liked him perhaps as well as he liked any one out of his own family. But to repine—why should he repine, or Patty any more, who stood anxiously reading his face, and only more anxious not to betray her anxiety than she was to hear what, perhaps, he might tell? But he did not do this. Nor would he continue the conversation, nor be persuaded to sit down. He asked that he might be sent for, at any moment, if Sir Giles expressed a wish to see him again. "I will come at a moment's notice—by telegraph," he said, with a gloomy face, that intended no jest. And he added still more gloomily, "I believe it will be for your advantage, too."

"I am thinking of my father-in-law and not of my advantage," Patty said with indignation. The anxiety in her mind was great, and she could not divine what he meant.

CHAPTER XL

Margaret Osborne had lost no time in settling down in a cottage proportioned to her means, with her little boy and the one maid, who did all that was necessary, yet as little of everything as was practicable, for the small household. The place she had chosen was not very far from Greyshott, yet in the impracticability of country roads, especially during the winter, to those who are out of railway range, almost as far apart as if it had been at the other end of England. The district altogether had not attained the popularity it now enjoys, and the village was very rural indeed, with nobody in it above the rank of the rustic tradesmen and traffickers, except the inevitable parson and the doctor. The vicar's wife seized with enthusiasm upon the new inhabitant as a representative of society, and various others of the neighbouring clergywomen made haste to call upon a woman so well connected, as did also the squire of the place, or, at least, the ladies belonging to him. But Mrs. Osborne had no such thirst for society as to trudge along the muddy roads to return their visits, and her income did not permit even the indulgence of the jogging pony and homely clothes-basket of a little carriage, in which many of the clerical neighbours found great comfort. She had to stay at home perforce, knowing no enlivenment of her solitude, except tea at the vicarage on rare occasions. Tea at the vicarage in earlier and homelier days would have meant a quiet share of the cheerful evening refreshments and amusements, when the guest was made one of the family party, and all its natural interests and occupations placed before her. But tea, which is an afternoon performance and means a crowd of visitors collected from all quarters, in which the natural household is altogether swamped, and the guest sees not her friends, but their friends or distant acquaintances, of whom she neither has nor wishes to have any knowledge—is a very different matter. At Greyshott there had been occasional heavy dinner-parties, in which it was Margaret's part to exert herself for the satisfaction, at all events, of old friends, most of whom called her Meg, and had known her from her girlhood. These were not, perhaps, very entertaining evenings, but they were better than the modern fashion. She lived, accordingly, very much alone with Osy, and the maid-of-all-work, whom, knowing so little as she did of the practical arrangements of a household, she had to train, with many misadventures, which would have been amusing had there been anybody with whom she could have laughed over her own blunders and Jane's ignorance. But alas! there was no one. Osy was too young to be amused when his pudding was burned or his potatoes like stones. He was more likely to cry, and his mother's anxiety for his health and comfort took the fun out of the ludicrous, yet painful, errors of her unaccustomed house-keeping. It depends so much on one's surroundings whether these failures are ludicrous or tragical. In some cases they are an enlivenment of life, in others an exaggeration of all its troubles. These, however, were but temporary; for Mrs. Osborne, though she knew nothing to begin with, and did not even know whether she was capable of learning, was, in fact, too capable a woman, though she was not aware of it, to be long overcome by troubles of this kind; and it soon became a pleasure to her and enlivenment of her life to look after her own little domestic arrangements, and carry forward the education of her little maid-servant. There was not, after all, very much to do—plenty of time after all was done for Osy's lessons, and for what was equally important, Margaret's own lessons, self-conducted, to fit her for teaching her boy. At seven years old a little pupil does not make any very serious call upon his teachers, and though Margaret was aware of having no education herself, she was still capable of as much as the little fellow wanted, except in one particular. Osy had, as many children have in the first stage, a precocious capacity for what his mother called "figures," knowing no better; for I doubt whether Margaret knew what was the difference between arithmetic and mathematics, or where one ends and the other begins. Osy did in his own little head sums which made his mother's hair stand erect on hers. She was naturally all the more proud of this achievement that she did not understand it in the least. She was even delighted when Osy found her all wrong in an answer she had carefully boggled out to one of those alarming sums, and laughed till the tears came into her eyes at the pitying looks and apologetic speeches of her little boy. "It isn't nofing wrong, Movver," Osy said. "Ladies never, never do sums." He stroked her hand in his childish compassion, anxious to restore her to her own esteem. "You can wead evwyfing you sees in any book, and write bof big hand and small hand, and understand evwyfing; but ladies never does sums," said Osy, climbing up to put his arms round her neck and console her. These excuses for her incapacity were sweeter to Margaret than any applause could have been, and such incidents soon gave pleasure and interest to her life. It is well for women that few things in life are more delightful than the constant companionship of an intelligent child, and Margaret was, fortunately, capable of taking, not only the comfort, but the amusement, too, of Osy's new views of life. These, however, we have not, alas! space to give; and as she was obliged to engage the instructions of the village schoolmaster for him in the one point which was utterly beyond her, Osy's mathematical genius and his peculiar phraseology soon died away together. He learned to pronounce the "th," which is so difficult a sound in English, and his condition of infant prodigy in respect to "figures" and all the wonders of his mental arithmetic came to an end under the prosaic rules of Mr. Jones, as such precocities usually do.

Margaret's life, however, had thus fallen into a tolerably happy vein, full of cheerful occupation and boundless hope and love—for what eminence or delight was there in the world which that wonderful child might not reach? and to be his mother was such a position, she felt, as queens might have envied—when the news of her cousin's death broke upon her solitude with a sudden shock and horror. She had heard scarcely anything about him in the interval. One or two letters dictated to Dunning had come from her uncle in answer to her dutiful epistles, but naturally there was no communication between her and Patty, and Gervase had scarcely ever written a letter in his life. Sometimes at long intervals Lady Hartmore had taken a long drive to see her, but that great lady knew nothing about a household which nobody now ever visited. "I might give you scraps I hear from the servants," Lady Hartmore said,—"one can't help picking up things from the servants, though I am always ashamed of it,"—but these scraps chiefly concerned the "ways" of Mrs. Piercey, which Margaret was too loyal to her family to like to hear laughed at. Gervase dead! it seemed one of those impossibilities which the mind feels less power of accustoming itself to than much greater losses. Those whom our minds can attend with longing and awe into the eternal silence, who are of kin to all the great thoughts that fill it, and for whom every heavenly development is possible, convey no sense of incongruity, however overwhelming may be the sorrow, when they are removed from us. But Gervase! How hard it was to think of him gaping, incapable of understanding, on the verge of that new world. Who could associate with him its heavenly progress, its high communion? Gervase! why should he have died? it seemed harder to understand of him whose departure would leave so slight a void, whose trace afar would be followed by no longing eyes, than of one whose end would have shaken the whole world. The news had a great and painful effect upon Margaret, first for itself, and afterwards for what must follow. She wrote, as has been said, to her uncle, asking if she might go to him, if a visit from her would be of any comfort to him; and she wrote to Patty with her heart full, forgetting everything in the pity with which she could not but think of hopes overthrown. Patty replied with great propriety, not concealing that she had kept back Margaret's letter to Sir Giles, explaining how little able he was for any further excitement, and that all that could be done was to keep him perfectly quiet. "He might wish to see you, but he is not equal to it," Patty said; and she ended by saying that her whole life should be devoted to Sir Giles as long as he lived, "for I have nothing now upon Earth," Patty said, with a big capital. All that Margaret could do was to accept the situation, thinking many a wistful thought of her poor old uncle, from whom everything had been taken. Poor Gervase, indeed, had not been much to his father, but yet he was his son.

The winter was long and dreary—dreary enough at Greyshott, where the old gentleman was going daily a step farther down the hill, and often dreary, too, to Margaret, looking out from the window of her little drawing-room upon the little row of laurels glistening in the wet, with now and then a passer-by and his umbrella going heavily by. There are some people who have an invincible inclination to look out, whatever is outside the windows, were it only chimney-pots; and Margaret was one of these. She got to know every twig of those glistening laurels shining in the rain, and to recognise even the footsteps that went wading past. There was not much refreshment nor amusement in it, but it was her nature to look out wherever she was. And one afternoon, in the lingering spring, she suddenly saw a figure coming up the village road which had never been seen there before, which seemed to have fallen down from the sky, or risen up from the depths, so little connection had it with anything there. Mrs. Osborne owned the strangeness of the apparition with a jump of the heart that had been beating so tranquilly in her bosom. Gerald Piercey here! He had been for a long time abroad, travelling in the East, far out of the usual tracks of travellers, and had written to her three or four times from desert and distant places, whose names recalled the Arabian Nights to her, but nothing nearer home. The letters had always been curt, and not always amiable: "I note what you say about having settled down. If you think the stagnant life of a village the best thing for you, and your own instructions the best thing for a boy who will have a part to play in the world, of course it is needless for me to make any remark on the subject." Margaret received these missives with a little excitement, it must be allowed, if not with pleasure. She confessed to herself that they amused her: "a boy who will have a part to play in the world!" Did he think, she asked herself with a smile, that Osy was seventeen instead of seven? At seven what did he want beyond his mother's instructions? But it cannot be denied that letters, with curious Turkish hieroglyphics on the address, dated from Damascus, Baghdad, and other dwellings of the unknown, had an effect upon her. To receive them at Chillfold, in Surrey, was a sensation. The Vicarage children, who collected stamps, were much excited by the Turkish specimens, and she could not help a pleasurable sensation as she bestowed them. Even Osy's babble about Cousin Colonel was not unpleasing to his mother's ears. Gerald was far away, unable to take any steps, or even to say much about Osy. She liked at that distance to have such a man more or less belonging to her. The feeling of opposition had died away. He had been fond of Osy, wanted to have him for his own—as who would not wish to have her beautiful boy?—and what could be more ingratiating to his mother than that sentiment, so long as it was entertained by a man at Baghdad, who certainly could not take any steps to steal the boy from his mother? Into this amicable, and even vaguely pleased state of mind she had fallen—when suddenly, without any warning, without even having seen him come round the corner, Gerald Piercey stood before her eyes.

Margaret went away from the window and sat down in the corner by the fire, which was the corner most in the shade and safe from observation. That her heart should beat so was absurd. What was Gerald Piercey to her, or she to Gerald Piercey? He might make what propositions he pleased, but he could not force her to give up her boy. At seven it was ridiculous—out of the question! At seventeen it might be different, but that was ten long years off. If this was what his object was, was not her answer plain?

He came in very gravely, not at all belligerent, though he looked round with an air of criticism, remarking the smallness of the place, which recalled to some extent Mrs. Osborne's old feelings towards him. He had no right to find the cottage small. She thought him looking old, worn, and with care in his face. He, on the other hand, was astonished to see her so young. The air of Chillfold, the tranquillity and freedom, had been good for Margaret. The desert sun and wind had baked him black and brown. The quiet of the cottage, the life of a child which she had been living, had brought all her early roses back.

"I have come," he said, taking her hand in his, "on a sad errand." And then he paused and cried hurriedly, "What have you done to yourself? Why, you are Meg Piercey again."

"Margaret Osborne at your service," she said, as she had said before; but with a very different feeling from that which had moved her on the previous occasion: to be recognised with surprise as young and fair, is a very different thing from being accused angrily of having lost your freshness and your youth,—"but what is it, what is it?"

"Uncle Giles is dying, Cousin Meg."

"Uncle Giles!" She drew her hand from him and dropped back into her chair. For a moment she did not speak. "But I am not surprised," she said. "I looked for it: how could he go on living with nobody—not one of his own?"

"He might have had you. Poor old man! it is not the time to blame him."

"Me?" said Margaret. "I was not his child; nothing, and nobody, can make up for the loss of what is your very own."

"Even when it is—Gervase Piercey?"

"Poor Gervase!" said Margaret. "Oh, Gerald Piercey, you are a man with whom things have always gone well. What does it matter what our children are? they are our children all the same. And if it were nothing but to think that it was Gervase—and what poor Gervase was."

Though she was perhaps a little incoherent, Gerald did not object. He said: "At all events, I am very sorry for my poor old uncle. Mrs. Gervase wrote to me to say that he was sinking fast, should I like to come? and that she was writing to you in the same sense. I had only just arrived when I got her letter, and I thought that the best thing was to come to you at once, in case you were going to see him."

"Of course, I should wish to go and see him; but I have had no letter. I must see him if she will let me. Dear old Uncle Giles, he was always good and fatherly to me."

"And yet he let you leave your home—for this."

"Cousin Gerald," said Margaret, "don't let us begin to quarrel again. This is very well—it suits me perfectly—and I am very happy here. It is my own. My dear old uncle was not strong enough to struggle in my favour, but he was always kind. I must go to see him, whether she wishes it or not."

"I have a carriage ready. I thought that would be your decision. We shall get there before dark."

"We?" she said, startled; then added, almost with timidity, "you are going—?"

"Certainly I am going. You don't, perhaps, think what this may be to me. My father will be the head of the house—"

"And you after him. I fully understand what it is to you," she said.

He gave her a singular look, which she did not at all understand, except that it might mean that with this increased power and authority he would have more to say about Osy. "And to you too," he said.

CHAPTER XLI

Patty received her two visitors without effusion, but with civility. Her demeanour was very different from all they had known of her before. She had been defiant and impertinent, anxious to offend and disgust, rather than to attract, with the most anxious desire to get rid of both, and to make them feel that they had no place nor standing in Greyshott. She had, indeed, been so frightened lest she herself should be overthrown, that all the "manners" in which Patty had been brought up deserted her, and she behaved like the barmaid dressed in a little brief and stolen authority, which they believed her to be. Indeed, the "manners" which Patty had been taught chiefly consisted in the inculcation of extreme respect to her "betters;" and her revolt from this, and conviction that she had now no betters in the world, carried her further in the opposite direction than if she had had no training at all. But in her calm tenure of authority for nearly a year, Patty had learned many things. She had learned that the mistress of a house does not need to stand upon her authority, and that a right, acknowledged and evident, does not require to be loudly asserted. It might have been supposed, however, that a certain awe of the heir-at-law—a humility more or less towards the man to whom shortly she must cede her keys, her place, and all the rights upon which she now stood, would have shown themselves in her. But this was not at all the case. She was quite civil to Colonel Piercey, but she treated him solely as a guest—her guest—without any relationship of his own towards the house in which she received him. To Margaret she was more friendly, but more careless in her civility. "I ordered them to get ready for you the room you used to have. I thought you would probably like that best," she said. Colonel Piercey was lodged quite humbly in one of the "bachelor's rooms," no special attention of any kind being paid to him, which was a thing very surprising to him, though he could scarcely have told why. To be aware that you are very near being the head of the house, and to be treated as if you were a very ordinary and distant relation, is startling in a house which is full of the presence of death. That presence, when it brings with it no deep family sorrow, brings a sombre business and activity, a sense of suppressed preparations and watchfulness for the end, which is very painful to the sensitive mind, even when moved by no special feeling. Waiting for an old man to die, it is often difficult not to be impatient for that event, as for any other event which involves long waiting. Patty went about the house with this air of much business held back and suspended until something should happen. She was called away to have interviews with this person and that. She spoke of the "arrangements" she had to attend to. "Would it not be better that Colonel Piercey should relieve you of some part of the trouble?" said Margaret. "Oh, no; one should always do one's own business. Outsiders never understand," said Patty, with what would have been, had she been less dignified, a toss of her head in her widow's cap.

Was Gerald Piercey an outsider in the house that must so soon be his own? He had given Margaret to understand during their long drive that his father would not change his home or his life, and that it was he, Gerald, who would occupy Greyshott. I think Colonel Piercey was of opinion that he had made something else clear, though it had not been spoken of in words—namely, that there was but one mistress possible for Greyshott in its new life; but Mrs. Osborne did not by any means clearly understand him, having her mind preoccupied by the belief that his feelings to her were not of an affectionate kind, and that his first object was to deprive her of her child. She felt, however, that he was kind—bewilderingly kind, and that there was something in him which wanted explanation; but all the more, Margaret was anxious and disturbed by this attitude of "outsider" attributed to him. If Gerald Piercey was an outsider in Greyshott on the eve of his uncle's death, to whom he was natural heir, who else could have any right there? He did not remark this, as was natural. He was not surprised that Patty should hold him at arm's length. It was quite to be expected that she should feel deeply the mere fact that he was the heir. Poor girl! He wondered what provision had been made for her—if any; and if there should be none, promised himself that his father's first act, as Sir Francis, should be to set this right. He was, in fact, very sorry for Mrs. Patty, whose ambitions and schemes had come to so summary an end. She should never require to go back to the alehouse, but should be fitly provided for as the wife of the once heir of Greyshott ought to be. He confided these intentions to Margaret at the very moment when Mrs. Osborne's mind was full of Patty's speech about the outsider. "You mean if Uncle Giles has not done so already," Margaret said.

"It is very unlikely he should have done so. Of course there could be no settlement; and who was there to point out to him that such a thing was necessary?" Colonel Piercey was so strong in his conviction that Margaret did not like to suggest even that Patty might herself have pointed it out. But her own mind was full of vague suspicion and alarm. An outsider! Gerald Piercey, the natural heir of the house?

Late that night the two visitors were called to Sir Giles' room. "He is awake and seems to know everybody; I should like you to see him now," Patty said, going herself to Mrs. Osborne's room to call her. Colonel Piercey was walking up and down in the hall, with an air of examining the old family pictures, which Patty had not thought it necessary to meddle with, though she had removed those that had been in the library. He was not really looking at them, except as accessories to the scene—silent witnesses of the one that was passing away, and the other that was about to come. Gerald Piercey had a deep sadness in his heart, though he could not keep his thoughts from the new life that was before him. The very warmth of the rising of that new life and all its hopes made him feel all the more the deep disappointment and loss in which the other was ending. Poor Gervase would never have been a fit representative of the Pierceys, but as Margaret said, as she had always said, he was his father's son, and the object of all the hopes of the old pair who had reigned so long in Greyshott. And now this branch was cut off, their line ended, and the old tree falling that had flourished so long. He wondered if it would really be any comfort to poor old Sir Giles, dying alone in his desolate house, that there were still Pierceys to come after him: the same blood and race, though not drawn from his source. It seemed questionable how far he would be comforted by this; perhaps not at all, perhaps rather embittered by the fact that it was a cousin's son and not his own, who should now be the head of the house.

"Come now, come now," cried Patty eagerly, "as long as he is so conscious and awake. He sleeps most of his time, and it's quite a chance—quite a chance. I want you to see with your own eyes that he's all himself, and has his faculties still." She had an air of excitement about her perhaps not quite appropriate to the moment, as if her nerves were all in motion, and she could scarcely keep her fingers still or subdue the quiver in her head and over all her frame. She led the way hurriedly, opening the doors one after another in an excited way, and pushing into the sick room with a "Look, dear papa, who I've brought to see you." Sir Giles was sitting up in his bed, his large ashy face turned towards the door, his dim sunken eyes looking out from fold upon fold of heavy eyelid, his under-lip hanging as that of poor Gervase had done. "Ah," he stammered, "let 'em come in—to the light, my dear. I'm not in a state—to see strangers; but to please you—my dear."

"Uncle Giles," said Margaret, with an exclamation of pain, "surely you know me?"

"Eh? let her stand—in the light—in the light; why, why, why—Meg: it's Meg,—that's Meg." She kissed him, and he made an effort to turn his feeble head, and with his large moist lips he gave a tremulous kiss in the air. "I'm—I'm glad to see you, Meg. You were the first to—tell me—to tell me: I'll be always grateful to you—for that."

"For what, dear uncle? It is I who owe everything to you. Oh, Uncle Giles, if I could only tell you how much and how often I think of it! you were always kind, always kind; and dear Aunt Piercey; you gave me my home, the only home I ever had."

"Eh! eh! What is she saying, my dear? You'll—you'll look after Meg—never let her come to want. She was the first to tell me. The greatest news that has come—to Greyshott. You remember, Meg—and Osy, bless him, how he cheered! There's—there's something for Osy. He cheered like a little trump, and he gave—he gave my boy his only wedding present, the—the only one. Dunning, where is my purse? Osy must have a tip—two tips for that."

"Dear papa," cried Patty, "don't disturb yourself; oh, don't disturb yourself! I'll see to it."

"My—my purse, Dunning!" The purse was procured while they all stood by, and the old man fumbling, got with difficulty, one after another, two sovereigns, which fell out of his trembling fingers upon the bed. "One for—for cheering; and one for—for the other thing. Give 'em to Osy, Meg, bless him; and my blessing. When It comes and all's right, that'll be a friend for Osy—always a friend, better than an old man."

"Dear papa," cried Patty, pushing forward again, "here is some one else to see you—Colonel Piercey, dear, don't you remember? Colonel Piercey—Gerald—that once paid you a long visit; I know you'll remember if you try. Here," she said, seizing his arm, pulling him forward, "stand in the light that he may see you."

She was vibrating with excitement like a creature on wires. The touch of her hand on Gerald's arm was like an electric cord; and to be pushed forward thus, and accounted for as if he had been an absolute stranger, to be brought with difficulty to the mind of the dying man, was to Gerald Piercey, as may well be supposed, an insupportable sensation. He drew back, saying hastily, "I cannot disturb him. I will not have him disturbed for me—let him alone, let him alone."

"Eh? what? who's that? somebody else? Gerald?" said Sir Giles. He held out his hand vaguely into the air, not seeing where his attention was called, the large old limp grey hand, with so little volition or power left in it. "Ah, Gerald, come to see the end of the old man? that's kind! that's kind! My poor wife and I used to think if our first boy had lived, don't you know, he might have been a man like you. Well, Gerald, I've nothing to give you, but my blessing—but my blessing. You won't mind if your nose is put out of joint, you know, as the old folks say. And you'll stand by It, Gerald, a—a good fellow like you."

"Dear papa, I think they'll go now; it's late, and you ought to go to sleep."

"Not yet," said Sir Giles, who had fallen into the old strain of faint sobbing and laughing; "plenty—plenty of time for sleep. Thousands of years, don't you know, till it's all—all over. Where are they? eh, Meg. I scarcely see you; eh!" he kissed the air again with his hanging, lifeless lips, "good-night; and t'other man. Gerald, be kind to her, my boy; a good girl, Meg, a good girl. She's been married, which some might think a drawback; but if you're fond of her, and she's fond of you. Eh, Dunning? well I'm not tired, not tired a bit—let him be the god-father, my dear; and good-night to you, good-night to you—all."

He died in the night.

The third funeral within a year from Greyshott! What a melancholy record was that—father and mother, and the only child! Sir Giles was the only one of the three who could be said to have been beloved. His wife had always been an imperious woman, his son had been a fool; but the old man was full of gentleness and kindness, and had been a model country gentleman in his day, known to everybody, and always genial to rich and poor. Once more the avenue was full of carriages, and the house of mourners, and there were some tears, and many kind recollections, and a great deal of talk about him as they carried him away. "It will be a long time before we see the like of him again," the country folk and tenants said, while the gentlemen of the county congratulated themselves that the old name was not to be extinct nor the land transferred to other hands. The new baronet was not there; he was also an old man, and not fond of much movement, but Colonel Piercey was his representative, and an excellent representative, a man of whom the whole district might be proud. He was looked to by every one, pointed out to those who did not know him, and surrounded by a subtle atmosphere of suspended congratulation and welcome, notwithstanding the universal grief for Sir Giles. The old man's dying words had not made a very deep impression on Colonel Piercey, except those which concerned Margaret. He had not understood the allusions, nor indeed thought of them, save as the wanderings of weakness. It seemed all of a piece to him—the thought that Sir Giles' firstborn, the boy dead some thirty years ago, might have grown such a man as he, and his nose being put out of joint, and the petition that he should be good to some one, and stand by it. All these wild and wandering words Gerald Piercey put out of his head as meaning nothing. It was, perhaps, the "first boy," whom he had never heard of before, whom he was to be good to, yet who would put his nose out of joint. It was all a muddle, and Gerald did not attempt to grope his way through it. He was deeply impressed and touched by the image of the old man dying; but he had no doubt as to his own prospects, and thought of no disaster. How could there be any doubt? If there had been a new will made since the death of Gervase, no doubt the estate had been charged with an adequate provision for Gervase's wife; if there had been no will made, his father and he, as the next-of-kin and heir-at-law, would of course take that into their own hands, and secure it at once. Beyond this and the natural legacies, Gerald suspected no new thing.

Margaret, on the other hand, had been deeply alarmed and startled by what she heard. She did not remember what she had said on the occasion to which her uncle referred, but she remembered his outburst of cheering, and Osy, with his legs wide apart and his hat waving in his hand, giving forth his hip, hip, hurrah. Was it possible that the old man had made out to himself some fiction of what might be going to happen, some illusion which buoyed him up with false hopes? Was it possible that Patty—? Margaret did not know what to think. She would fain have confided her alarm to Gerald, and taken counsel with him; but those other words of Sir Giles had been too broadly significant, and he was the last person in the world to whom she could talk on any subject that would recall them. She had avoided Gerald, indeed, since that scene, and it had not been referred to again between them. But her mind was full of perplexity and doubt. The bearing of Patty (always digne, always just what a daughter-in-law's chastened grief should be,—not too demonstrative), so confident, so authoritative, so determined to do everything herself, without assistance from an "outsider," increased this sensation of alarm and uncertainty in Margaret's mind. She did not know in the least what was coming. But it seemed to her certain that something was coming which was not in the course of nature, or according to the common expectation. Her mind grew more and more confused, yet more and more certain of this as the crisis approached; for Patty never had been so independent, so confident, so sure of being the head of everything, as on the funeral day.

Yet Patty had her troubles, too, which she had to bear alone, and without any aid at this crisis of her career. Miss Hewitt, whose indignation at her reception on her first visit had been so great that she had made a vow never to see her ungrateful niece again, had, by the time that Sir Giles' dangerous condition had become publicly known, got over her fury. She had been paid her fifty pounds, and she had begun to believe in Patty's continued success and in her cleverness and power. There had been a pause of alarm in the family after the death of Gervase, when they had all feared (little knowing her spirit) that Patty would be sent back on their hands. But when that alarm was well over and Patty was found to hold her own, the admiration of her relations was doubled. Her father was the first to claim a renewal of friendship; but his reception was so alarming, and his daughter poured forth upon his head such torrents of wrath, telling him that, but for the exposure of family affairs, she would have him tried for manslaughter, that the landlord of the Seven Thorns slunk off completely cowed and without a word to say. This added to Miss Hewitt's regard for her brave and victorious niece, who feared no one, and she had in the meantime made many attempts to obtain a footing at Greyshott. Partly to impress still more sensibly upon her father her utter and unchangeable hostility, and partly because some one to speak to became a necessity, Patty had admitted her aunt on various occasions; and now Miss Hewitt demanded, with a persistence which all Patty's spare moments had been spent in resisting, first an interview with Sir Giles, and then a place in the carriage which conveyed her niece to his funeral. Patty had not yielded in respect to the first, but in the extreme state of mental excitement in which she was, her resolution gave way before the second prayer. It had not been her intention to "mix herself up with any of the Hewitts," but in face of the scene which she anticipated at the reading of the will, it gradually came to appear more and more desirable to her to have some one to stand by her, some one to be dazzled by her position and good fortune, and to take her part whatever opposition she might meet with. Patty did not know what might happen at the reading of the will. She had a prevision, but not even now any absolute certainty, what the will was. And if it were as she believed, she did not know what powers might be brought into action against her, or what might be done. She decided at last that to have her aunt, who at bottom was a thoroughly congenial spirit, to defend and stand by her, would be an advantage. And this was how it was that Miss Hewitt attained the lugubrious triumph of her life, the satisfaction of following her former lover in his old carriage, his wife's carriage, whom she considered her triumphant rival, to his grave.

CHAPTER XLII

It was a strange triumph, and yet it was one. Miss Hewitt closely followed her niece, once more wrapt in a new extravagance of crape; and these ladies had the satisfaction of seeing Mrs. Osborne quietly take her place opposite to them on the front seat of the carriage. This gave both to Patty and her aunt an acute sensation of pleasure, which would have been greater, however, had the victim seemed in any way conscious of it. But Margaret was full of many thoughts, recollections, and anticipations. She, too, looked forward to the disclosure of her uncle's will with a curiosity and anxiety which had nothing to do with any expectations of her own. She had put away the two sovereigns so tremulously extracted from his purse by the dying man with a half smile and a tear. That, she concluded, was all that Osy would ever have from his great-uncle, who might so easily have made a provision for the boy. She had never expected it, she said to herself, but that was a different thing from this certainty that it never would be; still there was a tender familiarity about the "tip" for the child which went to Margaret's heart. Poor old uncle! If he had been left to himself, if he had been able to think, he would have acted differently. She put away the two pieces of money for Osy without any grudge, with a tender thought of the old man who had been as good as a father to her all her life. And now was this the end of Greyshott so far as she was concerned? or was there a strange something looming out of the clouds, another life of which she would not think, which she could not understand, to which she did not consent? She put all thought out of her mind of anything that concerned herself, or tried her best to do so—but the family was dear to her still. Was there any plot threatening the name, the race, the old, old dwelling of the Pierceys? There was a subdued triumph in Patty's look, a confidence in her voice and step, and the authoritative orders she gave, which did not look like a woman who after to-day would have no real authority in Sir Francis Piercey's house. She could not imagine what it could mean; but the advent of the elder woman, also in crape, and full of ostentatious sympathy and regret, strengthened all her apprehensions, though she did not know of what she was afraid.

One or two of the oldest friends remained for the reading of the will. It was felt on all sides that the grief which attended Sir Giles to his tomb was of a modified kind. No one except Mrs. Osborne could be supposed to regard the old gentleman with filial love or sorrow, and the party which assembled round the luncheon table was serious, but put on no affectation of woe. Patty took her place at the head of the table with a quiet assurance to which nobody objected. She had too much sense to talk of "dear papa" before all these people, and if she showed the composure of an authorised and permanent mistress of the house, it was probably because she had been accustomed to do so. Lord Hartmore, if his sympathies were not so much aroused as on the day of Gervase's funeral, still retained a sort of partisan feeling for the young widow. She was his protégée. His wife had not fallen in with his views, except in the most moderate way, merely to honour the promise he had made for her. Lady Hartmore did not attempt to improve her acquaintance with Patty. She was quite at her ease at the other end of the table by the side of Colonel Piercey, who now was de facto, in her assured belief, the master of the house. Margaret was not present at the luncheon, and Miss Hewitt, who was elated beyond expression by finding herself seated among all the great people, on the other side of Lord Hartmore, felt herself the principal person at table, and demeaned herself accordingly. "To think," she said, "my lord, that I should find myself 'ere on such an occasion; me that once thought to be the mistress; but oh! the ideas of the young is different from what comes to pass in life. 'Im as we have laid in his grave, dear gentleman, was once—Well, Patty, love, as you say, this ain't a time to talk of such things. Still, it do come upon me sitting at 'is table, and 'im not 'ere to bid me welcome. But it's a mournful satisfaction to see the last of 'im all the same."

"Aunt was an old friend of my dear father-in-law," Patty explained, curtly. "I believe, Lord Hartmore, that you know more of Margaret Osborne than I do. Margaret Osborne has not shown very much sympathy to me, and all this winter I have never been able to get out for such a purpose as making calls. I couldn't have taken a three hours' drive to be away so long, not if it had been a matter of life and death. That means almost a whole day, and dear Sir Giles never liked to let me out of his sight."

"Ah, 'e always knew them that were really fond of 'im," said Miss Hewitt. "You couldn't blind 'im, my lord, with pretences. I was kep' back by my family, and thoughts of what the world might say; but 'e knew that Patty was the same stuff like, and 'e took to her the double of what 'e would have done on that account. Oh, your lordship, what a man 'e was! You're too young to remember 'im at 'is best: 'andsome is as 'andsome does, folk say—but a gentleman like 'im can't always act as 'e would like to. You must know that from yourself, my lord. Sometimes the 'eart don't go where the 'and 'as to be given."

"Well, that is certainly sometimes the case," said Lord Hartmore, with a subdued laugh, "though I don't think I know it by myself."

"Aunt's so full of her old times," cried Patty. "If there was anything that was ever wanted for the little Osborne boy, Lord Hartmore, I should always be pleased to help. He got too much for my dear father-in-law latterly, being noisy, and such a spoiled little thing; but he was fond of him, and spoke of him at the very last." "I can never forget that," said Patty, putting her handkerchief lightly to her eyes. "And if there should be need of a little help for his education, or setting him out in life—but I should have a delicacy in saying so to Margaret Osborne, unless you'd be so good as to do it for me."

"Oh, you're very kind, Mrs. Piercey," said Lord Hartmore, confused. "Our dear Meg is rather a formidable person to approach with such a proposal."

"Yes, isn't she formidable?" cried Patty, eagerly. "That's just the word; one is frightened to offer to do her a good turn."

"Let us hope," said Lord Hartmore, "that her good uncle has left her beyond the need of help."

"Oh, I don't know about that," said Patty, with a very serious face.

"I feel sure of it," said Lord Hartmore, with genial confidence. "He was far too good a man, and too kind an uncle. Mrs. Piercey, I see my friend Gerald looking this way, and Mr. Pownceby wriggling in his chair, as if—" He made a slight movement as if to rise—which perhaps was not the highest breeding in Lord Hartmore; but it was very slight and accompanied by a look of deference, suggesting a signal on her part.

"Mr. Gerald Piercey is not master here, nor is Mr. Pownceby," said Patty, with dignity. "They may look as they please, but in my own house it's my part to say when people are to leave the table."

"She do have a spirit, Patty does," Miss Hewitt murmured under her breath.

Lord Hartmore settled himself in his chair again, abashed. "I beg your pardon," he said; and then, in a subdued tone, "Most likely Pownceby has a train to catch."

"In that case I don't mind stretching a point," said the lady of the house, "though Mr. Pownceby is no more than a hired servant paid for his time, and it is no business of his to interfere."

A hired servant! Old Pownceby, who had all the secrets of the county in his hands, and most of its business! Lord Hartmore grew pale with awe at this daring speech. He looked straight before him, not to see the signals of his wife telegraphing to him from Gerald Piercey's side. "I'll have nothing to do with it," he said to himself; and, indeed, in his consternation, Lord Hartmore was the last to get up when the movement of the chairs convinced him that Mrs. Piercey had condescended to move. He offered that lady his arm humbly, on an indication from her that this was expected. "I suppose we shall see Mrs. Osborne in the library?" he said.

"Oh, Margaret! I suppose she'd better be there for form's sake, though I don't suppose it matters much. Aunt, will you tell Margaret Osborne to come directly, please? I have never," said Patty, with a smile, "got into the way of calling her Meg, as you all do."

Lord Hartmore could scarcely dissimulate the little start of consternation with which he heard this. The forlorn young widow, for whom he had been so sorry, was appearing in a new light; but, of course, it was only her ignorance, he said to himself. The party had all assembled in the library when the voice of Miss Hewitt was heard outside calling to some one who seemed to be following: "This way, Margaret—this way. They're all in the library. I don't know the 'ouse so well as I might, but this is the way. Come along please, quick, and don't keep the company waiting," Miss Hewitt said.

Gerald Piercey started forward to open the door, for which Miss Hewitt rewarded him with an "Oh! thank you, but I'm quite at 'ome, quite at 'ome." Margaret came in in the wake of that bustling figure, pale, and with an air of suspense. "Was it necessary to send for me in that way?" she said to Gerald. He had placed a chair for her beside Lady Hartmore. "Oh, Heaven knows what is necessary!" said that lady. "You know the proverb about beggars on horseback." She was not so careful to subdue her voice as she might have been, but in the commotion it was not observed. Gerald Piercey stood with his hand on the back of his cousin's chair. They were the family, the only persons present of the Piercey blood. The old friends of the house stood near them. At the upper end of the room were Patty and her aunt. Mr. Pownceby stood in front of the large fireplace with a paper in his hand.

"I must explain," he said, "how the will I have to read is so very succinct a document. Sir Giles had made his will like other men, and as there was a good deal to leave, there were a number of bequests. The late Mr. Gervase Piercey was, of course, the heir, under trustees, as he was not much—acquainted with business. Sir Giles thought fit to change this, as was to be expected, after his son's death. He sent for me hastily one day, and gave me instructions which surprised me. I begged him to allow me to take these back with me in order that the new will should be properly written out, proposing to come back next day to execute it, and, in short, hoping that he might reconsider the matter; but he would hear of no delay. This document I will now read."

Gerald Piercey stood quite undisturbed, with his hand on the back of Margaret's chair. He was not anxious. It had not occurred to him that the house of his fathers could be alienated from him, and short of that, his poor old uncle's wishes would, he sincerely felt, be sacred whatever they were. He was glad to hear that there was a new will made, which, no doubt, provided for Mrs. Piercey; and waited with an easy mind to hear what it was. As for Margaret, the event about to happen began to dawn clearly upon her. She saw it in Patty's eyes, in her pose, sitting up defiant in Lady Piercey's chair. She looked up at her cousin with an eager desire to warn him, to support him, but was daunted by the calm of his look, fearing no evil. "Gerald, Gerald," she said, instinctively. The lines of his face melted suddenly; he looked down upon her with an encouraging, protecting smile, and took her hand for a moment, saying "Meg!" and no more. He thought she was appealing to him for his care and protection in face of a probable disappointment to herself.

Mr. Pownceby cleared his throat and waved his hand. He ran over the exordium, name, and formula, of sound mind, etc., etc., to which everybody listened impatiently, "do give and bequeath the whole of my estates, property, real and personal, etc., to—" here he paused a little, as if his own throat were dry—"Patience Piercey, my daughter-in-law, and companion for the last six months, to be at her entire disposal as it may be best for the interests of the family, and in remainder to her child. This I do, believing it to be best for meeting all difficulties, and in view of any contingency that might arise.

"Signed, Giles Piercey," added the lawyer, "and dated Greyshott, 16th June, just a fortnight ago."

There was a pause. Even now it did not seem to have struck Colonel Piercey what it meant. He listened with a half smile. "And—?" he said, waiting as if for more.

"That is all, Colonel Piercey, every word. The house, estates, money, everything. Even the servants are cut out. He said she'd look after them. Mrs. Piercey takes everything—house, lands, money, plate, everything. It is a very unusual and surprising will, but that is all."

And then there was another pause, and a general deep-drawn breath.

"It is a very surprising will indeed," said Lord Hartmore.

It was a sort of remark to himself, forced from him by the astonishment of the moment; but in the silence of the room it sounded as if addressed like an oration to all who were there.

"Pardon me," cried Colonel Piercey, "but Greyshott? Do you mean that Greyshott, the original home of the family—?"

"I represented that to Sir Giles, but he would hear nothing. It is Mrs. Piercey's with all the rest."

"It is the most iniquitous thing I ever heard," cried Lady Hartmore, rising quickly to her feet. "What! not a word of anybody belonging to him, nothing of Meg and her boy, nothing of his natural heirs, nothing of old Dunning even, and the old servants?—The man must have been mad."

Here Patty rose and advanced to the conflict. She was very nervous, but collected. "Mr. Pownceby can bear me witness that I knew nothing about it," she said. "I wasn't there."

"No, you were not there," said the lawyer.

"I thought it right I should have a provision," said Patty, "and so it was right; and if my dear father-in-law thought that the one that stood by him, and nursed him through all his illness, when everybody else forsook him, was the one that ought to have it, who's got anything to say against that? I didn't want it; but now that I've got it, I'll stick to it," cried Patty defiantly, confronting Lady Hartmore, who had been the only one to speak.

"I have no doubt of it," cried that lady, "but if I were Colonel Piercey, I shouldn't stand it; no, not for a moment! Why, the old man was in his dotage, no more equal to making a will than—than his son would have been."

"Mary!" cried her husband in dismay.

"Well!" said Lady Hartmore, suddenly brought to herself by the consciousness of having said more than she ought to have said, "I am glad, I am quite glad, Hartmore, for one thing, that you'll now see things in their proper light."

"And a very just will, too," cried Miss Hewitt, coming to her niece's side,—"just like 'im, as was a very right-thinking man. Patty was an angel to 'im, that she was, night and day. And it is nothing but what was to be expected, that 'e should give 'er all as 'e had to give. And not too much, neither, to the only one as nursed 'im, and did for 'im, and gave up everything. Oh! I always said it—'e was a right-thinking man."

Colonel Piercey said nothing after that exclamation of "Greyshott!" but he retired with the lawyer into a corner as soon as the spell of consternation was broken by the sudden sound of these passionate voices. He had seized Margaret by the arm and drawn her with him. "We are the representatives of the family," he said, hurriedly; and Mrs. Osborne was too much startled (though she had foreseen it), too sympathetic, and too much excited, to object to the manner in which he had drawn her hand within his arm. "Our interests are the same," he said, briefly, with a hurried nod to Mr. Pownceby; and they stood talking for some minutes, while a wonderful interchange of artillery went on behind. This was concluded by a sudden clear sound of Patty's voice in the air, ringing with passion and mastery. "I believe," she said, "Lord Hartmore's carriage is at the door." And then there arose a laugh of sharp anger from the other side. "We are turned out," cried Lady Hartmore, "turned out of Greyshott, where we were familiar before that chit was born." It was a little like scolding, but it was the voice of nature all the same.

"And I think," said Colonel Piercey, "Meg, that you and I had better go, too."

"Oh, as you please!" cried Patty; "Meg can stay if she likes, and I've already said I shouldn't mind giving any reasonable help to educate the little boy. And as for you, Gerald Piercey, you can do what you like, and I can see you are bursting with envy. You can't touch me!"

CHAPTER XLIII

It was thus in wrath and in consternation that the party dispersed. Patty stood in the hall, flushed and fierce, with defiance in every look, supported by her aunt, who stood behind her, and gave vent from time to time to murmurs of sympathy and snorts of indignation. Patty had almost forgotten, in her mingled triumph and rage, the anxiously chastened demeanour which she had of late imposed upon herself. She was a great deal more like Patty of the Seven Thorns than she had ever been since her marriage. The opposition and scorn of Lady Hartmore had awakened all her combative tendencies, and made her for the moment careless of consequences. What did she care for those big wigs who looked down upon her? Was she not as good as any of them, herself a county magnate, the lady of Greyshott? better than they were! For the Hartmores were not so rich as comported with their dignity; and Patty was now rich, to her own idea enormously rich, and as great a lady as any in England. Was she not Mrs. Piercey of Greyshott, owning no superior anywhere? It is curious that this conviction should have swept away for the moment all her precautions of behaviour, and restored her to the native level of the country barmaid, as ready to scold as any fishwife, to defy every rule of respect or even politeness. She waited to see Lady Hartmore to the door, having swept out of the room before that astonished lady with a bosom bursting with rage. Truth to tell, Lady Hartmore was much disposed to fight, too. She would have liked, above all things, to give the little upstart what humbler persons call a piece of her mind. Her pulses, too, were beating high, and a flood of words were pressing to her lips. It was intolerable to her to accept the insult to herself and the wrong to her friends without saying anything—without laying the offender low under the tempest of her wrath. As for Lord Hartmore, it must be owned that he was frightened, and only anxious to get his wife away. He held her arm tightly in his, and gave it an additional pressure as he led her past the fierce little adversary who, no doubt, had a greater command of appropriate language than even Lady Hartmore had, whose style was probably less trenchant, though more refined. "Now, Mary, now, my dear," he said soothingly. The sight of the carriage at the door was delightful to him as a safe port to a sailor. And though the first thing Lady Hartmore did when safely ensconced in her corner, was to turn upon him the flood of her suppressed wrath with a "So this is your interesting little widow, Hartmore!" he was too glad to get away from the sphere of combat to attempt any self-defence. He, too, was saying "the little demon!" under his breath.

Patty still stood there, when Margaret, who had hastily collected the few things she had brought with her, came down to join Colonel Piercey in the hall. He had been standing, as he had been on a previous occasion, carefully examining one of the old portraits. It was not a very interesting portrait, nor was he, I suppose, specially interested in it; but his figure, wrapt in silence and abstraction, made a curious contrast to that of Patty, thrilling with fire and movement. It was evident that she could not long restrain herself, and when Margaret appeared coming down the great stairs, the torrent burst forth.

"Oh, you are there, Meg Osborne: I wonder you didn't go with your great friends, the first people in the county, as you all think, insulting me in my own house! Ah, and I'll teach you all it's my own house! I won't have nobody here turning their backs to me, or going out and in of my place without as much as a thank you! You're studying my pictures, Colonel Piercey, are you? They're my pictures, they're not yours; and I'll have you to know that nobody sha'n't even look at them without my consent."

Colonel Piercey turned round, almost angry with himself for the fury he felt. "I beg your pardon," he said, very gravely, yet with a sort of smile.

"Oh, you beg my pardon! and you laugh as if it were a joke! I can tell you it's no joke. They're all mine, willed by him as knew best who he wanted them to go to; and I'll keep them, that I will, against all the beggarly kinsfolk in the world; coming here a-looking as soon as the old man's in his grave for what they can devour!"

"Are you ready, Margaret?" Colonel Piercey said.

"Don't you turn it off to her, sir: speak to me! It's me that has to be considered first. You are going off mighty high: no civility to the head of the house, though I've taken you in and given you lodging in my house, at least Meg there, near a week? Oh, you laugh again, do you? And who is the head of the house if it's not me? I'm Mrs. Piercey of Greyshott. The pictures are mine, and the name's mine, as well as everything else; and you are nothing but the son of the younger brother, and not got as much to do with it as Pownceby there, the lawyer."

"My dear Mrs. Piercey," said Mr. Pownceby, "however much you may despise Pownceby the lawyer, he knows a little more on that subject than you do: a lady is rarely, if ever, the head of a house, and certainly never one who belongs to the family only by marriage. One word, if you please: Colonel Piercey's father, now Sir Francis Piercey, is the undoubted head of the house."

"Oh, you'll say anything, of course, to back them up; you think they're your only friends and will pay you best. But you'll find that's a mistake, Mr. Pownceby the lawyer, just as they'll find it's a mistake. What do you want here, Dunning? What business has servants, except my footman to open the door, here? You've been a deal too much petted in your time, and you'll find out the difference now."

"Mr. Pownceby, sir," said Dunning, who had suddenly appeared on the scene, exceedingly dark and lowering, "Is it true, sir, what I hear, that none of us old servants, not me, sir, that looked after him night and day, is named in my old master's will?"

"I am sorry to say it is quite true, Dunning," Mr. Pownceby said; "but I don't doubt that Mrs. Piercey will remember your long service, as Sir Giles wished her to do."

"How do you know what Sir Giles wished? I know best what Sir Giles said I was to do," cried Patty. "As for long service, yes, if holding on like grim death and taking as little trouble as possible is what you mean."

"Me take little trouble!" cried Dunning, foaming. "I've not had a night's rest, not an unbroken night, since Lady Piercey died—not one. Oh, I knowed how it would be! when she come about him, flattering him and slavering him, and the poor dear old gentleman thought it was good for Mr. Gervase; and then after, didn't she put it upon him as she was in the family-way, and she never was in the family-way, no more than I was. Hoh! ask the women! Hoh! look at her where she stands! He thought as there was an heir coming, and there ain't no more of an heir coming than—"

"Let us go, please, let us go," cried Margaret, in distress. "Cousin Gerald, Mr. Pownceby, we have nothing, nothing surely, to do with this. Oh, let us get away."

"Put that fellow out of my house!" cried Patty, "put him out of my house! You're a nice gentleman, Gerald Piercey, to stand there and encourage a man like that to insult a lady. Robert, take that man by the shoulders and put him out."

"He had just best try," said Dunning, squaring his shoulders. But Robert, who was young and slim, knew better than to try. He stood sheepishly fumbling by the door, opening it for the party who were going out. Dunning was not an adversary to be lightly encountered. Colonel Piercey, however, not insensible to the appeal made to him, laid his hand on Dunning's shoulder.

"This lady is right," he said; "we must not insult a woman, Dunning. You had better come with us in the meantime. It will do you no good to stay here."

"Ah, go with them and plot, do," cried Patty; "I knew that's how it would end. He knows I can expose him and all his ways—neglecting my dear old father-in-law; he knows he'll never get another place if people hear what I've got to say of him! Oh, yes, go with 'em, do! They thought they were to have it all their own way, and turn me out. But all of you, every one, will just learn the difference. If he had behaved like a gentleman and her like a lady, I might have given them their old rubbish of pictures. I don't care for that trash; they're no ornament to the place. I intend to have them all taken down and carted off to the first auction there is anywhere. I don't believe they'd bring above a few shillings; but all the same they are mine, and I'll have no strangers meddling with them," Patty cried. "Oh, for goodness' sake, Aunt Patience, hold your tongue, and let me manage my affairs myself."

"The only thing is just this, ladies and gentlemen," said Miss Hewitt. "She's got put out, poor thing, and I don't wonder, seeing all as she's 'ad to do; but she don't mean more than a bit of temper, and she'll soon come round if you'll have a little patience. This is the gentleman that come to me, and that I first told as my niece was married to Gervase Piercey, and no mistake. 'E is a very civil gentleman, Patty, and, Lord, why should you go and make enemies of 'im and of this lady, as I should say was a-going to be 'is good lady, and both belonging to the family! Nor I would not go and make an enemy of Mr. Pownceby, as 'as all the family papers in his 'ands and knows a deal, and could be of such use to you. I'd ask them all to stay, if I was you, to a nice bit of family dinner, and talk things over. What is the good of making enemies when being friends would be so much more use to you?" said Miss Hewitt, with triumphant logic. But Patty, who had heard with impatience and many attempts to interrupt, turned away before her oration was over, and, turning her back upon her recent guests, walked away as majestically as was possible, with her long train sweeping over the carpet, to the drawing-room, where she shut herself in, slamming the door. Miss Hewitt threw up her hands and eyes. "That's just 'er," she cried, "just 'er! Thinks of nothing when 'er temper's up; but I 'ope you won't think nothing of it neither. She'll be as good friends in a hour as if nothing had 'appened; and I'll go and give her a good talking to," the aunt said.

When Miss Hewitt reached the drawing-room she found Patty thrown upon the sofa in the second stage of her passion, which was, naturally, tears. But these paroxysms did not last long. "I let you talk, Aunt Patience," she said. "It pleased you, and it looked well enough. But I know my affairs better than you. Enemies! of course they're all my enemies, and I don't blame them. What I said I said on purpose, not in a temper. I had them here on purpose to see the old gentleman before he died, so that they might know for themselves that he was in his right mind, and all that; and old Pownceby knows; and I wanted to show them that I wasn't afraid of them, not a bit. However, that's all over, and you needn't trouble your head about it. I have a deal to do before the trial—"

"The trial!" said Miss Hewitt, in consternation. "Is there going to be a trial?"

"Of course there will be a trial. They won't let Greyshott go without a try for it, and you'll see me in all the papers, and the whole story, and I don't know that there's anything to be ashamed of. The thing I've got to find out now is who to have for my lawyers. I want to have the best—the very best; and some one that will make it all into a story, and tell all I did for the poor old man. I was good to him," said Patty, with an admiration of herself which was very genuine—"I was indeed. Many a time I've wanted to get a little pleasure like other folks—to enjoy myself a bit. Oh, there was one night! when Roger Pearson was here and had been at a dance, and I knew all the girls were at it, and all as jolly as—, and me cooped up, playing backgammon with the old gentleman, and—and worse beside."

"Good Lord, Patty!" cried Miss Hewitt. "Roger Pearson! where ever did you see Roger Pearson? I thought that was all over and done with!"

"What did you please to mean by that remark?" said Patty, with great dignity. "It doesn't matter where I saw him. I did see him; and there's not many girls would have gone on with the backgammon and—the rest, as I did, just that night. Aunt Patience, you may know a few things, but you don't know the trials of a married woman."

"The trials!" said Miss Hewitt. "I've known a many that have boasted of the advantage it was. But trials—no. You'll be very willing, I shouldn't wonder, to have 'em again."

"That depends upon many things; but I think not," said Patty.

"You mightn't be lucky the first time, and yet be lucky the second," said her aunt; "but it can't be said to be unlucky, Patty, when it leaves you here, not twenty-five yet, with this grand property all to yourself. Lord! I thought you was lucky at the first, when you got 'im; for I knew they couldn't put 'im out of 'is rights, Softy or no Softy; but just think the luck you've had since; 'is mother dead afore you come home, and that was a blessing, and then 'imself just a blessed release, and then—"

"I'll thank you, Aunt Patience, not to speak of my husband in that way. A release! Who'd have dared to say a word if Gervase had been here? Oh!" she said, springing up from her seat, and stamping her foot upon the carpet, "and here I am for ever and ever just what I am now, when I would have been my lady all my life, and nobody to stop me, if he had lived but six months more!"

"Dear, and that's true," said Miss Hewitt deeply struck with the tragedy of the event. "I do pity you, my pet! my poor darling! That's true, that's true!"

While this scene was going on in Greyshott, Gerald and Margaret were jogging on towards Chillfold in their hired chaise. They had a great deal to say, and yet there were long silences between them. Gerald was more angry, Margaret more sad.

"I should have minded nothing else," the Colonel said, "if he had kept the old house for us, the house that has produced us all—Greyshott, that has never belonged but to a Piercey; and, Meg, if he had done justice to you."

"There was no justice owing to me," she said. "I left the house at my own free will. I belong to another house and another name—"

"That might have been true," said Colonel Piercey, with something of his old stiffness and severity, "if—"

"It is true," she said, "I am of the family of my child."

"Oh," he cried, "what folly, at your age! I was angry to have lost you; but now, I can't tell how it is, you are Meg Piercey again."

"You have got used to my changed looks," she said. "You have accepted the fact that I am no longer in my teens. But this is not worth discussing when there is so much more to think of. What shall you do? or, indeed, what can you do?"

"Fight it, certainly," he said. "As soon as I have taken you home, I am to meet old Pownceby, and lay the whole case before the best man we can get. Thank Heaven, I am not without means to fight it out. Poor Uncle Giles! It is hard to call him up to a reckoning before all the world; but he could not have meant it; he could never have meant it."

"I have his little tip for Osy," said Margaret, with tears in her eyes.

"His little tip! when he ought to have provided for the boy!"

"Poor Uncle Giles! He was never very strong: and I believe she was very kind to him, and he was fond of her."

"Do you want me to accept this absurd will, this loss to the race, because she was kind to him (granting that)—and an old man, in his dotage, was fond of a scheming woman?"

"Don't call names," said Margaret. "He was not in his dotage. We saw him—"

"Ah—called on purpose, that we might help to establish the fact," said Colonel Piercey, fiercely. "What do you call it but dotage—that tip over which you are inclined to weep; and the reason alleged for it, that you had been the first to tell him something? Yes, I know what that means. Pownceby told me. That's—how long since? But he believed it, just the same as ever, in the same kind of distant hope. What is that but dotage, Meg?"

"And must it all, everything—the mere foolish hope I expressed to please him, and anything she may have said—must it all be dragged before the public, and poor Uncle Giles' foolish hopes?"

"Would you like me to throw it all over, and leave that woman to enjoy her ill-gotten gains? Do you say I am to do that, Meg?"

"I—say? Oh, no. What right have I? No, Cousin Gerald, I do not think you should give up your claim. I think"—she paused a moment, and her face lighted up, the words seemed to drop from her lips. Other thoughts flashed up in her eyes—an expectation, the light of happiness and peace. The carriage had turned a corner, and Chillfold, with her cottage in it, and her boy, brought the relief and ease of home to Margaret's face. Her companion watched her eagerly. He saw the change that came over her. His thoughts followed hers with a quick revulsion of sympathy. He laid his hand upon hers.

"Meg," he said, "do you know there has never been anybody in the world whose face has lighted up like that for me?"

"You had a mother, Gerald," she said quickly, almost ashamed of her self-revelation; "but you forget—as Osy also will forget."

"At my age one wants something different from a mother," he said, "and one does not forget."

She did not say anything. She did not meet his look; but she gave a little pressure, scarcely perceptible, to the hand that held hers. Their long duel had come, at least, to peace—if nothing more.

CHAPTER XLIV

Patty had a great deal to do before the trial; for it is needless to say that no time was lost in bringing the matter to a trial. It was in some respects an unequal contest, for, clever as she was, she knew no more to whom she should apply, or in whose hands she should place her cause, than any other person of her original position. Mr. Pownceby was the only representative of law with whom she was acquainted, he and the shabby attorney of the village, who was the resort of litigious country folk. And Mr. Pownceby, whom she had insulted, was, as she had foreseen, on the other side. There was no help to be found in Miss Hewitt for any such need, except in so far that after many years' strenuous reading of all the trials in the papers, the names of certain distinguished advocates in various causes célèbres and otherwise were at that lady's finger ends. The idea of the two women was to carry their business at once, without any intervention of an intermediate authority, to one of the very greatest of these great men, with whom, indeed, Patty herself managed to obtain an interview, with the boldness of ignorance. The great man was much amused by Patty, but he did not undertake her case. He even suggested to her that it would be a good thing to compromise matters, and agree with her adversary in the way, which did not at all commend itself to Mrs. Piercey. She would rather, she declared, spend to the half of her kingdom than tamely compromise her "rights," and leave Greyshott to the heir-at-law. The Solicitor-General (I think it was that functionary) was very kind. He was amused by her story, by her youth and good looks, by her fierce determination and her ignorance. It was seldom that he had so genuine a study of human nature before him, and that instinct of human nature which makes our own cause always seem the one that is most just and right. He was moved to advise her to avoid litigation rather from a desire to keep that piquant story for his private gratification, instead of casting it abroad to all the winds, than from any higher motive. And yet he did a great deal for her, telling her who were the solicitors in whose hands she ought to place herself, with a sense that Mrs. Piercey would not be too particular about the means used to secure her success; and suggesting counsel with something of the same idea, and a somewhat malicious amusement and delighted expectation of what would be made of the case by such advocates. He would no more have suggested either the one or the other to Margaret Osborne, than he could have justified himself on moral grounds for recommending them to Mrs. Piercey. Like clients like advisers, he said to himself. He felt that Patty in the witness-box, manipulated by his learned brother, would be a sight for the—well, not perhaps for the gods, unless it were the gods of the shilling gallery, whom such an advocate would cause to weep over the young widow's woes—but for the delectation of the observant and cynical spectator. How wicked and wrong this was it is needless to say; and yet in the mingled issues of human concerns it was very kind to Patty, who was not, as he divined, particular about the modes to be employed in her campaign.

I will not enter into all those preparations for the trial which brightened life immensely to Mrs. Piercey, and made her feel that she had scarcely lived before, and that, however the trial might turn out, this crowded hour of glorious life was worth the age without a name which would have been her fate had all been peaceful and undisturbed. She had constant visits from her solicitors or their emissaries; constant correspondence; a necessity often recurring for running up to town, which opened to her many new delights. No expense was spared in these preliminaries, the lawyers, to whom the speculative character of the whole proceedings was clearly apparent, thinking it well (they were, as has been said, not scrupulous members of their class) to make as much out of it in the meantime as possible; and Patty herself having, in a different degree, something of the same feeling. She was ready, as has been said, to sacrifice half of her kingdom in order to win her plea, and, at the same time, she indulged freely in the pleasure of spending, with the idea before her that even in the event of losing, that pleasure could not be taken from her. Whatever she acquired now would, in that respect, be pure gain. Therefore there can be no doubt that she enjoyed her life during this interval. She had committed one or two imprudencies, which her advisers much regretted and gently condemned. She had made an enemy of Dunning for one thing, which they blamed greatly, and she had alienated the sympathies of her neighbours by her behaviour in the first flush of her triumph, which Lady Hartmore did not fail to publish. But if the client were not foolish sometimes, to what good would be the cleverness of her guides and counsellors? Patty, for her part, declared that she had no fear of Dunning. What could Dunning say that could affect her position? He could describe Sir Giles' hopes, which, it was evident, must have been mistaken; but she could swear, with a good conscience, that she had never said anything about those hopes to Sir Giles. Patty's modesty, the instinct that had made her really incapable of taking advantage of Sir Giles' delusion, had, it is to be feared, by this time, by dint of familiarity with the subject, become much subdued. She had shrunk with a blush from any such discussion, even with her old father-in-law; but she was not afraid now of the ordeal of being examined and cross-examined on the subject before all the world. She was not, indeed, at all afraid of the examination which nowadays frightens most people out of their wits. This, no doubt, was partly ignorance, but it was partly also a happy confidence in her own power to encounter and discomfit any man who should stand up to question her. This confidence has been seen in various cases of young women who have encountered jauntily an ordeal in which it is difficult for the strongest not to come to grief; but an ignorant girl often believes in her own sharp answers more than in any inquisition in the world.

Except these advisers-at-law, however, and her aunt, whom she by no means permitted to be always with her, Patty had actually no supporters or sympathisers. She lived in her great house alone: nobody entering it save one of these advisers; nobody sitting at her table with her; nobody taking any share in the excitement of her life. She had indeed waylaid the rector one day, and compelled him to come to her carriage door to speak to her, which he did with great reluctance, being openly and avowedly on the other side. "What have I ever done to you that you should be against me?" she said; "you used to be my friend once—"

"I hope I am everybody's friend—who does well," said the rector.

"And haven't I done well? If to nurse old Sir Giles night and day, and lay myself out in everything to please him wasn't doing well, why, then I must have been taught my duty very badly, for I thought it was 'I was sick and ye—'"

"Oh! that is how people force a text and put their own meaning to it," said the rector, with a gesture of impatience. "But," he added, in a more subdued tone, "nobody denies, Mrs. Piercey, that you were kind to the old man."

"And wasn't that my duty?" said Patty, triumphantly; but though she silenced her spiritual instructor she did not convince him that it was his duty to support her. No text about the wrongs of the widow had any effect upon him. He stood and looked down at the summer dust in which his feet were planted, and shook his head. It is a great thing to have the enthusiasm of a cause to prop you up, and to have lawyers coming and going from town, and a great deal of business on hand; but to have nobody to speak to, nobody to give you either help or sympathy at home, is hard. When Patty came home from London, after one of the expeditions in which she had been more or less enjoying herself, the blank of the house, in which there was not a soul who cared whether she won or lost, whether she lived or died, was sometimes more than she could bear. One evening, late in July, she went out for a walk, which was a very unusual thing with her, upon the great stretch of common land which lay outside the beech avenue. Patty had begun by this time to grow so much accustomed to the use of a carriage, that she no longer felt it the most delightful mode of conveyance. She had at first, when she came into the possession of that luxury, felt it impossible to walk half a dozen steps without her carriage at her heels; but now she became a little bored by the necessity of a daily drive, and loved to escape for a little walk. She had been in town all day, and it had been hot and uncomfortable. Patty had nowhere to go to in town for a little lunch and refreshment, as ladies have generally. It seemed a wrong to her that ladies had that; that they went in twos and threes enjoying their shopping and their little expedition, laughing and talking to each other, as some did who had gone to town in the same carriage with her, and again had travelled with her coming down, full of news and chatter and purchases. Patty had no one to go with her—there was no house in town where there were friends who expected to see her at lunch; and when she came back, though she might have bought the most charming things in the world, though there might be diamonds in her little bag, there was nobody to wish to see them, to exclaim over their beauty, and envy their happy possessor. These ladies sometimes spoke to her when they did not know her, but often looked askance and whispered to each other; and anyhow, the contrast they made with herself inflamed her very soul with anger. They could wander out, too, in the cool of the evening, still talking, laughing over their adventures, while she was always alone. It was soothing to see that many of them drove home from the station in a bit of a pony carriage or shabby little waggonette with one horse, while her carriage waited for her in lonely grandeur. Sometimes, even, they walked, carrying their parcels, while Patty looked down upon them with immeasurable contempt. But a carriage is not good for everything, and Patty sometimes strayed out alone, thinking the exercise would be good for her, but in reality hoping to escape a little from herself.

It was seldom that she met any one on that lonely moor, but on this particular evening there came towards her, with the glow behind him of the setting sun, a figure, which Patty felt to be, somehow, familiar; though as she did not expect to meet with any one here equal to her quality, she was not at all curious, but even contemptuous of any pedestrian who was not, like herself, walking for pleasure, but might probably be obliged to walk. He carried a long cricket-bag in his hand, and was in white flannels, which made a little brightening in the dimness of the evening, and had a light cap of a bright colour on his head. A well-made, manly figure, slim but strong, and a long swinging step clearing the intervening distance swiftly, made Patty think of some one who had been like that, who would not have let her, in other days, be alone if he could have helped it. She remembered very clearly who that was, and with a little shiver how she had last seen him, and the dance he had been to, and how the thought of that dance moved her to the depths. But this could not be Roger. He had always been fond of cricket—too fond, the village said—liking that better than steady work. But to be dressed like this, in flannels, and a cap of a "colour," was not for common men like him; that was the dress gentlemen put on for the play which was their only work to so many. Indeed, Patty was close upon him before she saw that it was indeed Roger, who took off his cap when he saw her, and would have passed on with that respectful salutation had, not Patty stopped almost without meaning it, in the start of recognition. "Is it you?" she said in her surprise, upon which Roger took off his cap again.

"Seems as if I'd risen in the world," he said, "but it's more seeming than fact. I've been playing for the county," he added, with scarcely concealed pride. "It don't do a man much good, perhaps, but we're pleased enough all the same."

"It's a long time since I have seen you," said Patty, scarcely knowing what she said. "I—I took you for one of the gentlemen."

"And it's a long time since I've seen you—and I'd like to say that I'm sorry, Pa—, Mrs. Piercey, for all that's happened—and for the trouble, if it is a trouble, you're in now."

"It is no trouble," said Patty, hotly. "I'm going to defend my rights, if that's what you mean."

"Well, I hope that's what it is," said Roger, "but I don't like to hear of any one I care for beginning with the law. It just skins you alive and wastes good money that might be spent far better—bring you in a deal more pleasure, I mean."

"You don't know very much, Roger, about the pleasure money brings in!"

"Oh, don't I, Patty! Well, if one of us remembers the old days the other must, too. Cricketing about all over the place as I'm doing, runs through a good lot, I can tell you, if it didn't bring a little more in."

"Don't you do anything but cricket, nowadays?" she said.

"Not much; but it pays well enough," said Roger, pushing back his cap from his forehead.

The evening, it is true, was getting a little dim, though not dark; but didn't he look a gentleman! No one would have guessed he wasn't a gentleman, was the thought that passed through Patty's mind like a dart.

"And I live a lot among the swells, now," he said, "and I hear what they say; I don't want to offend you, Patty, far from it—but ain't it a bore living all by yourself in that big lonesome house, with all the deaths and things that have happened in it?"

"You forget it's my home," said Patty, drawing herself up.

"Well, is it your home? All right if it had been your husband's or if there had been an heir; but I don't hold myself with a place going out of the family like that—that has been in it for hundreds of years. I don't like the thoughts of the Seven Thorns even going out o' the name of 'Ewitt. It's no concern of mine, but I don't."

"Perhaps you think I should go back there, out of my own place, and keep it up!"

"I don't say as I meant that," said Roger, turning his cap, which he had taken off, round and round in his hands, "but I wouldn't be the one to take it out of the family if it was me. I'd say, Look here now, what'll you give me? You be happy in your way, and I'll be happy in mine."

"Well, I shall take your advice, Mr. Pearson. I'll be happy in my own way. It's not yours, and never will be. But that don't matter, seeing we've nothing on earth to do with each other, and are in quite different ranks of life. I wish you good-night, and I hope the cricketing business will be a good one and pay, or else I might say, 'Mind, there's the winter coming on'—if a lady could take upon her to give advice to a sporting man."

"Patty," he cried, calling after her, "don't part with a fellow like this; I didn't mean to offend you—far from it. I only thought I'd warn you what folks said."

"Folks is fools for the most part," cried Patty fiercely, using a much-cited sentiment, which she had never heard of, by the light of nature, "and I don't want to hear what they say. Mr. Pearson, I wish you good-night."

"There! I've been and put my foot in it—I knew I should," Roger said. He stood, the image of despondency, in the middle of the moor, his white figure standing out against the western light as Patty turned at a sharp angle to go home. She could see him with the corner of her eye without looking at him. He stood there silent for a moment, and then dashed his fist into the air with a profane exclamation. "That's not what I meant at all," he said, and lifted his cricket-bag and sped away.

What was it that went out of the evening with him, when Patty, venturing to glance round, saw the landscape empty of the man who had offended her so deeply, who had ventured to blame her—her a lady so far above him—Mrs. Piercey of Greyshott, while he was only a cricketer, an idle fellow about the country, no good, as even the village people said? But yet a dreariness settled down upon the world; night came on and that loneliness which seemed now Patty's fate. Well, she said to herself, what did she care? She had her fine estate, her name that was as good as the best, her grand house, as much money to spend as she chose, and nobody to dictate to her what she should do—no, nobody to dictate to her—nobody even to advise, to say, "That's right, Patty!" Her Aunt Patience did that, it was true, but then Aunt Patience's approval, save in the very extremity of having nobody else, did not count for much. She hurried in; but it was lonely, lonelier even than the moor—nobody to speak to, nobody to break the long row of chairs and sofas which were there with the intention of accommodating half the county, but now had nobody to sit down upon them but Patty's self, moving from one to another with a futile feeling of breaking the solitude. But nothing was to be had to break that solitude except Aunt Patience. Mrs. Piercey of Greyshott rang the bell, and ordered the carriage to be sent at once to the village to fetch Miss Hewitt immediately, without a minute's delay! That she could do—send out her carriage, and her horses, and her secretly-swearing servants for any caprice at any moment. For Miss Hewitt! It was what might be called an anti-climax, if Patty had known what that meant. She did know what it meant deeply to the bottom of her heart, though she was not acquainted with the word. To go through all that she had gone through, to do all she had done, for the sake of having the company of Miss Hewitt and her sympathy and encouragement! could there be a greater drop of deepest downfall from the highest heights than this?

But the trial was coming on, and soon all England would be ringing with Patty's name and story and fortunes. She would have crowds of people to admire and wonder at her. She would win her cause in the sight of all England. She would be the heroine of the day, in everybody's mouth. Surely there would be some compensation in that.

CHAPTER XLV

I refrain from attempting to describe the great trial Piercey v. Piercey, which made the whole country ring. It was, indeed, a cause célèbre, and may be found, no doubt, by every one who wishes to trace it, in the history of such notable romances which exists in the legal records. It was so managed by the exceedingly clever advocates whom Patty had been fortunate enough to secure, as to entertain the country, morning after morning in the columns of the Times, by a living piece of family history, a household opened up and laid bare to every curious eye, which is, perhaps, the thing of all others which delights the British public (and all other publics) the most. Poor old Sir Giles, in his wheeled chair, with his backgammon board and all his weaknesses, became as familiar a figure to the reader of the newspapers as anything in Dickens or Thackeray—more familiar even than Sir Pitt Crawley, because he reached a still larger circle of readers and was a real person, incontestable fact, and only buried the other day. England for the moment became as intimately acquainted with the Softy, as even the old labourers in the parlour at the Seven Thorns. The story, as it was unfolded by the prosecution, was one not favourable to the heroine—a girl out of a roadside tavern, who had married the half-witted son of the squire, who had almost forced her way into the house on the death of its mistress, who had contrived so to cajole the poor old gentleman that he gave himself up entirely to her influence, and finally left her his estates and everything of which he was possessed—leaving out even his old servants whom he had provided for in his previous will, and giving absolute power to the little adventuress. This was a story which did not conciliate the favour of the public. But when it came to the pleadings on the other side, and Patty was revealed as a ministering angel, both to her husband and father-in-law, as having worked the greatest improvement in the one, so that it was hoped he would soon take his place among his country neighbours; and as having protected and solaced the failing days of the other, and been his only companion and consoler, a great change took place in the popular sentiment. It soon became apparent to the world that this little adventuress was one of those rare women who are never out of place in whatever class they may appear in, the lowest or the highest, and are always in their sphere doing good to everybody. The drama was unfolded with the greatest skill: even those "hopes" which it was not denied Sir Giles had greatly built upon, and the disappointment of which, when the young widow found herself deceived in her fond anticipations, was the crudest blow of all. The women who were present shed tears almost without exception over poor Patty's delusion; and that she should have implored the lawyer not to dispel that delusion, to let poor Sir Giles die happy, still believing it, was made to appear the most beautiful trait of character. And indeed, as a matter of fact, Patty had meant well in this particular, and it would have been highly to her credit had it been separated from all that came after. Dunning's testimony, which had been much built upon by the prosecution, was very much weakened by the account given of his various negligences; especially of the fact proved by the lady herself that he had accompanied his master to Lady Piercey's funeral, without providing himself with any restorative to administer to the old gentleman on an occasion of so much excitement and distress, and of such unusual fatigue. "I would not permit it even to be thought of, that he should attend my husband's funeral. It would have been too much for him," Patty said, with all the eloquence of her crape and her widow's cap to enhance what she said. But, indeed, I am here doing precisely what I said I would not attempt to do—and I was not present at the trial to give the details with the confidence of an eye-witness. The consequence, however, was, as all the world knows, that the verdict was for the defendant, and that Patty came out triumphantly mistress of the field, and of Greyshott, and of all that old Sir Giles had committed to her hands.

A romance of real life! It was, indeed, a disappointment and loss to the whole country when the great Piercey case was over. Even old gentlemen who were supposed to care for nothing but politics and the price of stocks, threw down the Times with an angry exclamation that there was nothing in it, the first dull morning or two after that case was concluded. Thus Patty was a benefactor to her kind without any intention of being so. People were generally sorry for the Pierceys, who, there was no doubt, had a right to be disappointed and even angry to see their ancient patrimony thus swept away into the hands of a stranger. For nobody entertained the slightest doubt that Patty would marry and set up a new family out of the ashes of the old. And why shouldn't she? the people cried who knew nothing about it. Was it not the very principle of the British constitution to be always taking in new blood to revive the old? Was not the very peerage constantly leavened by this process; new lords being made out of cotton and coals and beer and all the industries to give solidity to the lessening phalanx of the sons of the Crusaders? Old Sir Francis Piercey, who was the plaintiff, was well enough off to pay his costs, and he ought to be able at his age to reconcile himself to the loss! To be sure, there was his son, a very distinguished soldier. Well! he had better marry the young widow, everybody said, and settle the matter so.

The county people did not, however, take this view. They were wroth beyond expression on the subject of this intruder into their midst. Nobody had called upon her but Lady Hartmore, whose indignation knew no bounds; who had never forgiven her husband, and never would forgive him, she declared, for having betrayed her into that visit. "But to be sure I never should have known what the minx was if I had not seen her!" that lady said. Patty was completely tabooed on every side. Even the rector turned off the highroad when he saw her carriage approaching, and ran by an improvised path over the fields not to meet her. Wherever she might find companions or friends it was evidently not to be in her own district. Her old friends were servants in one great house or another, or the wives of cottagers and labourers; and Patty was altogether unaware of their existence. When she drove about the county, as she did very much and often in the impulse of her triumph, her eyes met only faces which were very familiar but which she would not know, or faces glimpsed at afar off which would not know her. She was undisputed mistress of Greyshott, and all its revenues and privileges. All the neighbouring land belonged to her, and almost every house in the village; but except to Miss Hewitt, her aunt, and the servants of the house, and, occasionally, some much-mistaken woman from one of the cottages, who felt emboldened to make a petition to the lady of Greyshott on the score of having been at school with her, Patty spoke to nobody, or rather had nobody to speak to, which is a better statement of the case.

With one large exception, however, so long as the trial lasted, when lawyers and lawyers' clerks had constant missions to Greyshott, and the distinguished barrister who won her cause for her, came over on a few days' visit. That visit was, in fact, though it was the greatest triumph and glory to Patty, one of the most terrible ordeals she had to go through. He was a most amusing visitor, with endless stories to tell and compliments to pay, and would have made almost any party, in any country house which had the good fortune to receive him, "go off," by his own unaided exertions. But it is to be doubted if this brilliant orator and special pleader had ever in his life formed the whole of a country-house party, with a little, smart, under-bred person and a village spinster for his sole hosts. He was appalled, it must be allowed, and felt that a curious new light was thrown upon the story which he made into a romance of real life; but all the same, it need not be said, this gentleman exerted himself to make the three days "go off" as if the house had been full, and the Prime Minister among the guests. But to describe what this was to Patty would require something more than the modest store of words I have at my disposal. She was not so ignorant as Miss Hewitt, who enjoyed the good the gods had provided for her without arrière pensée, and began to laugh before the delighted guest had opened his lips. Patty knew that there should be people invited "to meet" a man so well known. She knew that there ought to have been a party in the house, or, at least, distinguished company to dinner. And she had nobody, not even the rector! She did her best to invent reasons why So-and-so and So-and-so could not come, and made free use of the name of Lord Hartmore, who, she thought, with the instinct of her kind, had been made to give her up by his wife. She even made use of the fact that most people in the county were displeased with her on account of the trial, and because they wished the Pierceys to be still at Greyshott. "And so they are, in the person of much the most attractive member of the family," the great man said, who would have been still more amused by his position between these two ladies if he had not been in his own person something of a black sheep, and a little on the alert to see himself avoided and neglected. Patty was not aware that he would not have ventured to pay these compliments to another kind of hostess; but she suffered intently from the fact that she had nobody to invite to meet him, nobody who would come to her even for a night, to keep her guest in countenance. She demeaned herself so far as to write to the rector begging of him to come. But the rector had another engagement and would not, or could not, consent. Poor Patty! She suffered in many ways from being thus, as it were, out of the bonds of all human society, but never so much as in that dreadful three days. He was (as she thought) old, and he was fat, and not at all well-looking, though he was so amusing; but he gave her to understand before he went away that he would not mind marrying Mrs. Piercey of Greyshott. And so did one of the solicitors who instructed him, the younger one, who was unmarried; and there was a head clerk, nothing more than a head clerk, who looked very much as if a similar proposal was on his lips. "Like his impudence!" Patty said, though she really knew nothing of the young man. Three proposals, or almost proposals of marriage, within a week or two! This pleased the natural mind of Patty of the Seven Thorns, but it gave Mrs. Piercey occasion to think. They were all concerned with securing property for her, and assuring her in its possession, and they thought naturally that nobody had so good a right to help her take care of it. But this reasoning was not by any means agreeable to Patty, who, flattered at first, became exceedingly angry afterwards when she found herself treated so frankly as an appendage to her property.

"Of course I knew it was always like that as soon as you had a little money!" she said, indignantly.

"Not with 'im, Patty, not with 'im," said Miss Hewitt, upon whom the brilliant barrister had made a great impression.

"Him!" cried Patty, "a fat old man!"

"You can't have everything," said her aunt. "For my part I'd rather 'ave a man like that, that's such fine company, and as you never could be dull as long as 'e was there, than a bit of a cock robin with an 'andsome face, and nothing behind it!"

"If you are meaning my Gervase, Aunt Patience, I—"

"Lord, I never thought o' your Gervase! Bless us, 'e 'ad no 'andsome face, whatever else!" the old lady cried. She was sent home that evening in the carriage, and Patty, angry, indignant, desolate, remained altogether alone. It was hard to say which was worst, the dreadful consciousness of having "nobody to meet" a guest, or being without guests altogether. She walked up and down her solitary house, entering one room after another; all deserted and empty. The servants, as well-bred servants should, got out of the way when they heard her approaching, so that not even in the corridor upstairs did she see a housemaid, or in the hall below a shadow of butler or footman to break the sensation of solitude. To be sure, she knew where to find Jerningham seated in her light and pleasant chamber sewing; but Jerningham was somewhat unapproachable, occupied with her work, quite above idle gossip, and indisposed to entertain her mistress; for Jerningham flattered herself that she knew her place. What was Patty to do? The under-housemaid was a Greyshott girl who had been at school with her; therefore it may be perceived how great was the necessity for remembering always who she was, and never relaxing her dignity. She might have gone abroad, which she was aware was a thing that was done with great success sometimes by ladies who could travel about with maid and footman, and no need to think of expense. But Patty felt that she could not consent to descend among the common herd in search of acquaintances, and that her grandeur was nothing to her unless it was acknowledged and enjoyed at home. And then the winter was coming on, Patty was not yet sufficiently educated to know that winter was precisely the time to go abroad. She knew nothing in the world but Greyshott, and it was only for applause and admiration at Greyshott that she really cared.

It was in these circumstances that the winter passed, the second winter only since Patty's marriage, which had lifted her so far above all her antecedents and old companions. It was a long and dreary winter, with much rain, and that dull and depressing atmosphere of cloud, when heaven and earth is of the same colour, and there is not even the variety of frost and thaws to break the monotonous languor of the long dead dark weeks. Patty did not bate an inch of her grandeur either for her loneliness or for the aggravation of that loneliness which was in the great rooms, untenanted as they were. She did not take to the little cheerful morning-room in which Lady Piercey had been glad to spend the greater part of her life in such wintry weather. Patty dined alone in the great dining-room, which it was so difficult to light up, and she sat alone all the evening through in the great drawing-room, with all its white and gold, where her little figure, still all black from head to foot, was almost lost in a corner, and formed but a speck upon the brightness of the large vacant carpet, and lights that seemed to shine for their own pleasure. Poor Patty! She sat and thought of the last winter, which was melancholy enough, but not so bad as this: of old Sir Giles and his backgammon board, and Dunning standing behind backs. It was not exciting, but it was "company" at least. She thought of herself sitting there, flattering the old gentleman about his play, smiling and beaming upon him, yet feeling so sick of it all; and of that night—that night! when Roger Pearson had been at the dance, and brought Gervase in from the moor, to be laid on the bed from which he was never to rise. Her mind did not dwell upon Gervase, but it is astonishing how often she thought upon that dance at which her rejected lover had been enjoying himself, while she sat playing backgammon with her father-in-law, and listening for her husband. What a contrast! The picture had been burned in upon her mind by the event connected with it, and now had much more effect than that event. She could almost see the rustic couples with their arms entwined, and the romping flirtations of the barn, and the smoky lamps hung about, so different, so different from the steady soft waxen lights which threw an unbroken illumination upon her solitary head! It was bad then, but it was almost worse now, when she had no company at all, except Aunt Patience from time to time, as long as Mrs. Piercey could put up with her. And this was all—all! that her rise in the world had brought her! She had done nothing very bad to procure that rise. If Gervase had lived it would have been good for him that she had married him, she still felt sure, notwithstanding that in actual fact it had not done him much good; and it was good for Sir Giles to have had her society and ministrations in the end of his life. Everybody allowed that—even the hostile lawyer at the trial, even the sullen Dunning, who had occasion to dislike her if anybody had, who had lost his legacy and almost his character by her means. Even he had been instrumental in proving to the world how she had cheered and comforted the old man. And she had got her reward—everything but that title, which it was grievous to her to think of; which, perhaps, if she had got it—if Gervase had only had the sense to live six months longer—would have made all the difference! She had got her reward, and this was what it had come to—a quietness in which you could hear a pin drop; a loneliness never broken by any voice except those of her servants, of whom she must not, and dared not, make friends. Poor Patty! once so cheerful, so admired and considered at the Seven Thorns, with her life so full of bustle and liveliness—this was all she had come to after her romance in real life.

I cannot help thinking that if there had been a lady at the rectory, this state of affairs would have been mended, and that a good mother, with her family to set out in the world, would have seen the advantage for her own children of doing her best to attract acquaintances and company to Greyshott. But the rector was only a man, and a timid one, fearing to break the bonds of convention, and his daughters were too young to take the matter into their own hands. They might have done it had Mrs. Piercey waited for a few years; but then Patty had no inclination to wait.

CHAPTER XLVI

Mrs. Piercey went to town after Easter, as she was aware everybody who respected themselves, who were in Society, or who had any money to spend, did. But, alas! she did not know how to manage this any more than to find the usual solace in country life. She was, indeed, still more helpless in town; for no doubt in the country, if she had been patient, there would at last have been found somebody who would have had courage to break the embargo, to defy Lord and Lady Hartmore and all the partisans of the old family, and to call upon the lady of Greyshott. But in town what could Patty do? She knew nobody but the distant cousins somewhere in the depths of Islington, to whom she had gone at the time of her marriage, but whom she had taken care to forget the very existence of as soon as her need for them was over. Mrs. Piercey went to a fashionable hotel, and engaged a handsome set of rooms, and sat down and waited for happiness to come to her. She had her maid with her, the irreproachable Jerningham, who would not allow her mistress to demean herself by making a companion of her; and she had Robert, the footman, and her own coachman from Greyshott, and a new victoria in which to drive about—all the elements of happiness—poor Patty! and yet it would not come. She had permitted herself, by this time, to drop the weight of her mourning, and to blossom forth in grey and white; and she drove in the Park in the most beautiful costumes, with the old fat Greyshott horses, who were in themselves a certificate that she was somebody, no mushroom of a parvenue. So was the coachman, who was the real old Greyshott coachman, and (evidently) had been in the family for generations. She drove steadily every day along the sacred promenade, and was seen of everybody, and discussed among various bands of onlookers, whose only occupation, like the Athenians, was that of seeing or hearing some new thing. Who was she? That she was not of the style of her horses and her coachman was apparent at a glance. Where had she got them? Was it an attempt on the part of some visitor from the ends of the earth to pose as a lady of established family? Was it, perhaps, a daring coup on the part of some person, not at all comme il faut, to attract the observation and curiosity of the world? Patty's little face, with its somewhat fast prettiness, half abashed, half impudent, shone out of its surroundings with a contradiction to all those suppositions. The Person would not have been at all abashed, but wholly impudent, or else quite assured and satisfied with herself; and in any case she would not have been alone. A stranger, above all, would not have been alone. There would have been a bevy of other women with her, making merry over all the novelty about them, and this, probably, would have been the case had the other idea been correct. But who was this, with the face of a pretty housemaid and the horses of a respectable dowager? Some of the gentlemen in the park, who amused themselves with these speculations, would, no doubt, have managed to resolve their doubts on the subject had not Patty been, as much as Una, though she was so different a character, enveloped in an atmosphere of such unquestionable good behaviour and modesty as no instructed eye could mistake. Women, who are less instructed on such matters, may mistake; but not men, who have better means of knowing. Thus Patty did make a little commotion; but as she had no means of knowing of it, and no one to tell her, it did her no good in the world.

And she went a good many times to the theatre, and to the opera, though it bored her. But this was a great ordeal: to go into a box all alone, and subject herself to the opera-glasses of the multitude. Patty did not mind it at first. She liked to be seen, and had no objection that people should look at her, and her diamonds; and there was a hope that it might lead to something in her mind. But how could it lead to anything? for she knew nobody who was likely to be seen at the opera. When she went home in the evening she could have cried for disappointment and mortification. Was this all? Was there never to be anything more than this? Was all her life to be spent thus in luxury and splendour; always alone?

At first she had dined in solitary state in her rooms, as she thought it right, in her position, to do. But when Patty heard that other people of equal pretensions—one of them the baronet's lady, whom it was her despair not to be—went down to the general dining-room for their meals, she was too happy to go there too, thinking she must, at least, make some acquaintance with the other dwellers in the hotel. But things were not much better there, for Mrs. Piercey was established at a little table by herself in great state, but unutterable solitude, watching with a sick heart the groups about her—the people who were going to the theatre, or to such delights of balls and evening parties as Patty had never known. There was but one solitary person beside herself, and that was an old gentleman, with his napkin tucked into his buttonhole, who was absorbed by the menu and evidently thought of nothing else. Patty watched the groups with hungry eyes—the men in their evening coats, with wide expanses of white; the ladies, who evidently intended to dress after this semi-public dinner. Oh, how she longed to belong to some one, to have some one belonging to her! And such a little thing, she thought, would do it: nothing more than an introduction, nothing beyond the advent of some one who knew her, who would say, "Mrs. Piercey of Greyshott," and the ice would be broken. But then that some one who knew her, where was he or she to be found?

Alas! there came a moment when both he and she were found, and that was the worst of all. She was seated listlessly in her usual solitude, when she saw a pair of people who were taking their seats at a table not far off. They had their backs turned towards her, and yet they seemed familiar to Patty. They were both tall, the gentleman with a military air, the lady with a little bend in her head which Patty thought she knew. There was about them that indefinable air of being lately married which it is so very difficult to obliterate, though they did not look very young. The lady was quietly dressed, or rather she was in a dress which was the symbol of quiet—quakerly, or motherly, to our grandmothers: grey satin, but with such reflections and shadows in it, as has made it in our better instructed age one of the most perfectly decorative of fabrics. Patty, experienced by this time in the habits and customs of the people she watched so wistfully, was of opinion that they were going to the opera. Who were they? She knew them—oh, certainly she knew them; and they evidently knew several of the groups about; and now at last Patty's opportunity had surely come.

I think by this time Mrs. Piercey of Greyshott had acquired a forlorn look, the consequence of her many disappointments. It is not pleasant to sit and watch people who are better off than we are, however philosophical and high-minded we may be; and Patty, it need not be said, was neither. Her mouth had got a little droop at the corners, her eyes a little fixity, as of staring and weariness in staring. She was too much dressed for the dining-room of a hotel, and she had very manifestly the air of being alone, and of being accustomed to be alone. I think that, as so often happens, Patty was on the eve of finding the acquaintance for whom her soul longed, at these very moments when her burden was about to become too much for her to bear; and she certainly had attained recognition in the world outside, as was to be proved to her no later than to-night. Such coincidences are of frequent occurrence in human affairs. It had become known in the hotel to some kind people, who had watched her solitude as she watched their cheerful company, who she was; and the matron of the party had remembered how much that was good had been said of Patty on the trial, and how kind she had been to the old man who had left her all his money without any doing of hers. "Poor little thing! I shall certainly take an opportunity of speaking to her to-morrow," this lady was saying, as Patty watched with absorbed attention the other people. Indeed, the compassion of this good woman might have hastened her purpose and made her "speak" that very night, had not Patty been so bent upon those other people whom she was more and more sure she knew; and what a difference—what a difference in her life might that have made! But she never knew—which was, perhaps, in the circumstances, a good thing.

It was while Patty's attention was called away perforce by the waiter who attended to her, that the other people at whom she had been gazing became aware of her presence. The gentleman had turned a bronzed face, full of the glow of warmer suns than ours, in her direction, and started visibly. He was a man whom the reader has seen habitually with another expression—that of perplexity and general discontent; a man with a temper, and with little patience, though capable of better things. He had apparently got to these better things now. His face was lighted up with happiness; he was bending over the little table, which, small as it was, seemed too much to separate them, to talk to his wife, with the air of a man who has so much and so many things to say, that he has not a minute to lose in the outpouring of his heart. She was full of response, if not perhaps so overflowing; but on her aspect, too, there had come a wonderful change. Her beautiful grey satin gown was not more unlike the unfailing black which Mrs. Osborne always wore, than the poor relation of Greyshott was to Gerald Piercey's wife, Meg Piercey once again. It would be vain to enter upon all the preliminaries which brought about this happy conclusion. Margaret had many difficulties to get over, which to everybody else appeared fantastical enough. A second marriage is a thing which, in theory, few women like; and to cease to belong solely to Osy, and to bear another name than his, though it was her own, was very painful to her. Yet these difficulties had all been got over, even if I had space to enter into them; which, seeing that Patty is all this time waiting, dallying with her undesired dinner, and wondering who these people are whom she seems to know, would be uncalled for in the highest degree.

When the waiter came up to the solitary lady at the table, and Colonel Piercey turned his face in that direction, he started and swore under his breath, "By Jove!" though he was not a man addicted to expletives. Then he said, "Meg! Meg!" under his breath; "who do you think is sitting behind you at that table? Don't turn round. Mrs. Piercey, as sure as life!"

"Mrs. Piercey?" She was bewildered for a moment. "There are so many Mrs. Pierceys. Whom do you mean?"

"One more than there used to be, for my salvation," the bridegroom said; and then added, with a laugh, "but no other like this one, Meg—Mrs. Piercey of Greyshott—"

"Patty!" cried Margaret, under her breath.

"If you dare to be so familiar with so great a lady—the heroine of the trial, poor Uncle Giles' good angel—"

"Oh, don't be bitter, Gerald! It is all over and done with; and who knows, if it had been otherwise—"

"Whether we should ever have come together?" he said: "you know best, so far as that goes, my love; and if it might have been so, good luck to Greyshott, and I am glad we have not got it. Yes, there she is, the identical Patty; and none the better for her success, I should say, looking very much bored and rather pale."

"Who is with her?" asked Margaret.

"There is nobody with her that I can see. No, she is quite alone, and bored, as I told you; and in a diamond necklace," he said with a laugh.

"Alone, and with a diamond necklace, in the dining-room of a hotel!"

"Well, why not? To show it and herself, of course; and probably a much better way than any other in her power to show them."

"Oh, Gerald, don't be so merciless. She has got your inheritance; but still, it was really Uncle Giles' will, and she was kind to him—even old Dunning could not deny that. And if Gervase had lived—"

"It was as well he did not live, poor fellow, for her as well as for himself, though I should certainly, myself, have preferred it; for then we should have had none of this fuss, either of anticipation or disappointment—and no trial, and no costs; and no useless baronetcy that brings in nothing."

"Don't say that; your father likes it, and so will you in your day."

"My father likes to be head of the family, and so shall I. We'll have our first quarrel, Meg, over that little hussy, then."

"Not our first quarrel by a great many," she said, letting her hand rest for a moment on his arm. "But don't call her names, Gerald: all alone in a hotel in London, in the middle of the season, without a creature to speak a word to her! And I heard she was perfectly alone all the winter at home. Lady Hartmore goes too far. She has made it a personal matter that nobody should call. Poor little Patty! Gerald—"

"Poor little Patty, indeed! who has cost us not only Greyshott, but how many thousand pounds; who has made you poor, Meg."

"There is poor and poor. Poor in your way is not poor in mine. I am rich, whatever you may be. Is she still there—alone—Gerald, with that white little face?" Margaret had managed, furtively, to turn her head, still under shadow of the waiter, and get a glimpse of their supplanter.

"What does it matter if her face is white or not? She has chalked it, perhaps, as she might rouge it on another occasion, to play her part."

"You have no pity," said Margaret; "to me it is very sad to see a poor woman like that alone, trying to enjoy herself. I think, Gerald, I will—"

"Will what? You are capable of anything, Meg. I shall not be surprised at whatever you propose."

"Well, since you have so poor an opinion of me," she said with a smile, "I think I'll speak to her, Gerald."

"Do you remember that she turned you out of your home? that she insulted you so that it was with difficulty I kept my temper?"

"You never did keep your temper, dear," said Margaret with gentle impartiality, shaking her head; "and," she added with a smile, "you insulted me far worse than ever Patty did. Should I bear malice? I will say a word to her before we go."

When they rose, and when Patty saw who they were, the chalk which Colonel Piercey thought she was capable of using to play her part, yielded to a crimson so hot and vivid that its truth and reality were thoroughly proved. She half rose, too, then sat down again more determinedly than before.

"Mrs. Piercey," said Margaret, "we saw you, and I could not pass you without a word."

"You are very kind, I am sure, Margaret Osborne; but you could have left your table very well without coming near me."

"Yes, perhaps," said Margaret; "I should have said that, seeing you alone—"

"Oh, if I am alone it is my own fault!" cried Patty, with a heat of angry despair which almost took away her voice. Then it occurred to her that to show this passion was to lessen herself in the eyes of those to whom she most wished to appear happy and great. She forced her cry of rage into a little affected laugh. "I don't often come here," she said; "I dine generally in my own apartments. But to-day I expected friends who could not come, and so I thought I'd amuse myself by coming down here to see the wild beasts feed."

As she said this, her eyes fell accidentally upon the kind lady who had made up her mind to make the acquaintance of this forlorn little woman, and startled that amiable person so that she sat gazing open-mouthed and open-eyed.

"In that case I am afraid I am only intruding," said Margaret; "but I thought perhaps—if you are alone here, I—or my husband," she added this with a sudden blush and smile, "might have been of some use—"

"Oh, your husband! I wish him joy, I am sure. So you stuck to him, though he hasn't got Greyshott? Well, he'll have the baronetcy, to be sure, when the old man dies—I hadn't thought of that—without a penny! You must have been dead set on him, to be sure."

And Patty, bursting with fury and despite, jumped up, almost oversetting the table, and with a wave of her hand as if dismissing a supplicant, but with none of her usual regard for her dignity and her dress in threading a crowd, hurried away.

"You got rather more than you looked for," cried Colonel Piercey, triumphant, as Margaret came back to him and hastily took his arm. He had not heard what passed.

"I suppose there was nothing else to be expected," Margaret said in a subdued voice.

Patty went to the opera that night, as she had intended, her heart almost bursting; for that she should have hoped to meet somebody who would introduce and help her, and then to find that somebody was Margaret Osborne, was almost more than she could bear; but soon she was soothed by perceiving that more opera-glasses were fixed on her than ever, and that the people in the boxes opposite, and in the stalls, were pointing her out to one another. She caught the sound of her own name as she sat well forward in her box, that her diamonds might be well seen and her own charms appreciated; and she almost forgot the indignity to which she had been, as she thought, subjected. But as she went out, poor Patty could not but hear some remarks which were not intended for her ear. "That was the woman," somebody said, "the heroine of the great case, Piercey versus Piercey; don't you remember? the woman who married an idiot, and then got his father to leave her all the property." "What a horror!" said the lady addressed: "a barmaid, wasn't she? and the poor creature she married quite imbecile—and now to come and plant herself there in the front of a box. Does she think anybody will take any notice of her, I wonder?" "Impudent little face, but rather broken down—begins to see it won't pay," said another man.

Patty caught Robert, her footman, by the arm, and shrieked to him to take her out of this, or she should faint, which the crowd around took for an exclamation of real despair, and made way for the lady, to let her get to the air. And Patty left town next day.

CHAPTER XLVII

She left town next day in a tempest of wrath and indignation, and something like despair. She said to herself that she would go home, where no one would dare to insult her. Home! where, indeed, there would be nobody to insult her, but nobody to care for her; to remark upon her even in that contemptuous way; to say a word even of reprobation. A strong sense of injustice was in her soul. I am strongly of opinion that when any of us commits a great sin, it immediately becomes the most natural, even normal thing in our own eyes; that we are convinced that most people have done the same, only have not been found out; and that the opinion of the world against it is either purely fictitious, a pretence of superior virtue, or else the result of prejudice or personal hostility. Patty had not committed any great sin. She had sought her own aggrandisement, as most people do, but she had gained wealth and grandeur far above her hopes by nothing that could be called wrong; indeed, she had done her duty in the position in which Providence and her own exertions had placed her. It was not her business to look after the interests of the Piercey family, but to take gratefully what was given her, which she had the best of right to, because it had been given her. This was Patty's argument, and it would be difficult to find fault with it. And to think that the whole cruel world should turn upon her for that; all those gentlefolks whom she despised with the full force of democratic rage against people who supposed themselves her betters, yet felt to the bottom of her heart to be the only arbiters of social elevation and happiness, the only people about whose opinion she cared! She came back to Greyshott in a subdued transport of almost tragic passion. She would seek them no more, neither their approval nor their company. She would go back to her own class, to the class from which she had sprung, who would neither scorn her nor patronise her, but fill Greyshott with admiring voices and adulation, and make her feel herself the greatest lady and the most beneficent. She called for Aunt Patience on her way from the station and carried her back to Greyshott. "You're going to stay this time," she said; "I mean to live in my own way, and have my old friends about me; and I don't care that," and Patty snapped her fingers, "for what the county may say."

"The county couldn't say nothing against your having me with you, Patty—only right, everybody would say, and you so young, and men coming and going."

"Where are the men coming and going?" said Patty; "I see none of them. I dare say there would be plenty, though, if it wasn't for the women," she added, with a self-delusion dear to every woman upon whom society does not smile.

"You take your oath of that!" said Miss Hewitt, who was naturally of the same mind.

"But I mean to think of them no more," cried Patty; "the servants shall say 'not at home' to any of those ladies as shows their face here! I'll bear it no longer! If they don't like to call they can stay away,—what is it to me? But I'm going to see my old friends and give dinners and dances to them that will really enjoy it!" Patty cried.

Miss Hewitt looked very grave. "Who do you mean, Patty, by your old friends?" she said.

"Who should I mean but the Fletchers and the Simmonses and the Pearsons and the Smiths and the Higginbothams?" said Patty, running on till she was out of breath.

"Lord, Patty! you'd never think of that!" cried Miss Hewitt, horrified.

"Why shouldn't I?—they'd be thankful and they'd enjoy themselves; and I'd have folks of my own kind about me as good as anybody."

"Oh, Patty, Patty, has it come to that? But you're in a temper and don't mean it," Aunt Patience cried.

It would, perhaps, have been better for this disinterested relation had she supported Patty in her new fancy, as undoubtedly it would have been glorious and delightful to herself to have posed before her own village associates as one of the mistresses of Greyshott. But Miss Hewitt had been influenced all her life by that desire for the society of the ladies and gentlemen which is so strong in the bosom of the democrat everywhere. She could not bear that Patty should demean herself by falling back upon "the rabble"; and many discussions ensued, in which the elder lady had the better of the argument. Patty's passionate desire to be revenged upon the people who had slighted her resolved itself at last into the heroic conception of such a fête for the tenants and peasantry as had never been known in the county before. Indeed, the county was not very forward in such matters; it was an old-fashioned, easy-going district, and new ways and new education had made but small progress in it as yet. The squires and the gentry generally had not begun to feel that necessity for conciliating their poorer neighbours, with whom at present they dwelt in great amity—which has now become a habit of society. And the fame of the great proceedings at Greyshott travelled like fire and flame across the county. No expense was spared upon that wonderful fête. Patty knew exactly what her old friends and companions liked in the way of entertainment. She made a little speech at the dinner, which began the proceedings, to the effect that she had not invited any of the fine folks to walk about and watch them as if they were wild beasts feeding (using over again in a reverse sense the metaphor which she had already found so effectual), but preferred that they should feel that she was trusting them like friends and wished them to enjoy themselves. And to see Patty and Miss Hewitt walking about, sweeping the long trains of their dresses over the turf in the midst of these revellers, with a graciousness and patronage which would have made Lady Hartmore open her eyes, was a sight indeed. No Princess Royal could have been more certain of her superior place than Patty on this supreme occasion, when, flying from the hateful aristocrats, who would not call upon her, she had intended to throw herself back again into the bosom of her own class. And Miss Hewitt looked a Grand Duchess at the least, and showed a benign interest in the villagers which no reigning lady could have surpassed. "Seven? have you really? and such fine children; and is this the youngest?" she said, pausing before a family group; to the awe of the parents, who had known old Patience Hewitt all their lives, and knew that she knew every detail of their little history; but this will show with what gusto and fine histrionic power she was able, though really almost an old woman, to take up and play her part. But had it not been the ideal and hope of her life?

There was, however, one person at the Greyshott fête whom it was difficult to identify with the heroes of the village. When Patty saw approaching her across the greensward a well-knit manly figure in irreproachable flannels, with a striped cap of red and white on his head, a tie of the same colour, a fine white flannel shirt encircling with its spotless folded-down collar a throat burnt to a brilliant red-brown by the sun, her heart gave a jump with the sudden conviction that "a gentleman" had come, even though uninvited, to see her in her glory. It gave another jump, however, still more excited and tremulous, when this figure turned out to be Roger Pearson—not a gentleman indeed, but a famous personage all over England, the pride of the county, whose rise in the world was now fully known to her. She had seen him before, indeed, in this costume, but only in the dusk, when it was not so clearly apparent. How well it became him, and what a fine fellow he looked! handsome, free, independent, as different from all his rustic friends as Patty was from her old school-fellows in their cotton dresses, but in how different a way; for Roger, it was well known, was hand-and-glove with many of the greatest people of England, and yet quite at home in the village eleven which he had come to lead in the match which was one of the features of the day. Patty, though she was the lady of Greyshott, could not but feel a pang of delight and pride when he walked by her side through the crowd. He was the only one whom she could not patronise. She thought furtively that any one who saw them would think he was the young squire; that was what he looked like—the master, as she was the lady. He had no need to put on those airs which Patty assumed. Nobody disputed his superiority, or even looked as if they felt themselves as good as him. And it seemed to be natural, as the afternoon went on, that he should find himself again and again by Patty's side, sometimes suggesting something new, sometimes offering his services to carry out her plans, sometimes begging that she would rest and not wear herself out. "Go and sit down quiet a bit, and I'll look after 'em; I can see you're doing too much," he said. It was taking a great deal upon him, Miss Hewitt thought, but Patty liked it! She gave him commissions to do this and that for her, and looked on with the most unaccustomed warmth at her heart while he fulfilled them. Just like the young master! always traceable wherever he moved in the whiteness of his dress, that dress which the gentlemen wore and looked their best in; and nobody could have imagined that Roger Pearson was not a gentleman, to see him. "Well! and weren't there ways of making him one?" Patty thought to herself.

But, notwithstanding her indignant determination to throw herself back into the bosom of her own class, it was to Roger alone that she made any overtures of further intercourse. He stayed behind all the others when the troops of guests went away, and told her it was a real plucky thing to do, and had been a first-rate success. He looked, indeed, like a gentleman, but he had not adopted the phraseology of the Vere de Veres; and perhaps Patty liked him all the better. She said, "Come and see me any day; come when you like," when he held her hand to say good-night; and she said it in an undertone, so that Aunt Patience might not hear.

"I will indeed," he said in the same tone, "the first vacant day I have—" Her breast swelled to see that he was a man much sought after, though this had not been her own fate.

But either he did not have a vacant day, or, what Patty's judgment quite approved, he did not mean to make himself cheap. And Patty fell into a worse depth of solitude than ever, notwithstanding the presence of Aunt Patience, to whom she had said in the rashness of her passion that she should henceforth stay always at Greyshott, but whom now she felt to be an additional burden when perpetually by her side. There had been a little quarrel between them after luncheon one day in July, for they were both irritable by reason of that unbroken tête-à-tête, and of the fact that they had said ten or twelve times over everything they had to say; and Miss Hewitt had flounced off upstairs to her room, where, after her passion blew off, she had lain down on the sofa to take a nap, leaving Patty to unmitigated solitude. It was raining, and that made it more dreary than ever: rain in July, quiet, persistent, downpouring; bursting the flowers to pieces; scattering the leaves of the last roses on the ground; and injuring even those sturdy uninteresting geraniums which are the gardener's stand-by—is the dreariest of all rains. It is out of season, even when it is wanted for the country, as there is always some philosopher to tell us; and it is pitiless, pattering upon the trees, soaking the grass, spreading about us a remorseless curtain of grey. Patty, all alone, walked from window to window and saw nothing but the trees under the rain, and a little yellow river pouring across the path. She sat down and took up the work with which Aunt Patience solaced the weary hours. It was the old-fashioned Berlin woolwork, which only old ladies do nowadays. She contrived to put it all wrong, and then she threw it down and went to the window again. And then she was aware of a figure coming up the avenue, a figure clothed in a glistening white mackintosh and under an umbrella. She could not see who it was, but something in the walk struck her as familiar. It looked like a gentleman, she said to herself; though to be sure, in these days of equality, it might be only the draper's young man with patterns, or the lawyer's clerk. Patty felt that she would have been glad to see even the lawyer's clerk.

But when it was Roger Pearson that came into the room, what a difference that made at once! It was almost as if the sun had come out from behind the clouds for a moment, although he was not a gentleman, but only a professional cricketer. He was not dressed this time in his flannels, which suited him best, but in a grey suit, which, however, was very presentable. Patty felt that if the first lady in the county was to choose this particular wet day to call, which was not likely, she would not need to blush for her visitor. And she was unfeignedly glad to see him in the desolation of her solitude. She could tell from the manner in which he looked at her that he was admiring her, and he could tell that she was admiring him, and what could two young people require more of each other? Roger told her quite frankly a great deal about himself. He acknowledged that he had been "a bit idle" in his earlier days, and liked play better than work; but that had all come in very useful, for such play was now his work, and he had a very pleasant life, going all over the country to cricket matches, and seeing everything that was going. "And all among the swells, too," he said, "which would please you."

"Indeed, you're mistaken altogether," said Patty. "Swells! I loathe the very name of them. Since I've lived among 'em I know what they are; and a poorer, more cold, stuck-up, self-seeking set—"

"I don't make no such objections," said Roger, who, it has been said, took no trouble to use the language of gentlemen. "They're good fellows enough. I don't want no more of them than they're willing to give me—so we gets on first rate."

"They try to crush your spirit," cried Patty, flaming, "and then, perhaps, when they've got you well under their fist, they'll condescend to take a little notice. But none of that sort of thing for me!"

"Well!" said Roger, looking round him, "this is a fine sort of a place, with all these mirrors and gilt things; but I should have said you would have been more comfortable with a smaller house, and things more in our own way, like what we've been used to, both you and me."

"I have been used to this for a long time now," said Patty, with spirit, "and it's my own house."

"Yes, I know," he said, "and it ain't for me to say anything, for I'm not a swell like these as you have such a high opinion of."

"I have no high opinion of them. I hate them!" cried Patty, with set teeth.

"Well, I've often thought," said Roger, "though I know I've no right to—but just in fancy don't you know—as Patty Hewitt of the Seven Thorns would have been a happier woman in the nice little 'ouse as I could give her now, and never harming nobody, than a grand lady like Mrs. Piercey, with so much trouble as you have had, and no real friends."

"How do you know," cried Patty, "that I have no friends?" and then, after a moment's struggle to keep her self-command, she burst into a violent storm of tears. "Oh, don't say anything to me!" she cried, "don't say anything to me! I haven't had a kind word from a soul, nor known what it was to have an easy heart or a bit of pleasure, not since the night you came to the little door, Roger Pearson—no, nor long before."

There was a silence, broken only by her passionate sobs and the sound of the weeping which she could not control, until Roger moved from his chair and went up to the sofa on which she had thrown herself, hiding her tears and flushed face upon the cushions. He laid his hand upon her shoulder with a caressing touch, and said, softly, "Don't now, don't now, Patty dear. Don't cry, there's a love."

"And when you think all I've gone through," said Patty, among her sobs, "and how I've given up everything to do my duty! When you said to me that night you had been at a dance—Oh! and me never seeing a soul, never anything but waiting on them, and serving them, and nursing them, or playing nonsense games from morning to night! And then when the old gentleman died and left me what I never asked him for, then everybody taking up against me as if I had committed a sin; and never one coming near me, never, never one, but Meg in London coming to speak out of charity, because I was alone. Yes, and I was alone," said Patty, raising herself up, drying her eyes hastily, with a nervous hand, "and I'll be alone all my life; but I'll never take charity as if I was some poor creature, from her or from him!"

"You needn't be alone a moment more than you like, Patty," said Roger. "I was always fond of you, you well know. You jilted me to marry 'im, poor fellow, but I'll not say a word about that. You're not 'appy in this great 'ouse, and you know it, nor you'll never be. I'm not saying anything one way or another about them ladies and swells: maybe they might have been a little kinder and done no 'arm. But you're an interloper among them, you know you are; and I'm not one as 'olds with putting another man's nose out of joint, or taking his 'ouse over 'is 'ead. I wouldn't, if it was a bit of a cottage, or your father's old place at the Seven Thorns; and no more would I here. There ain't no blessing on it, that's my opinion."

"I don't know, Roger Pearson, that your opinion was ever asked," Patty said.

"It wasn't asked; but you wouldn't cry like that before anybody but me, nor own as you were in trouble. Now, 'ere's my 'and, if you'll have it, Patty; I'll not come 'ere to sit down at another man's fireside, but I'll stand by you through thick and thin; and I'm making a pretty bit of money myself, and neither me nor you—we don't need to be beholdin' to nobody. Let's just set up a snug place of our own, and I'd like to see the man—the biggest swell in the world—or woman either, that would put a slight upon my wife."

"What!" said Patty, with a smile that was meant to be satirical, "give up Greyshott and my position and all as I've struggled so hard for, for you, Roger Pearson? Why, who are you? nobody! a man as is a good cricketer; and that's the whole when all's said."

"Well," said Roger, good-humouredly, "it's not a great deal, perhaps, but it's always something; and it's still me if I never touched a bat. You wouldn't marry my cricketing any more than you'd marry his parliamenteering, or sporting, or what not, if you did get a swell; and you take my word, Patty, you'll never get on with a swell like you would do with me. We've been brought up the same, and we understand each other. I know how you're feeling, just exactly, my poor little girl: you'd like to be 'appy, and then pride comes in. You say, 'I've worked hard for it and I'll never give it up.'"

"If you mean I'll not give up being Mrs. Piercey of Greyshott, with the finest house in the county, to go to a cottage with you—"

"Don't now, don't," said Roger, protesting, yet without excitement; "I never said a cottage, did I? What I said was a 'andsome 'ouse, with all the modern improvements and furnished to your fancy, instead of this old barrack of a place, and a spanking pair of 'osses, a deal better than them old fat beasts, as goes along like snails; and some more in the stable, a brougham, and a victoria, and a dogcart for me; that's my style. I don't call that love in a cottage. I call it love very well to do, with everything comfortable. Lord! if you like this better, this old place—full of ghosts and dead folks' pictures, I don't agree with your taste, my dear, and that's all I've got to say."

Patty looked at her matter-of-fact lover, raising her head high, preparing the sharpest speeches. She sat very upright, all the tears over, ready, quite ready, to give him his answer. But then there suddenly came over Patty a vision of the winter which was coming, the winter that would be just like the last—the monotonous, dreadful days, the long, lingering, mortal nights, with Aunt Patience for her sole companion. And her thoughts leapt on before to the 'andsome 'ouse; for being, as Roger said, of his kind, and understanding by nature what he meant, her imagination represented to her in a flash as of sunshine, that shining, brilliant, high-coloured house—with all the last improvements and the newest fashions, plate-glass windows, shining fresh paint which it would be a delight to keep like a new pin, everything new, clean, delightful; carpets and curtains of her own choosing, costing a great deal of money, and of which she could say to every guest, "It's the best that money could buy," or "I gave so much a yard for it," or "Every window stands me in fifty pounds there as you see it." All this appeared to Patty in a flash of roseate colour. And the pair of spanking horses at the door, and a crowd of cricketing men, yes, and cricketing ladies; and meetings in her own grounds, and great luncheon parties, and quantities of other young couples thinking of nothing but their fun and their pleasure, the wives dressing against each other, the young men competing in their batting and bowling, and in their horses and turn-outs, but all in the easiest, noisiest, friendly way, and all surrounding herself, Patty, with admiration and homage as the richest among them. Oh, what a contrast to grey old Greyshott, with its empty, echoing rooms and its dark solitude, and the pictures of dead people, as Roger said, and not a lively sight or sound, nothing but Jerningham and the other servants and Aunt Patience. To think of all that, and Roger added to it,—Roger, who sat looking at her so kindly, with his handsome good-humoured face, not hurrying her in her decision, looking as if he knew beforehand that she could not resist him and his offer of everything she liked best in the world.

All this came to Patty in a moment, as she sat with her sharp speeches all arrested on her lips. The pause she made was not long, but it was long enough to show him that she had begun to think, and we all know that the woman who deliberates is lost; and it was in the nature of the practical-minded lover, who was not given to the sentimental, as it was also in Patty's nature, to carry things by a coup de main. He sprang up from the seat he had taken opposite to her, and suddenly, before she was aware, gave Patty a hearty kiss which seemed to sound through all the silent house.

"Don't you think any more about it," he said, holding her fast; "you jilted me before, but you're not going to jilt me again. I 'ave the 'ouse in my eye, and I know the jolly life we'll live in it: lots of company and lots of fun, and two folks that is fond of one another; that's better than living all alone—a little more grand, but no fun at all."

And to such a triumphant and convincing argument, which her heart and every faculty acknowledged, what could Patty reply?

CHAPTER XLVIII

It was only a few weeks after this that there appeared in the newspapers, which had all reported at such length the great trial of Piercey versus Piercey, a paragraph which perhaps caused as much commotion through the county as the news of any great public event for many years. Parliament had risen, and the papers were very thankful for a new sensation of any kind. The paragraph was to this effect:—

"Our readers have not forgotten the trial of Piercey v. Piercey, which unfolded so curious a page of family history, and roused so many comments through the whole English-speaking world. It is seldom that so many elements of human interest are collected in a single case, and the effect it produced on the immense audience which followed its developments day by day was extraordinary. The public took sides, as on an affair of imperial importance, for and against the heroine, who, from the bar-room of a roadside inn, found herself elevated in a single year to the position of a considerable landowner, with an ancient historical house and a name well known in the annals of the country. How she attained these honours, whether by the most worthy and admirable means, by unquestionable self-devotion to her husband and father-in-law, or by undue influence, exercised first on a young man of feeble intellect, and afterwards on an old gentleman in his dotage, was the question debated in almost every sociable assembly.

"The partisans and opponents of this lady will have a new problem offered to them in the new and startling incident which is now announced as the climax of this story. Those who have all along believed in the disinterestedness of the young and charming Mrs. Piercey will be delighted to hear that she has now presented herself again before the public, in the most romantic and attractive light by freely and of her own will resigning the Manor of Greyshott, to which a jury of her countrymen had decided her to be fully entitled, to the heirs-at-law of the late Sir Giles Piercey, together with all the old furniture, pictures, family plate, etc., contained in the manor house—a gift equally magnificent and unexpected. It is now stated that this has all along been Mrs. Piercey's intention, and that but for the trial, which put her at once on her defence, she would have made this magnanimous renunciation immediately after coming into the property. Her rights having been assailed, however, it is natural that a high-spirited young woman should have felt it her first duty to vindicate her character; and that she should now carry out her high-minded intention, after all the obloquy which it has been attempted to throw on her, and the base motives imputed to her, is a remarkable instance of magnanimity which, indeed, we know nothing to equal. It is, indeed, heaping coals of fire on the heads of her accusers, for whom, however, it must be said that their irritation in finding themselves so unexpectedly deprived of the inheritance they had confidently expected, was natural and justifiable. It must be a satisfaction to all that a cause célèbre which attracted so much attention should end in such a fine act of restitution, and that an ancient family should thus be restored to their ancestral place. We are delighted to add that Mrs. Piercey, who still retains a fine fortune bequeathed to her by the love and gratitude of her father-in-law, whom she nursed with the greatest devotion till his death, is about to contract a second marriage with a gentleman very well known in the cricketing world."

"In the name of Heaven, what is the meaning of that?" cried old Sir Francis Piercey, who was a choleric old gentleman, flinging down the newspaper (which only arrived in the evening), and turning a crimson countenance, flushed with astonishment and offence, to his son Gerald and his daughter-in-law Margaret, who had returned to their home in the north only a few days before. Sir Francis was a very peppery old man, and constantly thought, as do many heads of houses conscious of having grown a little hard of hearing, that nothing was told him, and that even in respect to the events most interesting to the family he was systematically kept in the dark.

"The meaning of what?" Margaret asked, without excitement. She had no newspaper, being quite content to wait for the news until the gentlemen had read everything and contemptuously flung down each his journal with the remark that there was nothing in it. Mrs. Gerald Piercey did not imagine there could ever be anything in the paper which could concern her or her belongings; and it was a quiet time in politics, when Parliament was up, and nothing very stirring to be expected. She rose to put down by her father-in-law's side his cup of tea; for though he was so fiery an old gentleman, he loved the little feminine attentions of which he had been for many years deprived.

"Let me see, Grandpapa," said Osy, coming to the front with the air of a man who could put all straight.

"By Jove!" cried Colonel Piercey, who had come to the same startling announcement in his paper. And the father and son for a moment sat bolt upright, staring at each other as if each supposed the other to be to blame.

"What is it?" said Margaret, beginning to be alarmed.

She was answered by the sudden opening of the door, and the entrance, announced by a servant quite unacquainted with him, who conferred upon him an incomprehensible name, of Mr. Pownceby, pale with excitement and tired with a journey. He scarcely took time for the ceremonious salutations which Sir Francis Piercey thought needful, and omitted altogether the "how-d'ye-do's" owing to his old friends, Margaret and Gerald, but burst at once into the subject that possessed him. "Well, I can see you've seen it! Sharp work putting it in so soon; but it's all true."

"What is all true? We have something to do with its being false or true, I suppose?" cried Colonel Piercey, placing himself in a somewhat defiant attitude, in an Englishman's usual position of defence before the fire.

"What are you saying, sir? what are you saying? I am a little hard of hearing. I desire that all this should be explained to me immediately. You seem all to understand, but not a syllable has reached my ears."

"I assure you, Sir Francis," said Mr. Pownceby, "I started the first thing this morning. I have not let the grass grow under my feet. Her solicitors communicated with me only yesterday. It is sharp work getting it into the papers at once, very sharp work, but I suppose she wanted to get the honour and glory; and it is quite true. I have the deed in my pocket in full form; for those solicitors of hers, if not endowed with just the best fame in the profession, are—"

"But you're going a great deal too fast, Pownceby," cried Colonel Gerald. "I don't see that either my father or I can accept anything from that woman's hand."

"The deed in full form, Sir Francis," said the lawyer, too wise to take any notice of so hotheaded a person, "restoring Greyshott and all that is in it to the lawful heir—yourself. I don't pretend to know what is her motive; but there it is all in black and white: and for once in a way I can't but say that I admire the woman, Sir Francis, and that she's got perception of what is right in her, after all."

"God bless my soul!" was all Sir Francis said.

"But we can't take it from that woman, Pownceby! Why, what are you thinking of? Receive from her, a person we all despise, a gift like this! Why, the thing is impossible! It is like her impertinence to offer it; and how you could think for a moment—"

Margaret, who had hastily taken up the paper and read the paragraph, here put it down again and laid her hand on her husband's arm. "You must wait," she said, "you must wait, Gerald, for what your father says."

"The woman of the trial?" said Sir Francis, getting it with difficulty into his head, "the baggage that married poor Gervase, and made a fool of his father—that woman!" He added briskly, turning to his son: "I was always against that trial, you know I was. Don't throw away good money after bad, I always said: let be; if we don't get it in the course of nature we'll never get it, was what I always said. You know I always said it. Those costs which you ran up in spite of me, almost broke my heart."

There was a pause, and then Colonel Piercey said with a half laugh, "We all know, father, that you did not like the costs."

"I said so!" said Sir Francis, "I was always against it. I thought the woman might turn out better than you supposed. A very remarkable thing, Mr. Pownceby, don't you think it's a very remarkable thing? after she had won her cause and had everything her own way. Do you recall to memory ever having heard of a similar incident? I never did in all my experience; a very extraordinary thing indeed!"

"No," said Mr. Pownceby, "no; I don't think I ever did hear anything like it. They generally stick to what they have got like grim death."

"I think that must be rather a remarkable woman," said Sir Francis; "I retract anything I may have been induced to say of her in a moment of annoyance. I consider she has acted very creditably, very—very—I may say nobly, Mr. Pownceby. I beg that I may never hear a word in her disparagement from any of you. I hope that we might all be capable of doing anything so—so—magnanimous and high-minded ourselves."

"But, father," cried Colonel Piercey, "we can't surely accept a gift like this from a woman we know nothing of—whom we've no esteem for—whom we've prosecuted—whom—"

"Not accept it, sir?" cried Sir Francis—"not accept a righteous restitution? I should like to know on what principle we could refuse it? If a man had taken your watch from you, would you refuse to take it if he brought it back? Why, what would that be but to discourage every good impulse? I shall certainly accept it. And I hope, Mr. Pownceby, that you will convey my thanks—yes, my thanks, and very high appreciation to this young lady. I think she is doing a very noble thing. Whether I benefited by it or not, I should think it a very noble thing. Don't be stingy in your praise, sir! It's noble to say you've been wrong—many haven't the strength of mind to do it. I'll drink her very good health at dinner. We'll have a toast, do you hear?"

"Yes, Grandpapa," cried Osy, always ready; "and shall it be with what Cousin Colonel calls the honours? You give the name, and I'll stand up upon a chair and do the 'Hip, hip, hurrah!'"

Upon what rule it was that old Sir Francis, rather a severe old gentleman to most people, had become grandpapa to Osy, while Colonel Piercey remained only, as of old, Cousin Colonel, is too subtle a question to enter into; but it was so to the perfect satisfaction of the two persons chiefly involved. And thus for the second time Osy cheered for Patty with the delighted readiness of an unbiassed soul.

Mrs. Piercey left Greyshott shortly after this, having left everything in the most perfect good order, and all the servants in the house, without saying a word of any new arrangements, though I need not say they had all read that paragraph in the newspapers. She went to London, where she spent a few weeks very pleasantly, and ordered a great many new dresses. Here she dismissed Jerningham, who carried away with her a number of black and white gowns, and the best recommendations. Patty plunged into pinks and blues with the zest of a person who has long been deprived of such indulgences, and the world learned by the newspapers that, on the 20th of August, Patience, widow of the late Gervase Piercey, Esq., of Greyshott, was married at St. George's, Hanover Square, to Roger Pearson, Esq., of Canterbury House. The happy pair went abroad for their honeymoon, but did not enjoy the Continent, only entering into full and perfect bliss when they returned to the glistening glories of their new house. There had been various storms between them before the question of Greyshott had been decided, and it had required all Roger's power and influence to carry his scheme to a successful conclusion. His determination not to sit down by another man's fireside, and to have nothing to say to the old house, which he declared gave him the shivers to look at, were answered by many a scornful request to take himself off then, if he didn't like it, and leave it to those who did.

"That's just what I want—to leave it to those that like it: you don't, Patty, and never will!" cried the bold lover. "How do I know? Oh, I know! You've gone through a lot, and you think you'll have something for it, anyhow. Well, so you shall have something for it. Wait till you see the 'ouse that is just waiting till you say the word—ten times better an 'ouse, and folks all about us will be delighted to see you, and as much fun as you can set your face to!" Oh, how powerful and how sweet these arguments were! But to give Greyshott back was a bitter pill to Patty.

"I'll sell it, then," she said; "it'll bring in a deal of money;" and this was what Miss Hewitt, who was almost mad with opposition, advised, arguing and beseeching till the foam flew from her mouth.

But Roger was obstinate. He declared that he would not be instrumental in taking any man's home from him. "Money's a different thing," he said. "One sovereign's just like another, but one 'ouse ain't like another." The telling argument, however, was one which Roger had the cleverness to pick up from a cricket reporter on a daily paper, to whom he had confided his romance.

"By George!" cried the journalist, "what a paragraph for my paper!" He said "par," no doubt, but Patty would not have understood what this meant. When she did take up the idea, and understood that her praises were to be sung and her generosity extolled in every paper, and that the Pierceys would be made to sing small before her, Patty was overcome at last. Her heart swelled as if it would burst with triumph and a sense of greatness when she read that paragraph. She felt it to be altogether just and true. If they had not prosecuted, there was no telling what magnanimity she might not have been equal to, and she accepted the praise as one who had deserved it to the very utmost.

"They've been in it hundreds and hundreds of years," she said to the new friends to whom her bridegroom introduced her in London—among whom were several newspaper men, and one who insisted upon getting her portrait for an illustrated paper—"as we have been in the Seven Thorns. Being of an old family myself, I have always felt for them." This was reported in the little biographical notice which was appended to Mrs. Piercey's portrait in the illustrated paper, where it was also told that she had been known far and wide as the Lily of the Seven Thorns, and had been carried off by the Squire's son from many competitors. It made up for much, even for the fact, still bitter to her, that she had been cheated out of her title, and would never be Lady Piercey,—a loss and delusion which sometimes brought tears into her eyes long after she was Roger Pearson's wife.

But when Patty settled down in her own 'Andsome 'Ouse, it was soon proved that Roger had not said a word too much. The cricketing world rallied round him. He ceased to be a professional, and became a gentleman cricketer and a member of the M.C.C. The cricket pitch within the grounds of Canterbury House was admirable, and matches were played there, in which not only the honour of the county, but the honour of England, was involved. Patty gave cricket luncheons and even cricket dinners, to which the golden youth of England came gladly, and where even great ladies, watching the cricket for one side or another, were content to be entertained. Patty drove her two spanking horses over the county, calling at the best houses; while even Lady Hartmore, after the restitution as she called it, paid her a visit of ceremony, which Mrs. Roger Pearson, swelling with pride and triumph, never returned. Not to have returned Lady Hartmore's visit was almost as great a distinction as to have received one from the Queen. And all the lesser ladies in the county envied Patty the strength of mind which made her capable of such a proof of independence.

Colonel Piercey and his wife became shortly afterwards the inhabitants of Greyshott, which suited Sir Francis better than to have his long-accustomed quiet permanently disturbed. "Though I'd like to keep the boy," he said. It cost a good deal to Colonel Pierce's pride, but it lay with his father to decide, and there was nothing more to say. They were not rich, for Greyshott was a difficult place to keep up on a limited income; but it was something, no doubt, after the shock of the restoration, to have the old house still.

And Patty flourishes and spreads like a green baytree. She is not so careful of etiquette, so anxious to be always correct and do what other ladies do. She is beginning to grow stout; her colour is high; her nursery is full; and she is, beyond all question, a much happier woman than she ever could have been in Greyshott, even had Lady Hartmore called and all gone well—now that she and her husband live in continual jollity in their own 'Andsome 'Ouse.

Margaret Oliphant – A Short Biography

Margaret Oliphant Wilson was born on April 4th, 1828 to Francis W. Wilson, a clerk, and Margaret Oliphant, at Wallyford, near Musselburgh, East Lothian.

She spent her childhood at Lasswade, near Dalkeith, Glasgow before moving to Liverpool.

Her youth was spent in establishing a writing style so much so that, in 1849, she had her first novel published: Passages in the Life of Mrs. Margaret Maitland based on the Scottish Free Church movement. It met with some success and was a good start to her career.

Two years later, in 1851, her third book Caleb Field was published. It was also now that she met the publisher William Blackwood in Edinburgh and was asked to contribute to his well-received Blackwood's Magazine. It was to be a lifetimes endeavor. Over the course of the relationship she would have well over 100 articles published.

In May 1852, Margaret married her cousin, Frank Wilson Oliphant, at Birkenhead, and they settled at Harrington Square, Camden, London. He was an artist working primarily in stained glass. With the marriage she became Margaret Oliphant Wilson Oliphant.

Their marriage produced six children but three tragically died in infancy.

When her husband developed signs of the dreaded consumption (tuberculosis) they moved, on the advice of doctors, to warmer climes. In January 1859 it was to Florence, and then to Rome where, sadly, he died.

Margaret was naturally devastated but was also now left without support and only her income from her writing. She returned to England and took up the task of supporting her three remaining children by her literary activity.

By now she was being published both as an established novelist and regularly in Blackwood's Magazine, amongst others. Her incredible and prolific work rate increased both her commercial reputation and the size of her reading audience.

Against this her domestic life continued to be tragic, full of sorrow and disappointment.

In January 1864 her only remaining daughter Maggie died and was buried in her father's grave in Rome. Her brother, who had emigrated to Canada, was shortly afterwards involved in financial ruin. Margaret generously offered a home to him and his children, adding another demand to her already heavy responsibilities.

In 1866 she settled at Windsor to be closer to her sons, who were being educated at near-by Eton School. That year, her second cousin, Annie Louisa Walker, came to live with her as a companion-housekeeper. Windsor was now to be her home for the rest of her life.

Her literary career for three decades was one of constant delivery and success. Whether she wrote historical works or across several genres in fiction: domestic realism, historical, romance or supernatural she was successful.

For more than thirty years she pursued a varied literary career but family life continued to bring problems.

The literary ambitions she wished for her sons were unfulfilled. Cyril Francis, the eldest, died in 1890, leaving a Life of Alfred de Musset, incorporated in his mother's Foreign Classics for English Readers. The younger, Francis, who she nicknamed 'Cecco', collaborated with her in the Victorian Age of English Literature and won a position at the British Museum, but was rejected by Sir Andrew Clark, a famous physician. Cecco died in 1894.

With the last of her children now lost to her, she had but little further interest in life. Her health steadily and inexorably declined.

Margaret Oliphant Wilson Oliphant died at the age of 69 in Wimbledon on 20th June 1897. She is buried in Eton beside her sons.

At her death, Margaret was still working on Annals of a Publishing House, a record of Blackwood's Magazine with which she had enjoyed such a successful relationship.

Her Autobiography and Letters, which present a thoughtful picture of her domestic anxieties, was published in 1899. Only parts were written with a wider audience in mind: she had originally intended the Autobiography for her son, but he died before she could finish it.

Opinions on Oliphant's work are split, with some critics seeing her as a 'domestic novelist', while others recognize her work as influential and important to the Victorian literature canon. Critical reception from her contemporaries is also divided. John Skelton took the view that Oliphant wrote too much and too quickly. Writing a Blackwood's article called 'A Little Chat About Mrs. Oliphant', he asked, "Had Mrs. Oliphant concentrated her powers, what might she not have done? We might have had another Charlotte Brontë or another George Eliot." However not all of the contemporary reception was negative. The esteemed M. R. James admired Oliphant's supernatural fiction, concluding that "the religious ghost story, as it may be called, was never done better than by Mrs. Oliphant in 'The Open Door' and 'A Beleaguered City'. Mary Butts lavished praise on Oliphant's ghost story 'The Library Window', describing it as "one masterpiece of sober loveliness".

More modern critics of Oliphant's work include Virginia Woolf, who asked in Three Guineas whether Oliphant's autobiography does not lead the reader "to deplore the fact that Mrs. Oliphant sold her brain, her very admirable brain, prostituted her culture and enslaved her intellectual liberty in order that she might earn her living and educate her children."

Whatever the merits of their cases Margaret Oliphant has been shamefully neglected in modern years. She is now becoming more widely recognised as a leading writer of her day.

Margaret Oliphant – A Concise Bibliography

A canon of more than 120 works, including novels, travel books, histories, and volumes of literary criticism.

Novels

Margaret Maitland (1849)
Merkland (1850)
Caleb Field (1851)
John Drayton (1851)
Adam Graeme (1852)
The Melvilles (1852)
Katie Stewart (1852)
Harry Muir (1853)
Ailieford (1853)
The Quiet Heart (1854)
Magdalen Hepburn (1854)
Zaidee (1855)
Lilliesleaf (1855)
Christian Melville (1855)
The Athelings (1857)
The Days of My Life (1857)
Orphans (1858)
The Laird of Norlaw (1858)
Agnes Hopetoun's Schools and Holidays (1859)
Lucy Crofton (1860)
The House on the Moor (1861)
The Last of the Mortimers (1862)
Heart and Cross (1863)
Salem Chapel (1863)
The Rector (1863)
Doctor's Family (1863)
The Perpetual Curate (1864)
Miss Marjoribanks (1866)
Phoebe Junior (1876)
A Son of the Soil (1865)
Agnes (1866)
Madonna Mary (1867)
Brownlows (1868)
The Minister's Wife (1869)
The Three Brothers (1870)
John: A Love Story (1870)

Squire Arden (1871)
At his Gates (1872)
Ombra (1872
May (1873)
Innocent (1873)
The Story of Valentine and his Brother (1875)
A Rose in June (1874)
For Love and Life (1874)
Whiteladies (1875)
An Odd Couple (1875)
The Curate in Charge (1876)
Carità (1877)
Young Musgrave (1877)
Mrs. Arthur (1877)
The Primrose Path (1878)
Within the Precincts (1879)
The Fugitives (1879)
A Beleaguered City (1879)
The Greatest Heiress in England (1880)
He That Will Not When He May (1880)
In Trust (1881)
Harry Joscelyn (1881)
Lady Jane (1882)
A Little Pilgrim in the Unseen (1882)
The Lady Lindores (1883)
Sir Tom (1883)
Hester (1883)
It Was a Lover and his Lass (1883)
The Lady's Walk (1883)
The Wizard's Son (1884)
Madam (1884)
The Prodigals and their Inheritance (1885)
Oliver's Bride (1885)
A Country Gentleman and his Family (1886)
A House Divided Against Itself (1886)
Effie Ogilvie (1886)
A Poor Gentleman (1886)
The Son of his Father (1886)
Joyce (1888)
Cousin Mary (1888)
The Land of Darkness (1888)
Lady Car (1889)
Kirsteen (1890)
The Mystery of Mrs. Biencarrow (1890)
Sons and Daughters (1890)
The Railway Man and his Children (1891)
The Heir Presumptive and the Heir Apparent (1891)
The Marriage of Elinor (1891)

Janet (1891)
The Cuckoo in the Nest (1892)
Diana Trelawny (1892)
The Sorceress (1893)
A House in Bloomsbury (1894)
Sir Robert's Fortune (1894)
Who Was Lost and is Found (1894)
Lady William (1894)
Two Strangers (1895)
Old Mr. Tredgold (1895)
The Unjust Steward (1896)
The Ways of Life (1897)

Short stories

Neighbours on the Green (1889)
A Widow's Tale and Other Stories (1898)
That Little Cutty (1898)
The Open Door (1918)

Selected Articles

Mary Russel Mitford (Blackwood's Magazine, Vol. 75, 1854)
Evelin and Pepys (Blackwood's Magazine, Vol. 76, 1854)
The Holy Land (Blackwood's Magazine, Vol. 76, 1854)
Mr. Thackeray and his Novels (Blackwood's Magazine, Vol. 77, 1855)
Bulwer (Blackwood's Magazine, Vol. 77, 1855)
Charles Dickens (Blackwood's Magazine, Vol. 77, 1855)
Modern Novelists—Great and Small (Blackwood's Magazine, Vol. 77, 1855)
Modern Light Literature: Poetry (Blackwood's Magazine, Vol. 79, 1856)
Religion in Common Life (Blackwood's Magazine, Vol. 79, 1856)
Sydney Smith (Blackwood's Magazine, Vol. 79, 1856)
The Laws Concerning Women (Blackwood's Magazine, Vol. 79, 1856)
The Art of Caviling (Blackwood's Magazine, Vol. 80, 1856)
Béranger (Blackwood's Magazine, Vol. 83, 1858)
The Condition of Women (Blackwood's Magazine, Vol. 83, 1858)
The Missionary Explorer (Blackwood's Magazine, Vol. 83, 1858)
Religious Memoirs (Blackwood's Magazine, Vol. 83, 1858)
Social Science (Blackwood's Magazine, Vol. 88, 1860)
Scotland and her Accusers (Blackwood's Magazine, Vol. 90, 1861)
The Chronicles of Carlingford (Blackwood's Magazine 1862–1865)
Girolamo Savonarola (Blackwood's Magazine, Vol. 93, 1863)
The Life of Jesus (Blackwood's Magazine, Vol. 96, 1864)
Giacomo Leopardi (Blackwood's Magazine, Vol. 98, 1865)
The Great Unrepresented (Blackwood's Magazine, Vol. 100, 1866)
Mill on the Subjection of Women (The Edinburgh Review, Vol. 130, 1869)
The Opium-Eater (Blackwood's Magazine, Vol. 122, 1877)

Russian and Nihilism in the Novels of I. Tourgeniéf (Blackwood's Magazine, Vol. 127, 1880)
School and College (Blackwood's Magazine, Vol. 128, 1880)
The Grievances of Women (Fraser's Magazine, New Series, Vol. 21, 1880)
Mrs. Carlyle (The Contemporary Review, Vol. 43, May 1883)
The Ethics of Biography (The Contemporary Review, July 1883)
Victor Hugo (The Contemporary Review, Vol. 48, July/December 1885)
A Venetian Dynasty (The Contemporary Review, Vol. 50, August 1886)
Laurence Oliphant (Blackwood's Magazine, Vol. 145, 1889)
Tennyson (Blackwood's Magazine, Vol. 152, 1892)
Addison, the Humorist (Century Magazine, Vol. 48, 1894)
The Anti-Marriage League (Blackwood's Magazine, Vol. 159, 1896)

Biographies

Edward Irving (1862)
Francis of Assisi (1871)
Count de Montalembert (1872)
Dante (1877)
Cervantes (1880)
Life of Sheridan in the English Men of Letters series (1883)
John Tulloch (1888)
Laurence Oliphant (1892)

Historical & Critical Works

Historical Sketches of the Reign of George II (1869)
The Makers of Florence (1876)
A Literary History of England from 1760 to 1825 (1882)
The Makers of Venice (1887)
Royal Edinburgh (1890)
Jerusalem (1891)
The Makers of Modern Rome (1895)
William Blackwood and his Sons (1897)
The Sisters Brontë. In: Women Novelists of Queen Victoria's Reign (1897)